INTERCEPTED

DOUG VEEDER

VEEDER MEDIA

Published by:
Veeder Media
PO Box 1862
Apex, NC 27502

Publisher's Note: This novel is a work of fiction. Names, characters, places, businesses, events, and incidents are either products of the author's imagination or used in a fictitious manner. All characters are fictional, and any parallels or similarities to people living or dead is purely coincidental.

ISBN: 978-1-7374597-0-5 (Paperback)
ISBN: 978-1-7374597-1-2 (eBook)

Library of Congress Control Number: 2021912440

The cover art is by Tom Derosier.
© 2021 Tom Derosier
Used with permission.

All Bible quotations are from the HOLY BIBLE. The New International Version and the King James Version.

This book is dedicated to my wife, Stephanie. For all the roads we have traveled and for all the interceptions we have faced along the way, you have been my ride-or-die through it all. I thank God for you being in my life every single day.

1985

CHAPTER 1

I t was a glorious summer morning in Goldston. The sun was shining down from heaven. It filled the morning drive through the small North Carolina town with a kaleidoscope of radiant colors bursting forth to greet the day. Fragrant mixtures of sweet smells wafted across the rolling hills from the display of beauty that lined the roadway.

The caravan of cars that brought the McLean family into town on Sunday morning grew longer every year. When the motorcade pulled into the church parking lot, Pastor Davis was always happy to walk out and greet the whole clan.

James McLean, the patriarch, stepped out of his car and walked hand-in-hand with his wife Colleen, as he led his loved ones through the sanctuary doors. James and Colleen, who had celebrated forty-one years of marriage earlier in the year, were followed by the families of six of their eight children. They gathered every week to celebrate their faith, family, love for one another, and the blessings they all had received from their Lord and Savior, Jesus Christ.

Paul McLean, their oldest, and his wife, Jill followed James and Colleen into the church. High school sweethearts, Paul and Jill, had been married for twenty years. They were followed into the church by their seven children. JJ, their oldest, was a towering young man, who was an All-American football player, hoping to lead his high school team to their first-ever State Championship. The pride of the local community, JJ was the love interest of every eligible teenage girl in town.

JJ was followed into the chapel by his younger brothers. Sean was the closest in age to JJ and did everything he could do to follow in JJ's footsteps. Colin, Michael, and Liam were younger. They were still finding their way in life and on the football field. All the McLean boys were budding football stars, but they all paled in comparison to JJ. The brothers were followed into the church by their seven-year-old twin siblings, Mary Katherine and Veeder.

The McLeans were a traditional Irish American family. A hard-working clan that put their faith in God and each other. It was a beautiful sight to encounter when the entire McLean family came to worship. They filled the sanctuary with a cacophony of sounds that delighted and surprised the rest of the parishioners as they filled in the pews.

The McLeans were Catholics who had converted to Protestantism when James' father immigrated to the United States with his brothers and sisters at the turn of the twentieth century. Farmers by trade in Ireland, the family settled in the tenements of New York.

James's father tired of city living. So, he and his wife packed up everything they had and headed south to begin a new life. They ended up settling down on a little plot of land in Goldston in 1910. Without a Catholic church in town, the family found a home in a local Baptist church. As the years passed, and a few more churches sprang up around their quaint community, the McLean family joined a nondenominational evangelical church where their faith and family flourished.

The McLean family could only purchase a few acres of land when they arrived in Goldston. Over the seventy-five years they lived in the sleepy little hollow that was nestled in the brilliance of God's tapestry, the family prospered. Today, their family farm sprawls out over a vast seven hundred acres of land that James farms with his remaining six children, his friends, and their families.

Goldston is a rural oasis settled among the rolling hills an hour outside of Raleigh. Time seemed to pass their community by as decadence and progress engulfed the rest of the world. Their days started before the sun rose and ended well after the sunset. They worked the land. They tended to their animals. They provided for their families and shared their abundance with those in need.

The McLean children were your typical American children. They went to school, were involved in extra-curricular activities, and every Sunday, they came to church with their parents. The kids loved coffee hour after service. It allowed them to hang out with their friends. The teenage girls swooned over JJ and even though he protested, he loved the attention.

After church, the family members went to their respective homes, changed into casual attire, loaded their vehicles up with a bounty of food, and went to James and Colleen's house for Sunday dinner, an all-day barbecue with family and friends.

By mid-afternoon, the yard was filled with a throng of people who were laughing, having fun, listening to music, dancing, playing games, and sharing God's love. The girls settled into smaller groups and played with each other. The boys picked teams for the football game that would be played for the rest of the afternoon.

Colleen walked across the yard. She brought James a cold drink while he tended to the barbecue pit. He took the drink from her, took a sip, and slipped his arm around her waist. He looked out over the yard and whispered in Colleen's ear, "We are truly blessed by Almighty God. I love you."

Colleen smiled, nodded, and agreed. They were blessed. It was the simple life. They believed in faith, family, farming, and football. They worked hard, supported their church, community, friends, and poured love out on the community. They tried to live a life worthy of the blessings they had received.

Colleen kissed James. "I love you too."

Colleen stepped away from the barbecue and made her way to the far end of the yard. She sat down at a picnic table away from the hustle and bustle of the frenzied activity going on in the yard, picked up her cards, and resumed playing the game with her smallest grandson, Veeder.

Veeder was not like the rest of the boys in the family. His brothers and cousins were all big, strong, tough kids who grew like weeds. Veeder was short and slight. He was watched like a hawk by his mother when it came to his safety and well-being.

Seven years earlier, when Jill was carrying the twins, she developed complications with the pregnancy. Within hours of being admitted to the Medical Center in Chapel Hill, Jill went into labor and delivered the twins ten weeks early. Mary Katherine was the first of the twins to be delivered and she came by natural birth.

Veeder, however, managed to get himself into a breech position. They tried to deliver him naturally, but it became apparent that he was in distress. So the doctors performed an emergency C-section.

Mary Katherine and Veeder were whisked away to the neonatal intensive care unit where nurses tended to them around the clock. Mary Katherine, by the grace of God, responded to medical treatment, started to gain weight, and went home after ten days.

Veeder didn't fare as well. His lungs weren't developed. So the doctors intubated him. They gave him a round of medicine known as surfactant. It was touch and go for several nerve-wracking hours. The treatment was a success, but Veeder wasn't out of the woods yet. Because of his medical complications, he ended up staying in the NICU much longer and Jill refused to leave his side.

The family set up a twenty-four-hour schedule to support Jill and Veeder. It was a grueling six-and-a-half-week ordeal. When the doctors told them that their son could go home, Jill and Paul broke with their tradition of naming their kids with a traditional Irish name and named their son after the doctor who had labored over their son's medical trauma: Dr. Michael Veeder.

After forty days of worry and prayer, Paul and Jill loaded Veeder into the car seat and started the journey home. On the way, Jill broke down in tears in the passenger seat. Paul pulled the car over to the side of the road to console his wife. Jill shared a dream she had with Paul. A premonition. And because of it, Jill made Paul promise that Veeder would never play football.

So, as Veeder sat at the end of the picnic table, watching all of his brothers, cousins, and friends having a great game of football, he got angry.

"It's not fair, Grandma."

"Whoever said that life was fair?"

"Mom lets JJ, Liam, Colin, Michael, and Sean play football."

"They're much bigger than you are."

"She even lets Mary Katherine play when she wants to."

"And what's wrong with that?" Colleen stared at him with raised eyebrows.

"Mary Katherine's a girl!"

"Girls can do anything boys can do."

"But if she can play, why can't I?"

"Your mom has her reasons."

"Stupid reasons." Veeder pouted, crossing his arms.

"We don't use that word, young man," Colleen admonished. "Besides, you were born to live a different life than your brothers."

"I know I was born early, and I'm small, but I'm tough Grandma!" Veeder flexed his muscles.

"No one said you weren't tough."

"I'd show 'em!" Veeder puffed out his chest. "I'd knock them all on their asses."

"Veeder!" Colleen raised her finger to scold him. "We don't talk like that in this family!"

"I would, though!"

"Who taught you that word?"

"JJ uses it."

"He shouldn't speak like that." Colleen glanced at JJ playing across the yard, storing away the information for later in the evening. "I'll have a talk with him about that language and he'll have to ask God for forgiveness. As will you, young man."

"Still doesn't make it fair that they can play and I can't."

"You may be right, but we get what we can handle in this life. You have a different path you'll need to walk."

"But I want to play football!"

"I know what you want young man, but it's at times like this that I am reminded of a quote from the book of Ecclesiastics..."

"Ugh!" Veeder dropped his head into his hands in frustration. "Not another Bible quote."

"You will face other things under the sun. Don't be confident in yourself. You don't have to be the fastest, the strongest, the wisest, or the most brilliant mind. The time will come, and you will have your chances. Look to God and thank Him for your blessings," Colleen paraphrased.

"I don't even know what that means, Grandma." Veeder rolled his eyes, putting his elbows on the table, and his hands on the side of his face.

"It means that life is what happens to you as you live it. Take your time. You have your own path. And always, thank God for your blessings."

"But I don't get to live it, Grandma. I am stuck on the sidelines!"

"Sometimes we think it is fair and at other times we do not." Colleen reached across the table and touched the side of his face.

"It's not fair, Grandma, that's for sure."

"You are destined for something great. You just have to have faith in our Lord and know that Jesus will help you find the right path."

"I don't even believe in Jesus, Grandma."

"You don't?" Colleen sat back, staring at him in disbelief.

"I ain't never seen him."

"You don't have to see something to believe in it."

"Well, he hasn't ever done anything for me."

"That's where you're wrong. Jesus blesses you every day, Veeder. I don't know how you can say you have never seen him. You've surely felt him in your life."

"No, I haven't!" Veeder puffed out his chest. He was frustrated. "Where is he, Grandma? Where is Jesus?"

"He's sitting right next to you with tears in his eyes, praying for you. Saddened by your disbelieving heart."

"You see him, Grandma?" Veeder was sarcastic in his tone and his mannerisms, looking under the table before setting his arms on the table and staring straight into Colleen's eyes. "Because I don't!"

Colleen moved her gaze to the side of the boy, looking at an empty space and fighting back the tears forming in the corners of her eyes. "Promise me, Lord Jesus, that you will not let my grandson leave this earth without seeing you face-to-face. Promise me you will reveal your glory to him. Give him a chance to love you and honor you with all of his heart."

"What did he say, Grandma?" Veeder was wide-eyed with anticipation and honest wonder.

"He said, 'Amen.'"

As the words left her mouth, the football hit the table and careened off of it onto the ground. Veeder jumped off the bench, raced over to the ball, picked it up, and held it in his hands. While he was staring at the ball, the cluster of kids was yelling at him to throw it back.

Veeder was still staring at the ball like he was holding onto a piece of gold when Liam yelled out, "I better run over and get it! He's so weak, God only knows how long it would take him to roll it across the yard to us!"

The other kids laughed as Liam started jogging in Veeder's direction. Liam always felt Veeder was a baby and was always taunting his younger brother. As they grew, the animosity escalated between them.

Veeder wanted to prove Liam wrong. He wanted to prove he wasn't weak. He wanted to make Liam eat his words. Without hesitation, Veeder cradled the ball in his right hand, turned toward the group of boys, cocked his arm, and threw the ball.

A hush settled over the crowd of boys as the ball soared through the air. The perfect spiral floated on the tufts of the clouds as if angels were cradling the ball and delivering it some fifteen yards across the backyard. JJ ripped the ball out of the air and stared in disbelief at Veeder.

"Do it again!" JJ tossed the ball back to Veeder.

The ball landed on the ground a few feet away from Veeder and rolled around. He raced over and picked it up. He grasped the ball with both hands, cradled it in his right hand, and fired another perfect spiral across the backyard into the waiting hands of his older brother.

For fifteen minutes, Veeder and JJ played catch in the backyard. He continued to pepper JJ with perfect spirals. JJ was awestruck as he caught each pass. The brothers, cousins, aunts, uncles, grandparents, and family friends formed a semi-circle around the game of catch. They all watched in stunned silence at first, but soon the yard was filled with a growing chorus of cheers as the two boys threw the ball to each other.

"No!" Jill shouted across the yard as she came out of the house and saw Veeder playing catch with JJ.

"No, no, no, no!" Jill was angry as she marched across the backyard. "You all promised! You promised me and Paul that Veeder wasn't going to play this game!"

"But Mom!" Veeder argued.

"No more!" Jill grabbed Veeder by the wrist.

Veeder tried to break free of her grasp. "Mom, let me play! Let me play!"

"No! You're too small!"

"I am not!" It was too late, though. No argument was going to change Jill's mind. She had made her final declaration about the matter, and with Veeder protesting the entire way, Jill marched Veeder across the yard, and into his grandparents' house.

JJ stared at his mother dragging Veeder across the yard. He couldn't understand why she was so opposed to him playing football. As he stood there in shock at what he was witnessing, Colin grabbed the football out of his hands and returned to the game.

CHAPTER 2

—∽◉∾—

Veeder clashed with his mother over the humiliation of being dragged off the field for the next few days. His defiance was out of control. He wanted to play football like his older brothers, but the more he argued with her, the more she dug in her heels. She was not going to let him play.

JJ became Veeder's biggest advocate. He couldn't fathom her reasons for not letting Veeder play. One night, after dinner, while JJ was helping Jill with the dishes, he became indignant. "You're being ridiculous, Mom!"

"Just stop right there, JJ." Jill held up her hand, waving a finger at him. "I have had enough!"

"Why should I?"

"Because you have no idea what you're talking about!"

"You're denying him an opportunity, Mom. I don't get it! What am I missing?"

"Just leave it alone."

"You're being selfish."

"How am I being selfish?" Jill stared at JJ with fire in her eyes.

"Veeder has a God-given talent and you're squashing it."

"Throwing a ball is not a God-given talent!"

"Every good thing we have in life is a gift from God."

"Oh please, JJ," Jill chuckled, rolling her eyes at him. "Football is not Veeder's talent."

"How do you know?"

"Because I said it isn't!" Jill slammed down the pot she was drying. "Let it go, JJ!"

"You're denying him the chance to find out. How is that honoring God, Mom?"

"You have no idea what it is like to watch your child suffer, JJ. And I hope you never do."

"Then explain it to me."

9

"God gave Veeder a unique life and it doesn't involve football! Is that clear?"

"No! It's not. You're being selfish."

"Enough!" Jill threw the dishtowel on the kitchen counter and abruptly left the kitchen, mumbling under her breath.

JJ watched her leave, shook his head in frustration, and continued drying the dishes. A few minutes later, Paul stormed into the kitchen. "What was that all about, JJ?"

"I told her she was being ridiculous about Veeder playing football."

"And who are you to decide what's in your brother's best interest?" Paul asked, standing toe-to-toe with JJ.

"Why is everyone against him playing?"

"Because we decided he wasn't going to play!" Backing up, Paul raised his hand and pointed at JJ. "End of story."

"You're being irrational, Dad."

"Leave it alone, JJ," Paul yelled.

"Why?"

"Because I told you to do so!"

"Do you hear yourself?"

"Leave it alone!" Angry, Paul stormed out of the kitchen.

But JJ and Veeder didn't leave it alone. They continued the indignant onslaught all week. The more they argued, the more resolute Jill became. The more they pleaded, the more their requests were denied. Jill was not backing down. Veeder was not going to play football.

The week had been intolerable, but nothing prepared the family for Saturday night's dinner. It turned into a war zone. Veeder became incensed. He got angry at his parents and spewed forth another barrage of disparaging comments. When Paul couldn't take it any longer, he slammed his hand down on the table and sent Veeder to his room.

Veeder left the table and ran up the stairs with tears in his eyes. He slammed his bedroom door, turned on the little lamp next to his bed, and crawled under the sheets. Tears poured out of him. Thirty minutes later, there was a knock at his bedroom door.

"Can I come in?" Jill poked her head inside the door.

"No," Veeder said through gritted teeth.

Jill ignored his response, closed the door behind her, walked over to his bedside, and set a plate of food on the nightstand. "I brought you some food in case you get hungry."

"I don't want it." Veeder puffed out his lower lip.

"I know you're mad at me, Veeder." Jill sat on the bed next to him.

"You're mean."

"One day you'll have kids and you'll be in a similar situation. Maybe then you will understand."

"It's not fair, Mom."

"It's what's best for you."

Veeder sat up, pleading his case once again. "All the football teams start soon, Mom!"

"And so do a lot of sports."

"JJ, Sean, Colin, Michael, and Liam get to play. It's not fair."

"They're bigger than you."

"I'm tough, Mom."

"That's why we signed you up for soccer again."

"Soccer? Ugh!" Veeder threw his arms in the air, staring at his mother. "Really?"

"What's wrong with soccer?"

"It's for girls, Mom."

"It is not."

"There are only two boys on the soccer team!"

"See, it's not all girls."

"Right." Veeder rolled his eyes. "Me and the kid who does ballet! Great! All the other kids on our team are girls."

"I find that hard to believe, Veeder; you're exaggerating."

"Whether you find it hard to believe or not, Mom, it's true." Veeder slumped back into his pillow more dejected than ever.

"There's nothing wrong with soccer..."

"I get picked on and teased all the time."

"By whom?"

"My friends."

"They don't sound like friends to me if they would pick on you for playing soccer."

"I know I am smaller than most of the other kids, but I'm tough." Veeder contested, flexing his muscles. "One day my body will grow into my toughness."

"Nice try, Veeder, but it won't work. You're not playing football. End of story."

"If you don't let me play, Mom, I'll continue to get picked on by all of my friends."

"And if all of your friends jumped off the Brooklyn Bridge…"

"Yes, Mom, I would jump!" Veeder interjected before she could finish her sentence. "I would jump and as I did, I would turn my head and find you, so you could watch me. I'd be the one smiling and waving at you until I slammed into the water!"

A tear formed in Jill's eye. "You would want to hurt me that much?"

"Do *you* want to hurt me, Mom?"

"I am not hurting you." Jill fought back the tears.

"You are, Mom. You might not think so, but you are."

"I don't know what to say to help you understand how I feel."

"I wish you would just tell me the truth."

"What truth do you want from me, Veeder?"

"I want the real reason why you won't let me play."

Jill slunk back against the headboard, lifting her feet onto the bed, and putting her arm around Veeder's shoulders. "You really want to know?"

"I do, Mom."

Jill stared off into the darkness. She fought against the lump that had formed in her throat and took a deep breath. "When you were born, I sat next to you day after day, night after night, in the NICU, praying continually as you fought with every ounce of your little body to survive.

"Long after Mary Katherine had gone home, I was still by your side. Listening to the sensors that were attached to your body, staring at the tubes that fed you and helped you to breathe. Being unable to hold my precious baby took a toll on my heart. While

12

the world went on around us, nothing else mattered to me except my baby boy, who was lying in a cold, heartless incubator. Alone."

"Mom, I'm not a weak little baby anymore." Veeder put his head on her chest. "I'm bigger. Stronger."

Tears started rolling down her face. "You know, there were many nights when I wondered if you ever saw me sitting in that rocking chair. I wondered if you knew I was there and how much I loved you."

"I knew you were there, Mom. I don't remember it, but I am sure I knew."

"I am glad you think that but every time I reached into the incubator, you jumped. Startled like when a stranger touches you." Jill got lost in reminiscing. "I spent so many sleepless days and nights by your side. Loving you. Praying for you. Just wanting to hold you."

"I know you did, Mom, but what does this have to do with me playing football?" Veeder's patience was waning.

Jill ignored his question. "One night, for no other reason than sheer exhaustion, God finally gave my worn-out body some respite, and I fell asleep in that chair. And I had a dream.

"I dreamt that God took me by the hand in the darkness and walked me across a football field. The stadium was empty. It was cold. It was scary. And as much as I wanted to ask God why we were walking across that field, I knew I wasn't supposed to speak. I was there to witness something.

"So we walked. We crossed that cold, desolate field. And after we had walked the whole hundred yards, we turned, and it all changed. And it was amazing."

"What was?" Veeder stared at her with a confused look on his face.

"The whole field was lit up. Thousands, no tens of thousands of people were cheering for you. It was wonderful. You played the most amazing game I had ever seen. You scored a touchdown and ran by me with the most beautiful smile. It was glorious."

"So I am supposed to play football, Mom, don't you see?"

"That's when I felt it."

"What?"

"The Lord grabbed my arm and held me tight. He whispered in my ear 'Be strong now.' I turned to ask why I needed to be strong, and you were in a hospital surrounded by doctors. The field was gone. The fans were gone. The beauty was gone. It had all gone dark. It was all gone, except for the doctors who were trying to save your life.

"The doctors were all screaming. They were in a panic. The more I tried to see what was happening, the farther away I was. The more I tried to be strong, the weaker I felt. The more I prayed, the more alone you felt to me.

"I woke up in a complete sweat. I was panicked. I never knew what happened to you. I don't know if you ever went back on the field again. I don't know if you died. I just knew I had to be strong, but I didn't know why.

"All I knew is that football had taken everything from you. It may have even taken your life. So, I placed my hands on your weak little body inside the incubator, and I made a promise to you and God. I promised that if you ever left the hospital, football was never going to be a part of your life. Whatever God was trying to show me in my dream would never happen to you."

"It was just a dream, Mom, that's all," Veeder pleaded, but his words fell on deaf ears.

"I prayed harder for your healing than I had ever prayed in my life. So, when you finally turned the corner, got healthier, and were strong enough to come home, I knew I was blessed with an amazing gift.

"As your father and I drove home from the hospital, I made him promise me that he would never teach you to play football."

"That's not fair, Mom. You don't have the right. It's my life."

"And not just him, I made your father promise that he wouldn't let grandpa, your uncles, your cousins, your brothers, or any of his friends teach you to play the game of football. And to this day, he has kept that sacred promise to me.

"And I have kept my promise to you too, Veeder. I promised you that no one would ever teach you that game so you could never get hurt. I don't want anyone to ever hurt you." Jill wrapped Veeder in her arms, tears flowing down her cheeks.

For the first time all week, Veeder returned her embrace. He held onto his mother tighter than he had ever held her before. At that moment, they both found the solace of a quiet love between a mother and a son.

Five minutes passed as they just held each other in the quiet darkness of Veeder's room. Then Veeder tilted his head and looked up into his mother's loving eyes. "Mom, you're the only one who is hurting me."

CHAPTER 3

─◦◉◦─

The sun shone bright in the Carolina sky as the workweek got started. The farm was abuzz with activity. In addition to her work on the farm, Jill was preparing to send the kids back to school. She was busy mending and buying new clothes, organizing school supplies, and coordinating all of the kids' various schedules.

In the hustle and bustle of a chaotic Monday morning, Veeder found a quiet place on the front porch to play with his matchbox cars. Lost in his imagination, he didn't notice JJ jog across the yard and stop at the bottom of the steps.

JJ smiled to himself as he watched Veeder playing with his cars. He missed the days when he could get lost in the world of his own imagination. A part of him wished he could go back to simpler times when every encounter with the world was caught up in the wonder and mystery of mere innocence and creativity.

But he wasn't a child anymore. The world had changed for JJ. He had expectations to meet and God willing, he would fulfill those expectations. He would meet those promises that he prayed would open up a world of possibilities for a brighter future.

In that moment, though, JJ envied Veeder. Watching his little brother play on the porch made him smile. It reminded him that innocence ruled the day. That imagination and creativity opened up a world of endless possibilities. Possibilities that would allow him to love as wide, as long, and as deep as his heart was willing to explore, teaching him about life.

Today was not about innocence, though, and JJ knew it. Today was about looking towards the future and embracing destiny for both of them. JJ sat down on the top step. "Hey, Veeder, what are you doing?"

"Playing with my cars."

"Sounds like fun."

"It is." Smiling, Veeder looked up at JJ. "Want to play with me?"

"I would love to, Veeder." A hint of sadness rifled through his soul, the past tugging on his heart in a moment of nostalgia. "Unfortunately, I don't have time to play with toy cars."

"Gotta work with Dad on the farm?"

"Actually, tryouts are next week. I have to get ready for football."

Veeder went back to playing with his cars. "You guys gonna win the championship?"

"You bet we are! It will be the first time in the history of Goldston Regional High School."

"How many touchdowns are you going to run for this year?"

"I don't know, buddy, that's up to God." JJ rubbed his hands together.

"I bet you run for twenty touchdowns."

"That might be a little much." JJ laughed.

"I don't think so."

"Well, I like the way you think. I hope you're right."

"You'll do it."

"Hey, you want to get out of here?" Veeder stopped playing with his cars and looked at JJ. "I've got something better we could do together."

"Really, JJ?" Veeder was bursting with excitement. "You want to do something with me?"

"I do. I want to show you the coolest thing." JJ played up his enthusiasm. "So what do you say? Do you want to go?"

"You bet I do!" Veeder put his cars into a box, picked up the box, ran into the house, and put the box at the bottom of the stairs. "See you later, Mom!"

"Where are you going?" Jill yelled from the kitchen.

"Out with JJ!" Veeder ran through the front door. It slammed behind him as he bounded down the stairs.

"I'll race you." JJ took off, running across the yard. Veeder chased after JJ as fast as his little legs could carry him. He chased JJ through the yard and out into the fields, laughing the whole time.

Veeder loved running with JJ. It was hot. It was humid. Sweat poured off their foreheads as they raced through the fields. The corn stalks whipped across their legs and faces. The dirt kicked up from JJ's feet with every step and Veeder did everything to avoid the dust that was flying in his face.

A quarter of a mile later, JJ and Veeder stopped running. They bent over, putting their hands on their knees, trying to catch their breath. Their shirts hung heavy with sweat.

"Wow! I am out of shape." JJ stood straight up, interlocking his fingers behind his head, and looking around in every direction.

"Me too!" Veeder mimicked JJ, a big grin plastered across his face.

JJ smiled at Veeder. *Out of the mouth of babes*, he thought to himself, awestruck by Veeder's sense of innocence and wonder.

"I bet you are." JJ laughed, lowering his hands. He put one hand on Veeder's shoulder. "Come on, we'll walk the rest of the way."

The two boys walked through the fields for a while. JJ took in the sunshine that illuminated the land in amazing golden beauty. He listened to the birds singing. In the distance, he could hear the roar of a tractor. A gentle breeze tickled his face. The wind felt refreshing as it cooled his skin.

The haze of the sun covered the rolling hills and the trees in the distance. He was mesmerized by the colorful tapestry that God had woven together. Luscious green leaves were set against the bright blue Carolina sky that was filled with white puffy clouds. There was a vast array of yellows and browns that darted across the fields. Vibrant purple, blue, white, and pink flowers dotted the landscape. All woven together to make a perfect, beautiful picture of the true glory of God's word springing forth from the land and filling the world with a glimpse of His Spirit.

It was beautiful and JJ savored every moment of the silent walk. When they reached the far end of the field, JJ led Veeder into the woods. "Be careful, Veeder. Keep an eye out for snakes."

Veeder closed the gap between him and JJ, keeping an eye out for snakes. The two boys stepped into the woods, walking the trails, climbing over rock formations, and fallen trees. The trek seemed easier now. The shade of the trees made it feel a good twenty degrees cooler and much more bearable than the walk through the cornfield.

Veeder wasn't sure where JJ was taking him, but he didn't care. JJ was his idol. He revered his older brother and looked up to him with pride. The fact that JJ wanted to spend any time with him was a gift. Whatever they were out in the middle of the woods to see was just *the whip cream on top of his chocolate sundae kind of a day.*

They climbed up one last incline and into a clearing when JJ announced, "We're here!"

Veeder looked around, perplexed. "Where are we?"

"Your training grounds."

"My training grounds?" Veeder scratched his head and crinkled his nose. "What am I training for?"

"Football, dummy."

"What?" Veeder raised his eyebrows and tilted his head, staring at his brother.

"This is where I train for football. I made it for myself years ago."

"But what does that have to do with me?"

"This is where you are going to learn what it takes to play football. We are going to get your heart, mind, and body prepared to play! Are you ready?"

"I am!" Veeder shouted with exuberance, raising a fist high above his head.

"Good!"

"But what about mom?"

JJ stared at Veeder for a moment. "What about mom?"

"She'll never let me play."

"You worry too much!" JJ messed up Veeder's hair.

"I don't know how things work in your world, JJ, but in my life, mom is a pretty big force to be reckoned with!"

"You worry about football and let me worry about mom, okay?"

"But what about dad?"

"Dad?" JJ shook his head back and forth, placing his hands on his hips.

"Yes. Dad!"

"Why are you worried about dad?"

"He'll kick your butt!"

"Dad isn't going to kick my butt, Veeder." JJ chuckled.

"Yes, he is," Veeder said, kicking at a small rock on the ground. "Why do you think that?"

"I told you how mom made dad promise to never let anyone teach me how to play football." Veeder inched closer to JJ, looking around to make sure no one was listening. "Between you and me, I think she has something on that guy. Whatever she says, he does."

"Okay, you're right," JJ laughed. "Dad will kick my butt if I teach you how to play."

"Oh good, I'm glad we're on the same page." Veeder was dejected, kicking another pebble lying at his feet.

"Doesn't mean you can't learn how to play."

"How?" Veeder threw up his arms in frustration. "How are you going to teach me? Because it would be mean to drag me all the way out here just to tease me."

"You're right, it would be cruel of me to do that." JJ knelt, placing a hand on Veeder's shoulder, and looking into his younger brother's eyes.

"So what's your plan, JJ?"

"Do you remember the story mom told you about the promise she made dad keep?"

"Yes."

"Who did mom make dad promise would never teach you how to play football?"

Veeder started listing off people by counting them on his fingers. "Let's see; there was grandpa, dad, our uncles, you, our brothers, our friends, dad's friends, our uncle's friends."

JJ waited as Veeder paused to think. "Is that everyone?"

Veeder ran through the list on his fingers. "Yes. She covered just about everyone except the Pope. Did I miss anyone?"

"No, buddy, you didn't." JJ laughed and tussled Veeder's hair.

"Why are you laughing?"

"Because while I listened to you tell me her story, I found a loophole in her promise."

"You did?" Veeder was excited. "Tell me!"

"You see Mom said I couldn't teach you how to play football…"

"But she never said I couldn't teach you how to play," Colleen interjected, stepping out from behind a tree.

"You, Grandma?" Veeder turned around, dropping his head in defeat as JJ stood up behind him.

"Yes. Me." Colleen was a little hurt as she walked toward her grandsons.

"What do you know about football?"

"A lot more than you think."

"Really?"

"Yes. And here's the best part." Colleen stopped in front of Veeder. "You want to tell him, JJ?"

"I have the rest of the week off to get ready for my high school season. So we figured that while I'm out here training, grandma could learn from me."

"I can learn what he does and teach you how to do the same exact things."

"Do you think it will work?" Veeder was hopeful. "Won't mom get mad?"

"Mom never said we couldn't work out together." JJ winked at Veeder. "She just said I couldn't be the one training you."

"Are you sure you're up to this, Grandma?" Veeder looked at Colleen with a skeptical eye. "Are you sure you aren't too old for all of this?"

"I'll be sixty on Thanksgiving Day. If Sarah was able to give birth to Isaac when she was ninety, I am sure I can help train you for football."

"But we still have one major problem."

"What's that?" JJ asked.

"Mom won't let me play. What good is training if I can't play?"

"You worry about playing football," Colleen said, "and let me worry about your mother, okay?"

"You got it!" Veeder pumped his fist in celebration. "Let's go!"

They didn't waste any time. They got right to work. They spent the next few hours teaching, learning, and working together. And for the rest of the week, Veeder was attached to JJ at the hip. When JJ got up in the morning to go for a run, Veeder ran with him. The farther JJ ran, Veeder tried to match him, step for step. He never went as far as JJ did, but he went as far as his legs would take him.

When JJ went out to his workout area, Colleen and Veeder went with him. When JJ lifted logs off the woodpile and carried them forty yards just to stack them in a new pile, Colleen had Veeder move smaller logs. Once the logs were stacked in a pile, they moved the wood back to its original location.

Colleen paid close attention to everything JJ told her. She taught Veeder with perfection, preparing him for what he would face on the field. They ran Iron Man drills three to four times every day. They performed ladder drills. JJ flipped a tractor tire across the clearing while Veeder flipped a Jeep tire at his side. They did pull-ups, sit-ups, push-ups, jumping jacks, sprints, shuttle runs, and climbing drills. They worked hard to increase their strength and endurance. When they finished the physical training, they threw the football together as they worked on Veeder's form and footwork.

As each day passed, the two boys, although ten years apart in age, were like two peas in a pod. They did everything together. They learned from each other and they grew closer. They forged a connection in that clearing that would forever bond them together.

When Veeder and Colleen met up with JJ in the clearing on Thursday morning, JJ had hung a car tire from a tree branch. He swung it back and forth while Veeder worked on his timing and accuracy by throwing the football through it. JJ told Colleen what she needed to do to work on Veeder's throwing and she executed the coaching plan to perfection.

When they finished practicing each day, Colleen made the boys take a knee as she gave thanks to God for His grace and guidance. It was her way to embrace her faith in a God who had blessed her family with more than they ever deserved. It was also a reminder to the boys that God is everywhere in the world and He makes a way through all things.

Colleen believed that God deserved thanks for His blessings and provisions. If her grandchildren were allowing her to join them in their lives, she was going to teach them to praise God with all of their hearts.

When JJ and Veeder came back from their run on Friday morning and sat down in the kitchen to eat breakfast with the family, Paul came into the kitchen. "Alright boys, you have fifteen minutes to be in your mother's minivan."

"What are you doing Paul?" Jill asked.

"I am taking the boys to Chapel Hill to buy them new football gear for the season."

JJ, Sean, Colin, Michael, and Liam all started talking at once about what they were getting. It was an annual rite of passage in the McLean house to head out to Chapel Hill before the football season and buy new gear.

Mary Katherine and Veeder sat and ate their breakfast while the brothers ran to get their shoes on. Paul kissed the twins on the top of their heads, kissed Jill, and headed out to the vehicle.

The boys ran out behind him and piled into the minivan. Veeder followed them, stopping on the porch, and watching as they drove out of sight. The second the minivan disappeared down the driveway, Veeder ran off, met Colleen on the pathway to the woods, and headed out to JJ's workout area.

Colleen made sure Veeder put in a hard day's work in JJ's absence. She pushed him beyond his limits, and every time she thought he would quit, he pushed himself harder. He never complained. He never blinked at any of her requests. The harder she pushed, the harder he worked. He loved the game and was willing to do whatever it took to be the best.

When Colleen was tired of watching the boy work so hard, she decided it was time to reward him. "Go grab a couple of footballs, so I can push the tire swing for you."

"Yeah!" Veeder pumped his fist and ran over to the lockbox JJ kept in the clearing.

"We have to keep working on your accuracy," Colleen said, crossing the clearing towards the tire swing. "I don't want you to get lazy out there."

"Me?" Veeder puffed out his chest. "Never!"

Colleen laughed at Veeder's confidence. She wasn't paying attention to her surroundings when she kicked a four-foot-long copperhead that was in her path.

"Don't move, Veeder." Colleen froze in her tracks as the angered copperhead coiled, brought his neck above its body, and stared her down.

"What's wrong, Grandma?"

"Stay back, Veeder." Colleen was afraid. "I just angered a copperhead and I don't know what it's going to do."

Veeder grabbed a football out of the locker and moved around to the side of Colleen to get a better look at the snake. "Okay, Grandma, relax. You're going to be okay."

"Veeder, stop moving." Colleen stared down at the angry snake.

"Move away from the snake slowly, Grandma."

"I can't move, Veeder, it might strike."

"I see him, Grandma." Veeder cocked his arm, creeping closer to his grandmother. "Move back slowly."

"What are you doing? Don't come any closer." Colleen was frozen with fear.

"I've got you covered, Grandma, just step back slowly."

Colleen started to slide her foot backward. As she did, the snake raised his head a little and leaned toward her. "I don't think I should move any further."

"Grandma, if you don't back out of there, that snake is going to bite you."

"He might go away if I stay perfectly still."

"The only reason he hasn't struck is because he is watching both of us. You stand there any longer, he's going to strike." Veeder crept a little closer.

"I don't know if I can move." Colleen was paralyzed with fear.

"Don't be scared, Grandma, I've got this."

"What are you going to do?"

"I won't have to do anything if you stop wasting time." Veeder crept a little closer, his arm cocked, and ready.

Colleen took another half step backward and as she did, the snake pitched his head back. With laser focus, a keen sense of anticipation, and a cool, calm, collected resolve, Veeder fired the football at his grandmother's knee.

A split-second after the ball left Veeder's hand, the snake lurched forward at Colleen. When its open mouth was a couple of inches from Colleen's knee, the football connected full force against the head of the snake, launching the leviathan ten feet sideways across the clearing. Colleen fell onto on the ground with a loud scream of terror, her heart racing.

Veeder raced over to Colleen. "Are you okay, Grandma? Did he hurt you?"

"I'm fine, Veeder, I'm fine." Colleen wrapped the boy up in her arms, her heart pounding against her chest, breathing hard, tears of joy rolling down her face. "How did you do that?"

"I didn't do anything."

"You stopped the snake from biting me!"

"I just threw the football."

"How did you know when he was going to strike? And where the ball needed to be?"

"I just knew."

"Thank God you were here." Tears streamed down her face. "You saved my life. Praise be to God! Thank you, God!"

"All I did was throw the football, Grandma, God didn't have anything to do with it."

"That's where you are wrong." Colleen took the boy's face in her hands and looked into his eyes. "God had everything to do with what just happened. He was with you as you threw the ball."

"No, Grandma. I just did what my gut told me to do."

"God gave you a gift, Veeder. I don't know many people who could've made that throw."

"If you say so." Veeder shrugged his shoulders.

"God gave you the talent to be able to see things so much better than the rest of us. He gave you the ability to use that football like he directed David to use his slingshot. Without God bestowing you with the talent you have, that snake would have bitten me."

"I just did what my brain told me to do."

"No. You did what He told you to do. I am so proud of you!" Collen kissed Veeder on the cheek. "Thank you!"

The run-in with the copperhead rattled both of their nerves. Veeder and Colleen decided to call it quits for the day. As they walked along the pathway back to the farm, Colleen put her arm around Veeder's shoulders. She said a prayer of thanksgiving for her grandson's gift and for his courage to act in a dangerous situation. She thanked God for protecting her, and she prayed that Veeder would open his heart and accept the love of our Lord and Savior, Jesus Christ.

It broke Colleen's heart that Veeder didn't believe in God, but she was confident that one day he would. She knew it was a matter of time and whatever path God had planned for him, she believed He would find him at the right time in his life.

CHAPTER 4

—☙❧—

The next morning, Veeder was finishing up his breakfast when JJ walked into the kitchen and sat down at the table. "What's up, buddy?"

"Good morning."

"What are you doing today?"

"Nothing."

"Want to have some fun?"

"Yes!" Veeder was always up for an adventure.

"Go put on your hiking boots."

"Why?"

"It's a surprise."

"Be right back!" Veeder jumped up from the table, threw his plate into the sink, and ran out of the kitchen.

JJ got up from the table, went into the pantry, grabbed a handheld cooler, and walked back into the kitchen. He packed a lunch for the two of them. Just as he closed the cooler, Veeder came running back into the kitchen.

"I'm ready, JJ!"

"Good." JJ picked up the cooler. "Let's get out of here."

JJ started for the front door. Veeder walked next to him, engaging him in a game of twenty questions about their destination. He smiled at his little brother, ignored the questions, and put the cooler into the back of his Jeep. They climbed in and after they were buckled into their seats, he took off down the driveway.

JJ had taken off the top to his Jeep and had turned up the volume on the radio, the latest country songs blasting through the radio speakers. The wind whipping through their hair, they sang along with the radio. They were laughing and singing when he turned off the main road.

He pulled onto a one-lane, dirt path that led back into the woods. Cutting speed while passing under the low-hanging branches that loomed over the pathway, JJ paid close attention as he drove along the road that climbed up a steep hill.

Veeder reveled in the moment, laid his head against the headrest, wind rushing past his face. This had been the greatest week of his life. He got to spend time with JJ. He learned more about football, but he also got to know JJ better as a person. He smiled. It was the perfect week. He never wanted it to end.

JJ pulled into a small clearing deep in the heart of the woods, shut down the engine, and set the emergency brake. "We're here."

"We're here?" Veeder looked around with a raised eyebrow.

"Well, not exactly here. We're traveling the rest of the way on foot."

"Where are we going?"

"Up the hill." JJ pointed toward an overgrown footpath.

"Why?"

"You'll have to see when we get there."

"How far do we have to go?"

"To the top!"

"Really? How long is that gonna take?"

"If we move quickly, about an hour." JJ jumped out of the Jeep and slammed the door. "But I promise it will be the most beautiful sight you have ever seen. It's amazing."

"Cool." Veeder jumped out of the Jeep.

"But you can only come on one condition."

"Sure, anything."

"You have to promise me you won't tell anyone about this place. I've never taken anyone up here. It's my private getaway."

Veeder smiled and promised. JJ grabbed the cooler out of the Jeep, and they started walking up the winding path. It was a humid day, and it took the boys ninety minutes to traverse the steep trails. They were sweating when they stepped into the clearing on top of the peak.

It was beautiful. Veeder could see for miles in every direction as he looked out over the valley below. He felt like he was a few feet away from being able to touch the sky. He tried to reach up and run his hands through the cool, refreshing clouds that floated by on the breath of the slight wind that was pushing them along.

JJ walked over to the edge of the peak and sat on a boulder that looked out over the valley. Veeder stepped out of the shade and followed. He sat next to JJ, closed his eyes, and enjoyed the peaceful tranquility.

He could hear the rhythmic flapping of wings as birds flew by with love songs on their beaks. He could hear the wind whistle through the treetops before kissing his cheeks. He could hear the squirrels dancing on the leaves in a game of tag that made him smile. He could feel the sun cascading down the side of the peak, bringing life and warmth to everything below.

The air was fresh and clean. His senses rejoiced as they were engulfed in the euphoric, aromatic fragrances of the flowers that wafted up the side of the ridge, carried on the soft hands of the wind. The scents and sounds of the world swirled around his head.

"You really get a sense of how beautiful God's creation is from up here," JJ said, breaking the silence.

"Maybe."

"Maybe?" JJ was perplexed, staring at his little brother. "How do you look out on all of this and not see the loving hand of God everywhere?"

"I don't believe in God." Veeder shrunk, hiding his face from JJ's gaze.

"You don't?" JJ was shocked at the revelation. "Since when?"

Veeder turned his head, looked at his brother, and shrugged his shoulders. "I don't know."

"You're telling me that you can see all of this beauty, all this majesty, and you don't believe God is real?"

"I want to believe he's real. I do." Veeder panicked. He felt like his brother might stop loving him. "Trust me, JJ, I try. I go to church every Sunday, I go to church school every Wednesday night, but nothing ever changes. I just don't believe in Him."

"But He's always with us."

"I've just never seen Him or felt Him."

"Seen Him?" JJ chuckled, running his hand through his hair. "What about air? You can't see air, but you know it's real."

"But I can feel air when I breathe. I can feel it when the wind blows."

"God is in everything, Veeder. He is in the wind. When you feel each breath or the wind blowing against your face, you're feeling the presence of God."

"I wish I could believe that JJ, but I don't."

"Okay, what about your God-given talent to throw a football? If there isn't a God, where do you think that talent came from?"

"I don't know." Veeder shrugged his shoulders. "I was just born with it."

"You weren't just born with it; God gave you your talent."

"You're saying that God gave it to me before I was born. If that were true, then God knows everything that is going to happen in my life?"

"Haven't you ever read Psalm 139:16? That's kind of the point. He knew you before you were formed."

"Then if that is so, why does everybody always talk about free will?"

"Don't get me wrong, buddy, you have free will. The enemy is here to kill, deceive, and steal you away from God."

"How is the enemy involved if it's my free will?"

"That's a complicated answer."

"Try, JJ." Veeder was genuine in his request, he wanted answers. "Help me understand."

"The enemy lies to you and tries to convince you that those thoughts are your own."

"So, I don't have free will?"

"You do."

"I am so confused."

"You have the right to follow your own path in life. You can believe or not believe, but at some point, you will have to realize that there is a path that God has laid out for your life."

"How do we know what the right path is?"

"We know when we find it."

"Oh." Veeder looked down at his hands, feeling disappointed.

"Look, Veeder, God has a plan for you and whatever that plan is, I pray that God will help you find it. I pray you find His love and grace and that you fulfill His purpose for your life."

"Me too." Veeder looked out over the valley below.

"You will." JJ was confident, placing his hand on Veeder's shoulder. "In His time, you will."

"Can I ask you a question, JJ?"

"Sure. Anything."

"How can you be so sure there is a God?"

"Faith."

"Faith?"

"Yes." JJ nodded, patting Veeder on the back. "You have to have faith, Veeder."

"How do I find faith?"

"There is no simple solution to that question."

"You see why I have such a hard time? Everyone says you have to have faith, but no one tells you how to find it."

"You find it in your heart."

"But how?"

"That's a great question." JJ paused. "It's different for everyone."

"How did you find yours?"

"My story is complicated, but I have faith that God has a plan for me. In Jeremiah 29:11, it says that He has a plan for you. For all of us. That verse gives me the faith I need to believe He has my future worked out for me."

"We just learned about that verse in church school."

"Then take solace in the truth that God has a plan for you."

"But after Jeremiah wrote that, didn't it take another seventy years of captivity before the Jewish people returned to Jerusalem?"

"You're right." JJ smiled, patting Veeder on his back. "It did take them seventy years."

"I don't get your point, JJ. Are you saying I have to wait seventy years to play football? Because I might be too old."

"You would be buddy." JJ laughed, draping an arm around Veeder's shoulder. "But this plan for your life didn't just start when you were born. This plan has been in motion for years."

"That's ridiculous."

"I'm serious. God has been working on all of this for hundreds of years now. We're reaping the fruits of His labor."

"We weren't even alive hundreds of years ago."

"But our family was."

"What does our family have to do with this?"

"Everything."

Veeder scratched his head. "Now I'm really confused."

"Our family settled here in 1910."

"So?"

"Like in Jeremiah, that was seventy-five years ago."

"That has nothing to do with today, JJ."

"It has everything to do with today." JJ pulled Veeder close to him, using his other hand to point down into the valley. "When our family moved here, we had nothing. A measly few acres of land, but look out over the valley now. The farm is over seven hundred acres and growing every day."

"Our family has worked hard over the years."

"We have, but God has blessed us. He had a plan to prosper us, to give us hope, and a future."

"You mean our relatives worked hard for what they got."

"No, Veeder. We had faith in God and followed His plan. And look around, we did all right. We are living proof of that prosperous future that God promised."

"That's crazy, JJ." Veeder looked up at his brother and shook his head in disbelief.

"Why is that so hard to believe?"

"You really believe God started this plan for our family over seventy years ago?"

"I believe it goes farther back than that but yes, I do. I believe God has been providing for our family for the past seventy-five years."

"You're starting to sound like grandma."

"Good. She is the keeper of our family story."

"What does the past have to do with the future?"

"Everything!" JJ got animated.

"How do you know?"

"You don't know our family history, Veeder, do you?"

"Should I?"

"If you understood where we came from, you might understand all of the gifts God has bestowed upon us."

"And you know our family history?"

"Yes."

"How?"

"When you're as old as I am, you'll have heard all of the stories grandpa, grandma, dad, and mom have told about how we came to this little piece of Heaven."

"Like what?"

"Like how our family immigrated to New York City from Ireland."

"Everyone knows that."

"Or about how great-grandpa and great-grandma left the rest of the family behind in New York and planted roots in this little corner of North Carolina."

"You've got the 'little' part right."

"It's much more than that, Veeder. Haven't you ever heard Grandpa say, 'This is God's country and we are just stewards of his land'?"

"He was being sentimental."

"Hmm." JJ rubbed his chin with his fingers, thinking of a way to convey his point. "Do you think everything you have is yours? Or is it a gift from God?"

"It's mine."

"I believed that when I was your age too." JJ laughed. "But it's a gift."

"It's mine!"

"Everything we have is a gift from God. He showers us with His goodness. And for you and me, those treasures started over seventy years ago."

"It did?"

"It did." JJ reached into the cooler, grabbed two ice-cold water bottles, and handed one to Veeder.

"Thanks." Veeder opened the water bottle and took a sip.

"Things were bad in Ireland when our great-grandfather lived there. His family decided to sell everything they had and moved to America.

"They lived in Hell's Kitchen, which was the Irish part of New York City. It was deplorable. He lived in a house with his three brothers, two sisters, their spouses, and crying babies. Work was scarce. But great-grandpa was a hard worker and he saved all of his money."

"Why did he save all of his money?"

"Because he and great-grandma hated New York City. It wasn't a place to start a family. So they prayed every day for wisdom."

"Did they find it?"

"They both said that God came to them in a dream and told them, 'Go South. Farm the land. It won't be easy. There will be good times and bad times, but go south.'"

"You're trying to tell me that they both had the same dream." Veeder stared at JJ with a skeptical expression.

"I don't know. That detail was sketchy, but I do believe God told them to 'Go.' And they went. They took every penny they had saved up, found a small plot of land, built a small house, bought some equipment, and started farming.

"By the first harvest, they saw God's goodness firsthand. It was just the two of them. They worked hard and made enough to live. Any extra was used to buy more land, to share with the community and the church. And with each successive harvest, their blessings grew.

"And with each passing year, they always thanked God. Bought more land and they always gave more than their fair share to the church and the community. They shared their provisions with everyone. And as they started to have children, they hired people to help great-grandpa work the fields."

"Children?" Veeder was surprised. "Grandpa has brothers and sisters?"

"You really need to start paying attention at family gatherings." JJ laughed, taking a sip of his water. "Grandpa is the sixth of nine children."

"Sixth?" Veeder's jaw dropped open. "Where did they all go?"

"Grandpa doesn't talk about his older brothers. All five were killed in World War II."

"Wasn't grandpa in the army?"

"He was. Grandpa married grandma in 1944. He was twenty. Two months later, he shipped out to Europe. Dad was born while he was overseas."

"He wasn't here when dad was born?"

"Nope. He was in Europe."

"That must have been tough."

"Grandpa doesn't talk about the war much."

"Why did he go if all of his brothers died?"

"He believes that when God blesses you with a country where you are free to worship, free to live, free to love, and free to be whatever you want as long as you respect the rights of everyone, well, those are principles worth defending and dying for.

"He also says that God blessed him on his tour of duty. He said he leaned heavily on Jeremiah 1:19. They might have fought against grandpa, but they were never going to beat him because God was with him. Rescuing him. He honestly believes he only returned because God protected him when he was overseas defending our country."

"Wow!" Veeder was astonished. "What happened to his other brothers and sisters?"

"His younger brother died in a boating accident. His two younger sisters hated farming. When they were old enough, they moved back to New York City to live with their cousins.

"Grandpa used to get Christmas cards and occasional letters, but they chose a different path. Over the years, he fell out of touch with them."

"I wouldn't ever want to live without you guys."

"It happens, Veeder. Families grow apart when they get older."

"I hope we don't, JJ."

"We won't," JJ reassured him. "You don't have to worry about that."

"So, is that how grandpa ended up with the farm?"

"Not right away."

"No?" Veeder stared at JJ. "Why not?"

"When the war ended, grandpa came back and started working on the farm. Great-grandpa had hired more people. Most of the workers were down on their luck and facing hard times when they were hired. Grandpa felt like his father shortchanged these men and took advantage of their situation."

"They weren't paid enough?"

"Great-grandpa said they agreed to their wages before they came to work for him."

"Sounds like a big disagreement between them."

"It was, but grandpa was not the boss. It was the family farm and great-grandpa was in charge. It was his father's decision."

"So what happened?"

"Nothing. Grandpa worked the fields just as hard as anyone else. He did so out of reverence and service to God. He followed his father's lead. He worked hard. It wasn't easy but they made a good living, and after the harvest, they shared their abundance with those less fortunate."

"So, when did grandpa take over the farm?"

"In October of 1952, there was an accident."

"What happened?"

"One of the tractors flipped in the mud and pinned great-grandpa underneath it. By the next morning, they had to amputate great-grandpa's right arm. He was grateful to be alive, but he knew he was never going to be able to work the farm like he always had.

"So, at Thanksgiving Dinner that year, great-grandpa turned the family farm over to grandpa. He and grandma were in charge and you know what the first thing grandma and grandpa did when the farm was turned over to them?"

"No. What did they do?"

"Grandma says they got down on their knees together and prayed to God for His grace, wisdom, guidance, and clarity."

"Sounds like grandma."

"Well, grandma says that God gave them a heavy dose of clarity."

"How?"

"A few weeks later, grandpa and grandma went to help the church distribute holiday baskets for the less fortunate families in the community. Most of the families who showed up for assistance were the same people that worked on the farm. It broke their hearts."

"What did they do?"

"They did what they have always done, they asked God for a solution and He provided one."

"What was it?"

"Grandpa invited everyone to a New Year's Day dinner in the big barn. He had decided it was time to forge a new partnership with his friends who worked on the farm. He has always been very deliberate about using the word friend. Grandpa has never called anyone an employee. He has always believed that you are either friend or family. If you're neither, you don't belong here."

"Grandpa has always been nice to everyone."

"And he was on that day too. He told them that God had blessed all of them. They prayed for a good year ahead and they ate. Later that evening, he gave every friend a check for what they rightfully should have been paid for every year they worked on the farm."

"Wow! That's amazing!" Veeder interjected. "Grandpa and grandma did that?"

"And not only that, grandpa gave each of his friends an acre of land and helped them all build a house. None of his friends would ever be in need again. God would bless all of them and all of us."

"And God has blessed us." JJ took a sip of water, staring out over the valley. "For thirty-three years, our family has been blessed under their stewardship. The farm has grown. And every year, we share our abundant resources with the community and the church. And all of this exists because God told two people to 'Go South' and they went."

"Wow, that's amazing!" Veeder stared in awe at the valley. "I never knew that about our family. It makes you think."

"And God was right there in the middle of it all. Was it easy? No. Were there good times? You bet. Were there bad times?

Unfortunately, there were. But our family remained faithful through all of the storms."

"That's a great story, JJ."

"It's our story, Veeder. Our family owns all of this land because of a promise made over seventy years ago when our great-grandfather followed God's direction. And because of it, we all have been blessed."

Veeder grew silent and hung his head. "Do you hate me because I don't believe?"

"I could never hate you." JJ pulled Veeder into a hug. "I love you and thank God for you. It is by His grace and providence that He brought us closer together."

"I love you too." Veeder wrapped his arms around his older brother.

"Just do me a favor."

"Anything, JJ, name it."

"You said you keep trying to believe in God."

"I do."

"I call that faith."

"But I don't believe."

"But if you keep trying to find Jesus, I am sure God will reveal Himself to you when the time is right and open your heart. God's timing is perfect. Just don't give up looking for Him."

"I promise! I won't stop trying."

"Good." JJ grabbed the small cooler. "Let's eat! I am starving!"

CHAPTER 5

—⁓◉⁓—

It was a hot afternoon. It had been a crazy day. There were a million things to get done before school started. So when Jill found a few minutes to sit and relax on the front porch, she took advantage of the luxury.

Rocking in a chair, she watched Mary Katherine playing in the yard with a friend. It was in these rare, quiet moments when she was able to thank God for all of His blessings. She had a big, beautiful family. She had an amazing husband who worked hard to provide for her and her children. A man who was devoted to her and was a precious gift to her children. She had seven beautiful children who were her pride and joy.

"God is good!" she whispered, smiling as she continued to rock in her chair. A light breeze blew across the porch. She cradled the ice-cold glass of sweet tea in her hands, closed her eyes, and embraced the moment of peace.

"Good afternoon, Jill." Colleen walked up the steps of the porch.

"Mom?" Jill's eyes flew open, clutching her chest with her free hand. "You startled me!"

"Sorry, I didn't mean to scare you."

"No worries." Jill took a deep breath, chuckled in embarrassment, and regained her composure.

"How are you doing today?"

"Enjoying a few minutes of quiet."

"I remember how awesome those moments were."

"Aren't they?"

"Don't get me wrong." Colleen sat in the chair next to Jill. "I love my kids, but I do not miss the days of cleaning up after them all day."

"It's tiring." Jill laughed, sighing. "Isn't it?"

"And yet, I miss having all of my kids under my roof."

"You do not."

"I do." Colleen shook her head back and forth with a smirk on her face. "As crazy as these days seem, you will miss them when they all move out. The quiet will be deafening."

"I don't know about that."

"It will be, trust me."

"How?" Jill laughed, raising her arms, and looking around. "Your kids never move that far away."

"Be that as it may, you'll still miss it."

"Please forgive me, Mom, where are my manners today?" Jill stopped rocking in her chair and put her glass on the table. "Can I get you a glass of sweet tea?"

"That would be lovely. Please."

"I'll be right back."

Colleen rocked in her chair and watched Mary Katherine playing in the yard. A few moments later, the door slammed. Jill returned carrying a glass of sweet tea and a plate of homemade chocolate chip cookies.

"Here you go." Jill handed Colleen the glass, placing the cookies on the table between the two rocking chairs.

"Thank you, Jill." Colleen took a sip and placed the cold glass against her cheek.

"You're welcome."

"Homemade cookies?" Colleen took one off the plate and bit into it. "Mm. So good."

"I made them with Mary Katherine and her friend."

"Who is her friend?"

"A girl she met at church."

"Look at those two."

"Not a care in the world."

"The wonder of a child's imagination on a summer afternoon."

"Now, that I miss!" Jill took a bite of a cookie as they both chuckled.

They sat, rocking in their chairs, drinking sweet tea, and watching Mary Katherine play in the yard. Enjoying the moments of quiet that passed, they took in the sights and sounds of the world around them.

Colleen nibbled on her cookie, contemplating how to broach the conversation. Hoping it would go well, she asked the Holy Ghost for guidance and wisdom.

"Jill, can I ask you a question?" Colleen stopped rocking her chair, turned to face Jill, and placed her glass on the table.

"Sure, go ahead." Jill was caught off guard.

"Are you really going to stop Veeder from playing football for the rest of his life?"

"Et tu, Brute?" Jill was blindsided by Colleen's bluntness.

"I'm not your enemy here, Jill."

"Sure doesn't sound like you're my ally." Jill was irritated and she gave Colleen a disapproving glare.

"I am asking for my own understanding."

"You know how I feel about him, Mom."

"I do."

"He was a preemie."

"He was." Colleen nodded.

"He is smaller than the other boys."

"But he's not in the incubator anymore."

"I have always been honest with you about the dream I had and how I felt it was a warning from God." Jill's blood was starting to boil under her skin.

"I know about the dream, Jill, but sometimes a dream is just a dream."

"It was a warning!" Jill yelled before regaining her composure. "I believe that with all of my heart."

"Or maybe it was just a nightmare that you had in the middle of the nightmare you and Paul were living through at the time."

"Really, Mom?" Jill couldn't believe what she was hearing from Colleen. She was visibly upset and shocked by the stance her mother-in-law was taking. "Forgive me for being upset but, as a mother and a grandmother, you are the last person I expected to question my decision."

"I'm just trying to understand your rationale."

"I'm going to protect him from going through that pain if I can."

"You know you can't protect him from life."

"I can try."

"You can't stop bad things from happening to anyone," Colleen laughed, rolling her eyes.

"You bet I can!" Jill shot Colleen an icy glare.

"No. You can't, and you know it," Colleen said with biting acrimony. "Life happens. Adversity will come. And by our faith in God, we weather the storms."

"Sometimes, though, as a mom, you stop the storms from coming."

"I know you want to control life, Jill, but you can't. Life finds all of us whether we like it or not. We do our best for our kids and prepare them for what lies ahead."

"If I don't let him play, the reality of the dream can never come true."

"Is denying him of a game he loves really in the best interest of your son?"

"As far as I'm concerned, it is."

"Then I am going to overstep my bounds here." Colleen leaned closer to Jill and lowered her voice. "You're wrong."

"How can you say that to me after everything we have been through with that boy?"

"I get it, Jill. I do." Colleen sat back, throwing up her arms.

"Obviously, you don't!"

"Veeder is smaller than all of the other kids. He put you and Paul through forty days of hell. But he's not in the incubator anymore."

"That's not fair!"

"No, Jill," Colleen said with determination. "What isn't fair is making him watch his brothers play football and making him hear stories of his father's glory days, then forcing him to sit on the sidelines without any glory days of his own."

"Do you hear yourself?" Jill shot back in anger. "I'm protecting the boy! How is that unfair?"

"He deserves to prove to you he is just as tough as they are."

"And that's all it is!" Jill had found her *aha moment* and drove the point home. "It's not about football, Colleen! He wants to prove how tough he is, so his brothers won't pick on him."

"Oh, please." Colleen scoffed at Jill's assertion, chuckling at her conclusion. "You really don't believe that?"

"He doesn't love the game, he's in love with gaining their approval."

"That's garbage, Jill, and you know it! He loves the game."

"How do you know?"

"Because I've been playing football with him every day for the past week."

"What?" Jill was shocked, hurt, and disgusted. "How could you do that knowing how I feel?"

"I'm not sorry, Jill, I'm not." Colleen stared at Jill. "The boy has a gift. I nurtured it."

"Why would you defy me like that?"

"I know how you feel about Veeder playing football, but after I saw him play catch with JJ, I knew he had a God-given talent. I had to find out for myself how good he is."

"You had no right, Colleen!"

"I had every right!" Colleen's temper flared, she refused to back down.

"No, you didn't!"

"He's my grandson!"

"And he's *my* son!"

"You're right," Colleen acquiesced. "He is your son, Jill. I'm not going to argue that point with you."

"At least you realize that, Colleen," Jill fired back with biting acrimony.

"But you can't control Veeder forever."

"Watch me."

"Sooner or later, Jill, he's going to play, with or without your consent. Would you rather support him in his efforts? Or fight him?"

"If I point Veeder in the right direction, he will never turn from it."

"Not in this case, Jill." Colleen gave her a disapproving stare.

"I started Veeder off on a different path than one that involves football and if you don't interfere with me, he will stay on this path and never turn from it."

"Stop worrying about tomorrow, Jill, today has enough trouble for you to handle."

"I can stop bad things from happening if I don't allow him to be in a position to get hurt."

Colleen stared into Jill's eyes. "You can't control his life and you can't worry about what hasn't happened. God will take care of tomorrow. You can only focus on today."

"It's my decision and I have made it!"

"For now." Colleen struck a conciliatory tone. She turned and looked out over the yard. "Veeder wants to play football and the more you interfere, the more he will resent you for it."

"That's ridiculous. You don't know what you're talking about."

"I do know what I'm talking about, Jill." Colleen stared at Jill with contempt in her eyes. "I tried to control my son's life too, remember?"

"That's different."

"Is it?" Collen took a deep breath, trying to remain calm. "I denied him his dream, and in his defiance, he enlisted. A year later they sent him to Vietnam. He never came home."

"That is a completely different situation."

"I wonder what would have happened if I just let him do what he wanted." Colleen fought back the tears. "Would he still be alive today?"

"He was patriotic. He would have enlisted anyway."

"Well, we'll never know, will we? And I live with that guilt every day." Colleen wiped away a tear. "I don't want you to ever feel that guilt."

"You can't blame yourself, Mom. He made his own decision."

"And one day, so will Veeder." Colleen patted Jill's knee and looked into her eyes. "So will Veeder one day."

"You really think he will?" Jill's heart sank at the thought of Veeder defying her wishes.

"I do. And then, whether he gets hurt or not, he will never share it with you, and you will feel guilty for that every single day."

"I really don't want him to play."

"And if that is your final decision, I will respect it."

"Thank you."

"I won't agree with it, but I will respect it."

"But you won't agree with it?"

"No."

"Why not?"

"Just make sure you're making decisions for him and not for you."

"I am, Mom. I really am."

"I know you believe that." Colleen sat back in her chair, running her hand over her mouth.

"What would you do in my situation?"

"I've said too much already, Jill. That's for you to decide."

"You choose this point in the conversation to withhold your thoughts?"

"Just do me a favor and pray about it."

"I will."

"Not just you. You and Paul. Pray about it. Talk about it. Together. And if God stirs your heart just a little, maybe you could let Veeder play in the family game on Sunday."

Jill paused for a moment, taking a deep breath. "They're so much bigger than he is, they'll hurt him."

"They are bigger but they're family. They'll take it easy on him."

"How can you be so sure?"

"Just pray on it." Colleen rose to leave. "Listen to what God says in your heart."

"I will."

"Then I promise, I will respect whatever you decide."

"Thank you."

"Have a good night, Jill." Colleen turned, walked down the front steps, and headed for home.

Later that evening, Paul sat in the little alcove of their bedroom reading his Bible. Jill walked into their bedroom and stood in front of the mirror that was attached to the top of their oak dresser. She pulled the pins out of the bun and let the auburn tresses fall below her shoulders.

She stared into her own tired eyes as she reflected on the last ten years of her life. The conversation with Jill had rattled her. She began to second guess the decisions she had made for all of her children. With a crooked smile and a loud sigh, Jill walked across the bedroom and sat down in the chair next to her husband. "Excuse me, Paul, but can we talk for a few minutes?"

"Absolutely, Sweetheart." Paul set his Bible down on the table next to his chair. "I noticed you have been pensive all night and was wondering what was bothering you."

"Your mom came to see me today. She brought up Veeder playing football."

Paul rolled his eyes, looked away for a second, and let out a long, loud sigh. "Would you like me to talk to her?"

"Paul, I don't know if she was wrong."

"What did she say?"

"She wanted to know why I wouldn't let him play. For my protection? Or for his?"

"The reason doesn't matter. It's none of her business. We made a decision; she should respect it."

Jill grimaced and turned her head. "Did we really make that decision together?"

"Yes."

"But we never talked about it. We never prayed about it…"

"We made a decision. End of story. I will reiterate that to mom in the morning."

"Paul," Jill paused for a moment, "your mom has been playing football with Veeder."

"What?" Paul's jaw dropped wide open. "Since when?"

"Does it matter?"

"Yes!" Paul was angry. "She shouldn't have done that!"

"Apparently, Veeder's really good."

"She should have respected our decision."

"Paul, I love you for sticking by me, but it wasn't something we decided together. I made you do it."

"I love you, Jill. I will always support you."

"But what if I was wrong?"

"It's our mistake to make. Not hers! She had no right."

"Pray with me?" Jill took Paul's hand in hers. "Maybe God will provide us with some clarity."

"I will always pray with you." They knelt together, bowed their heads, held hands, and prayed.

CHAPTER 6

It was another glorious Sunday afternoon in God's country. A day when the family would remember, celebrate their humble beginnings, and rejoice in how the farm had grown over the years. A day where they thanked God for blessing them, but it was also a time to come together to share their faith, their love of family, and the relationships that God had blessed them within their lives.

Paul pulled into the driveway with JJ, Colin, Michael, and Sean. He parked the truck. They jumped out, grabbed the coolers, a couple of footballs, and headed toward the backyard. Jill pulled in behind Paul with Liam, Mary Katherine, and Veeder. When parked, Veeder and Liam jumped out and ran off. In their excitement, they didn't hear Jill yell for them to help her unload, which left Mary Katherine to help carry the platters of food.

"Hi, Grandma! Hi, Grandpa!" Mary Katherine said as she and Jill put the platters of food down on the center island of the kitchen.

"Hi, Mary Katherine. How are you today?" Colleen asked.

Jill sorted out the platters and started putting food into the refrigerator.

"Are you ready for school?" James asked.

"I'm good, Grandma. And yes, Grandpa." Mary Katherine rolled her eyes. "I wish school lasted all year. Summer break is such a waste of time."

"That's because you're the smart one." James winked at her.

"Mom, can I go outside and play?"

"Yes, Mary Katherine. Thank you for your help."

"Thanks, Mom." Mary Katherine raced out the door.

"Good afternoon, Jill," Colleen said, trying to get Jill's attention.

"Good afternoon, Mom… Dad. Great sermon this morning, don't you think?"

"I think Pastor Steve hit it out of the park today," James answered. "I am truly inspired by his words. Very powerful."

"I agree," said Colleen.

"So do I." Jill placed the last platter in the refrigerator and closed the door.

"Did you get a chance to think about what we talked about yesterday, Jill?" Colleen blurted out.

"I did, Mom. Paul and I had a long talk last night." Jill was frustrated that Colleen brought up the topic of Veeder playing football again, and she shot her mother-in-law an icy glare.

Colleen ignored Jill's facial cues. "What did you decide?"

"We decided to do what was best for our son." Jill walked out of the house and into the backyard.

"What was that all about?" James asked.

"Nothing."

Jill walked down the steps of the back porch and across the backyard to the coolers. Agitated, she reached into one and grabbed a bottle of coke, opened it, and took a long, hard swig, trying to calm her nerves. The music played, helping steady her resolve. Her gaze swept over the yard. Paul and his brothers were standing around the barbecue pit, talking and laughing. The boys were picking teams for football. The girls were off to the side playing. The other wives ate and chatted. No one was aware of the turmoil growing inside of Jill.

Jill took a deep breath, walked over to her husband, and planted a big kiss on his lips. "I love you, baby, you better be right about this."

"Right about what?" Paul asked as Jill turned around and walked away from him. "What did I do?"

Jill walked with determination across the backyard. All her fears, trepidations, and nerves were welling up inside her body. She was in uncharted waters. She was afraid, confused, and conflicted. As she reached the table, she fought back the fears. "Get behind me, Satan."

Jill sat down next to Veeder, put the coke bottle on the table in front of her, and looked across the backyard. "What are you doing?"

"Nothing." Sadness enveloped his voice.

"Why not?"

"Nothing to do." Veeder planted his chin squarely on the palms of his hands, defeated.

"Are you trying to tell me, that between all of the toys you have in our house and over here, that you have nothing to do?" Jill asked, trying to inject a little levity into the situation.

Veeder shrugged his shoulders. "Nope. These parties aren't fun for me."

"Why not?"

"No one to play with."

"Did you ask anyone?"

"Everyone I want to play with is playing football."

"I'm sure there is someone else to play with."

"Everyone here gets to do whatever they want while I sit here and do nothing."

"You'll find something to do."

"Yes, Mom, in about five minutes, grandma's going to come over with a deck of cards because she feels sorry for me."

"She doesn't feel sorry for you."

"Yes." Veeder sounded pitiful. "She does."

"Maybe she likes spending time with you." Jill poked his side with her elbow. "Did you ever think of that?"

"Nope, Mom, she doesn't. I am *that* kid. The sad little cousin that grandma *has* to play with, so he doesn't sit alone all afternoon."

"I think that's nice of her."

"It is." Veeder rolled his eyes, frustrated with the conversation.

"Then why knock it?"

"Because she gets mad at me because I'm not faithful enough! I'm not perfect!"

"Nobody's perfect."

"You should tell her that."

"Or… maybe you should count your blessings."

"Why?"

"Because your grandmother loves you."

"I know she does, Mom, but would you want to be the kid who only hangs out with his grandmother every Sunday?"

"To be honest with you, Veeder, I would."

"That's because you're weird." Veeder chuckled, poking his mom in the arm.

"You think so? Don't you?" Jill chuckled as well.

"You've always been weird."

"You might be right about that, Veeder." Jill lowered her head, placing her hand on the back of his neck. "Where you're involved, I just might be the weirdest mom in the whole world."

"You really are, Mom. I'm glad you're finally seeing it."

"Do you think you could find it in your heart to forgive me?"

Veeder was puzzled as he turned and looked at her with a furrowed brow. "Forgive you for what?"

"What do you want to be doing right now?"

"Playing football." Veeder sighed, gazing across the yard.

"And you're not playing because I won't let you?" Jill took her son's hands in hers.

"Basically."

"I'm willing to work with you, Veeder, if you promise me one thing."

"Work with me?"

"I'm thinking about letting you play football today."

"You mean it?" Veeder was trying to contain his excitement.

"Will you promise me you won't get hurt?" Jill knew it was a promise he could never keep, but she asked him anyway.

Veeder squirmed in anticipation. "I promise, Mom! I promise I promise, I will never, ever get hurt!! I will never, ever, ever, ever, ever, ever, get hurt! I promise! Can I play? Can I please, please, please, please, pretty please, with sugar on top, pretty please, can I play, Mom?"

Jill chuckled. She felt insane for contemplating it but as she stared into the excitement and the passion of her sons' request, compassion overtook her heart. "Yes. Go play with your brothers."

Veeder didn't need any more encouragement and he sure wasn't going to hang around for her to change her mind. He threw his arms around her in a big embrace with a bunch of kisses, thanking her before running to join the game. "JJ, mom said I could play! Mom said I could play!"

JJ looked over at his mother who nodded in the affirmative and gave JJ a nervous thumbs up. He smiled, turning to the rest of the group. "Veeder's on our team."

Liam yelled from across the line, "Good! You can have him! I can't wait to knock him on his butt all day."

JJ smiled back at Liam, flexed his muscles, and chuckled. "If that's the way you want to play, I can't wait to knock you on yours!"

Liam thought twice before opening his mouth again. The teams took their places on opposite ends of the field and readied for kick-off.

Paul approached the table and sat next to Jill. He draped his arm around her shoulders. "Are you sure you want to do this?"

"No," Jill said as nervous laughter overtook her.

"Then why do it?"

"Because I'm not really sure about anything right now. But your mom's right, I can't worry about what might happen. What kind of life is that for a kid?"

"He could get hurt."

"He could fall down the stairs tomorrow. Do I ban him from using stairs?"

"No," Paul guffawed. "But I see your point."

"Go ahead, say it," Jill said, looking at Paul with a weird expression. "I'm crazy, aren't I?"

"I'm proud of you."

"That's one of us."

"I hope you don't mind, but I'm going to sit here all afternoon while you grit your teeth and hide your eyes."

"Thank you." Jill was nervous, folding her hands together in front of her.

"And promise me one thing?"

"What?"

"Please don't tell my mother she was right? We'll never hear the end of it."

"Deal!" Jill chuckled, leaning her head on Paul's shoulder to watch the game.

The game was exciting. It was a back and forth battle all afternoon. It didn't take long for the family to realize that Veeder was a pretty good quarterback. He picked apart the defense all game and made some great downfield throws for touchdowns.

JJ decided early in the game that Veeder wasn't going to play defense. Michael and Liam were knocking him down whenever they had the chance. So JJ did his best to limit those opportunities. That didn't stop Michael and Liam, though. When they would knock him down, they taunted Veeder. They tried their best to intimidate him. But every time they knocked him down, he jumped right back up and smiled.

Every time Michael and Liam knocked Veeder down, Jill became agitated. Paul kept her from running onto the field and punishing both of them in front of everyone. But under her breath, she was developing a bunch of extra chores for them to do. It would be their penance for their ill-advised decision to beat up on their younger brother.

Near dinner time, the game was tied. It was decided that the next team to score would win the game. Liam's team had the ball and was driving down the field for the winning score when JJ intercepted an errant pass, and returned the ball to midfield, before being run out of bounds.

Veeder came back onto the field in hopes of leading his team to victory. Excited, he got close to the huddle, strutting the last few yards in front of Liam and Michael. JJ set up the play, they broke the huddle, and approached the line of scrimmage. Veeder came up to the line under center, barked out a made-up cadence, and yelled, "Hike!"

The ball was snapped and the defense blitzed. The left side of the offensive line couldn't hold back the rush as Veeder dropped back. Forced from the pocket, Veeder scrambled to the right side of the field. Out of the corner of his eye, he caught a glimpse of his cousin running uncovered across the middle of the field. On a dead run, Veeder stuck his right leg in the ground, fired the ball across his body moments before Liam wrapped him up, and took him to the ground.

Veeder never saw the near-impossible pass fly across the middle of the field over the heads and outstretched arms of a couple of leaping linebackers. The ball dipped towards the ground as it split the safeties and was caught by a diving receiver for a completion. Before the receiver could get up to advance the ball, he was tagged down where he laid on the field.

Players on the field, and family members watching the game, started talking about the amazing throw Veeder had just made. They were dumbfounded that he would have had the presence of mind, or the arm strength, to make such an amazing pass.

"Didn't I tell you not to run in my direction?" Liam stood over Veeder, taunting him.

Veeder rolled over and jumped up, clutching his left arm. "Bring it, Liam! I'm not afraid of you!"

"Oh, I'm bringing the pain next time."

"You hit like an old lady!"

"Oh yeah?" Liam puffed out his chest, flexing his muscles, trying to intimidate his brother.

"Yeah!" Veeder pushed him out of his way.

Liam pushed Veeder in the back. "You'll wish you never played after I knock you down next time."

"Good luck, buttercup!" Veeder yelled, grabbing Liam, and starting to wrestle with him.

"You wait! I'm going to make you cry for mommy!"

"You'll be the one crying when I stick the ball in the end zone and rub the win in your face!"

"Cut it out!" JJ had had enough. He was angry, pulling them apart and separating them.

"He started it!" Liam and Veeder yelled in unison.

"Get back on your side, Liam!"

"That's right, take the baby's side!" JJ flexed and Liam ran back to his side of the line.

"You're the baby, Liam!" Veeder taunted, standing behind JJ's protection.

"Get in the huddle, Veeder!" JJ yelled, turning to Veeder, and pointing towards the huddle.

When Veeder got back to the huddle, he got an earful from JJ. "Winners don't play like that!"

"Sorry, JJ."

"Beat him with your arm. Don't be a punk!"

"What about him?"

"If he wants to be a punk, let him. Walk away! You're better than that!"

"Got it!"

"I better not see that again!" JJ said, patting Veeder on the back. "That was a great throw."

"Thanks."

"Now let's win this thing so we can go eat!"

"You bet!"

JJ set the play and the team broke the huddle. Headed back to the line of scrimmage, Veeder went under center, made up a cadence, and yelled, "hike!"

He dropped back, but he couldn't find anyone open. A second later, one of his cousins broke through the right side of the line and was about to sack Veeder. He spun away from the tackle and rolled to the right. He drifted closer to the sideline, saw JJ break free from his defender, and head for the end zone. Veeder cocked his arm and launched a deep pass down the field.

As Veeder let the ball fly, he saw Liam sprinting at him with the intent of knocking him down. Veeder braced himself and as Liam was about to hit him, Veeder lunged towards Liam and brought his elbows up to defend himself. The two boys collided and fell to the ground.

Veeder rose to celebratory cheers, JJ had caught the winning pass. His elation over having won the game was short-lived, though. Liam was rolling around on the ground next to him and screaming, "He broke my nose! He broke my nose!"

Jill and Paul bolted across the backyard. They assessed the injury as Colleen handed Paul a hand towel filled with ice. They were unable to tell whether Liam's nose was broken, so Paul and Jill helped Liam to his feet. They held the ice on his nose and walked him to Paul's truck. They all got in and drove to the nearest emergency room.

After dinner, the family helped get things cleaned up. James and Colleen took the rest of Paul and Jill's kids' home and waited at the house for them to return. As the night wore on, most of the McLean children went to bed. Veeder laid awake in his bed listening for the hum of his father's truck. He relived the whole day in his mind. He loved the feel of the ball in his hand, he loved how the ball felt when it left his hand, he loved how it looked soaring through the air towards its intended target, and how much of an adrenaline rush it was every time he completed a pass. He reveled in all of the touchdowns he threw, and he even reminisced about the fleeting euphoria he felt when he threw the winning touchdown to JJ.

It was somewhere around midnight when Veeder heard Paul's truck pull into the driveway. His parents helped Liam into the house. Paul helped him up the stairs and into his bedroom. Jill talked to Colleen and James, thanking them for looking after the rest of the kids. James and Colleen passed on the invitation to stay the night and went back to their home.

Paul and Jill locked up and went upstairs to go to bed. Veeder slipped out of his bed and crept down the hall to his parent's room. He knocked on the door and pushed it open. When he popped his head inside the door, Paul was sitting on the edge of the bed staring at him. "What are you doing up at this hour of the night?"

"I couldn't sleep." Veeder entered the room and sat on the bed next to Paul.

"Worried?"

"Is Liam okay?"

"Your brother is going to be fine." Paul put his arm around Veeder's shoulders.

"Did he break his nose?"

"He did not."

"That's good."

"His nose is bruised and swollen, he has a black eye, and the doctor said he will not be able to play any contact sports for at least a week."

"I didn't mean to hurt him, Dad, honest I didn't."

"I know you didn't, the two of you got carried away. That happens sometimes."

"Did it ever happen to you?"

"Your mother will kill me for telling you this, so we have to make this our secret," Paul said, leaning closer to Veeder.

"Cross my heart." Veeder made an x over his heart.

"We got into so many fisticuffs; grandpa was always on the field pulling us off of each other."

"Is mom mad at me?" Veeder asked, nervous his mother would never let him play again.

"I will be if you don't get your backside off to bed," Jill said, walking out of the bathroom and sitting down on the bed.

"I'm sorry, Mom."

"What are you still doing up?"

"I couldn't sleep. I was worried about Liam."

"He'll be just fine."

"Are you mad at me, Mom?"

"You and Liam got a little carried away out there today."

"I didn't mean to hurt him."

"Accidents happen, but you two went too far. We'll talk about that later."

Veeder hung his head low. "Will I ever be able to play again, Mom?"

"If you don't go to bed right now, no, you will never be able to play again." Jill laughed, wrapping him up in her arms and giving him a big hug.

"Thanks, Mom."

Jill turned her head and whispered into Veeder's ear, "It was fun watching you out there on the field. I loved watching you smile and enjoy yourself. I love you. Now get to bed!"

"Love you, Mom."

Veeder jumped off the bed and raced down the hall to his bedroom. Jill followed, tucked him into his bed, and kissed his cheek. "Good night, my little quarterback."

CHAPTER 7

—◦◦—

The whistle blew, the lights illuminated the creeping darkness of dusk. The coaches called the varsity team to huddle up, and they took a knee at the center of the practice field. It was the end of the final practice before the biggest game of their young lives.

JJ sauntered to the center of the field and knelt. Filled with a plethora of emotions, sweat pouring off his body, he was excited for the last game of the season on Friday night, but sad to see four years of hard work, and a record-setting career come to an end. He was also inspired by thoughts of the future and the amazing opportunities that awaited after graduation.

It had been a wild season. JJ had set record after record on the field. Coaches from several universities scouted him. They visited JJ and his family with promises of glory in an effort to recruit him to play for their teams. He was overwhelmed by the attention he had garnered from the best football programs in the country, but he knew he was prepared for the trials and tribulations that awaited him in college.

JJ accepted a football scholarship to attend Chapel Hill University. He couldn't wait to be a Cobra. He couldn't wait to represent the state that had blessed his entire family since his great-grandfather had settled down in Goldston. Playing for the Cobras had always been his aspiration, and it was going to be a true honor to live out his dream as a native Carolinian and the first member of the McLean family to go to college.

JJ's teammates were psyching each other up, excited for the big game. Coach McCarthy walked over to the team and stood in the middle of his players. Having been the football coach of the Goldston Regional Gators for twenty-five years, he was a tall, burly man with graying hair, and a hardened face that looked like each year of those seasons had etched their place along his furrowed brow. He was a no-nonsense, tough man who pushed his players hard, asking nothing more than excellence and expecting true loyalty among his coaches and players. He took one last moment to collect his thoughts. He wanted to savor every minute and make it last. He looked at all the players' faces, cleared his throat, and gave his final speech before the much-anticipated game.

"Men, this is what we have worked so hard for all season. It's why we conditioned for hours back in August. It's why we had two-a-day practices and it's why we spent hours in the classroom studying our opponents. We had to prepare our hearts, our minds, our bodies, and our souls, so we could rise to the challenge of the season.

"And rise to the challenge you did! You went out on the field every Friday night and won every single game! We played against teams that were bigger and stronger on paper, but they failed to understand the one thing that you all have that they didn't—heart!" Coach McCarthy pounded his chest with his fist.

"You believed in your hearts that you were tougher than the guy across the line from you. You believed in your brothers who stood shoulder to shoulder with you on every play. And you believed in your coaches who worked to prepare you each week. And as we get prepared to go out and face Bryson City on Friday night for the State Championship, I, and the rest of the coaching staff, are proud of each and every one of you!

"We have had our bumps and bruises. We have played sore and we have played in pain, but you all rallied around one another. You picked each other up when one of us was hurting. You believed in each other. Supported each other. And in the end, came together as a family!

"And now, you have an opportunity to do something that has never been done at Goldston Regional!" Coach McCarthy yelled, becoming animated. "You have an opportunity to go out and win the State Championship on Friday night! Are you ready?"

"Yes!" the players all roared, while whooping, hollering, and jumping up and down.

They reveled in the moment, and Coach McCarthy traveled around the circle giving high-fives and saying repeatedly, "Get excited boys! Get excited boys! Get excited!"

After a few moments of celebration, Coach McCarthy stood in the center again and quieted down his team. When they were attentive, he continued, "Men, go home tonight and enjoy the Thanksgiving meal with your families tomorrow. Thank God for your families, for your blessings, and your opportunities! Enjoy the day off!

"But on Friday night, I expect you to come back here as focused and determined. On Friday night, you will get to live a dream that very few people get to live because you will get to represent the Goldston Regional Gators for the state championship!

"Win, lose or draw, no one can ever take that honor away from you. I want you to play the best game of your lives!" Coach McCarthy yelled, amping up his rhetoric. "And God willing, we *will* hoist the championship trophy on Friday night!"

The team reignited their celebration full of whoops and hollers of "Let's Go!" and a ritualized chant of "Championship!" giving themselves another round of high-fives, fist bumps, and chest bumps.

Coach McCarthy yelled, "Team, bring it in!!"

The players crowded around their coach, putting their hands in on top of his, as he knelt in the center of the team. Coach McCarthy yelled his final words for the team, "I am proud and honored to be your Coach! I am proud to lead you on the field on Friday night! And I am proud of every one of you! Now let's go win this thing!"

"Yeah!" They all erupted as they crowded closer chanting "Championship! Championship!"

"Captains," Coach McCarthy yelled above the fracas. "Call out your final practice!"

JJ stepped into the middle of the huddle with the other captains, held their hands high as all of the players crowded around, and JJ yelled out, "Championship on three!! One! Two! Three! Championship!"

JJ stood in the center of the field, taking in the scene as his teammates ran, excited to the locker room. He embraced the gravity of the moment in a fit of nostalgia. This would be the last time he would ever walk across this practice field as a member of the Goldston Regional Gators.

He thought back over the hard work and practices. Amassing many of the school's football records, he had grown up over the past four years. No longer the low man on the totem pole as a cocky freshman who still needed to learn how to play the game, he had grown up to be a disciplined player who was respected. His time on the Gators was coming to an end, and JJ wanted to go out on top as a champion.

JJ's emotions got the best of him. Before turning around, he took one, long last look at the field, wiping a tear from the corner of his eye. He patted his chest three times with his fist and pointed a finger toward the sky. "Thank you, God. Thank you for four great years and thank you for blessing me with your grace. Amen."

JJ lowered his arm, looked around, turned, and jogged into the locker room.

CHAPTER 8

—◦◦◦)—

Veeder woke up on Thanksgiving with his olfactory senses pinging off the charts. The delicious aromas of turkey, homemade puddings, and pies wafted throughout the house. He climbed out of bed, raced down the hall to JJ's room, flung open the door, and ran across the room. He started shaking JJ's shoulder. "JJ, get up! Get up!"

"Veeder, why are you waking me up?" JJ rolled over, trying to open his eyes.

"There are football games to watch!"

"The football games don't start until 12:30 pm, buddy." JJ rubbed his face.

"Oh!"

"Besides the Giants aren't even playing today."

"I know, but the Cowboys play the Rams, and we need the Rams to win."

"That we do."

"Plus the Jets play the Lions and let's be honest, nobody I know likes the Jets."

"You're right about that, Veeder." JJ laughed, sitting up in bed. "I don't know anyone either!"

"Get up, JJ!"

"Not yet."

"Why not?"

"I'm tired." JJ rubbed his eyes and yawned. "Go downstairs and bother mom and dad so I can get another couple of hours of sleep."

"Alright, JJ, but you're missing out." Veeder raced out of the room, being sure to slam the door behind him. He bounded down the stairs and into the living room, excited for the day ahead. He couldn't wait to celebrate Thanksgiving with his family.

The house was quiet, though. His dad was half asleep on the couch, Mary Katherine watched the Macy's Thanksgiving Day Parade on television, and his mom was in the kitchen cooking.

"Good morning, Veeder," Jill yelled from the kitchen.

"Good morning, Mom!" Veeder responded, climbing onto the couch.

"One of these days, Paul." Jill walked into the living room. "I want to go to New York City and experience the parade in person."

"Why would you want to do that, Jill, when you can watch it on a perfectly good TV?"

"Can you imagine us in New York City?" Jill got lost in her imagination. "The wind whipping down the street as marching bands, floats, entertainers, and those large balloons pass us by. And at the end of the parade, Santa Claus comes down the street to ring in the Christmas season."

"That sounds awesome, Mom." Mary Katherine said, looking at Paul. "Can we go to New York to watch the parade, Daddy?"

"Yeah, Dad, can we go?" Veeder chimed.

"You see what you started, Jill?" Paul moaned, sitting up on the couch.

"It would be magical." Jill was daydreaming of that perfect day she knew would never come.

"I don't know if we will be able to go kids."

"Aww," Veeder moaned.

"Why not?" Mary Katherine fired back.

"Yeah, Paul, why not?" Jill shot back at him, winking at him playfully.

"Because why would I spend thousands of dollars on a trip where my children spend the whole time complaining about how cold it is, Jill?"

"Bah-humbug!"

"You know I am right."

"You, my dear," Jill said, walking across the living room to where Paul was sitting, "are Ebenezer Scrooge."

"Really, Jill?"

"Yes, Ebenezer." Jill bent down and kissed him on the cheek. "I am just being practical."

"Well, Mr. Practical, get your butt into the kitchen so you can help me with the food because football doesn't start for another two and a half hours."

"Only if you give me another kiss," Paul said with a devilish grin. Jill bent down to oblige. He wrapped her up in his arms, pulled her down on the couch, and as Jill tried to turn her face from side to side to avoid kissing him, he planted a bunch of kisses all over her face.

"Gross!" Mary Katherine and Veeder screamed in unison.

"You know I love you, sweetheart?" Paul asked, holding her in his arms.

"Baby," Jill replied, "after twenty years of marriage and seven kids, I don't care whether or not you love me. You are stuck with me!"

"Well, sweetheart," Paul said, staring into Jill's eyes, "After twenty years of marriage and seven kids, you are more beautiful today than the day I met you. In case I don't say it enough, I am most thankful that you are my wife, my best friend, and the most amazing mother to our kids. I love you."

"Aw, baby, I love you too."

They embraced in a long, deep kiss which prompted Mary Katherine and Veeder to yell "gross" again.

"And I am thankful that you're getting off your butt to help me with the cooking today."

"Do I have to?"

"Yes. Now get up off this couch, old man, and get in that kitchen!" They got up together and went into the kitchen to prepare the family feast.

When the football games came on the television, the boys piled into the living room to watch the Lions play the Jets. Each child took their turn getting washed up and complaining about the clothes they had to wear to grandma and grandpa's house.

In the second half of the game, the Jets mounted a comeback. Paul abandoned the kitchen and joined the boys on the couch.

Jill was about to go into the living room and put her foot down when the Lions quarterback threw a forty-four-yard touchdown that sealed the win.

Jill was getting last-minute help from the kids when Paul came into the kitchen trying to adjust his tie. Jill stopped what she was doing and walked over to him. "Let me help you with that, baby."

"Thank you, sweetheart," Paul said as she took his tie and started to fix the knot.

"You're very welcome."

Paul admired his wife. "You look beautiful today, Jill."

Jill blushed. "Thank you."

Paul wrapped his arms around Jill for a quick hug, whispering, "They really are good kids."

"I know," Jill whispered back. "I love these days together."

"Me too."

"As chaotic as they are, watching our family loving each other reminds me of how much God has blessed us."

"I thank God for you and them every day, sweetheart."

"I love you too." Jill kissed Paul.

"I love you more."

"Now," Jill said, breaking the quiet embrace. "As much as I want to stand here like this for the rest of the day, we must load up the kids and the food."

"Really?"

"It's time to go to your parents' house."

"Couldn't we just…"

"No, we can't!" Jill cut Paul off with a simple hand motion.

"Fine." Paul feigned a weak attempt at levity. "We'll go."

"Good boy."

"I love you." Paul kissed Jill one more time. Then he turned and yelled, "Okay, kids, it's time to get moving!"

The next twenty minutes were hectic as the kids made multiple trips into the kitchen to take bowls, dishes, and trays of food to the cars. Paul and Jill coordinated the kids and the food between his truck and her minivan for the short drive to James and Colleen's house for Thanksgiving dinner. When they arrived, the whole ordeal became a full-blown comedy of errors as each of Paul's brothers and sisters arrived at the same time. Food was going in every direction. James tried to get everyone situated in the barn next to his house.

He had renovated the barn to accommodate his growing family. He and Colleen wished they could hold large family dinners in their home, but it wasn't possible anymore. Their family accounted for forty-seven people at dinner before any of their friends came over for dessert.

Veeder was lost in the frenzy of activity. His mom, aunts, and the older cousins were shuffling food between the main house, cars, and warming ovens that had been installed in the renovated barn. After having to move out of the way many times, he sat on a couch at the far end of the barn and watched the football game on television.

Veeder was used to assuming his place on the couch with the younger kids when the barn was being used for big family get-togethers. But he started getting hungry as he saw the long train of tables filling up with platters of food. He couldn't wait to find his seat and start eating.

Once all the food was set out on the buffet and the last-minute details were attended to, James and Colleen called the family to find their places at the table. Once everyone was seated, they engaged in small talk. Veeder was quiet, sitting at the far end of the table waiting for dinner to begin.

James stood up and used a spoon to tap the side of his glass until he had the attention of those gathered. He smiled. "Thank you all for coming today. Happy Thanksgiving!"

"Happy Thanksgiving!" came the response from his family.

"It is on days like this when I gather together with my beautiful sons and daughters, their beautiful spouses, and my wonderful, amazing, beautiful grandchildren that I understand how blessed Colleen and I truly are. Of course, I am doubly blessed today as we also get to spend this day celebrating the sixtieth birthday of my elegant wife."

"Here, Here," everyone yelled. Colleen blushed from all the attention.

James bent down and kissed Colleen. "Happy Birthday, my love."

"Thank you, James," Colleen said through her glowing smile.

James put his hand up and waited for everyone to quiet down before he continued, "This truly is a beautiful day that God has prepared for us. Let us bow our heads in a moment of prayer and thanks." He bowed his head and offered up a wonderful prayer.

"Amen," everyone said in unison, lifting their glasses, and toasting one another.

"Happy Thanksgiving! Dinner is served! Feel free to dig in!" James announced. And like a stampede of cattle, the family got up from their seats and descended upon the buffet table.

Throughout the afternoon, the barn became crowded as many friends joined the celebration. They spent the day eating, laughing, singing, watching football on television, talking about football, and sharing life stories. And through it all, they were thankful and remembered to praise God, who had blessed their family, their friends, and their community.

They spent most of the day talking to JJ about the championship game. They reveled in stories of his football exploits. They gushed over his rushing records and all the touchdowns. They were all talking about winning the state championship and JJ was the centerpiece to accomplishing that feat.

JJ tried his best to change the conversation. He spent a good part of the evening talking about Sean's exploits as a standout wide receiver. He regaled them with tales from Michael and Liam's undefeated season on the middle school team. And he praised Veeder for making a name for himself as a star quarterback in Pop Warner.

Veeder loved the attention JJ heaped on him. As the season went along, the opportunities to work out with JJ became far and few between. The tensions between Michael, Liam, and Veeder subsided, and the three of them started working on their football skills together. So listening to JJ, a football great in this part of the state, talk about them, made them all feel proud of their older brother. They all loved hanging out with JJ, but at times like these, they also saw how humble his heart truly was, and they loved him for it.

After the late afternoon football game ended, James called everyone back to the dinner table. James stood up. "My beautiful family and all of my beautiful friends who have joined us here today, we have truly been blessed this year. As I look out over this wonderful crowd of people, I thank God for all of you. But today is also another special day, so if my helpers could please bring in the cake."

James paused while some of his friends brought in a large cake and placed it on the table in front of Colleen. Before he lit the candle on top of the cake to celebrate Colleen's birthday, he said, "I want to thank my beautiful wife of forty-one years for the amazing life she has given me. Thank you, my love."

"Here, Here," they all yelled out.

"I thank God for you every day. I am humbled by how graciously and beautifully you have stood by my side. So I ask everyone in the room to join me in a toast." They all stood and raised their glasses in honor of Colleen.

"To my beloved wife, Colleen, on your sixtieth birthday, my prayer is that God would grant your every wish. May God always fill your life with His grace! I love you with all my heart. Happy Birthday!" James held his glass, toasted the crowd, and then Colleen.

"Slainte" they all yelled.

James took Colleen by the hand, pulled her up into his arms, and kissed her. He then took a lighter out of his pocket, lit the candle on top of the cake, and started singing happy birthday until a semi-harmonious rendition of the song filled the room.

Colleen stood at the head of the table beaming, her heart filled with love and grace. Everything she had ever wanted was in that room. As they all sang to her, she thought about the sixty years of life that God had blessed her with, and it brought tears of happiness to her eyes.

As her family and friends finished singing, she wiped away her tears, leaned over the candle, took a deep breath, and blew it out. Cheers erupted around the room followed by repeated calls for a speech.

"They are not going to stop until you oblige them," James whispered in her ear.

"I know." She blushed once again, kissing her husband before turning to the chanting crowd, and raising her hand in an attempt to quiet them down.

When the room was quiet, Colleen raised her voice. "You all know that I am not one for big speeches, so I won't be long. Standing here, in front of all of you, I am overwhelmed and overjoyed. God is great! He has blessed me with my amazing husband, my beautiful children, their spouses, and my amazing grandchildren. And the cherry on top of this day is the love of all of our friends, who have come to celebrate with us. Thank you. I love you all. Now let's cut up some cake and eat!"

Cheers and applause erupted, but before anyone could step away from the table, James signaled for their attention once again. "Please forgive me, I don't want to get in the way of the cake."

They all laughed.

James continued, "I promise you all, especially the kids, that there will be cake in a few moments, but I have a gift for my wife that I would also like to share with all of you too."

James turned to face Colleen, placing his hands on her shoulders. "Colleen, I promised you a long time ago that when the time was right, we were going to go out into the world and enjoy the rest of our lives. We have run this farm since 1952 and for thirty-three years, we have stewarded it through good and bad times. Because of you, our children, and our friends who have worked tirelessly alongside us, the farm has grown every year. That, my dear, is mainly a testament to you as the anchor and foundation of our family.

"So I plan to make good on my promise. My birthday present to you is that while we are still young and still have life in our veins, I want to see the world with you and travel to the places we have always dreamed of going. I have decided to spend the next few months turning the farm over to the children, and when that transition is complete, I will officially retire."

Colleen was speechless at the announcement. She leaped into James' arms and gave him a big kiss, oblivious to the gasps and chatter of their guests. They were happy for James and Colleen, but with change comes a sense of nervousness and uneasiness about what the future might bring.

CHAPTER 9

The high school band marched through the parking lot as the excitement of those tailgating for the North Carolina state championship game reached a fever pitch. For the families living in Goldston and the surrounding communities, a trip to the state championship game was their Super Bowl. Families filled up the parking lot early in the morning and shared stories of their glory days along with embellished stories of the season at hand. Their hearts were filled with excitement, joy, and great anticipation.

Grills and smokers lined the parking lot. Food, drinks, and community embodied the spirit of the day. Fans from the rival team, Bryson City, filled in around the families from Goldston Regional and the real fun began. Taller tales began to surface, touch football games started, and far-fetched prognostications were shared. Perfect strangers became friends, brought together by the impending football game that was still hours away from being played.

The frenzy of celebrations taking place outside the stadium was far removed from the mindset of players and coaches settling into their pre-game routines. Game plans were finalized. Players stretched and took the field for warm-ups. This was the biggest game of their lives and they were ready. Then came the long period of waiting before the teams were announced and herded down the long tunnels back out onto the field.

The gates opened and thousands of fans descended upon the stadium with chants, cheers, and support for their favorite team. Excitement electrified the crowd unlike any other game they had ever attended. For the fans of the Goldston Regional Gators, this was a historic moment. It was their first trip to the championship game, and they couldn't wait for the game to get started.

The McLean family had spent the entire day in the parking lot celebrating and praying for an amazing end to JJ's record-setting season. Family filled an entire section of the stadium for the crowning moment in JJ's career. The tension was high. The nerves of Paul and Jill overtook their excitement. They prayed for JJ to finish strong and that the state championship title would be coming home with them at the end of the night.

The crowds erupted when both teams were introduced and burst onto the field. The captains met for the coin toss. After the singing of the national anthem and a few other ceremonial performances, it was time to play the game. All the pomp and circumstance, all the hype, and all of the carnival-style celebrations were over. It was time to play. The crowd electrified the stadium with a loud celebratory roar as Bryson City kicked the ball off.

Bryson City came out strong. The perennial powerhouse was business as usual against Goldston Regional who let their nerves get the best of them. Bryson City's defense shut down the Gators who were losing ten to nothing by the end of the first quarter.

Coach McCarthy and the offensive coordinator made some adjustments heading into the second quarter. JJ exploded for a ninety-two-yard touchdown and a forty-six-yard touchdown reception before Bryson City's kicker split the uprights with a field goal as time expired in the first half. Goldston Regional clung to a fourteen to thirteen lead as both teams headed into the locker rooms.

The halftime performances did nothing to quell the excitement in the air. For the fans of Goldston Regional, this was turning into the type of game that they had come to expect. For the powerhouse Bryson City fans, though, they were surprised by how much fight Goldston Regional had in the first half. This was going to become a bruising battle that would be hard-hitting for the rest of the night.

The second half turned into a defensive battle. Both offensive units were shut down as the teams traded field position. Bryson City retook the lead with a field goal in the waning minutes of the third quarter. A Bryson City interception early in the fourth quarter gave them great field position. Goldston Regional clamped down on defense and forced Bryson City to kick another field goal which extended their lead to a score of nineteen to fourteen.

JJ rewarded the Goldston Regional faithful with another touchdown, but Bryson City blocked the extra point attempt. After the ensuing kick-off, Bryson City only needed a field goal to win the game, so they drained precious time off the clock. On third and long, in the face of a sellout blitz, the Bryson City quarterback threw an ill-timed interception. The Goldston crowd erupted in jubilation while Coach McCarthy called the entire offensive unit to huddle up around him on the sideline.

"Listen up men." Coach McCarthy barked over the deafening crowd. "Don't celebrate yet! This game isn't over. We have five minutes left. No mistakes. Protect the football. And no heroics. Just ground and pound. A couple of first downs and we win! Now go get it done!"

With their marching orders in hand, the team broke the huddle and made their way to the line of scrimmage. Bryson City clamped down on defense and made it hard for Goldston Regional to find room to run. Both teams battled for control of the line of scrimmage while precious time ticked off the clock. With each successive play, the fans of Goldston Regional's nerves welled up as the team inched closer to victory.

Goldston Regional picked up a much-needed first down, allowing them to burn more time off the clock. They came to the line of scrimmage; the quarterback took the snap and handed the ball off to JJ. He followed his fullback to the right side of the line but when he saw a hole developing to his left, thoughts of a game-ending touchdown filled his mind. JJ reversed field and burst through the hole. The defense responded and attacked. He was exposed without blockers leading the way. The Bryson City defense swallowed him up. Four or five players landed crushing blows and wrapped his body in their grasp while he fought for more yardage.

His heart pounding, JJ pushed and drove as hard as he could. Lineman from his team pushed the pile from behind. More defenders made punishing contact with the pile. The scrum turned into an all-out battle of will and sheer determination as JJ fought for yardage. He pushed and drove and as a defender grabbed his leg, his right foot got planted in the turf. His leg jerked and his body spun from the force of another defender tackling him. He felt one pop and then another below his waist. Excruciating pain radiated throughout his body. Another defender crashed into his body and spun his leg again. JJ was on the way to the ground in inexplicable pain when he realized that he had fumbled the ball.

A mad dash of players from both teams chased the football that danced along the field. They ran over JJ, diving past him, and kicking his leg as they dove after the fumble. Referees pulled players off the pile trying to determine who had gained possession of the ball.

JJ never heard the call. The only voice he heard was his screaming out in agonizing pain. Pandemonium gave way to a deafening silence after the referees whistled for a stoppage of play. The Goldston Regional coaches and team trainers raced across the field to attend to JJ. Coach McCarthy knelt beside his hyperventilating star running back.

Coach McCarthy looked up from his inconsolable player and noticed that the team trainer was already signaling to the booth for immediate medical assistance. Within minutes, the screams of the siren grew louder. Jill raced onto the field and consoled JJ as the first responders went to work. They wasted no time preparing JJ for transit. As they loaded him onto the stretcher, one of the coaches helped Jill into the ambulance.

Jill held JJ's hand, knelt beside him, and prayed with him as she did her best to comfort him while tears streamed down his face. Moments later, the ambulance screamed towards the hospital.

CHAPTER 10

—⌒◎⌒—

The ride to the hospital felt like an eternity. Jill was living in a hypnotic dream state as the sirens echoed in her ears. She held JJ's hand and consoled him. She had to be strong. The Emergency Medical Technicians were attending to her son and she was doing her best to stay out of their way.

Entering the emergency room brought about another level of frenzied activity. Doctors and nurses attended to JJ while she stood back and watched. They yelled out medical terms to one another that she did not understand. Panic and fear gripped her heart. She bowed her head. "God, may Your loving hands protect JJ. Lord, give me strength. May Your will be done. Amen."

Dr. Guidry turned from the table, touched Jill's arm, and as she lifted her head from prayer, he stared into her eyes. "Mrs. McLean, we have to take your son up to surgery right now."

"Is he going to be okay?"

"He will be okay, but there is a lot of damage to the leg. I won't know the extent of the damage until I open it up and see for myself."

"Do what you need to do to help my son, Doctor."

Dr. Guidry turned around, barked orders to his medical team, unlocked the wheels to the gurney, and headed for the surgical unit. Jill started to follow Dr. Guidry and his team, but a nurse stepped in front of her with a clipboard. "Ma'am, I need you to fill out these consent forms before Dr. Guidry can operate."

Jill watched them wheel JJ onto an elevator and disappear. She filled out the consent forms, then was directed to admissions where she filled out more paperwork. When she completed the registration process, she was escorted to the pre-operation unit to see JJ before they took him into surgery.

She caught her breath when she saw him. She swallowed her fears and put on a brave face. She was not expecting to see all the tubes and gadgets that had been attached to her son's body. She held his hand and they whispered to one another. The anesthesiologist interrupted their conversation to explain his role and to start the medications for surgery.

Jill held JJ's hand and talked with him until it was time for his surgery. She exuded strength when he needed it most. Her heart was breaking because of the pain he was in, knowing there was nothing she could do to help him.

The nurses came into the room to take JJ to the operating room. Jill prayed with JJ, and then the nurses wheeled him away. She held his hand until they reached a point where Jill had to stop walking. As the door to the surgical unit closed, she felt alone. Her son was in the hands of God and the precious gifts He had given to the surgeon.

A nurse walked her to the waiting room where the McLean family had taken up residence. Paul wrapped her up in his arms and for the first time all night, she let her guard down as the tears trickled down her cheeks.

A petite blond woman in a business suit walked up to Paul and Jill. "Mr. and Mrs. McLean, my name is Beth. I am the hospital social worker assigned to JJ's case. If you have a few minutes, can we talk?"

"No!" Jill was irate, turning and staring down the woman. "I have had enough with forms, medical billing, nurses, procedures, and all of the other people who have accosted me with trivial matters since I have arrived!"

"Jill…" Paul put his arms around her to calm her down, but she cut him off and pulled away from his arms.

"No, Paul! Stop!" Jill yelled, turning to face Beth. "I don't care about the forms, the billing, the minute details to run this hospital. I care about my son. So unless you have news about his surgery, leave us alone!"

Jill stormed off down the hallway while Paul tried to ameliorate the situation. "I am sorry for that, Beth. It's been a long night. Excuse me."

Paul and Jill found the hospital chapel and took up residence in the front row. They talked, cried, consoled each other, and prayed. Jill remained in the chapel seeking solace while Paul made multiple trips to the waiting room for any news.

Jill awaited the unknown. The seconds ticked by on the clock. The feeling of helplessness tugged at her heart. She tried to cajole God into giving her the best possible outcome. She contemplated the concept of "His will" because she knew there was a big difference between "His will" and "her will." She could try to convince God to do her bidding, but she knew in the end that God had this. She knew that whatever plan He had for JJ would always result in a more beautiful world.

Paul bought Jill a large cup of coffee. It was the darkest moment of their lives and yet, their love for one another grew as each hour passed.

Jill was resting her head on Paul's shoulder when a nurse came into the chapel. "Excuse me."

"Yes?" Paul and Jill turned to look at the nurse.

"Do you have any news about our son?" Jill asked.

"I do," the nurse responded. "The doctor would like to talk to you."

"Where?" Paul asked.

"He will meet you in the waiting room shortly."

"Thank you," Jill said.

"I'll let him know you're on your way," the nurse said before leaving the chapel.

"I'm scared, Paul."

"I know." Paul pulled Jill into his arms, squeezing her tight. "God has this. He will take care of JJ."

Paul kissed Jill on the forehead before they left the chapel and walked back to the waiting room. They sat next to Colleen and James. Jill was shocked to see all the players, coaches, families, and school officials still packed into the hallways of the hospital waiting for any news about JJ.

"Mr. and Mrs. McLean?" Dr. Guidry called, walking into the overcrowded waiting room.

"I am Paul McLean." Paul stood up, extending his hand toward the doctor.

"Mr. McLean," the doctor said, shaking Paul's hand.

"This is my wife, Jill."

"Yes, we met earlier tonight." He shook Jill's hand.

"How is my son, Doctor?" Jill was stoic, keeping her emotions in check.

"Your son, Mrs. McLean, is a trooper."

"Is he okay?" Paul asked, fearing the worst.

"The surgery was not easy. The x-rays confirmed our worst fears. JJ broke his femur, his tibia, and his fibula."

Jill put her arm around Paul's waist, bracing herself. "Will he walk again?"

"He will." The doctor paused. "In time."

"Thank God," Paul exhaled.

"I'm not going to lie to you, he has a long road in front of him. Recovery will not be easy."

"But he will walk again?" Paul reiterated.

"Yes," Doctor Guidry said before adding, "after a lot of physical therapy."

"How long, Doctor?" Jill asked.

"We had to insert some rods and pins to set the three breaks in your son's leg. When the swelling goes down, it will need to be placed in a cast."

"When can he come home?" Jill asked.

"He's going to be here for a while, Mrs. McLean. He will most likely need another surgery, but we won't know that for a while."

"Will he need any help walking? Braces? Crutches?" Paul asked.

"Currently, I don't see why he would. I believe he will recover and have full use of his leg, although there will be some limitations."

"Thank God," Paul said, letting out a loud sigh.

Tears filled Jill's eyes. "How long will recovery take?"

"That depends solely on JJ, Mrs. McLean."

"Will he ever play football again?" Veeder asked, sidling up next to Jill.

"That depends, young man." Dr. Guidry knelt in a catcher's squat. "Do you promise to take it easy on him?"

"I'm not worried about me." Veeder gritted his teeth, clenching his fists. "He has a scholarship to play at Chapel Hill University next year. Will he ever play football again?"

Dr. Guidry jerked upright. His face paled. He turned to face Jill and Paul. "I didn't know JJ was planning on playing college football."

"He's never playing again, is he?" Jill choked up, knowing his scholarship would be rescinded.

"He has a scholarship," Paul said.

"I'm sorry," Doctor Guidry said. "JJ's playing days are over. The damage is too extensive for him to play at that level ever again."

"No!" Veeder yelled, racing out of the waiting room in tears.

"Veeder!" Jill chased after him.

"I'll go get him." Colleen intercepted Jill. "You stay here."

"Thank you, Mom."

Colleen didn't say a word as she turned and chased after Veeder.

"When can we see him?" Paul asked, fidgeting with his hands.

"He's in recovery now and will be there for a few more hours before we move him to a private room. You might want to go home, get some sleep, and come back in the morning."

"We won't be going home, Doctor. When my son is awake, come find us." Jill was frustrated. "We will be in the cafeteria or the chapel."

"And if you have any more questions or if there is anything I can do, please have the nurses page me."

"Thank you, Doctor," Paul said, shaking Dr. Guidry's hand.

Doctor Guidry turned and walked back into the surgical unit. Paul turned to face Jill and wrapped his arms around her. They had to be strong. The surgery was over, but the long, hard journey of recovery was just beginning.

Jill tracked down Veeder an hour later. He had gone to the chapel with Colleen after bolting out of the waiting room. James and Colleen had been in the chapel with Veeder but when he said he wanted to be left alone, they sat in a couple of chairs in the hallway.

"Is he in there alone?" Jill said, hugging both of them.

"Yes. That's what he wanted," James said.

"Do you think he is praying?" Jill asked, hoping for a miracle.

"He's not the most faith-filled child, Jill," Colleen interjected.

"The Lord works in mysterious ways," Jill responded.

"How is JJ?" James asked.

"He's still in recovery."

"How are you holding up?" Colleen asked.

"I'm not thinking about it," Jill said, a wave of fatigue washing over her. She was drained but she knew this was just the beginning. Weariness was not an option. "Coffee and prayer. That's how Paul and I are coping with this right now. Coffee and prayers are about all I can handle."

"Where is Paul?"

"In the cafeteria with the rest of the family," Jill responded. "You should go join them."

"Are you sure you don't want any help with Veeder?" Colleen asked.

"I'm good. Go get something to eat. I've got this." Tears formed in the corners of Jill's eyes. Colleen and James hugged Jill and made their way to the cafeteria. As they walked down the hall, Jill took a deep breath and walked into the chapel.

"I hate what you did to my brother!" Veeder yelled at the cross, tears streaming down his face. "You say you're good and you help good people! Well, JJ is good, and look what happened? Where were you? Huh? Where were you? Why didn't you help him?"

Jill walked up behind Veeder. She put her hands on his shoulders, then fell on her knees to receive his hug when he turned and collapsed into her arms in a puddle of tears.

"I hate God, Mom! I hate God, Mom!" Veeder bawled through his tears. "Why did God do this to JJ, Mom? Why?"

"I don't know why this happened, baby. I don't know."

Jill knew she didn't have the answers Veeder needed. So she sat there on the floor and held him as he cried on her shoulder. The best she could do was just to be present in his pain. Jill leaned back against the pew, closed her eyes, and asked God for strength and wisdom. She knew there would be a long journey ahead for all of them and she was going to need His loving hands to guide her every step of the way.

1992

CHAPTER 11

Veeder sat in the passenger seat of Liam's beat-up Ford Mustang and stared out the open window at the world, enjoying the wind whipping across his face.

Veeder reminisced about the good old days when he and his brothers played football on the farm, dreaming of playing professional football together. Their days would start when the sun rose. They bounded down the stairs and out the door to play football. They laughed, they grew, and they pushed themselves to be better players and better people. It was their collective dream. It was what bonded them together when they all still lived under the same roof.

Those dreams changed over the past seven years. It started when JJ's dreams disappeared in the blink of an eye. One catastrophic hit changed his life forever, leaving him to endure multiple surgeries, physical therapy, counseling, and a spiritual journey to discover his new reality.

Veeder and Liam drove through the countryside reminiscing about childhood stories and sharing the latest news of their siblings.

"Going to see Anna?" Liam asked.

"Yeah." Veeder turned, looked at Liam, and nodded.

"Her father still dislikes you?"

"That's a nice way of putting it." Veeder chuckled.

"How are you going to solve that little problem?"

"I don't know, Liam." Veeder turned and laid his head against the headrest, wind whipping across his face while he stared out at the fields. "I don't know."

Veeder closed his eyes and remembered the day he first laid eyes on Anna. He was walking down the street with his friends at Goldston's Old Fashioned Days when she walked right past him. She was headed in the opposite direction and didn't notice him, but Veeder saw her. His heart skipped a beat. He was smitten. One look at her smile and he knew he had to meet her, so he ditched his friends.

"Sorry guys." Veeder turned around and followed Anna down the street. "I've got to go."

"Where are you going?" His friends yelled after him.

"I just saw an angel."

"What?" Mark asked, raising his arms, and furrowing his brow.

"You don't believe in angels," Brett added.

"There's a first time for everything!" Veeder laughed while skipping backward down the street. "If there is a God, I just saw one of his angels."

Veeder raced off while his friends made fun of him for flaking out on them, but he didn't care. He had just seen the most beautiful girl in the world, and he chased her down the street. He wracked his brain trying to find a way to break the ice.

Anna stopped at a booth to look at some crafts. Veeder stood on the other side of the table, pretending to be interested in the merchandise, stealing moments to stare at her. Anna wasn't fooled. She knew what he was doing and decided to have a little fun with her admirer.

"Find something you like?" Anna asked, mischief in her voice.

"Yes," Veeder's voice squeaked.

Anna chuckled at the high-pitched sound that left his mouth. "You're into dolls?"

"Not me." Veeder fumbled with the dolls on the table. "My sister has a collection. I'm looking for her."

"Mm-hmm." Anna raised a suspicious eyebrow, walking away to peruse the merchandise at another table.

Veeder was frustrated with himself for failing to make a good impression but wasn't going to give up. He wanted to meet this beautiful girl but struggled with how.

"Come here often?" Veeder stepped next to her, looking at some of the items for sale.

"Smooth." Anna blushed, turning and looking at him.

"Well, you know, I try," Veeder responded, trying to play it cool.

"See something you like at this booth?" Anna was suspicious.

"I do now." Veeder turned and look at her.

"You're incorrigible." Anna walked away.

"You know, you shouldn't do that," Veeder quipped, racing to catch up with her.

"Walk away from you?"

"Well, you shouldn't do that either, but you shouldn't use words I don't know," Veeder smirked.

Anna stopped and looked at him puzzled. "Are you really that daft?"

"When I get a chance to look that word up," Veeder winked. "I'll let you know."

Anna rolled her eyes, turned, and walked away shaking her head in disbelief. Veeder followed her.

"Are you going to follow me all day?"

"I was hoping I wouldn't have to."

"So don't."

"Well, that kind of depends upon you."

"How so?"

"Let me take you to Lizzie's." Veeder smiled. "We could split an ice cream sundae."

"Why would I do that?"

"Because I'm cute and you're still talking to me."

"You don't lack confidence, that's for sure."

"But you're interested!"

"How do you figure that?" Anna laughed.

"If you thought I was a creep, you would have told me to get lost by now."

"Maybe I'm being polite."

"Just another good reason to get to know you."

"You really are incorrigible."

"I thought we agreed not to use words I don't understand," Veeder said with sarcasm, making Anna blush again.

"See, you blushed."

"So?"

"You like me." Veeder teased.

"Like you? I don't even know you."

"Split a hot fudge sundae with me?"

"And if I agree…"

Veeder cut her off, puffing out his chest. "You would make me the happiest man in the world."

"That's not what I was going to say."

"No?" Veeder paused. "What were you going to say?"

"If I agree to go to Lizzie's with you." Anna stopped walking and turned to look at him. "Will you stop following me around like a lost puppy dog?"

"If that's what you wish."

Anna smiled, tilted her head, and ran her fingers through her hair. "I do. I really do."

"But you won't."

"There's that confidence again." Anna blushed, biting her lip.

"What can I say? It's part of my charm."

"Do you promise?" Anna pressed the issue. "Will you stop following me around like a lost puppy dog?"

"Fine," Veeder conceded. "If that's what you want, I'll stop following you."

"Good." Anna smiled, winking at him. "I like chocolate sprinkles on my sundaes."

They walked to Lizzie's and ordered a hot fudge sundae. Then they got lost in conversation, losing track of time, and ended up spending the rest of the day together.

Liam pulled up in front of Lizzie's and stared at Veeder, who was lost in his thoughts. "Veeder, we're here."

"Huh? What?" Veeder jerked in the seat as Liam shook his shoulder.

"We're here."

"Sorry." Veeder unbuckled the seat belt. "I was lost in a daydream."

"I figured." Liam laughed. "You need any money?"

"I'm good."

"How are you getting home?"

"Mom."

"Cool."

Veeder got out of the car and shut the door. "See you tomorrow."

"Have a good night." Liam pointed at Veeder, winking at him, before pulling away from the curb, and driving away.

Veeder walked into Lizzie's and stopped in the doorway. He saw Anna Kelly sitting in a booth waiting for him. His heart skipped a beat when Anna waved to him. He walked over to the table and slid into the booth next to her.

"Waiting long?" He kissed her.

"Ew, gross!" Mary Katherine squealed from across the booth. "It's bad enough you date my friends. Please don't get mushy in front of me."

"Hey, Sis," Veeder said, taking ahold of Anna's hand.

"Not long," Anna said. "I ordered the usual."

"A hot fudge sundae with chocolate sprinkles?"

"Yes."

"You read my mind." Veeder smiled.

The three teens sat in the booth, laughed, and talked about everything that was happening in their quiet little town. Veeder was thankful to Mary Katherine for her help since his relationship with Anna had hit a bump in the road. If it had not been for her, afternoons like this might not be possible. It warmed his heart that his two best friends in the world were best friends as well.

Veeder paid the bill. He and Anna walked to the playground nearby, like they had on the day they met. While the two of them wandered off, Mary Katherine sat on the bench in front of Lizzie's and read a book.

"When does football start?" Anna held his hand.

"Two days."

"Are you ready?"

"For high school ball? Please. I was born ready."

"It's not going to be the same as middle school and Pop Warner."

"The real question is; is high school ready for me?"

"Okay, you big stud!" Anna was being facetious and he knew it.

"You know it!" Veeder puffed out his chest.

"I'm serious, Veeder. I'm worried."

"Why, Anna? In a town like this, no one scares me."

"But it's a regional school."

"I've played against them all before."

Anna bit her lip and said with a devilish grin, "I hear the starting quarterback is pretty good."

"Johnny Peterson?"

"He's had a couple of good seasons."

"Not good enough."

"I hear he is pretty good-looking." Anna teased, spying him out of the corner of her eye to see his reaction.

"Not good enough!"

Anna stopped walking, turned, and looked into his eyes, frustrated with Veeder's bravado. "I wish you would stop doing that; I'm worried about you."

"There's nothing to worry about, Anna."

"They're all so much bigger than you are."

"Everyone has always been bigger than me. That has never stopped me before."

"It doesn't worry you?"

"They might be bigger, but they're not tougher."

"There you go again." Anna sighed. "Why do you do that?"

"I'm being serious. No one's tougher than my brothers. I trained with the best."

"Promise me nothing will happen to you?"

"I promise." Veeder wrapped Anna up in his arms in a reassuring hug. She melted into his embrace.

"I don't know what I would do if anything ever happened to you."

"Nothing to worry about. Number nineteen is invincible."

"I see my vocabulary is rubbing off on you." Anna's sarcasm was biting.

"It is!" Veeder smirked. "Thank you."

"You never told me why you choose number nineteen."

"Johnny Unitas."

"Who?"

"Johnny Unitas." Veeder pulled back and stared at her. "Only the greatest quarterback to ever play the game."

"Until you?" Anna smiled.

"Exactly!"

"That overconfidence is going to get you into trouble one day." Anna swatted at him. Veeder pulled Anna closer. The two of them stood swaying back and forth in each other's arms, the rest of the world faded away. It was late. They kissed, then walked hand-in-hand back to Lizzie's, taking their time to return.

Veeder and Anna had only been joking around with Mary Katherine for five minutes when Anna's mother pulled up to the curb and honked the horn. Anna gave Veeder a quick kiss before dashing into the car.

"Thank you, MK." Veeder sat down next to his sister and waved to Anna before the car pulled away from the curb.

"For what?"

"I don't have enough time to list everything."

"I have time." Mary Katherine chuckled, looking at her watch. "Where would you like to start?"

Veeder paused for a moment. "Thank you for being my best friend."

Mary Katherine was taken aback by her brother's humbleness. "Best friend?"

"You were there for me when JJ got hurt."

"It was a tough time for all of us."

"You were my rock. I don't know if I would have gotten through it without you."

"I know how close you two are. I wanted to help."

"You help me with my school work."

"Someone has to or you would never be allowed to play football."

"True." Veeder laughed. "And you always make me laugh."

"That's an easy one." Mary Katherine rolled her eyes, pushing his shoulders. "You laugh at everything."

"Well, you always try to get me out of trouble when I don't think things through."

"Try?" Mary Katherine laughed. "Try? I try to get you out of trouble?"

"Fair enough." Veeder laughed.

"Honestly." Mary Katherine struck a serious tone "You should be paying me for that one. You get into *a lot* of trouble."

"I do not."

"I call them as I see them, and from where I am sitting, you get into *a lot* of trouble."

"Fair enough." Veeder stared out at the street. "Thank you for helping me out with Anna."

"I didn't do much there."

"Because of you, MK, Anna and I are able to hang out."

"Well, you didn't help yourself in that department."

"Hey," Veeder exclaimed. "You were the one who told me to be honest!"

"But telling her father that you don't believe in God? Really? What were you thinking?"

"I was doing what you told me to do!"

"Her father's our pastor, Veeder!" Mary Katherine rolled her eyes. "What were you thinking?"

"Not my brightest move, huh?"

"Um, no!" Mary Katherine laughed. "Even I would have told you to lie about that one."

"Now you tell me!"

"Sorry. I thought you would've figured that one out on your own."

"Did you forget the part about keeping me out of trouble?" Veeder teased.

"Yeah." Mary Katherine shrugged. "Not much I could do about that one."

"Well, thank you." Veeder humbled himself. "Because of you, we are still able to see each other."

"Don't think anything about it."

"I have to. I know you could be doing better things than hanging out with us."

"It's what twin sisters do." Mary Katherine put her arm around Veeder's shoulders.

"No. It's what best friends do."

"You're not so bad yourself."

"Thank you, MK. I love you."

"Love you too, little brother."

"Aw!" Jill yelled from the car, pulling up to the curb.

"Mom, stop!" They both yelled in unison.

"I wish I had my camera to commemorate this moment," Jill responded. Seeing her youngest two children being so kind to one another filled her heart with joy. Veeder and Mary Katherine rolled their eyes and made some snide remarks as they got into the car.

CHAPTER 12

Veeder was always the first one to arrive at practice and the last one to leave the field at the end of the day. Working on his craft of being a football player and being in top physical condition was a priority. Practice was part of the job. Preparation was the key ingredient in having passion for the game. His heart, mind, and soul were focused on being the best football player to ever play the game. He would spend hours correcting, refining, and perfecting his skills.

Veeder had already been on the field running wind sprints for an hour when the coaches and the other players reported to campus for the first day of tryouts. After a summer filled with voluntary workouts, the team held two-a-day practices for the first two weeks of the official season, and the coaches put the players through the most grueling two weeks of their lives. They believed it separated the true players from the want-to-be players who thought high school football was a steppingstone to instant popularity.

The team conditioned, worked on position-specific skills, worked out in the weight room, spent time in the classroom learning the playbook, studying film, and getting mentally prepared for the season ahead. And when there was a lull in the day, they conditioned some more. It was two weeks of intense preparation for the season as the coaches prepared a roster that would give them the best opportunity to win a state championship. Veeder loved every minute of the physically demanding camp. He wasn't the biggest player on the field, but he wasn't going to let anyone beat him. He was never going to quit.

The varsity team already had an established quarterback. There were four other quarterbacks, including Veeder, who were competing to make the team. By the end of the second week of camp, the battle for varsity quarterback came down to three players.

Johnny Peterson was the returning quarterback. He had led the team for two years and was entering his senior season as the odds-on favorite to be the starter. He was a game manager who wasn't going to electrify the offense. His goal was to have another solid season and to earn a college scholarship.

Joel Harper had spent his freshman year on the junior varsity team. He had a decent season, but he didn't have a strong arm. He was a good fit for Coach McCarthy's offense, though. He would manage the game, handing off the ball. He only had to throw the ball to keep opposing defenses honest; otherwise, they would stack the box and stuff the run.

Well known in the local football community, Veeder was the third quarterback on the list and was a long shot to make the roster. He was making the transition to high school football with a big arm and a bigger ego. But it was his work ethic that impressed the coaching staff. He never quit and as final cuts loomed, Veeder hoped that the other two qualities would trump his ego.

Coach McCarthy loved Veeder's arm but could do without his attitude. He would remind Veeder to be a leader, not a problem. The directive was hard for him. He was fearless. Nothing stood in his way, and the more the veteran players harassed him, the harder he worked. It paid off on the field. He would make a show of his arm strength and pinpoint accuracy.

"How's the JV bench looking, McLean?" Johnny teased Veeder while they jogged to the next station. The upperclassmen laughed and pointed fingers at Veeder. Johnny traded high fives with others for the glib remark.

"Why don't you send me a postcard when you get there, Johnny?"

"Oooh!" The crowd of players cooed, now pointing at Johnny.

"You think that's funny."

"Not for you!" Veeder smiled.

"You think you can outplay me, rookie?" Johnny stepped up to Veeder and stood face to face with him.

"Outplay, outrun, out throw, and out-think."

"You think so?"

"Know so." Veeder pushed past Johnny, bumping his chest as he walked past. Agitated with Veeder's bravado, Johnny turned and pushed Veeder to the ground. The receivers crowded around and egged on the situation. Veeder jumped up, throwing a punch at Johnny. The two quarterbacks started to tussle. The other players stepped in and tried to break it up. Coach McCarthy and Coach Reeves, the offensive coordinator, yanked the players apart by their jerseys.

"What are you two doing?" Coach McCarthy yelled.

"Proving who's boss!" Veeder squawked.

Johnny yelled, "Defending myself!"

"Zip it!" Coach McCarthy commanded.

"Coach…" Johnny tried to interject.

"I said zip it!" Coach McCarthy barked. "You two are supposed to be my leaders. Leaders don't act like toddlers. Now get it out of your system before I get rid of both of you! Is that understood?"

"Yes, Coach," Johnny conceded.

"Yes, sir." Veeder stared at the ground.

"Now shake." The boys were reluctant to shake hands. "I said shake!"

They shook hands and mumbled apologies to each other.

"Now get back to work!" Coach McCarthy yelled.

Veeder and Johnny glared each other down as they went back to the station. Veeder felt that Johnny's time in the top spot was fading. If he was given a fair shot, he would prove he was the best player on the field.

Coach Reeves huddled up the players and explained the drill. Johnny was the first quarterback up to throw. Veeder watched for the next few minutes while Johnny hit each of his receivers as they ran their routes. Then, Joel took his turn at quarterback.

Johnny strutted back and stood next to Veeder. "That's how the pros do it."

Veeder chuckled but didn't say a word. He waited while Joel took his turn. Coach Reeves called Veeder onto the field. With the precision of a laser surgeon, Veeder threaded the needle on every pass, throwing with perfection every time. When done, he strutted across the field. As he passed Johnny, Veeder quipped, "It's easy without pressure."

Coach Reeves changed the routes from short to mid-range passes. Johnny completed about eighty percent of his passes. Whenever a pass fell to the ground, he would get frustrated and make a disparaging comment to the receiver about making better adjustments.

Joel missed half of his targets. Veeder could tell he was frustrated but was impressed with how well he kept his composure and continued to fight through the adversity.

"I'm betting Veeder completes twenty percent of his passes," Johnny joked when Veeder took his turn on the field. He and other veterans laughed and joked until Veeder shocked them by completing every pass with pinpoint accuracy.

Impressed with Veeder's accuracy, Coach Reeves had the receivers run more difficult routes, but Veeder continued to deliver an accurate pass every single time. Proud of his accomplishment, he nodded and winked at Johnny as they switched places.

Johnny took the field frustrated, mumbling profanities. He was frustrated at being beaten out by a freshman. Coach Reeves had the receivers run routes beyond thirty-five yards. Johnny struggled, completing fifty percent of his passes. His calm demeanor peeled away along with his accuracy, leaving only anger. Joel fared even worse, completing only twenty percent of his passes, none of them over forty yards.

When it was his turn, Veeder launched a fifty-five-yard pass with laser-guided accuracy that hit his receiver in stride. Astonished, Coach Reeves took off his hat and rubbed his eyes. "Can you do that again?"

"All day, Coach! Deeper too!"

"Show me."

Veeder dropped bombs from fifty-five to seventy yards downfield. A crowd developed behind him. The other players were mesmerized at the passing clinic Veeder was putting on.

When the whistle blew, Veeder turned and strutted toward the sideline with a sly grin on his face. He passed Johnny, bumping him with his shoulder.

Angry, Johnny jumped Veeder from behind, dragging him to the ground. They started throwing punches as players and coaches did their best to pull them apart.

"Cut it out!" Coach McCarthy yelled, standing between both players, his outstretched hands pressed against their shoulder pads.

"He's a showboat, Coach!" Johnny yelled.

"You're a baby and a whiner!" Veeder retaliated.

"Shut up!" Coach McCarthy yelled. "Both of you!"

"He's angry because I'm better than him!" Veeder instigated.

"Veeder!" Coach McCarthy barked. "Come with me! The rest of you, laps! Run them for the rest of practice, coaches!" The team groaned and complained but started running laps around the football field.

Coach McCarthy all but dragged Veeder over to the baseball field. He made Veeder run an Iron Man drill for forty-five minutes. Veeder gritted his teeth through the drill, every muscle in his body hurting. He was exhausted but refused to quit, refused to let Coach McCarthy see that he had gotten the best of him. He would run the drill all night if that was what his coach intended.

When the drill was over, Veeder collapsed, gasping for air. Coach McCarthy threw him a water bottle. Veeder opened it and chugged some of it down before pouring some on top of his head.

Coach McCarthy knelt next to him. "You have talent, son, but a bad attitude."

"He threw the punch, Coach!"

Coach McCarthy put his hand on Veeder's shoulder. "And somehow, you still think I care about that."

"So this is all my fault, Coach?"

"You're undisciplined, Veeder." Coach McCarthy stared across the field.

"I'm better and you know it."

"Does it matter, Veeder?"

"Yes!"

"No, it doesn't, son." Coach McCarthy turned his head, looking into Veeder's eyes. "On that you're wrong."

"I'm the best player on the field."

"That may be true, but your teammates don't like you."

"Who cares?" Veeder was defiant. "When did football become a popularity contest?"

"They won't play for you, son."

"What does that matter?"

"If you want to be great, you have to get the team to play for you. They *have* to want to block for you but with your attitude, all they want to do is destroy you."

"But Coach…"

"But nothing," Coach McCarthy interrupted. "The quarterback is supposed to be a leader. If you're not, you're no good to me or the team."

Without another word, Coach McCarthy got up and walked off the field. Veeder knelt on the ground and stared at Coach McCarthy walking away. He drank the rest of the water. To avoid going back to the locker room, he spent an hour running laps around the baseball field until he couldn't run any further. Then Veeder dragged himself to the locker room.

The final roster was posted on the locker room door. Veeder took a deep breath and read the list. Panic settled into the pit of his stomach as he got closer to the bottom. Then he saw it.

Veeder McLean, QB. It was the last name on the list. Relief washed over his body before letting out a long sigh. He had made the team.

CHAPTER 13

—⟨◦⟩—

Liam drove Veeder and Anna through the winding country roads. They listened to the radio until they arrived at a deserted spot. Veeder pointed to a grassy patch a few hundred feet up the road. "Stop right up there."

"Where are we going?" Anna was intrigued.

"It's a surprise."

"Are you sure you want me to drop you off here?" Liam questioned, pulling the Mustang to a complete stop, and looking around.

"We're fine." Veeder and Anna exited the car. "Thanks for the ride, Liam."

"Not a problem," Liam responded before driving away.

"What are we doing here?" Anna looked around.

"You'll see." Veeder grinned, grabbing Anna's hand, they ran across the street. It took a few minutes but Veeder found the overgrown dirt road that led back into the woods. Anna walked alongside him, looking around for clues.

Veeder made small talk as they strolled through the woods. They talked about football tryouts, the farm, Anna's music lessons, and life in general, enjoying the scenery and fighting the humidity.

They took in the sights, sounds, and smells that greeted them on the trail. It was a cornucopia of aromas and sounds that wafted through the dry, humid air. They reveled in the rare moments when a slight breeze would rustle through the treetops and give them a little bit of relief from the afternoon heat.

It took a little more than two hours to hike to the top of the trail but when they made it to the apex of the path, Veeder pulled back the branches, clearing the way onto the top of the peak. "This is what I wanted to show you."

"It's beautiful," Anna gasped in delight. Anna looked out over the valley below them in awestruck wonder. A smile brightened her face. She could see for miles in every direction. She closed her eyes and breathed in the floral feast that was floating up the side of the peak from the valley below. "How did you ever find this place?"

"I didn't." Veeder stepped beside her. "JJ did."

"That figures. I should have known."

"He brought me here when I was little." Veeder slipped his arm around her waist.

"That must have been awesome."

"It was."

"You and JJ have always had this special thing between you, haven't you?"

"He was always my hero, but it was here that we became close friends."

"You miss him?"

"He writes." Veeder shrugged his shoulders. "He calls when he can."

"But it's not the same."

"No, it's not." Veeder paused. "It is what it is."

"I bet he's proud of you for making the football team." Anna grabbed his arm, slipped her hand into his, and they intertwined their fingers.

"He said very few freshmen ever make the varsity team. He said we are in a select club."

"Sounds like he is really proud of you."

"You know, I am breaking a promise I made to JJ."

"You are?" Anna was perplexed.

"He made me promise that I would never bring anyone up here."

"I know you shouldn't break promises." Anna turned, wrapping her arms around him. "But I am glad you did."

"I'm sure he wouldn't mind." Veeder smiled and put his arms around her.

"I won't tell him if you don't."

"I promise."

"When did he find this place?"

"I don't know." Veeder kissed Anna, took her hand, and walked over to the rock where he sat with JJ years earlier. He sat on the rock before helping Anna settle in with her back to him. He scooted up behind her and wrapped his arms around her waist. She reached down to hold his hands as he rested his chin on her shoulder. "He took me to this very rock when I was seven. We sat here and he told me about the history of our family."

"Sounds like an amazing day." Anna smiled.

"It was." Veeder hesitated. "But that was before he broke his leg and everything changed."

"That was a rough time for you, wasn't it?"

"What?"

"JJ's injury."

As the words left Anna's mouth, a familiar pain gripped Veeder's heart. He was transported back to the hospital. He remembered the moment he walked into JJ's room and saw him lying there with his leg suspended above the bed. It was a tough juxtaposition for Veeder to swallow. His invincible hero laid up in a hospital. Broken. Weak. Vulnerable in a way he never imagined possible.

"Hey buddy, how are you doing?" JJ asked. Veeder crept cautiously towards the hospital bed. Veeder mumbled something under his breath. He wasn't ready for the reality of what he was seeing. He didn't know what to think and he sure didn't know what to say.

Veeder was angry. He was scared. While the rest of the family was saying prayers, he was cursing God for what he had done to JJ. Seeing his older brother laid up like this just made his anger burn hotter.

"This is nothing." JJ tried to reassure Veeder. "I'll be up and around before you know it."

Veeder stood by the side of the bed staring at JJ's leg and all of the monitors. He wanted to cry but he fought back the tears. He knew he needed to remain strong.

"Get up here." JJ reached over the side, grabbed Veeder, and pulled him onto the bed. He gave Veeder a huge bear hug, kissed the top of his head, and messed up his hair, trying to lighten the moment. "You want to watch some TV? There are some good college games on."

"No." Veeder pouted, lowering his chin to his chest.

"I know this is hard for you to understand, Veeder, but trust me, God has a plan."

"How can you say that God has a plan?"

"Because He does. God will see me through this setback."

"It's more like God messed up your plan!" Veeder shot back. "You had a plan to play college and pro football."

"I guess I have a new plan to look forward to."

"How are you so calm about this?"

"What do you want me to do?"

"Why aren't you angry? God took everything away from you!"

JJ pulled Veeder into a tight embrace. "God didn't take everything away."

"You can't play football again."

"True."

"So what's left?"

"I'm still living. I'm still breathing." JJ patted his chest. "And unluckily for you, I'm still here to make your life very, very difficult!"

Veeder chuckled for a moment. "You never made my life difficult."

"Yeah, I was never really good at that, was I?"

"You're the one who makes my life better." A tear rolled down Veeder's cheek.

"Nah, you're just being kind now."

"You do." Veeder's emotions got the best of him, and the tears flowed down his cheeks, falling off onto the bed below.

"There's no reason to be upset."

"Everything's changed."

"The only thing that has changed is that I won't be able to play football anymore."

"I want it to go back to the way it used to be."

"Everything else in my life will stay the same."

"You were supposed to go pro!"

101

"I was never promised a college or professional career."

"You had a college scholarship to CHU. They wanted you to play football."

"God gave me a gift, you're right about that, but I believe this is as far as the gift was supposed to take me. It doesn't look like playing college football was part of the plan."

"Because God took it away from you!"

"He didn't take it away from me." JJ smiled, shaking his head back and forth. "It was an accident."

"It sucks."

"Or maybe He has something better planned for my life."

"How can you say that?"

"I know this is hard to believe, Veeder, especially looking at me lying in this bed, but I know something good will come of this. I know God will use this for His glory and His good. You just have to have faith."

"I hate God!"

"Don't ever say that."

"Why not?" Veeder crossed his arms, sticking out his chin. "It's true. I do."

"I know it looks dark right now." JJ was patient, gentle, and kind. "But I am blessed. I have a bright future in front of me."

"That's not what mom says."

"What did she say now?" JJ chuckled, rolling his eyes upon learning there was family gossip.

"I overheard her telling grandma that you have a long, difficult road in front of you."

"Yeah? Well, I overheard mom tell grandma about a dream she had when you were in the incubator."

"What does that have to do with anything?" Veeder sat back, staring at him, perplexed.

"Think about it."

Veeder thought for a moment. "I don't get it."

"The dream wasn't about you. It was about me."

"You think?"

"The dream sounds a lot like what is happening right now."

"You're right!"

"So she spent all that time not letting you play and it looks like she was denying the wrong kid. Maybe it was me she shouldn't have let play football."

"But what does that have to do with what I heard mom telling grandma?"

"Don't ever tell mom I said this," JJ leaned in and whispered into Veeder's ear, "but mom's a worrier!"

"But she said you have to have more surgeries."

"I do."

"And you got PT?" Veeder shrugged his shoulders and contorted his face as though he had just eaten a big spoonful of lima beans.

JJ laughed because of the confused look on Veeder's face. "PT stands for physical therapy."

"Physical therapy?" Veeder titled his head, staring at his brother, confused. "Huh?"

"Yes." JJ laughed, tussling Veeder's hair. "I will have to go to physical therapy to strengthen my leg after my surgeries."

"And you're not mad?"

"Nope, I'm not." JJ smiled. "I have faith. I believe God has a plan for me."

"He stole your plan."

"We are never promised anything in this life, Veeder." JJ smiled, taking pity on his younger brother.

"But why would He take away what you had worked so hard for?"

"Because it wasn't the plan He had for me."

"His plan sucks."

"His plan is awesome!" JJ put his arm around Veeder's shoulders, pulling him closer. "It may not be what we wanted, but sometimes what we want and what we get are two very different things."

"Why did he have to take away football?"

"I don't know, but on the bright side, it looks like we'll get to find out together."

"You were a great football player, JJ."

"I had a Coach once who always said to us that one-day football will end. Whether at the end of middle school, high school, college, or if we were lucky enough, at the end of a pro career. It didn't matter when it happened, the fact of the matter is that football will end."

"What's your point?"

"He always asked us, 'When that day comes, what will you do afterward?'"

Veeder stared at JJ for a moment. "You were supposed to be one of the lucky ones."

"I wish that was true, Veeder, but that would be my will and not His will."

"What is His will?"

"Right now, surgeries and PT. I have some tough days in front of me."

"That stinks."

"Maybe. But as I recover, He will show me what I am supposed to do with my life. He has a path laid out for me."

"I hate God for doing that to you."

"I don't." JJ collected his thoughts. "I know one thing that I am surer of today more than any other day in my life."

"What's that?"

"That God loves me."

"He has a weird way of showing it."

"You might be right." JJ laughed, pushing Veeder in a playful manner. "But He has a plan for me. I am willing to accept what He has for my life, and when you see how glorious and awesome His plan is, maybe then you will stop hating God."

"That will never happen."

"You'll see! One day you will eat those words." JJ wrapped Veeder up in another great big bear hug. Veeder loved every minute of the time they spent together. He loved being in JJ's strong arms, even if it was in a hospital bed.

"Veeder! Veeder! Earth to Veeder! Where are you, Veeder?" Anna asked, reaching up and shaking his shoulders.

Veeder gave her a big hug and whispered in her ear, "Sorry, Anna. I was lost in thought about something that happened a long time ago."

"You were thinking about JJ, weren't you?"

"Yes." Veeder paused, smirked, and then pointed to the Valley below. "This peak is where I realized how beautiful this place is. My brother showed me that."

"He also made you promise to keep it a secret."

"He did." Veeder kissed her cheek. "But I couldn't think of a more beautiful place to bring the most beautiful girl in the whole world."

Anna blushed. "I don't know if I am the most beautiful girl in the world."

"I love you, Anna Kelly. I only wanted to share this with you."

Anna turned around, stunned by Veeder's proclamation, her heart pounding hard against her chest. "You love me, Veeder?"

Veeder put his hands on her face and stared into her eyes. "I love you with all of my heart." Then he leaned in and kissed her.

"I love you too," she whispered, opening her eyes after the kiss. They both sat on the rock, staring out over the valley, smiles brightening both of their faces. Their hearts raced in the quiet solitude of the moments that followed their mutual confession.

Veeder put his chin on Anna's shoulder and whispered in her ear, "I have loved you since the moment I laid eyes on you."

Anna remained silent. She stared out over the horizon, her heart beating against the wall of her chest. She wanted to say so much in that moment. Instead, she sat there, her heart full of love, living in the moment.

"I know I'm stupid for saying this," Veeder whispered a few minutes later. "I went home after meeting you and as I skipped through the door, my mom asked me why I was so happy. I told her that I had just met the woman I was going to marry."

"How did you know that?"

"Know what? That I am going to marry you one day?"

"Yes?" Anna asked, blushing. "One day is so far away, how can you know something like that?"

"I just know."

"Did God whisper it in your ear?"

"What's any of this have to do with God?" Veeder asked in frustration.

"Because in Second Corinthians six it tells me not to marry an unbeliever. We won't have anything in common, and we'll have many difficult struggles."

"But I don't believe that Anna. You marry the person you love."

"But I do believe that. I can't marry somebody who doesn't love God."

"Why not?"

"We would be working against each other. The struggles of this world are hard enough to overcome. A lack of faith would destroy the marriage, but we would be bound together forever. I couldn't commit to that kind of life."

"And what if I never believe?" Veeder asked, fearing her answer. "How will we overcome that?"

"We're freshmen in high school, Veeder. I love you." Anna turned, held his hand, and kissed him. "God has a plan for us. We have time to figure that out."

"I guess we do," Veeder said. Anna turned, leaned back into him, and stared out over the Valley. He wrapped his arms around her waist again. This time, pulling her closer than before. He was afraid that he would lose the love of his life one day. The thought scared him, but he pushed those thoughts to the back of his mind.

He was in love. He knew that there wasn't anything that could ever take the love they had for each other away. Love was too strong. Love would conquer all. Ten years, a hundred years, it didn't matter. He loved Anna and she loved him. That would never change.

CHAPTER 14

—⌾—

It had been one of the craziest football seasons ever for Goldston Regional. Veeder took over as the starting quarterback in the first game of the season when Johnny Peterson was knocked out of the game with a concussion. The Gators had been losing 28-3 and decided that Joel wasn't going to be able to pass the ball. So, Coach McCarthy did the unthinkable. He unleashed Veeder McLean on the world of high school football.

On the second play from scrimmage, Veeder launched a sixty-three-yard bomb that Zane Farley caught in stride and took down the sidelines for an eighty-seven-yard touchdown. It electrified the crowd. When the final seconds ticked off the clock, Goldston Regional lost by a score of forty-eight to forty-five. It was the most exciting twenty-two minutes of football that the Gators had played in years. Veeder completed all twenty passes for six touchdowns and four hundred twenty-two yards. A football legend had been born on the field that night and the county was abuzz with stories of the comeback the Gators had mounted.

The Gators lost the second game of the season to the best team in their conference by a score of thirty-one to twenty-eight. Coach McCarthy's team was off to an 0-2 start, but he had hope for a great season nonetheless. His young quarterback had thrown for ten touchdowns and over nine hundred yards to start the season.

It was a new offense. Coach McCarthy had always been committed to the running game but Veeder was exciting to watch. He electrified the team and the fans. Friday night games were sold out every week and for the first time in years, Coach McCarthy was having fun.

Goldston Regional High School won their next five games. They had a five and two record with a five and one conference record. They were on their way to clinching a playoff berth if they could win the rest of their games. Coach McCarthy wanted another shot at a state championship before he retired and he could feel it within his grasp. Maybe not at the end of this season but soon. And with his newfound prized quarterback, he felt like anything was possible.

The whistle blew as the Goldston Regional Gators made another stop on fourth down. As the defense left the field and the offense ran onto the field, Coach McCarthy yelled, "Veeder!"

"Yes, Coach." Veeder held his helmet, standing on the sideline, before joining his teammates on the field for the final seven minutes of the game.

Coach McCarthy put his hand on Veeder's shoulder. "I'm putting Peterson in for the rest of the game."

It was the smartest decision Coach McCarthy could make as he looked forward to the end of the season. The game was over before it even started. Veeder had beaten the cornerbacks often and early with an aerial assault that made the defense shutter every time he dropped back to pass the ball. He was putting on a passing clinic and the other team was getting angrier as the Gators started running up the score.

"Coach, you promised!"

"I know, but the game is getting out of hand." Coach McCarthy knew he should have pulled the starting offense off the field in the middle of the third quarter, but he promised Veeder he wouldn't because JJ was back in town. Veeder wanted every minute of playing time he could get in front of his hero.

"This is the only game JJ is going to get to see me play in this season," Veeder protested. He knew he should have been pulled but his need to impress his older brother trumped the line between right and wrong. Even though the score was fifty-six to ten, he wanted to be on the field.

"Do you promise to run the ball?"

"Yes, sir."

"No heroics, Veeder, I mean it!"

"You got it, Coach!"

"Go!" Coach McCarthy rolled his eyes. He couldn't believe he had just been conned by a freshman but for the first time in his career, he had a freshman who had star power and would be the anchor of his team for the next three years.

Veeder put his helmet on and ran onto the field. The defense blitzed everyone on first down and swallowed up the running back for a five-yard loss. The defense drew a flag, though, when the middle linebacker lowered his shoulder and drove it into Veeder's back, planting the quarterback face-first into the turf. A skirmish broke out between the lineman and the defense. Veeder jumped to his feet and smiled at the middle linebacker, strutting back to the huddle.

The referees broke up the melee and ejected the middle linebacker. The opposing coaches argued while the linesman marked off the fifteen-yard penalty. Veeder knew the defense was pinning their ears back and coming after him. He was ready for them and was prepared to protect himself at all costs.

The offense came to the line, Veeder barked out the cadence and took the snap. Veeder dropped back and faked a handoff to his running back. Veeder bootlegged to the right and ran for six or seven yards until the safety hit Veeder. The safety landed on top of him and they both slid across the turf for five yards.

"Great hit, Man! Great hit! Love it!" Veeder patted the safety on the helmet, then hopped up, and ran back to his huddle. "Great hit!"

Veeder dropped back to pass on second down and short, but the defense sent eight men on an all-out blitz. Veeder spun out of the sack and scampered to the right side of the field. Without a receiver in sight, Veeder lowered the ball and took off at full speed.

The defense gave chase. Veeder had one man to beat as the safety was running him toward the sideline. Instead of running out of bounds for a huge gain, Veeder cut back and made a move that caused the safety to miss the tackle.

Veeder turned the ball inside and got obliterated when one of the linebackers drilled him in the center of his chest with the crown of the helmet. The collision knocked Veeder five yards backward. The rest of the defense piled on, planting him on the opponent's sideline.

Tempers flared, fights broke out, and flags flew all over the field. The coaches and referees tried to restore order. Veeder laid on the ground gasping for air. He looked up into the angry faces of the team he had been terrorizing all night. They yelled profanities and made disparaging remarks about him.

He looked past the mob that was taunting him and fixated on a bright blue star in the sky. The shenanigans on the field faded from his mind. He thought that Anna would love the star and promised himself that he would show it to her after the game.

"You okay?" Coach McCarthy and the team doctor were on their knees looking down at him.

Veeder looked up and smiled. "Fine, Coach!"

"Then why are you still on the ground?"

"Taking a break, Coach!"

"Taking a break?" Coach McCarthy was angry.

"Yeah, Coach. It's exhausting doing all this hard work."

"Get off my field," Coach McCarthy yelled at Veeder. He would've laughed if he wasn't so ticked off at the flippant attitude of his young quarterback. Veeder had almost incited a riot and all he could do was lie on the field and crack jokes. *Wait 'til Monday, son,* Coach thought, *we'll see who's laughing then!*

Coach McCarthy and the team doctor helped Veeder to his feet, but he walked across the field without any assistance. Veeder had to sit out for a play because of the injury time out, so Johnny took the field with the offense.

After the next play was whistled down, Veeder put on his helmet, but Coach McCarthy put his arm up to stop him from going back onto the field. "You're done for the night."

"Coach…" Veeder started to plead.

"You're done, Veeder!" Coach McCarthy barked.

"It's the only game JJ's going to see, Coach! Let me finish it!"

"No!"

"Come on, Coach!"

"If I let you on the field again," Coach McCarthy turned to stare down his quarterback, "they're going to kill you!"

"I promise I won't get hurt!"

"No!"

"Why not?"

"You taunted their safety and took a hit by their linebacker when you could've easily run out of bounds, Veeder! What were you thinking out there?"

"Sixty-three to ten, Coach!"

"For another touchdown?"

"I wanted the touchdown!"

"That was stupid, kid!" Coach McCarthy turned his back on Veeder. "Go take a seat! You're done for the night!"

Veeder was angry at being yanked. He went to the bench, threw his helmet on the ground, and then proceeded to the sideline to cheer on Johnny. He was the team leader and he was going to support them, even when he had to stand on the sidelines. The clock expired and the teams shook hands. Veeder was shielded by the coaches to limit any further shenanigans from happening between the two teams.

Veeder didn't waste any time with locker room celebrations after Coach McCarthy's post-game speeches. He left the field, showered, and changed. He exited the locker room while the rest of the team celebrated their sixth straight win.

CHAPTER 15

Excited to get home, Veeder urged Liam to drive faster. When the Mustang pulled into the driveway, Veeder jumped out of the car, slammed the door, ran across the yard, bounded up the front steps, threw his bag on the porch by the front door, and burst into the house. A raucous round of applause and cheers erupted.

Veeder wasn't paying any attention to the compliments, handshakes, high fives, and accolades. He was intent on finding out who the blonde-haired woman holding JJ's hand was and why she was in their house. When Veeder finally made his way through the crowd of people in his living room, he wrapped JJ up in his arms in a big, old bear hug.

"Great game, Veeder!" JJ congratulated him with a big smile.

"Thanks," Veeder said, staring at the woman standing next to JJ. "I'm glad you made it."

"I wouldn't have missed it for the world. You were awesome!"

"All thanks to you!" Veeder said, hugging his brother again.

"This is my girlfriend, Liz." JJ turned and introduced the woman standing next to him.

"You were great out there tonight." Liz smiled, holding out her hand.

"Thanks." Veeder was skeptical and jealous of Liz, looking her over while shaking her hand. "It's nice to meet you."

"The pleasure is all mine. I have heard so much about you. It's nice to finally meet you."

"Girlfriend, huh?" Veeder gave JJ an approving nod.

"Yeah." Liz blushed. "For a while now."

"I see." Veeder shot JJ a sideways look of disdain. "I wish JJ had told me. How did you two meet?"

"We were assigned to the same village in Africa."

"I can't wait to hear that story." Veeder clapped his hands, rubbing them together, and waiting for details.

"Trust me," JJ interjected. "It's not that exciting. You can definitely wait to hear that story."

"How long are you two in town?" Veeder was curt.

"A couple of days," JJ responded.

"Veeder!" Paul was waving his arms at him from across the room. "Get over here!"

"Go see dad," JJ said, pointing at Paul. "I'll catch up with you later."

"Okay." Veeder gave JJ another hug. "It was nice meeting you, Liz."

Veeder turned and crossed the room, pressing down the rising jealousy. He had waited for months to see JJ and the limited amount of time they had to spend together would now be impeded upon by his girlfriend.

JJ seemed happy, though, as he told wild tales about their excursions in Africa. Veeder wanted to hate Liz. He wanted to find flaws with her but couldn't. Liz was nice. She was funny, and most of all, Liz made JJ happy.

Veeder excused himself from the family gathering and went outside to sit in one of the rocking chairs on the front porch. He searched for the glowing blue star he had seen when he had been knocked down during the game. After about an hour, JJ came out and sat down next to him. "What are you doing out here?"

"Checking out the stars."

"You played one heck of a game out there tonight."

"Thanks."

"I'm serious, Veeder, I was impressed."

"I was hoping I would have a good game tonight."

"You did." JJ was beaming with pride. "You're better than I ever thought you would be."

"You taught me everything I know."

JJ chuckled. "If I remember correctly, grandma taught you everything I knew."

"That's right. She did." Veeder laughed.

JJ and Veeder spent the night laughing about the stories of their grandmother teaching Veeder how to play football. They laughed into the wee hours of the morning and went to bed long after everyone else had either left to go home or had fallen asleep.

Early the next morning, JJ crept into Veeder's room and woke him up for a run around the farm. The competition started as soon as they hit the bottom step of the porch. They raced each other across the yard and out into the fields. When they settled down into a slow jog, Veeder shared stories about Anna and after hearing about her, JJ was excited to meet her.

JJ shared stories about Liz. He told Veeder how they had met while digging latrines in a small village in Africa. They decided that if they could build sewage systems, they could achieve anything they set their minds to, together. He also told Veeder about her family back in Michigan and the many debates he had had with her father about college football.

JJ turned up the path that led back to the old football workout area. It wasn't used anymore. All of the brothers had moved on and Veeder used the training facilities at school. JJ stopped running when he got to the clearing. He walked around for a few minutes as his memories flooded back. Veeder sat down on the old box that used to house their football equipment.

"A lot of good memories up here." JJ walked around, lost in a moment of nostalgia.

"We had great times up here."

"I still don't believe the snake story," JJ teased, winking at Veeder.

"When have you ever known grandma to lie?"

"True." JJ laughed. "She never has, and I don't know if she ever will."

"It was a lucky throw."

"After watching you play, luck had nothing to do with it."

"Please." Veeder blushed. "It was a team effort. We have all worked hard."

"You have a God-given gift, Veeder. I can't wait to watch you on TV one day."

"That's a long way off."

"But it will happen. I know it."

"Maybe." Veeder smiled, thinking about the prospects of playing professional football. "One day."

JJ walked around a little more and reminisced, getting lost in his thoughts. It seemed like an eternity ago when he would spend his time preparing his body for the rigors of the gridiron. He loved every minute he spent working, preparing, and playing when he was younger, but it felt foreign to him now. Like it had been someone else's life and not his.

He wiped away a couple of tears that formed in the corner of his eyes, choked down the lump in his throat, turned around, walked across the clearing, and sat next to Veeder. "I was wondering if I could ask you for a favor?"

"Sure. What is it?"

"Well, to be honest, Liz and I are more than just dating."

"I wouldn't tell mom that." Veeder chuckled, sticking his elbow into JJ's side. "She'll tell you how many different ways you're going to Hell."

"No, no, no, nothing like that, Veeder. Get your mind out of the gutter." JJ laughed, pushing Veeder's shoulder.

"Hey, you're the one who made the inference."

"No, I didn't."

"Keep telling yourself that," Veeder teased.

"But you're right, Mom would tell me the various ways I would be going to hell if I did anything like that." They both laughed.

"Yes, she would."

JJ paused, taking a deep breath. "Liz and I are getting engaged."

"What?" Veeder was shocked at JJ's declaration. "When?"

"Well, technically, we are already engaged."

"Wait a minute," Veeder said, scratching his head. "When did you get engaged?"

"A couple of weeks ago."

"But only technically?" Veeder stared at JJ, he was confused.

"Yes."

"Wait, I'm lost."

"Liz's father is old-fashioned. She wants me to ask her father for her hand in marriage before we 'officially' get engaged."

"Oh." Veeder laughed. "I can understand that. Dad will want that when MK gets engaged."

"So even though we are engaged, we're getting formally engaged when we go back to Michigan."

"That's awesome, JJ! Congratulations!" Veeder hugged JJ.

"You think so?"

"Wait," Veeder said, teasing JJ. "You don't know if it's awesome?"

"I know it's awesome." JJ pushed him again. "I'm just nervous. It's such a big step."

"Well, I don't know her well enough to tell you what's wrong with her yet. But she makes you happy, right?"

"She does." JJ's eyes lit up in a way Veeder had never seen before.

"You love her?"

"I love her with every ounce of my being." JJ beamed as he talked about Liz. "She has made my life worthwhile. I am the happiest man on earth. Nothing could take away my joy."

"Then what are you nervous about?"

"I know, right?" JJ chuckled. "God brought us together and I am just so blessed."

"I am happy for you." Veeder left out any commentary on God.

JJ paused for a moment and started rubbing his hands together. "I was wondering if you would be my best man?"

"Me?" Veeder was shocked.

"Who else would I ask?"

"Sean, Colin, Liam, Michael," Veeder said, listing them off on his fingers. "One of your friends."

"I could ask one of them if you want me to," JJ said, staring at Veeder with a furrowed brow.

"I didn't say I wanted you to ask one of them, I'm just a little shocked that you would ask me."

"I know this seems crazy but for as long as I can remember, you have been my sidekick. We bonded over football. You helped Mom nurse me back to health. You're kind of like one of the coolest people I know."

"You must not know a lot of people."

"Well, there is that." JJ laughed, poking Veeder.

"Hey!"

"I'm kidding."

"What does Liz say about me being your best man?"

"She's excited. She can't wait to get to know you better. She has heard all your stories, although she might be tired of them. So if I were you, I wouldn't bring them up."

"Oh good," Veeder said, rolling his eyes. "Your wife hates me already!"

"Yeah, just a little bit." JJ teased.

"Really?"

"Yes, but regardless of that, what do you say? Will you be my best man?"

"Not if your wife hates me."

"She doesn't hate you." JJ laughed, tussling his hair. "I'm teasing you."

"Good."

"So you'll do it?"

"Even if she hated me, I'd be honored to do it. Yes."

"Thank you." JJ gave Veeder a big hug.

"The bachelor party is going to be kind of lame."

"That's just the way I like it."

"Really?" Veeder was taken aback.

"I live in Africa, in a tent, Veeder. A night at McDonald's with running water and an indoor toilet, sharing stories of the glory days is a major celebration for me!"

"That's true." Veeder chuckled.

"Kind of lame, huh?"

"It's different, I'll give you that," Veeder put his hand on the center of JJ's back. "But it also sounds cool when you think about all the good you're doing in the world."

"Thanks." JJ smiled. "That means a lot."

"I mean it," Veeder said, he was awestruck by JJ. "I'm really proud of you."

"Look at the time," JJ said, checking his watch and changing topics. "Breakfast will be hitting the table soon. Race you back to the house?"

"You're on!" JJ took off down the trail and Veeder ran after him. They were in an all-out sprint to the house. Veeder slowed down as they neared the house, only beating JJ by twenty yards. But that didn't stop him from rubbing it in JJ's face at breakfast.

Anna came over and joined the family for breakfast. Veeder introduced her to JJ and Liz. They spent the day getting to know each other. The more he learned about Liz, the more Veeder understood why JJ loved her so much. She was perfect for him. They were like two peas in a pod, and he couldn't wait to celebrate their wedding.

The next morning, the whole family took JJ and Liz to the airport so they could visit her parents. It was a tear-filled goodbye because the family would have to wait until Christmas before they would return. It would be their last extended trip in the states for a while as JJ and Liz were planning on returning to Africa in the New Year.

CHAPTER 16

⁃◦⟨◎⟩

I t was pitch black when Jill stumbled into the kitchen, flicked the light switch, and squinted her eyes, adjusting to the light. She crossed the kitchen floor mumbling to herself about needing a strong cup of coffee. Jill loved these quiet moments of solitude in the morning. She thanked God for His grace. She praised Him for another day of His love and wisdom. And she thanked Him for His creation of coffee. Oh, how she thanked Him for coffee!

The kitchen was soon a flurry of activity. Mary Katherine and Veeder came downstairs, rustled up their school supplies, and ate a hot breakfast. Jill whipped up a platter of pancakes, scrambled eggs, toast, sausage, and bacon. Veeder piled his plate with more food than he should have eaten, mumbling something about "being a growing boy" as he wolfed it all down. Mary Katherine had some eggs and toast while reading a book about reconstructive surgery. Paul sat at the table, drinking a cup of coffee, eating scrambled eggs with dry toast, and reading the newspaper.

Jill loved the moments when her family was gathered together. She turned on the radio and made some small talk as she sat down to eat. She bowed her head and said a quiet prayer of thanks when there was a knock at the door.

"Did you hear that?" Jill asked.

"Hear what?" Paul responded.

"I thought I heard a knock at the door." Before Paul could respond, there was a louder and longer knock. "Who could that be at this hour of the morning?"

Paul and Jill got up from the table, rushing to the front door. They opened the door, and a soldier was standing in front of them, holding a bouquet, and smiling from ear to ear.

"Is breakfast still at oh five hundred?"

"Sean!" Jill squealed, pulling him into the biggest hug he had ever received. Tears of joy streamed down her cheeks.

"It's good to have you home, son." Paul stepped onto the porch, wrapping Jill and Sean in his arms. Mary Katherine and Veeder raced to the front porch to greet their older brother. They all stood on the porch in a massive group hug, showering Sean with love. Once inside, they peppered him with a plethora of questions.

"Look." Sean held up his hands to get them to stop talking for a moment. "I promise I will answer all of your questions, but not until I have had some of mom's amazing coffee."

"I just made a fresh pot." Jill's smile stretched across her face. They went into the kitchen. Sean sat down at the table and Jill placed a large cup of coffee in front of him. He took a big sip, savored it, and swallowed with his eyes closed.

"Better than I remember, Mom."

She smiled, ran her hand over his head, and kissed his cheek. "Glad to have you home, Sean. Want some eggs?"

"Please."

"We didn't know you were coming, Sean," Paul said, sitting down at the table.

"I wanted to surprise you."

"Mission accomplished," Mary Katherine said with a sly smile.

"Good one, MK," Sean responded, winking at her.

"How long are you back for this time?" Jill asked.

"Our unit is back in the States for a couple of months."

"How long can you stay?" Paul asked.

"I got a two-week pass."

"That's great!" Jill put a plate of eggs in front of Sean.

"These are so good, Mom. Thank you." Sean said between mouthfuls of eggs.

"You can make my game this week?" Veeder asked.

"Make it?" Sean stared at him, shaking his head in disbelief at the question. "That's the whole reason I came home."

"Really?" Veeder was excited.

"I called JJ the other day. He went on and on about the star quarterback of the Gators."

"He's had a great season," Paul added. Veeder beamed with pride listening to his brother talk about JJ's analysis.

"He must be. They never let freshman play." Sean winked at Veeder.

"He's got forty touchdown passes so far this year," Mary Katherine added.

"Thirty-nine, MK," Veeder corrected. "But who's counting?"

"How many games?" Sean asked.

"Eight," Jill said.

"Yikes!" Sean was in awe. "Really? That's awesome, bud!"

"Nobody can believe it," Paul interjected. "He's been lighting it up all season."

"Well, I can't wait to see you play."

"Thanks." Veeder smiled, finishing his breakfast.

"You better throw a lot of touchdowns in the next two games," Sean chuckled. "I need something to brag about when I get back to the base."

"I promise," Veeder said, confident.

The family loved having Sean home. They hung on every word while he shared stories from his excursions in the Army. He shared his exploits on peacekeeping missions, humanitarian aid missions, and about the time he was deployed to the Middle East during Desert Storm. Ultimately, though, the conversation returned to the usual McLean family topics. They talked about the blessings of God, the farm, and how the business had grown.

As Jill was getting ready to take Veeder and Mary Katherine to school, Sean shared with them that he was going to re-up his commitment with the Army. He was up for a promotion to Captain and a career in the military suited him. He wanted to spend his life serving his country and defending the nation that had been so good to his family. Paul and Jill worried about their son committing his life to the military, but they understood his decision. They respected him. They were impressed with how much he had grown as a man and as a man of God.

While Veeder and Mary Katherine were at school, Sean went with Paul for a tour of the farm. They took a long walk around the grounds before hopping in Paul's truck and driving out to the added acreage. They talked about life, business, and how the farm had continued to grow. And with that growth, the family was able to do even more to support the church and the local community.

They joined Jill for a late-day lunch that was filled with more love, laughter, and stories of their lives. It was a godsend to have Sean home, even if for a short period of time, and they were going to savor every moment. After lunch, Jill suggested that Sean go watch Veeder at practice.

Sean planned on doing just that and then taking Veeder and Mary Katherine to dinner. He wanted to know more about this six-game winning streak and about how Veeder had revived a team that had languished in the basement of the conference for the past six seasons.

Sean got a dose of sentimentality when he stepped on campus for the first time since graduation. He forgot how small their school was in comparison to other schools around the state. There were a little over five hundred kids from the surrounding towns that fed into Goldston Regional High School. Sean remembered only having ninety-three kids in his graduating class. Other schools had a couple of thousand students to draw from for their football team so as he walked out to the practice field, he knew how hard a six-game win streak was for such a small school.

Sean knew that it would have taken a spark plug to electrify the team. He also knew that it took hard work, commitment, tenacity, and faith in a common goal. But he never thought it would be his little brother who brought about a revival of the football program and with it, a rejuvenation of the school and the community.

Sean showed up at the field for the last hour of practice. He had played for Coach McCarthy, who was old school. He had been coaching this team for over thirty years; things were not going to change in the twilight of his career. He worked his players hard every single day. He didn't believe in walkthroughs before game day. Coach believed in working hard until game day and then on game day, you went out and executed. No more, no less. As Sean stepped out on the field and watched the players, he chuckled to himself, *Nope. Nothing ever changes.*

When practice ended, Sean spent some time catching up with the coaches. He milled around the school grounds remembering old times until Veeder was ready to leave. They hopped into Sean's rental car and raced back to the farm to pick up Mary Katherine. Veeder convinced Sean to make another stop at the church so he could introduce him to Anna.

Veeder introduced Sean to Pastor Kelly and his wife. They spoke for a few minutes about the church, his military service—Pastor Kelly had been an Army Chaplain—and about life in general. Sean asked if Anna could join them for dinner and a rented movie back at the farm. Pastor Kelly agreed as long as Anna was home by midnight… it was a school night.

As they walked to the car, Pastor Kelly stood on his front porch with his wife and remembered the difficult path they had all walked to get to this moment. It wasn't easy watching his daughter date someone who didn't believe in God, but he liked Veeder. Veeder was good to Anna, but he also knew that Anna had a strong love of the Lord, and he trusted her to make the right decisions.

They all piled into the car and drove into town to have dinner at Lizzie's. All of their stories shared an eerie sense of familiarity. They laughed and joked about all of the tales they had of high school. Sean shared chronicles of his time at Goldston Regional while Mary Katherine, Anna, and Veeder shared accounts of their brief time at the upper school. It was a great conversation that left all of them with the sense that time may change, the people at the school may change, but not much else changes.

Sean paid for dinner, stepped out onto the sidewalk, and stared at his surroundings. He looked to his left and then to the right, embracing the welcoming feeling this one-street little town gave him. Sean stood there taking in the sights and sounds as a large grin crept across his face.

"What's up, Sean?" Veeder asked as Mary Katherine and Anna stood next to him, wondering why they were just standing there.

"This place is a sight for sore eyes," Sean replied nostalgic. "I never thought I'd miss it. It's good to be home."

"It's good to have you home," Mary Katherine interjected, slipping her arm around Sean's waist, and hugging him.

"I agree," Veeder added, putting a hand on the center of Sean's back. "It's great to have you here with us."

"Let's go home." Sean pulled them both into a hug. Then they all climbed back into his car. Mary Katherine rode in the front seat while Veeder sat in the backseat with Anna. Anna rested her head on Veeder's shoulder and leaned into him. He put his arm around her shoulders, stroking her arm while looking out the window and taking in the scenery. *It's not a bad little place to live* he thought to himself.

His heart was filled with an overwhelming sense of happiness and contentment. He was prepared for the game, was dating the most beautiful girl he had ever seen, and Sean was home. If all went well, he would finish what JJ and Sean had started seven years ago when they almost brought home a state championship.

Sean drove up the driveway and noticed a state trooper's patrol car parked in front of the house. He sped up a little and came to a screeching halt, sending sand and dirt flying everywhere. He hadn't even turned off the engine before Veeder, Mary Katherine, and Anna were out of the car and running across the driveway. The state trooper was speaking with Paul and Jill on the front porch. As they reached the bottom steps, they heard the state trooper's last sentence. "I'm sorry to inform you that your son, James, has died."

Jill collapsed on the porch—an agonizing scream escaped her mouth. Paul dropped to Jill's side, pulling her to him—their tears joining in a stream down Jill's cheek. Mary Katherine was hysterical as Sean wrapped her up in his arms, just holding her. It must have been a minute or two before Veeder realized he had been screaming "No! God no!" as Anna tried to hold him in her arms and comfort him.

Sean and the officer tried to console everyone. Paul took Jill into the house and Mary Katherine went with them. Veeder sat on the wicker couch on the front porch in tears. Anna sat next to him, holding him in her arms. Sean walked the state trooper back to his patrol car.

"I don't know if what you told my parents has registered with them, Officer," Sean said as they reached the patrol car. "Do you mind telling me what happened?"

"All I know is that your brother, James, had rented a car at the airport earlier this afternoon. He was driving on the highway when a drunk driver lost control of his car. The drunk driver's car hit the middle barrier and careened across the highway in front of an eighteen-wheeler. The driver of the truck reacted to the car skidding in front of him and turned the wheel to avoid a collision. The truck struck the front end of your brother's car. Your brother's car was knocked across the lane and was hit by two more cars before exiting the highway, hitting a tree head-on at a pretty high speed."

"Do you know if he died instantaneously?" Tears streamed down Sean's cheeks. He was hoping that his brother had not suffered.

"I'm sorry, Lieutenant, I don't know."

"Thank you, Officer," Sean said, shaking hands.

"I'm sorry for your loss." The state trooper said with compassion.

"Thank you."

The officer got into his patrol car and drove away. Sean took a moment for himself, wiped the tears from his eyes, and walked back to the porch. He knew what he had to do next, and he did not enjoy the fact that he was the one who had to call Liz.

Sean walked up the steps to the porch, walked over to Veeder, pulled him up into his arms, and held him in his embrace for a long time while the two of them cried. Sean broke the embrace and looked Veeder in the eyes. "He loved you so much."

"I loved him, Sean."

"I know." Sean pulled Veeder back into a hug. "And most importantly, JJ knew that."

"This is not happening, Sean, it's not!"

"I wish it wasn't, buddy."

"Please tell me this is all a bad dream and when I wake up, JJ will be here."

"I wish it was, Veeder, I wish it was," was all that Sean could say, holding Veeder in his arms. As he broke the embrace, he smiled at Anna, bent down, kissed her on top of her head, and said, "Thank you."

"I am so sorry, Sean," Anna replied, tears in her eyes.

"I know. Thank you," Sean replied, mustering up a halfhearted smile. "I'll call your parents in a little bit and let them know what happened."

"Thank you."

Sean patted Veeder on the side of his face and gave him another hug. "I have to go call Liz."

Veeder said nothing, falling back into the chair, and staring out into the darkness. He barely felt Anna put her arms around him. He was numb. His heart was broken. His hero was gone.

Sean went into the house and called Anna's parents to tell them what had happened. Then he called Liz. She was inconsolable. Liz's father got on the phone and they had a long talk about what had happened and why JJ was in North Carolina.

Liz's father explained that JJ was excited about Sean getting a fourteen-day pass. He was jealous that Sean was going to get to see two games. So he decided to surprise the family and head home for a couple of weeks. He wanted to join Sean in the stands, rooting for Veeder over the last couple weeks of the season. Liz wanted to join them too, but she had come down with a bad case of the flu. She was in no shape to travel. Liz implored JJ to wait until the weekend so she could join them, but he was so excited about Friday night's game. So they decided he would fly down and surprise everyone. He was just so sure that Veeder would lead the team to a state championship, and he wanted to be there to witness it.

Sean thanked Liz's father for talking with him and for helping him to understand JJ's last mission to support his family, especially Veeder. It would be their lasting memory of their beloved son and brother. They prayed together. Then Sean hung up the phone, went to his room, and cried himself to sleep.

Veeder woke up the next morning on the porch where he and Anna had fallen asleep. His heart ached. He didn't want to move and wake her up. As the birds started to sing, the events of the night before hit him like a ton of bricks and the tears started to flow again. His life had changed. *His hero had died. How could he ever recover from this devastating event and move forward?*

Anna felt him rustling and woke up. Her body ached from having slept on the uncomfortable chair, but her heart broke. The love of her life was devastated. Anna wiped his tears away. "I love you, Veeder."

He turned, looking at her with grief-filled eyes. "Why JJ, Anna? Why him? Why couldn't it have been me?"

Anna didn't have any words. She just wrapped her arms around Veeder, pulling him into her chest, and just held him. She tried her best to console him. She was heartbroken and prayed in that moment for God's strength, for both of them and the whole McLean family.

CHAPTER 17

—◦◦◦—

The next few days passed by in a blur for Veeder. The entire family descended on the house to offer their condolences, to help with funeral arrangements, to pray, and to offer their support.

The football team took the field on Friday night in search of their seventh consecutive victory. Expectations were high but their hearts were heavy. Johnny Peterson led the offense and the team put forth a valiant effort. As the final seconds ticked off the clock, the other team scored a last-minute touchdown to win the game by a score of twenty-seven to twenty-four. They lost their quest for a seventh straight victory. And with the loss, the team put their playoff hopes on life support.

Liz flew into town with her family on Saturday afternoon. Veeder spent the weekend avoiding her. He didn't know what to say. His heart was broken. JJ wasn't coming home again. What could he say to the woman who loved him more than anyone else in the world? He had no words that could ever mend her broken heart, nonetheless his own.

Anna was by Veeder's side, day and night, supporting him, helping out the family, and doing whatever was needed to help them get through the darkest of days. Breathing was as much as Veeder could handle, but Anna kept him going. He had no idea how he would ever be able to thank her for all of the love she showered upon his family.

Monday afternoon came way too soon. Veeder pulled up his tie and went downstairs to wait for the rest of the family. He walked out onto the porch and saw Anna standing alone, by the railing, in a black dress, staring out at the farm. He walked over, stood behind her, placed his hands on her sides, and stared out at the farm. "Thank you, Anna."

"You have nothing to thank me for." Anna turned around, staring into his eyes. "I have no words. There is nothing I could ever say."

"I don't know if the pain will ever go away."

"One day. It will." Anna half-smiled, reaching up and fixing his tie.

"I love you."

"I love you, too." Anna kissed him. "I always will."

Veeder put his arms around Anna, pulling her into him. He held her for the longest time. She put her head on his shoulder and melted into him, and for the next few minutes, the world spun to the beat of their hearts. They stood silent in the immensity of the day ahead of them.

The drive to the church was the longest, hardest drive Veeder had ever taken. He sat next to Anna in the back seat of his father's truck, held her hand, and stared out the window in silence. The closer they got to the church, the harder his heart pounded against the wall of his chest. The tears started to fall when they pulled into the driveway of the sanctuary. It was becoming too real, and he knew that when he walked through those hallowed doors, he would have to face his worst nightmare. He would have to say farewell to his hero.

The first hour of the wake was a private viewing for the family. Veeder sat stoic in the last pew of the chapel, staring at the open casket at the front of the room. He watched his mother and father greet relatives, share hugs, tears, and laughter. One by one, they all said goodbye to JJ.

"You should go up there and say goodbye," Colleen said, sitting down next to Veeder, and taking his hand in hers.

"I can't, Grandma." The pain in Veeder's voice broke her heart while watching the tears roll down his cheek.

"I know it's hard."

"It's not fair."

"Whoever said life was fair?"

"Why did JJ have to die so young?"

"God has His reasons."

"Stupid reasons."

"You may feel that way, but God created us all to live vastly different lives. As difficult as it is to believe, this is how JJ's life was supposed to go. We celebrate his life, love him, and commit him to God for all eternity."

"Huh, God?" Veeder quipped. "I'd like five minutes to knock Him on His ass right now."

"We don't talk like that Veeder!" Colleen was shocked at his choice of words in church. "Who taught you that word anyway?"

"JJ did." Veeder chuckled through his tears. "JJ did, Grandma."

"Well, he'll have a chance to explain that one to Jesus on his own."

"I still don't believe in Jesus, Grandma." Veeder shook his head in anger. "How could anyone believe in a God who would take someone like JJ when he was in the prime of his life?"

"I don't have any explanations, Veeder. I don't. I grieve with you and I celebrate JJ's life with the family."

"Celebrate?" Veeder scoffed, angry at her choice of words.

"Yes, celebrate."

"His life was just getting started. How can we celebrate that he was ripped away from us?"

"I know it is difficult, but I am secure in the blessing that JJ is with God for eternity."

"I wish I could believe that."

"I wish you would open your eyes because Jesus loves you. He blesses you every day."

"Where was Jesus when JJ needed him?"

"Where he needed to be." Colleen paused. "Comforting JJ in his final moments."

"Really?" Veeder turned, staring at Collen with contempt. "Where is he now, Grandma? Where is Jesus right now?"

"He's sitting right next to you with tears in his eyes. He is holding you up because your heart is breaking, and He prays for your disbelieving heart."

"Why would He do that?"

"Because He loves you."

"My condolences, Mrs. McLean." Anna stepped into the last pew, hugged Colleen, and sat on the other side of Veeder.

"Thank you, Anna."

"I know this isn't easy." Anna sat down and held Veeder's hand.

"Difficult times but God will provide."

"One day at a time," Anna said with compassion. "God heals all wounds."

"You don't have to tell me that, Anna," Colleen said, tilting her head toward Veeder. "Tell that to your boyfriend, here."

"Grandma," Veeder interjected. "Enough already! Just stop!"

"I've said my peace." Colleen stood and shuffled down the pew.

"How are you doing?" Anna asked.

"Not good."

"Are you going to say goodbye to JJ?"

"I can't." Veeder sniffled, wiping away his tears.

They sat silent, watching Colleen kneel in the pew, and pray out loud. "Thank you for your love, Lord Jesus. As we commit our beloved child, JJ, to your loving care, promise me, Lord Jesus, that you will not let my grandson, Veeder, leave this earth without seeing you face-to-face. Promise me that you will reveal your glory to him. Please give him every chance to love you and honor you with all of his heart. Amen."

Veeder looked over at Colleen in disbelief as she lifted her head and stood up. "Really, Grandma?"

"I will pray for you for the rest of my life." Colleen stood and walked down the center aisle of the church to go pay her last respects to JJ.

When the private viewing was over, Veeder felt odd standing in a line at the center of the church. They waited for the church doors to open so that the community could pay their final respects to JJ. Veeder still hadn't found it in his heart to kneel in front of the casket and look at JJ lying there. It was too much for him to handle. He was happy that Anna was allowed to stand next to him at the end of the line. She shielded him from seeing JJ.

The doors opened and Anna squeezed his hand. It gave him strength as a few of their friends came walking down the center aisle. They walked through the line of family members, offering hugs and condolences. When they passed through and moved onto the casket to pay their last respects to JJ, Veeder turned and faced the next person in the line of mourners.

Veeder broke into tears and hugged Johnny Peterson who led the entire football team, dressed in their game day jerseys, down the center aisle. Veeder held tight to each of his brothers on the football team as they passed through the line. He felt and heard their condolences in each of their embraces. He apologized to each one of his teammates for letting them down on Friday night. He knew they understood, but he needed that moment with each one of them to let them know how much he appreciated their support.

Veeder lost control of his emotions and wept when Coach McCarthy put his arms around his young quarterback. "I'm so sorry" was all Coach McCarthy could say. Veeder held onto him and cried on his shoulder. When Coach McCarthy knelt at the casket, he placed two footballs inside the casket with JJ. The footballs were signed by every member of JJ's high school team for all four years that he had played for the Gators. Not only did they all sign the football, every one of those players followed Coach McCarthy through the receiving line to pay their final respects to JJ.

Veeder was so overtaken with emotion that he excused himself from the receiving line. He slipped out the side door of the chapel and walked into a small courtyard. He sat down on a bench and starting weeping, his heart was overwhelmed by the kindness and compassion of the people who had come to show their love and respect for his brother.

Liz sat next down to him, wiping her tears away with a handkerchief. "I know why you are avoiding me this weekend and I completely understand."

"I'm sorry, Liz," Veeder said, wiping away his tears with the back of his hand.

"You don't need to be, I'm kind of relieved that you have."

"You are?" Veeder asked, looking at her. "Why?"

"Because I didn't know what to say to you." Liz dabbed the tears forming in her eyes with the handkerchief.

"Really?" Veeder chuckled a little bit. "I had no idea what to say to you. You must be devastated."

"I feel the same way about you."

"Really?" Veeder laughed for a second and Liz joined him.

"Your brother loved you so much, Veeder." Liz took his hand in hers and fought back against the lump that had lodged in her throat.

"Please don't." Veeder begged, choking on his words.

"I have to, Veeder," Liz said with compassion.

"No, you don't. I know how much he loved you."

"There was something JJ always wanted to tell you, but he could never find the words."

"I don't know if I am ready." Veeder clenched his free hand into a fist and took a deep breath.

"I know you thought JJ was your hero, but the truth of the matter is, you were his. He loved getting letters from your parents telling him about everything you did on and off the football field."

"Please don't, Liz," Veeder whimpered, trying to hold back the flood gates.

"I have to. JJ would be disappointed in me if I didn't share this with you."

"I loved him so much." Tears started streaming down his cheeks again.

"I remember the day we got engaged. We were in the middle of Africa. The first person he wanted to call and tell was you."

"I never got the call."

"We had no cell service and since we were going to come home a few weeks later, we decided to wait. For the weeks leading up to us coming home, he just couldn't wait to tell you."

"He was never very patient."

"Well, one night, in a heavy downpour, our Jeep got stuck in the mud, so he told me all about the story of your birth."

"He loved telling that story for some crazy reason."

"He told me about the whole ordeal and how little you were, but it wasn't until you got older when he finally realized that you were born to save him from himself."

"What?" Veeder looked at her, wiping the tears from his cheek. "How?"

"Your brother, according to him, was a bully when he was a kid."

"No he wasn't."

"According to JJ, he was. He was bigger and stronger than everyone. He teased the little kids mercilessly. He was mean to them. He wouldn't give details. He was ashamed of his actions but as he told me the story, he wept."

"JJ never cried."

"I know," Liz said, wiping away her tears. "So I know his story had to be true."

"But JJ wasn't a bully," Veeder lamented. "He was kind to everyone."

"Because of you."

"Because of me?"

"He said he was watching you one day on the playground. He saw some kids bullying you. They were treating you the way he treated others and it broke his heart."

"JJ was never mean to anyone, Liz." Veeder was stunned by her revelation. "Are you sure you have the story right?"

"JJ swears he was, and it was that day on the playground that showed him who he really was. He said that was the day he started going to youth group. He started reading his Bible more. He started learning about God and the love of Jesus. It was because of what he witnessed that day, in the park, that he decided to change the way he lived his life."

"I never knew any of this."

"Because he never told you," Liz said, squeezing Veeder's hand. "He said you changed his life. That if you had not struggled so much early in life, he never would have changed. You were the reason he found Jesus and gave his life over to Him. Because he saw himself in those boys who bullied you, he turned his life around, and got saved."

Veeder sat on the bench frozen, staring down at his feet while Liz continued. "He felt like God gave him a second chance when he started teaching you about football. He felt like he had a chance to redeem himself. He just never imagined you would become as good as you are."

"JJ was the reason I am any good."

"He was your biggest fan," Liz chuckled, wiping away her tears. "Oh, how he loved hearing about your games, and he praised God for the talent He gave to you."

"I don't believe in God," Veeder looked down to hide his face from Liz. "He knew that."

"He knew." Liz put her arm around Veeder's shoulders. "He was also sure that you would find God one day."

"But what if I never do?"

"Do you remember the night you visited JJ in the hospital and asked him why God had taken football away from him?"

"He told you about that?" Veeder asked, nodding his head.

"JJ told me everything. I loved hearing about his life." Liz paused, wiping her eyes. "Do you remember that day?"

"I remember."

"JJ was going to tell you that it was God's plan for him to go out into the world and help those who couldn't help themselves. He was supposed to help people much like those kids he used to pick on. He was supposed to love on them, help them, and bless them with the love of God."

"I am so sorry he left you, Liz," Veeder said, hugging her.

"Thank you. I miss him," Liz said, returning the hug. "He said I was the 'cherry on the top of his ice cream sundae of a life.' He said you would know what that meant."

"Yeah, I do." Veeder smiled, his heart climbing into his throat.

"He was happier than you could ever imagine. He wanted you to know he was blessed and he wanted you to search your heart. He wanted you to find God so you both could play football in heaven together, forever."

"I miss him so much." Veeder broke down again.

Liz held Veeder, cradling him against her body, rocking back and forth with him on the bench. "I do too, Veeder. I do too."

They sat together, for a long time, mourning the loss of JJ. They shared stories about JJ, laughing together as they recounted many of the adventures they had with him. The wake was drawing to a close. They decided it was time to join the rest of the family.

"I know you don't want to see him, Veeder, but you have to say goodbye to JJ." Liz put her arm around Veeder's shoulders.

"I don't know how."

"Just go talk to him." Liz fought back the tears and feigned a smile.

"I don't want to say goodbye, Liz," Veeder said, choking back the tears. "I don't want him to leave me."

"He'll never leave you, Veeder. He will always be with you in your heart. His love will always be with you."

"Thank you," Veeder replied. "What about you? Are you going to be okay?"

"I will be in time. It's going to be hard because I love JJ so much, but I know he would want me to go on living." They stood up and gave each other a long hug.

"I wish he was still here with you."

"Me too," Liz said through a faked smile. "Come on, let's go say goodbye to your brother."

Veeder and Liz walked into the chapel and over to the casket together. They hugged each other before Veeder knelt in front of JJ. He looked into the casket and broke down in tears. Anna started to walk over to Veeder to comfort him, but Liz stopped her. "Give him a moment. He has to say goodbye on his own."

Anna and Liz stood behind Veeder, holding each other, while Veeder said goodbye. When he was done, he stood up, hugged both women, then went and sat in the front row with Anna, while Liz said goodbye. When the sanctuary had emptied of friends and extended relatives, Pastor Kelly called the family together in the front of the chapel. They said a few prayers and then the family left.

Veeder walked over to the casket again, looked down, and said with tears running down his face, "Love you, JJ. I'll be seeing you around."

Veeder touched his hand, took another moment for himself, then walked to the back of the sanctuary, where Anna was waiting for him, and left.

CHAPTER 18

⟶⟲⟋

The overcast, gray, dreary clouds hung heavy in the cold afternoon sky. The funeral procession moved to the graveyard. Veeder's heart shattered into a million fragments and his knees buckled graveside when he placed flowers on JJ's casket. Anna and Mary Katherine grabbed his elbows and helped steady him, grief weakening every muscle in his body.

Once composed, Veeder muttered his final farewell to his brother. Turning from the casket, Anna and Mary Katherine helped him back to his seat. He spotted Johnny Peterson and his family in attendance. It touched his heart and gave him peace of mind to know they had come. When they returned to the chapel for the reception, he noticed the Peterson family was not in attendance.

The reception dragged on into the late afternoon. Veeder, tired of the condolences, slipped away to walk around the church grounds. A light drizzle, soon turning into a steady rain, forced him back inside. He hoped to find a quiet place to remember JJ while he dried off. Unfortunately, the solitude didn't bring him the peace he was hoping to find.

Veeder walked around the empty chapel, reading the plaques, and staring at the stained glass. Soon, he found himself standing at the steps to the altar. He stared for a long time at the cross that hung on the wall. Time dragged as he stood fixated, feeling nothing but bitterness. He had nothing to say to God, so he turned and slipped out of the sanctuary.

Veeder was about to walk back down the stairs to the reception hall when he noticed Pastor Kelly reading at his desk. He walked to the office door and spied on the Pastor for a few minutes before knocking. "Pardon me, Pastor Kelly."

Pastor Kelly looked up from his book. "Veeder."

"Do you mind if I come in for a minute?"

"Please, come in." Pastor Kelly stood up.

"Sorry for bothering you." Veeder walked toward the desk and extended his hand.

"No bother at all." Pastor Kelly took Veeder's hand and pulled him into a big hug. Veeder was dumbstruck by the gesture but felt a wave of comfort in the reassuring embrace of his minister. "Sit, please."

Pastor Kelly gestured toward four high-back leather chairs that surrounded a coffee table. Veeder walked over and sat down. Pastor Kelly followed and sat across the table from him.

"What can I do for you?" Pastor Kelly asked.

"I have a bunch of questions that keep pestering me, and I'm looking for answers."

"That's understandable, Veeder. You have been through a lot. You'll find answers to those questions in due time."

"I don't want answers in due time," Veeder barked in anger. "I want answers now!"

"I'm sorry, Veeder." Pastor Kelly was calm in the face of Veeder's anger. "It doesn't work that way."

"Why not?"

"It's one of the mysteries of life. Grief is different for everybody but through prayer, you will find peace."

"That's ridiculous!" Veeder fidgeted in his seat, rubbing his hands together. "I have listened to everyone say they will pray for us. Well, those prayers aren't working, Pastor!"

"I'm sorry you feel that way."

"I want to know why God took my brother! Why, Pastor? Why did God take him?"

Pastor Kelly took a moment to collect his thoughts. He could feel the anger in Veeder and prayed for guidance. "I don't have any words that will bring you comfort or resolution. There are no words. To be completely honest, I am trying to sort through my own feelings over the loss of your brother."

"That doesn't cut it, Pastor."

"I'm sorry, Veeder. I know death is hard to understand, but sometimes we don't have the words or the answers we seek."

"No!" Veeder yelled, slamming his hand down on the coffee table. "You parade around this church all the time with confidence, with the word, with the directions our lives are supposed to take, and now you tell me you don't have the answers?"

"Unfortunately, I don't."

"No, Pastor! I don't accept that answer! Tell me why God took JJ!"

"I don't know what to tell you, Veeder. This is one of the mysteries of life that even has me completely vexed and heartbroken."

"Tell me something, Pastor!" Veeder was desperate, seeking answers to grab onto for his peace of mind. "Tell me there was some greater purpose for JJ's death."

"I'm sorry, Veeder. I can't do that. It doesn't work that way."

"Why not, Pastor? You're on His payroll!"

"I wish it worked like that, son. I really do." Pastor Kelly paused for a moment. "I wish I could pick up the phone and call God. I wish I could ask him for all of the answers you seek but I can't. I'm sorry."

"It doesn't work like that, huh?" Veeder chuckled, leaning back in the chair, and staring at Pastor Kelly. "You're a hypocrite."

"I'm sorry you feel that way."

"You strut around church every Sunday telling people about God's love, His grace, His peace, and His wisdom, but when I come to you looking for some clarity about God's will, you don't have any insights to share with me."

"I will pray for you, Veeder."

"I don't want your prayers. I want answers!"

"You will have to ask God these questions yourself. You will have to ask Him for the answers you seek."

"Why would I do that, Pastor?" Veeder asked with contempt.

"For clarity. For peace."

"I don't need any more clarity, Pastor. I've gotten all the clarity I can handle over the past few days."

"You have?" Pastor Kelly was perplexed. "Do you care to share it with me?"

"This is a cruel world." Veeder's anger turned to sadness, tears started rolling down his cheeks.

"It is, Veeder. You won't get an argument from me."

"It's a mean, dark place. It steals your joy, your love. You're alive one moment and you're dead the next. Poof!" Veeder made a hand gesture to show the emptiness. "No answers. No Meaning. Life is nothing more than a cruel charade."

"Trust God, son," Pastor Kelly said with compassion. "You just have to have faith."

"There is no God, Pastor, don't you get that?"

"I understand that you are angry with God right now, Veeder. I do. And quite honestly, you have every right to be."

"I'm not angry with God, Pastor."

"You're not?" Pastor Kelly was confused because of Veeder's vitriol.

"No," Veeder said, staring down Pastor Kelly with conviction. "How can you be angry at something that doesn't exist?"

"Excuse me?"

"If I were angry at God, I would have to admit that He exists. I would have to believe my Grandma Colleen who keeps telling me that He's sitting next to me, holding me up, comforting me. But let's be honest, Pastor, I'm not angry at God because He just doesn't exist."

"Your grandmother is a smart woman, you should listen to her. The Lord is closer than you think. He is always there for those who are troubled in spirit."

"Please don't start getting all preachy with me, Pastor Kelly."

"I am going to, Veeder. It's what I do, I'm on His payroll." Pastor Kelly said with a hint of sarcasm, winking at him.

Veeder chuckled. "You're funny."

"I know this is tough for you to understand, but if you let God into your heart, this will get better in time. He makes all things good, even in the tough times. He is working, especially for those who love Him, and have been called to serve Him."

"And what good was my brother's death? JJ loved God."

"We all face death, Veeder. We all have hardships."

"It was all meaningless." Veeder wiped the tears from his eyes. "JJ traveled all over the world to help the less fortunate. He did it for the love of God. And what did it get him? Nothing."

"Everything in life has meaning, Veeder. We may not understand the reasons but everything in life has meaning."

"Then why did this happen?"

"I don't know."

"Hypocrite."

"You can be bitter if you want to, but how is that going to help you? Help JJ?"

"Nothing can help JJ!" Veeder threw up his hands in frustration. "That's kind of the point of death! And yes, Pastor, that makes me bitter."

"You just need time to heal, son. You need time to hurt, to question, to be angry, to grieve."

"I don't know if I will ever get past this stage."

"Why not, Veeder?"

"Why would I?" Veeder paused, wiping the tears away. "God stole my brother from me!"

"The Bible is full of people who hit rock bottom before God used their pain to make the world a better place."

"Not like this, Pastor."

"You don't think so?"

"No."

"What about Christ?"

"What about Him?

"Christ died on the cross."

"So?"

"They twisted thorns upon His head, they beat Him, and they killed Him. His death was supposed to end this rag-tag group of people who followed Him. Yet, Christ went through the indignity of the cross and defeated it. He conquered death for us. For you."

"What does that have to do with me?"

"God loves you. He knows you're in pain. He's with you in your adversity. Let Him in."

"I don't know if I can."

"God is going through all of this with you. He is standing next to you, tending to your pain, loving you."

"You're wasting your words, Pastor."

"If you mourn, He is going to comfort you. He is a living God. Believe it or not, Veeder, the Lord is comforting you right now. Open your heart and let Him in."

"I don't feel very comforted. I feel numb. I feel alone. I feel like my heart has been ripped out of my chest and stomped on."

"I know. I know you don't believe me, but I do." A tear crept down Pastor Kelly's cheek. "I didn't know your brother very well, but I know you are in crippling pain."

"How do you know?"

"When Anna comes home, she is brokenhearted. She mourns for your brother, but she grieves for you. She prays for you. Her heart is breaking because your heart is broken and I grieve with my daughter. I pray every night that God will take your pain away. I pray that He will heal you. Sometimes, quite selfishly, because I know God will have to take your pain away before Anna's pain will go away.

"I wish I could snap my fingers and take away the pain the death of your brother has caused you, but I can't. So, I get on my knees every night and ask God to heal your pain. I will keep praying until He does."

Veeder was caught off guard by the compassion of Pastor Kelly. He was humbled and didn't know what to say, so he lowered his head in shame, and stared at the floor. "Thank you, Pastor Kelly. I love Anna with all of my heart."

"I love Anna too, son, and I'm truly sorry for your loss."

"What do I do now?"

"What would JJ tell you to do?"

Veeder chuckled, smiling to himself, raising his head. "JJ would tell me to, 'Suck it up buttercup. Time to pick yourself up by your bootstraps, toss the self-pity in the trash can, and get back to work. Get back to living.'"

"Well, Veeder." Pastor Kelly leaned forward, looking Veeder in the eye with conviction. "Suck it up buttercup. Time to pick yourself up by your bootstraps, toss the self-pity in the trash can, and get back to work. Get back to living."

Veeder and Pastor Kelly laughed for a moment. "Anna didn't tell me you were funny, Pastor."

"Most teenage daughters don't find their fathers very funny."

"MK thinks my dad is hysterical."

"Well, Mary Katherine is a rarity. Most teenage girls think their dads are overbearing, strict, and a royal pain in the butt, among other things, but never funny."

"Well, I'll have to disagree with Anna about that. I think you're funny."

"Veeder, I know what you're going through is very hard. I'm not going to sugarcoat it and pretend that it is going to be easy, but in the twenty-third Psalm, it says that even on your darkest day, the worst day you could ever imagine, God is with you. And believe it or not, He will comfort you."

"Just when we were starting to find common ground, you bring in the Bible references."

"Come on, Veeder, humor me. I am on the payroll, it's what I do."

"Very funny, Pastor." Veeder chuckled because his words were used against him again.

"You're walking through the valley of darkness right now. Life isn't always going to be lollipops and rainbows, first downs and touchdowns."

"I never thought life would be easy, but this is unfair."

"You will have to walk every day in the valley of life and it will be tough. Darkness and tough times will come. It will be unfair. There will be times when you will have to punt the ball without knowing if you will ever get it back. Never knowing if you'll get another opportunity."

"JJ doesn't get another opportunity."

"But you do." Pastor Kelly's voice was filled with kindness. "Let me ask this, when you punt the ball away and you have to go stand on the sideline, do you worry?"

"No."

"Why not?"

"Because I have faith in my brothers. The defense will stop them and get the ball back."

"Faith in your guys, Veeder? Why?"

"Because I watch them work every single day. We believe in each other and we believe in a common goal."

"But is your common goal guaranteed?"

"No."

"Why not?"

"Because faith in your guys and executing against all adversity are two different things."

"Exactly, Veeder!" Pastor Kelly was filled with hope. "Right now, you're in the valley of darkness. Life is tough. Life is harder than it has ever been and not one of those guys on that field can change your heart right now."

"But they all have shown up for me."

"Sure they have. They can even pray for you but they can't heal you. I am telling you Veeder that if you have faith, you can start healing your heart right now. All you need is a tiny bit of faith and God will move mountains for you. Everything is possible with Him."

"More Bible talk, Pastor? Really?"

"Come on, Veeder, what do you have to lose? Have the same faith that you have on the football field, but this time, place your faith in God and the love of Jesus Christ. I promise He will deliver you from this valley. He will move this mountain."

"I don't know if I can, Pastor."

"Lean on God, son. Trust Him. Let Him care and comfort you." Pastor Kelly stood up and walked over to his desk. He opened the bottom drawer and pulled out a book. He walked back to his chair and sat down. "Read this Bible, the word of God, the heart of the Lord poured out for you. I promise you that your pain will be healed and you will rise out of the ashes."

"Can you promise me that He will tell me why JJ had to die?"

"I can't promise you that. That's up to God." Pastor Kelly paused. "Sometimes things happen, and we never know the reasons why."

"That doesn't sound very fair, Pastor."

"Let me try this from a different angle." Pastor Kelly sat back in his chair, rubbing his fingers under his chin. "What position do you play on the football team?"

"Quarterback."

"Pretty important position."

"Heart of the offense."

"Who calls the plays?"

"The Offensive Coordinator."

"What?" Pastor Kelly asked, staring at Veeder with a puckered face. "Is he on the field with you?"

"No."

"Where is he?"

"He's up in the booth overlooking the field, Pastor." Veeder started to get frustrated. "I don't get where you're going with this."

"Why don't you call the plays, Veeder? You're the quarterback."

"Because I can't see everything that is happening on the field. I look for open receivers but I can't see what everyone on the defense is doing. The Offensive Coordinator's job is to see the field, figure out the right plays so we can be successful, and to call them down to the huddle. My job is to see what is in front of me and to execute those plays."

"Hmm… Kind of like God then, huh?" Pastor Kelly leaned forward, grasping his hands together. "God's job is to see your whole life laid out before you. His job is to prepare you, protect you, and love you. Your job is to execute. Your job is to live in His grace and His wisdom. He knows your future, son, you don't. Sometimes, we won't have the luxury of knowing what He has prepared for us, what He sees. Right or wrong, we have to have faith that God has called the right play. Even when we disagree with Him."

"It's still not fair, Pastor."

"I agree with you. Life isn't fair. It's not a perfect world, but He is just."

"How can you say that?"

"Because God is love. He hurts when you hurt. He celebrates when you celebrate. Most importantly, He loves you every single day." Pastor Kelly offered the Bible to Veeder. "I know you don't believe that right now but if you read this book, I promise that some of this will start to make sense. I can guarantee that the hurt will go away if you just let God love you."

"You promise?" Veeder took the Bible and held it in his hands.

"I promise," Pastor Kelly said, pointing his finger toward the sky. "My boss is my witness. I am on the payroll."

Veeder laughed again. "No promises, Pastor, but I'll try."

"That's all I ask, and when you have questions, call me. We can sit down and work through them together."

"Thank you, Pastor Kelly."

Pastor Kelly stood up, walked around the coffee table, and hugged Veeder. "I'm sorry for the loss of your brother. My heart grieves with you and your whole family. God bless you."

CHAPTER 19

Veeder was sitting out on the front porch, his feet propped up on the railing, staring up at the stars. It was time to get back to school. *Suck it up buttercup. Time to pick yourself up by your bootstraps, toss the self-pity in the trash can, and get back to work. Get back to living.* It was time to get back to living. He felt better after the conversation with Pastor Kelly. He had even cracked the Bible a couple of times but nothing stuck. He hadn't found any comfort.

He had a hard time saying goodbye to Liz. She was supposed to be JJ's wife. His heart broke for her. He was thankful for their conversations. She had given him so many gifts by sharing her stories of JJ. Veeder smiled as he thought about them. He would miss Liz.

Bright headlights shimmered in the distance, making their way up the driveway. The car stopped in front of the house and Johnny Peterson hopped out. He grabbed a gym bag out of the backseat and sauntered across the front yard.

"Hey, Rook, what's up?" Johnny walked up the steps and across the porch.

"I took your job and you still call me 'Rook'?"

"You're a first-year player, Rook. You will always be a rookie until next season."

"That sucks."

"It does, but don't you love the irony?"

"You could at least show me a little respect."

"I do."

"How so?"

"By calling you 'Rook.' It would be disrespectful of me not to," Johnny said with a devilish grin. Veeder laughed. They exchanged a couple of fist bumps.

"What's up, Johnny?"

"Mind if I have a seat?"

"Pull up a chair."

Johnny sat down next to Veeder. "How have you been holding up?"

"I'm doing alright. Thank you for coming to the funeral."

"We're teammates."

"To the wake, maybe. The funeral was going above and beyond."

"Not at all. When one of us is down, we're all down."

"Thank you. It means a lot."

"Besides, my brother made the team as a freshman when JJ was a senior. We grew up knowing your brother. JJ was a good guy."

"He was a great guy."

"He was." They sat in silence at the declaration. Johnny was at a loss for words. He'd never known anyone who had died before. Not a young person at least.

Tired of the awkward silence that had enveloped the two of them, Veeder turned and asked, "So what brings you out to my neck of the woods?"

"I wanted to see how you are holding up."

"And?"

"It's good to see you are still impatient," Johnny laughed. "Are you going to play Friday night, Rook?"

"I don't know if I'll be back this season."

"Come on, Rook," Johnny pleaded. "We want you to play our last game with us."

"Even if it means you won't play?"

"Rook," Johnny said, swallowing his pride. "I loved playing last Friday night, but we lost."

"It was a tough loss."

"But a loss, nonetheless."

"That is true. You did lose."

"I can't complain, though. I got a scholarship offer on Monday."

"No, sir!"

"I'm serious."

"Where?"

"Mississippi Valley State University," Johnny announced with pride.

"The Alma Mater of the one and only Jerry Rice!"

Johnny puffed out his chest. "The Alma Mater of the *great* Jerry Rice!"

"That is awesome. How?"

"The head coach came to scout our receivers. He was impressed with my performance."

"And they offered you a scholarship?"

"I know, right? I'm as surprised as you are."

"You shouldn't be."

"I thought that ship had sailed after you took my job. I had some colleges sniffing around last year, but that dried up when you became the starter."

"You're a good player. It's everyone else's loss and Mississippi Valley State University's gain."

"Thanks." Johnny smiled. "I got lucky. He came to the right game."

"Luck had nothing to do with it. You deserve it, Johnny. Congratulations."

"So you see, I don't need to play this weekend."

"No?"

"I don't want to hurt my arm before I go to Mississippi Valley State University."

"I can understand that." Veeder rolled his eyes in feigned sarcasm.

"So what do you say, Rook? Join us Friday night?"

"I'm done for the rest of this season."

"Look, Rook, I know we have had our differences and I've given you a lot of grief, but you're the best quarterback I have ever seen…"

"Can I get that in writing?" Veeder joked. They both laughed.

"I'd love it if you would play on Friday."

"Bring home a win, Johnny. You've earned the start, make us proud."

"Come on, Rook, you know I am right."

"About being better than you?" Veeder winked at Johnny. "Yes, I am."

"If JJ were standing here, he'd tell you to play on Friday night."

"How do you know what my brother would say?"

"Because you're just like him."

"You don't know what you're talking about."

"You're a gamer, Rook. You always want the ball and you never quit."

"JJ was like that, not me."

"My brother was on the field during that championship game. All they had to do was run out the clock. Ground and pound. Chew up the clock. But JJ saw that hole and he wanted to seal the game with another touchdown."

"How did that work out for him?"

"JJ once told my brother that there is always going to be pain in glory."

"Why are you telling me this, Johnny?" Veeder was getting frustrated. "Why the trip down memory lane?"

"I met JJ after he broke his leg. He came to visit some of the coaches at practice. I asked him about his leg and you know what he told me?"

"Get away from me, kid?" Veeder chuckled.

"Funny, but no." Johnny paused. "JJ told me that football should be played on the edge. Always give one hundred percent. He had no regrets, Rook. He said that if he could do it all over again, he would run through that hole every single time."

"JJ and I are different people."

"You're such a liar, Rook." Johnny threw up his arms in disgust, sitting back in his chair. "Why are you fooling yourself?"

"I'm not."

"Sixty-three to ten. Remember that?"

Veeder stared at Johnny with a skeptical eye. "What?"

"I was standing there when Coach asked why you didn't step out of bounds. He was ticked off that you would risk an injury in a meaningless game and what did you tell him, Rook? What was your reason for allowing yourself to get creamed?"

151

"Sixty-three to ten," Veeder mumbled under his breath.

"You wanted the touchdown. You weren't going to quit." Johnny turned to face Veeder. "I would have stepped out of bounds and jogged back to the huddle. But not you, Rook, you went for the touchdown."

"I also got knocked out of that game if you don't recall."

"No, you didn't. You got yanked by Coach."

"Still got punched out."

"And you earned a hell of a lot of respect from every player on both teams."

"Means nothing."

"Really? Because I saw JJ when we left the field. He was fired up. He respected you."

"Be that as it may, he'll never see me play again."

"Then honor him." Johnny reached into the bag, pulling out a jersey with the number seventeen. "I've been holding on to this for way too long."

"What's that?"

"JJ wore number seventeen."

"Unitas wore nineteen."

"I know you love Johnny Unitas, Rook, but you love your brother more. It's time you honored him." Johnny hung the jersey over the railing in front of Veeder.

"Johnny, I can't." Veeder's heart jumped into his throat.

"Come play with us Friday night, Rook." Johnny pointed at the jersey. "Honor JJ."

Veeder grabbed the jersey and held it in his hands. "I don't know if I can."

"Go make JJ proud of you. If not for you, for him. For his memory."

"You're asking a lot, Johnny." Veeder stared at the jersey.

"There's pain in glory, Veeder," Johnny said, putting his hand on Veeder's shoulder and patting his back. "There's pain in glory."

Johnny stood up, walked off the porch, and across the front yard. He climbed into his car, started it up, honked the horn, and sped off down the driveway.

CHAPTER 20

—◦◦◉)—

Veeder tried to get back into the swing of things at school but everyone pitied him. They treated him with kid gloves, the joking around and bravado were gone. It made him feel pathetic because his brother had died, which made the day harder than he imagined. He knew people wanted to be supportive, but this was too much.

Anna reminded him that this would pass in time. Life would get back to a new sense of normal and everyone would soon start treating him the way they always had. Veeder didn't like her explanation, but he accepted it.

Gameday was tough. Veeder sat on his bed, staring at the number seventeen jersey that was draped over the dresser. He was thankful to Johnny for allowing him to honor JJ. The only question was *did he want to?*

Veeder was torn and conflicted, trying to decide what to do. The season was on the line and it all came down to this final game against the Robison Raiders. A win wouldn't guarantee a trip to the playoffs, but a loss would end their season.

Veeder thought about what Johnny told him about JJ; there's pain in glory. He thought about what Pastor Kelly had told him; to overcome adversity, you have to move mountains. He realized that you shed a lot of blood, sweat, and tears to reach the apex of joy. But if glory sat on the other side of the mountain, then Johnny was right, there's pain in glory.

The Raiders stadium was packed with fans from both schools when Veéder took the field alongside his teammates, donning the number seventeen jersey in JJ's honor. Robison honored JJ with a special tribute before the game started. It was a fitting testimony to one of the state's premier players who had passed too soon.

The crowd erupted in a raucous cheer when Veeder walked with the captains to midfield for the coin toss. That cheer was

153

followed by the fans breaking into a boisterous chant of his first name, followed by a louder chant for JJ. He smiled from ear to ear, looking around the stadium; tears dotting his eyes. Football was his respite, his refuge from the storm, and the one place where the worries of the world disappeared. Veeder called heads and won the coin toss. The Gators elected to kick-off and the Raiders started the game on their twelve-yard line.

Robison boasted one of the best running games in the state and put their powerhouse style of football on display. They burned ten minutes and fifty-five seconds off the clock on the first drive of the game, taking a seven to nothing lead.

Coach McCarthy was worried. Veeder hadn't thrown a ball in over forty-five minutes. He was afraid that the long drive by the Raiders would disrupt the rhythm of his offense.

The Raiders buried the kick-off deep into the end zone and the Gators kick returner took a knee. On first down from the twenty-yard line, the Raiders blew up the line on a sell-out blitz, driving Veeder into the turf for a loss of eight yards.

"What are you guys doing out here?" Veeder yelled, busting into the middle of the huddle, and taking a knee. "Is someone going to block for me tonight?"

The team was silent as he glared at them. Veeder decided to disregard the play that had been sent in from the sideline. *They might be able to see the whole field, but they didn't see what I saw as they broke through our line*, he thought to himself.

"Okay." Veeder calmed himself. "So we saw what they've got. Let's return the favor. Spread formation, all fly routes, and gentleman, I mean fly because I am going to launch one. You're gonna need to go get this one. Line, I need four seconds. Can you give me that?"

"Yes!" the linemen yelled in unison.

"On two!" Veeder barked. "Ready?"

"Break!" they all yelled, clapped their hands, and ran to the line in the shotgun formation. Coach McCarthy started screaming from the sidelines because it wasn't the play he had called. Veeder barked out the cadence with a couple of hard counts in hopes that he might catch the defense offsides. He took the snap and the defense sold out with another blitz. Veeder dropped back five steps, set his feet, and launched the ball down the field towards Zac Tyler who had beaten his defender off the line.

Veeder was already sprinting down the field with his arms raised before Zac hauled in the pass that had traveled sixty-two yards in the air. Zac took off for the end zone. Veeder ran by the Mustang's bench. "Hey Coach, thanks for the break. My arm was nice and rested!"

It took the Gators fifty-seven seconds to score, striking fear in the hearts of the Raiders. Robison might be able to chew up the clock with their running game, but the Gators could strike in the blink of an eye.

For the rest of the half, both teams played to their strengths. The Raiders ran the ball and chewed up time on the clock while Veeder led the Gators in an aerial assault that shredded the Raiders defense. When both teams headed to their locker rooms for halftime, the score was seventeen to fourteen in favor of the Raiders.

The second half turned into a back-and-forth affair between two very good football teams. Veeder continued picking apart the zone defense with his no-huddle offense while the Raiders brought their power running game back on the field. They chewed up yardage and the clock as they wore down the Gators defense.

Late in the fourth quarter, the Raiders led the game by a score of thirty-three to twenty-eight with a little over three minutes left in the game. The Gators special teams turned the kick-off into a big return that placed the ball on the Gators forty-seven-yard line. Veeder came out in the no-huddle offense and moved Goldston Regional down to the Raiders twenty-two-yard line. After a couple of hard-fought run plays, the Gators were facing first and goal on the nine-yard line. With a little over fifty seconds left on the clock, Veeder called a time out and walked to the sidelines.

"What do you say, Coach? Throw it?"

"We have them on their heels. Give it to Griggs."

"You sure?"

"Run it."

Veeder broke the huddle, called the cadence, and handed the ball off to Griggs who picked up two yards before being stood up by the Raiders defense. Veeder called the team to the line, took the snap from the center, and faked a throw outside before handing off the ball. Griggs fought for a tough two yards before being brought down. Veeder called a time-out and trotted over to the sidelines. "Third and goal, Coach."

"Stick with the run game."

"I can make the throws, Coach. They've got our run game shut down."

"Run the ball, Veeder!"

Veeder shook his head in disagreement but ran on the field and called the play in the huddle. The Gators broke for the line and as he handed the ball off, the defense stood up Griggs at the five-yard line and took him to the ground with six seconds left in the game. Veeder called their final time-out and trotted to the sideline. Before Coach McCarthy could say anything, Veeder said, "I have an idea, Coach."

"Shoot."

"Let's play a little backyard football."

"Think it will work?"

"You got a better idea?"

"Go for it, kid." Coach McCarthy closed his eyes and said a prayer of desperation while Veeder trotted back out to the huddle.

The team broke the huddle with four receivers to the left and one to the right. Veeder stood by himself in an empty backfield. It was a formation they had never run before and the Raiders defense was confused. They started to shift, calling out their coverages. They were out of time-outs, so they had to adjust to the new formation. Veeder stood four yards behind the center and barked out the cadence.

The ball was snapped into Veeder's hands. He dropped back and looked left. The receivers were covered. He faded to the right hoping someone would break free. With all of his receivers covered, he tucked the ball under his arm and took off for the end zone.

Veeder had one defender to beat. At the three-yard line, the Raiders linebacker dove at his legs, and Veeder hurdled him. He thought he had cleared the defender when his foot got hit and his body flipped, end over end. It felt like an eternity before his feet came back down on the ground. He landed on his feet, tumbling forward, but he caught himself with his free hand on the turf and sprinted for the end zone. He collided with the safety at the half-yard marker. When he finally landed on the ground, he had crossed the goal line for the touchdown.

The Gators crowd erupted in a loud cheer and rushed the field. The scoreboard flashed 34-33 with zero seconds on the clock. Veeder took a knee in the end zone and tucked his head. "That was for you JJ."

It was pandemonium as fans and players celebrated on the field.

After the celebrations ended and the locker room cleared out, Veeder was dropped off at the entrance to the cemetery by one of his teammates. He wanted to have a few moments alone with JJ. Walking to his brother's grave, his emotions got the best of him and tears started streaming down his face.

"Hey, JJ," Veeder said through the tears, kneeling in front of his brother's tombstone.

"I brought you something." Veeder laid the game ball on the ground in front of the headstone. "I wanted you to have this."

The tears fell harder, Veeder was openly crying. "I miss you. I miss you on the sidelines. I miss being able to call and tell you about my games. I'm sure you're watching from wherever you are, and I hope I make you proud because that's all I ever wanted to do. I just wanted you to be proud of me."

Veeder sat down, leaning his back against the headstone. "I never got to thank you, JJ. Thank you for believing in me. I'm where I am because of you and it hurts so much that you're not here to share it with me. I love JJ. I miss you."

Veeder sat in the cemetery talking to JJ, crying as he poured out all of his feelings to his brother's monument. Wishing he had said these things when JJ was alive, he would feel guilty for the rest of his life because he hadn't.

Veeder had fallen asleep leaning against JJ's grave and was startled when he felt someone nudge his shoulders. "Hey, Veeder."

"Dad?" Veeder looked up, wiping remnants of his tears from his eyes. "What are you doing here?"

"Preston called the house after he dropped you off."

"Why didn't you come right away?"

"I figured you needed some time to say goodbye to your brother," Paul responded, sitting on the ground next to Veeder.

"I miss him so much, Dad." Veeder's heart jumped into his throat.

"We all do, son."

"It all hit me at the end of the game tonight, Dad. I wanted to run home and call him, but I'll never be able to call him about a game ever again." Veeder fought back the tears. "I wish JJ could have seen the game."

"He was there," Paul said, putting his arm around Veeder's neck and staring off into the night, trying to choke down his tears.

"You think so?"

"He had the best seat in the house." Paul patted Veeder's chest with his free hand. "Your heart."

"Thanks, Dad." Veeder looked into his father's smile, which gave him comfort.

"I'm proud of you, Veeder. I know it wasn't easy going out there tonight."

"JJ would have wanted me to play."

"You're right." Paul nodded in agreement. "He would have, but it still doesn't make it easy. I don't know if I could have gone out and played like you did if my brother had died. I love you, son."

"I love you too, Dad." Veeder hugged his father.

Paul and Veeder sat in the cemetery for a long time, sharing their favorite memories of JJ. They talked about the future and why it was important to take every opportunity to tell your loved ones how much you love them, every chance you get. They laughed together, they cried together, and they said goodbye to JJ together.

1999

CHAPTER 21

Veeder waited while the NSBEN (National Sports Broadcasting and Entertainment Network) crew set up their cameras in the center of the Chapel Hill University locker room. This was the third consecutive year he had been nominated for the Heisman Trophy. He was used to the routine. NSBEN would conduct an interview and splice it together to air at a later date.

Veeder felt he had been snubbed with his previous nominations. He had a rocky relationship with the press, and when it came time for members of the media to vote, he felt like they punished him for his prior transgressions. He accepted their treatment. It was his fault and he knew it was his responsibility to repair the damage. He had to prove he had matured both on and off the football field.

Veeder had proved that on the field. His storied career at Chapel Hill University spoke volumes. He had led the team to four consecutive winning seasons, three consecutive bowl game victories, and a perennial appearance at the top of the national rankings.

Veeder continued to wear number seventeen throughout high school and at Chapel Hill University. His jersey set sales records since becoming the starting quarterback. He was reminded of his brother every time he slipped it over his head.

"We're ready for you, Mr. McLean." The young female assistant walked over to where Veeder was sitting.

"Veeder."

"What?"

"Please call me, Veeder." He stood up. "My dad is Mr. McLean."

"Okay." She blushed. "I'm sorry, Veeder. We're ready for you."

The young assistant led Veeder across the locker room. He sat next to Jack Johnson, who was the reporter conducting the interview. The assistant grabbed a small microphone and started placing it on his tie.

"Veeder!" Jack Johnson held out his hand. "Great to see you again. Awesome win last weekend."

"Thank you." Veeder reached around the assistant to shake Jack's hand.

"All set," she said, stepping away to stand behind the cameras.

"Thank you."

"Are you ready, Veeder?" Jack asked as they sat in their chairs.

"As ready as I'll ever be."

"Then, let's get started." Jack and Veeder sat up straight and stared into the camera. The cameraman counted down with his fingers and pointed at Jack when the red light on top of it turned on, signaling they were recording.

"Good evening, sports fans, Jack Johnson sitting here with Veeder McLean, the quarterback of the Chapel Hill Cobras and a 1999 Heisman Trophy candidate. We are coming to you from the locker room of the Cobras who are on the verge of earning a trip to the National Championship. Veeder, it is great to have you with us."

"Thank you, Mr. Johnson, it is great to be here representing my team, my coaches, and the awesome Chapel Hill faithful."

"Congratulations on the season you are putting together."

"Thank you." Veeder smiled. "It has been a great season, but we aren't done yet."

"Carolina is fighting to earn a trip to the national championship. Are you nervous?"

"The whole team is focused on the game against the University of Durham this week. So it is business as usual. We work hard and prepare to win every week."

"And as your fans know, a win against Durham this week would guarantee a national championship bid. Who do you hope to play in the championship?"

"We'll be honored to play any team in the national championship."

"But do you have a team you would prefer to play against in the big game? A team that might be easier to beat?"

"There are no easy wins in football, Jack, especially in the national championship. So we have no preferences for an opponent."

"Interesting." Jack Johnson realized Veeder was not going to take the bait and give him a sound bite he could use to create some controversy. So he pivoted to the Heisman trophy. "So you have been nominated for the Heisman Trophy?"

"Yes, sir. It is an honor to be nominated with so many great players."

"This is not your first time being nominated, is it?"

"No, Jack, this is my third nomination."

"And you haven't won it yet?"

"No, sir." Veeder felt his blood start to boil. "I have not. I have been lucky enough to have been nominated with some extraordinary players who deservedly earned the trophy."

"Are you going to win it this year?"

"I don't make predictions," Veeder said, controlling his emotions. "I am honored just to be nominated with such an elite group of athletes."

"But looking at your statistics, you would think you would be the odds-on favorite to win the Heisman. You have been a four-year starter at CHU. You have more touchdowns, the highest completion rating, more completions, and more passing yards than any other quarterback in college football."

"If you say so, Jack." Veeder chuckled.

"You don't agree?"

"Statistics are reserved for coaches, fans, and the press. The only things that matter to me are wins and losses."

"You have a forty-two and four record as a starter. Undefeated this year. Doesn't that, along with your other stats, qualify you as the best player in the nation?"

"Our team has won a lot of games." Veeder wrung his hands together. "But it's not just me, Jack. It takes an entire team to achieve the level of success we have had. Those wins aren't mine, those wins belong to our entire team. I am proud of our guys, our coaches, and all we have accomplished together."

"You just might have a career in politics when your playing career is over, Veeder," Jack quipped, becoming frustrated with Veeder's answers.

"I might consider that." Veeder winked at him, a sarcastic smile crossing his face.

"Your political answers aside, do *you* believe you will win the Heisman Trophy?"

"I don't predict what the voters will do."

"But after everything you have accomplished," Jack said, sitting back and laughing. "Come on, Veeder, a part of you has to believe you will win the Heisman this time."

"That's not my decision. It comes down to the voters and unfortunately, there has been a lot of animosity between the press and me over the years."

Realizing he touched a nerve, Jack pressed the issue. "Do you feel like there is a lot of animosity between you and the media?"

"I do." Veeder struck a conciliatory tone. "And I am solely to blame for that discord."

"You blame yourself?"

"Yes, Jack, I do." Veeder humbled himself. "I made a lot of mistakes as a freshman. I came from a small town, and we didn't have the kind of media coverage a large University has. I wasn't ready for the media attention, and I own the problems I created in my relationship with the press."

"It's good to hear you say that."

"I have grown up over the past four years, Jack. I haven't only matured into a good football player; I have matured into a good representative for my team and the University."

"You sound like that animosity with the media still exists."

"In some cases, maybe." Veeder shrugged his shoulders. "I made mistakes and readily admit that, but I am not the young, eighteen-year-old kid who made those mistakes years ago."

"That is a very mature attitude, Veeder."

"Thank you."

"But since you brought up your freshman year, let's talk about that for a moment."

"Do we have to relive it, Jack?" Veeder laughed, trying to brush the topic aside.

"You went through some struggles or shall we say, some growing pains, and the press took you to task over it. Does it make you angry?"

"At myself? Yes." Veeder rubbed his hands together. "I should have handled myself more professionally."

"But not the media?"

"How can I be mad at the members of the media for doing their job? I made the mistake. I wish I could go back and do things differently, unfortunately, I can't."

"So it doesn't still bother you?"

"I have moved on."

Veeder smiled to himself as Jack brought up the game that caused his career-long war with the national media. He remembered the brash, entitled eighteen-year-old farm boy who came to college thinking the world owed him something.

He worked hard when he got to Chapel Hill University. He wore his heart on his sleeve. He wasn't willing to back down to anyone, which created some problems with the veteran players. No one doubted his talent. He was a great player but his temperament started to wear thin on coaches and players. They needed him to take it down a notch and get with the program, but he was not willing to kowtow to anyone. *Put up or shut up* was his mantra and he lived it as a freshman.

By opening weekend, he had frustrated the coaching staff and they buried him on the roster. He was the third-string quarterback, the guy who carried the clipboard.

In the first game of the season against Tigerville University, starting quarterback, Lane Brockman was knocked out of the game. Daniel Spiers took over at quarterback. He was sacked five times and threw three interceptions that were all returned for touchdowns. When the Cobras left the field at halftime, they were down by a score of thirty-four to seven.

The coaches were furious. They yelled at the team, especially the offensive line. They tried to motivate a team that hung their heads in defeat. It was apparent that even the players dreaded the prospect of taking the field for the second half. So Coach Mercer called Veeder into the training room along with Offensive Coordinator, Dillon Bentley.

"Veeder," Coach Mercer said with a scowl on his face. "I am putting you in to start the second half."

"I'm ready, Coach." Veeder was excited to get the nod to start the second half.

"We're going to run the ball and chew up clock, do you understand?"

"Yes, sir."

"Don't mess this up, Veeder," Coach Bentley yelled.

"I won't," Veeder said, glaring at his offensive coordinator.

"Get us out of this game without any more embarrassing blunders."

"Yes, sir!"

The Cobras left the locker room and lined up in the tunnel when Veeder heard Coach Bentley say, "With Veeder under center, God help us" to Coach Mercer. The comment angered him. He couldn't understand why they had no confidence in him after only a few weeks, but he didn't care. He was about to lead the team on the field. He was excited to be playing in his first college game.

Veeder had to wait on the sideline because Tigerville started the second half with the ball, but he didn't have to wait long. Tigerville University fumbled the snap, and the ball was recovered by the Cobras. Veeder ran onto the field with the offense, stepped into the huddle, and called the play.

The Cobras came to the line of scrimmage and Veeder counted nine men in the box. Realizing that Tigerville was coming on a blitz, Veeder audibled at the line of scrimmage. Before Coach Mercer could call a timeout, the ball was snapped. Tigerville blitzed, Veeder dropped back, set his feet, and fired a missile forty-five yards down the field for a touchdown. The Cobra faithful erupted and War Memorial Stadium came to life.

"What the heck are you thinking out there?" Coach Mercer barked at Veeder when he got back to the sideline.

"Scoring!" Veeder exclaimed, walking past the coaches. He went to the bench and Coach Mercer spent the next few minutes yelling at him for not listening.

Coach Mercer didn't get to yell at Veeder for long. The energized Cobra defense went out, stepped up their attack, and got the ball back.

Veeder spent the rest of the day carving up the Tigerville defense and putting points on the scoreboard. With twelve seconds left in the game, Coach Mercer called his final timeout. The Cobras were down by six points. It was fourth down on the Tigerville University four-yard line.

After the timeout, Veeder walked to the line of scrimmage in the shotgun formation. He barked out the cadence, took the snap, dropped back, and surveyed the field. His receivers were covered. Out of the corner of his eye, he saw the left defensive end break through the line. He dove at Veeder for the sack, but Veeder spun away from the tackle and bootlegged to his right.

Veeder continued to look downfield. The middle linebacker barreled down on him. Veeder lowered his shoulder and drove it into the sacking linebacker. The brunt of the collision knocked the linebacker backward.

The linebacker tried to pull Veeder to the ground with him but he ended up knocking Veeder sideways, hurtling towards the ground. Stumbling, he placed his left arm on the ground and was parallel to the turf, when he fired an ill-advised pass from under his body into the corner of the end zone. Two more defenders drove him into the grass and he laid there for a second until he heard War Memorial Stadium erupt.

Veeder jumped to his feet with a large piece of sod hanging off of his face mask and rushed to the end zone to celebrate with his team. He had gone from third-string quarterback to the most unlikely hero in Cobra history. His mind-boggling under the body pass was an instant highlight reel. He was thrust into the national spotlight, and he was not ready for the media attention waiting for him after the game. Raw emotion, adrenaline, and frustration coursed through Veeder's body in a moment that would later be dubbed by his family members as the quote heard around the nation.

"The coaches didn't even want me on the field!" Veeder yelled into the camera, sitting at his locker answering questions. "They buried me on the depth chart! They told me to 'run out the clock, don't to embarrass myself!' Well, you saw it with your own eyes! No embarrassment here, just pure talent! I showed the world and there's more magic just waiting to be unleashed, you just wait and see! I will take this team places they could only have dreamed of before I got here!"

"Are you claiming to be CHU's savior?" One of the reporters shot back while the cameras zoomed in on Veeder.

"Why do you have to do that?" Veeder asked, staring down the reporter.

"Do what?" The reporter asked.

"Put words in my mouth?"

"I didn't put words in your mouth."

"Yes, you did!" Veeder barked, standing up and pointing at all of them while his teammates tried to intervene. "You media whores are going to twist my words to sell a story! You're all the same! You'll ruin a career to make a dime! I don't need you! Get out of my face!"

It was an unfortunate incident. Veeder was a small-town farm boy who had not been schooled in the finer art of handling the press and the media had a field day with the quote.

The coaches were furious. His teammates were angry. His family was disappointed. It was supposed to be an amazing moment of a promising college career, but instead, Veeder created a public relations nightmare he had not been able to recover from for four seasons.

"I guess you could say that throw catapulted you to the starting role at CHU," Jack Johnson quipped as they finished reliving the story of the infamous game.

"Not really," Veeder said. "Spiers started the next game but had another tough day, so they put me in in the second half. I got the lead back late in the fourth quarter, but we lost the game after I threw an errant pass for an interception."

"I remember that game. It was a tough loss."

"Lane came back too soon for our third game and suffered another concussion in the second half. That's when the coaches reluctantly gave me the nod as the starting quarterback."

"And the rest, as they say, is history."

"You could say that." Veeder smiled. "I've had some great days as a Cobra, but my best days are still ahead with the National Championship. But that underhanded pass really defined my toughness on the football field and propelled me into the national spotlight."

"And with it came the infamous quote?"

"It wasn't my best moment," Veeder chuckled, shaking his head back and forth. "I think the quote has been played more times than the throw that caused the celebration."

"You might be right about that."

"But it was the wrong thing to say. I was an immature kid who was thrust into the spotlight and I made a mistake." Veeder was humble and conciliatory. "I apologized to my coaches, my teammates, and my family. They have forgiven me and we have all moved on."

"Do you think it will ever be forgotten?"

"As my grandmother always says, 'you can do everything right, but people will always remember the one thing you did wrong.' I'm living proof of that. I made the mistake. I own that mistake and I am moving on to brighter days."

"Great attitude, Veeder," Jack said. "Is your grandmother an important part of your life?"

"My whole family is an important part of my life. My grandmother was the one who finally convinced my parents to let me play football and she has never missed a game."

"If you make the national championship, will she be there?"

"She'll be there." Veeder smiled. "My parents and my siblings will all be there."

"Sounds like a great family."

"They are. They have always supported me. They are my rock and without them, I don't know if I would be sitting here today." Veeder smiled, looking into the camera. "I love you all."

"Speaking of your family, I hear there is a story behind your jersey number."

"There is." Veeder paused, taking a moment to collect his thoughts. "I always wore nineteen in honor of Johnny Unitas. During my freshman year of high school, a drunk driver killed my brother JJ. My friend and Mississippi Valley State starting quarterback, Johnny Peterson, who wore the number at the time, gave it to me. He told me I should wear it in honor of JJ. I did. And I have ever since. JJ was the definition of heart and perseverance. I take comfort in his strength when faced with adversity."

"That is a touching story, Veeder," Jack said, humbling himself for a moment. "Thank you for sharing. I am sorry about your brother."

"Thank you."

"You brought up Johnny Unitas but there are a lot of kids out there who think you are the greatest quarterback to ever play the game. They look up to you as a role model. Do you have any role models in your life?"

"My twin sister MK."

"Your twin sister?" Jack raised his eyebrows and tilted his head, astonished. "Really? That is a shocker. I never would have guessed that in a million years. Why is MK your role model?"

"Mary Katherine is a pre-med student. She has worked harder than anyone I know. She could be anything she wants to be in this world, but all she has ever wanted to do is help people. She is becoming a doctor to make the lives of other people better. To help them on their worst days and give them a chance to have better days. And there are millions of people like her. Doctors, policemen, firemen, EMTs, soldiers. These are the true role models in life. They are selfless. They honor life. They love and care for people. If you want a true role model, emulate these people who work anonymously in our communities every day to make the world a better place."

Veeder paused for a moment and then continued, "I'm just a football player, Jack. I entertain people. I am humbled that people think I am a role model and I take that responsibility seriously, but I want to let all of the real heroes in our community know I appreciate everything you do for all of us. Thank you for your service and your sacrifice. And to my sister, MK, thank you. You inspire me to be a better person every day."

"Great sentiments, Veeder," Jack said, staring into the camera. "I join you in thanking people like your sister MK who are selflessly giving of themselves in our communities."

"Thank you."

"Your name has been thrown around as the number one pick in the NFL draft, any thoughts about that?"

"I would love to play at the next level, Jack. Whether drafted first or last, it doesn't matter. I would like to help out a team that's committed to winning a championship."

"Thank you, Veeder, for your time today. We wish you the best of luck in the future."

"Thank you, Jack."

The light on the camera went dark. Jack thanked Veeder for the interview, took off his microphone, and walked away. The assistant walked over to Veeder and fumbled with the microphone on his tie. Once she took it off, Veeder thanked her and walked out of the locker room where Anna was waiting for him.

"How did it go?" She asked, throwing her arms around him and kissing him.

"I'll tell you at dinner," Veeder said, slipping his arm around her waist and walking off together.

CHAPTER 22

—❧—

Veeder and Anna were sitting in the café enjoying the evening. They were laughing about some of the craziest things they had done while they waited for Mary Katherine to arrive.

"Good evening." The waitress put menus on the table. "My name is Gina and I'll be your server. Will it just be the two of you tonight?"

"We're waiting on one more," Anna responded.

"Can I get you some drinks while you're waiting?"

"Sweet Tea," Anna responded.

"What do you have on tap?" Veeder asked.

"I need to see some ID."

"Not a problem." Veeder handed his license to the waitress. She looked at his license and got excited, handing it back to him.

"You're Veeder McLean. The CHU quarterback."

"Yes." Veeder blushed. "I am."

"I thought it was you. Can I have your autograph?"

"Sure," Veeder said, checking his pockets and looking around the table. "Do you have a pen and a piece of paper?"

"Waitress!" She held up her hands with a pad of paper in one hand and a pen in the other.

"Oh. Right."

The waitress handed Veeder a piece of paper and a pen. He wrote her a nice note to go along with his autograph. He handed the autograph to her while she ran down the list of beers they had on tap.

"Can I have a Guinness please?"

"One Guinness and one sweet tea coming right up." The waitress raced off to tell her coworkers who was sitting in her section. They were all pointing and gossiping while Anna and Veeder returned to their conversation. Anna blushed with a twinkle in her eye. She turned her head and stared out the window but as she did, her smile grew larger and brightened up her face.

"What are you thinking about?"

"Something," Anna responded, looking at Veeder and blushing.

"What is it, Anna? Out with it."

"Do you remember the night we drove down to Raleigh?"

"Summer of ninety-eight."

"We wanted to buy scalped tickets to the Jimmy Buffett concert at Carter-Finley Stadium for the Fourth of July?"

"I remember it well," Veeder said with a sparkle in his eye. It was a memory he would never forget.

Veeder decided he wanted to do something epic for the Fourth of July, so he drove Anna to Raleigh to buy scalped tickets for the concert. The tickets were scarce and Parrot Heads were not parting with their prized Independence Day seats. And the true scalpers were charging exorbitant prices. They were more than Veeder could afford, so he and Anna gave up their quest for tickets and decided to find a good place to watch the fireworks.

Anna and Veeder were trying to sing along with the radio in Veeder's truck. It was a series of chuckles intermixed with their poor attempts to sing the right lyrics. Anna turned sideways, resting her head against the headrest while she stared at the man she had been in love with since they met at Old Fashioned Days. She was lost in her thoughts when the sky lit up with a huge bolt of lightning and the heavens dropped a deluge of water.

Veeder felt the engine buck and a worried look replaced the smile that had been etched across his face.

"What is it?" Anna asked, worried about the change in his demeanor.

"Something's wrong with the truck."

"Can you fix it?"

"I don't know." He was concerned. "I'm looking for a safe place to park."

"It's pouring. Where are you going to find a place tonight?"

"Over there." Veeder pointed. He slowed down the truck, crossed the street, and pulled into the parking lot of Gypsy's Shiny Diner. He parked just as the truck sputtered out and quit.

"What do we do now?" Anna asked, concerned about the truck.

"We go in and eat."

"I mean about the truck."

"I'll borrow their phone and call Michael. He'll come help us."

Anna covered her head with a magazine she found on the floor of the truck. She hopped out and shrieked as she ran to the front door of the diner while Veeder followed her. They stepped inside the first set of doors, soaked. Laughing, they hugged each other and kissed.

Trying to shake off some of the water, they walked through the second set of doors and stood at the *Wait to Be Seated* sign. The diner was a throwback to the nineteen fifties. Anna and Veeder felt like they had stepped through a portal that took them back in time. The diner was even adorned with an actual, working jukebox playing music from the era.

The hostess took them to a booth with an open space in the middle of the floor near their table. The diner was almost empty. Most people had attended the Jimmy Buffet concert or one of the local fireworks shows so except for a few random patrons, they had the place to themselves.

"I'll be back in a minute," Veeder said while Anna sat at the booth.

"Where are you going?"

"I'm going to call Michael," Veeder responded before walking to the counter.

Anna sat at the table, perused the menu, and waited. She smiled and looked up when she heard "La Bamba" blaring from the speakers of the jukebox. It was one of her favorite songs. When she turned around, Veeder was standing in the middle of the diner holding a bouquet of red roses.

"What are you doing?" Anna asked, laughing at the sight.

"Giving you a romantic and memorable Fourth of July." Veeder walked to the booth and handed her the roses. "These are for you, my dear."

"We didn't break down, did we?" Anna blushed, closing her eyes and smelling the roses.

"Nope," Veeder said with a boyish grin.

"You planned all of this?"

"Everything except the rain."

"What about the Buffet concert?"

"We were never going."

"And the search for a fireworks display?"

"It was all a ruse to get you right here," Veeder said, pulling Anna to her feet and holding her in his arms.

"Why?"

"Because you love fifties music and diners."

"I do but this is…."

"Amazing! This place combines both of the things you love, and I love you," Veeder stepped back and bowed. "May I have this dance?"

Anna laughed at Veeder while dancing with him. "You're crazy. You know that, right?"

"Crazy in love with you."

They danced and laughed throughout the evening, ignoring the weird looks the other patrons gave them. They ordered some dinner and enjoyed each other's company while the rest of the world faded away. All that mattered was the music and the two of them. Veeder dumped a bucket full of coins into the jukebox and reveled in every dance they shared.

They had worked their way through just about every song in the jukebox as the evening flipped past midnight and crept into the wee hours of the morning. They were pressed together, swaying to another golden oldie, when the waitress came over and tapped Veeder on the shoulder. "I hate to interrupt you love birds, but we are getting ready to close up soon."

"That's not a problem," Anna whispered, wrapping her arms tighter around Veeder and sinking the side of her head deeper into his chest.

"Bring me the check. We won't hold you up. I promise," Veeder whispered. He followed Anna's lead and kept dancing. The song ended and they shared a long, deep kiss.

"Thank you." Anna smiled at him. "This has been one of the greatest nights of my life."

"Mine too."

"I wish it never had to end." Anna turned to walk back to the table.

"Anna, wait." Veeder took Anna's hand and she turned to face him. Veeder was caught up in his emotions. He took his high school ring off his finger and knelt in the middle of the diner. "I have loved you ever since I saw you walking down the street back in middle school. I knew then I would spend the rest of my life with you…"

"Veeder, what are you doing?" Anna interrupted.

"I want the rest of my life to start now." Veeder held out his high school ring. "Anna Kelly, will you make me the happiest man in the world by agreeing to spend the rest of your life with me? Will you marry me?"

Anna was shocked. She was not prepared for a proposal. She wasn't ready. Tears started rolling down her cheeks, she knelt on the floor. "I love you with all of my heart…"

"Is that a yes?" Veeder interjected.

"We're not ready for this, Veeder," Anna said with tears in her eyes. She saw Veeder deflate as her words enveloped him.

"I am, Anna," Veeder whispered.

"You're not." Anna held his hand, placing her other hand on the side of his face and looking into his eyes. "We're not."

"I love you with all of my heart. Nothing is going to change that."

"I know. I love you too, but we're not ready yet." Anna placed her forehead against his. Tears streamed down her face. "We're going to be juniors in the fall. I have a nursing program to get through. You have a football team to lead."

"But I love you."

"I will marry you one day, Veeder," Anna said, smiling through her tears.

"But not now?"

"I'm sorry, baby. I love you so much, but I don't want the emotions we feel after an amazing night to cloud our better judgment."

"Then when?"

"When we're ready to make that commitment, we'll know it in our hearts," Anna said, wrapping her arms around him.

Veeder smiled as he and Anna recounted the events of the night. He was embarrassed he had allowed himself to get caught up in his emotions.

"That was such a great night," Anna smiled as though it had just happened yesterday. "Remember how mad your parents were when we got home?"

"My parents?" Veeder exclaimed, raising his arms, befuddled.

"Yes!" Anna remarked. "Your mother gave me the cold shoulder for weeks."

"Yes, she did." Veeder chuckled. "She was mad we got home so late."

"It's not funny. That was hard for me."

"Well, what about your father? He was livid."

"He was, wasn't he?" Anna laughed.

"I was surprised he let you see me after that."

"He didn't want to, but my mom talked him into allowing you to see me again."

"She did?" Veeder paused. "I'll have to thank her the next time I see her."

"That was one of the greatest nights of my life." Anna held Veeder's hand.

"Mine too." Veeder smiled. "Although, if I remember correctly, the next weekend wasn't so great, though, was it?"

"Why did you have to bring that up?" Anna asked in frustration. "Way to kill the mood."

"Because your father used the old stumbling block to start another fight between us."

"It's not a stumbling block." Anna shot a look of disdain at Veeder. "God is important to me and my husband will have to believe in God."

"And what if I never do?"

"Sorry, I'm late," Mary Katherine said, racing into the café, pulling out a chair, and sitting down at the table. "I lost track of time. I hope I didn't keep you waiting long."

"No, MK," Anna said.

"Not at all," Veeder added.

"We were just reminiscing about an amazing night we had a while back," Anna responded.

"The Fourth of July story again?"

"Yes," Veeder and Anna replied in unison.

"Ugh!" Mary Katherine grimaced, hitting her forehead with the palm of her hand. "You two need some new stories."

"You're just jealous, MK," Veeder ribbed.

"Jealous?" Mary Katherine stared at him. "How so?"

"You wish you had what we have."

"Yeah," Mary Katherine said with sarcasm. "I don't think I do."

"Can I get you something to drink, Miss?" The waitress asked.

"A coke," Mary Katherine replied.

"And another Guinness."

"That's your fourth, Veeder," Anna said, concerned with the number of beers he was consuming.

"I'm not driving, my apartment is just around the corner."

"Not my point."

"I'm fine, Anna."

"MK, your parents said hello," Anna said, changing topics and shooting Veeder a disapproving glare.

"You saw my parents?"

"We go out to dinner after every game with grandma and grandpa," Veeder said. "Mom and dad made the last game, so they joined us."

"Sounds like fun."

"Not really." Veeder rolled his eyes. "It gives dad and grandpa a chance to tell me what I did wrong during the game."

"Dude, that sucks," Mary Katherine responded, laughing. "They are ruthless."

"I know, right?"

"Be that as it may, your mom wanted us to say hello," Anna added. "She said you haven't been home in about a month and she misses you."

"I'll call her," Mary Katherine said, perusing the menu. "I've been crazy busy with classes and my internship at the medical center."

The waitress came back with the drinks, took their orders, and the three of them had a wonderful dinner. Veeder and Anna were enthralled with Mary Katherine's stories from her pre-med program. They loved when she shared stories of her internship on the children's ward of the hospital. It was her respite from the long hours she spent on all of her schoolwork.

"Which reminds me, Veeder, I need a favor," Mary Katherine said.

"I knew that was coming, MK. What is it now?"

"When can you come back to the hospital to visit the kids?"

"I am really busy, MK."

"Come on, Veeder. The kids love it when you visit."

"I've got a game this week, and I have the Heisman dinner in New York."

"So you can come to visit the kids in between?"

"Or maybe after the season?"

"Come on, Veeder, the kids love you," Anna interjected, winking at Mary Katherine in solidarity.

"Okay, MK, I promise."

"Great! When?"

"I will have to get back to you. Either next week or after the Heisman dinner, okay?"

"I'm holding you to that," MK said.

"Unfortunately, I have to run," Veeder said, looking at his watch. "It's getting late and I have an early class tomorrow morning."

"I thought football players didn't go to class," Mary Katherine joked.

"Very funny, MK." Veeder pulled out cash and put it on the table. "This should be more than enough to cover dinner. Leave the rest for a tip."

Mary Katherine picked up the cash, counted it, and tried to hand some back. "Too much."

"It's fine, MK." Veeder leaned in and kissed Anna.

"I love you," Anna said.

"I'll see you tomorrow after practice."

"Ugh! PDA people." Mary Katherine interjected, pretending to put her finger down her throat. "Gross!"

"Sorry, MK, you're outnumbered." Veeder kissed Anna again. "Love you, sweetheart."

"Oh yeah, I forgot. Liam wants you to call him," Mary Katherine added.

"I'll see him after the game this weekend," Veeder said, heading towards the door.

"Call your brother!" Mary Katherine yelled after him.

"Do you see what I mean, MK?" Anna asked.

"What?"

"Did you see how many beers he had?"

"He had a couple," Mary Katherine said, staring at the cash on the table. "I lost count."

"Eight."

"He seems fine to me."

"He used to never drink."

"Have you talked to him about it?"

"He says it's not a big deal. All the guys on the football team drink beer."

"Well, that group is a bunch of drunkards, but Veeder seemed to be okay."

"I'm worried about him, MK."

"He'll be fine, Anna."

"You think so?"

"There are only two things he has wanted in life. Playing in the NFL and marrying you. I don't think he'll do anything to mess either of those up," Mary Katherine said, grabbing the money Veeder left on the table and fanning it in front of her face.

"I guess you're right." Anna was filled with doubt.

"I know I am," Mary Katherine said, raising her eyebrows a couple of times. "And if I am correct, my brother left us enough for dessert. Want to split a piece of Molten Lava Cake?"

"Yes!" Anna responded, excited. "I love their cake."

Anna and Mary Katherine ordered a piece of cake to share and spent another hour talking about everything that was happening in their lives.

CHAPTER 23

—⊙◦⊙—

The final game of the season against the University of Durham was over before the game even started. Veeder threw a long touchdown pass on the first play of the game. He had another career day, passing for over four hundred yards and five touchdowns, beating Durham by a score of 38-0. It was the exclamation point on his final season at Chapel Hill University.

When the game was over, Veeder stood shoulder to shoulder with his teammates, singing the Chapel Hill University Alma Mater with the fans for the last time. He was gripped with a sense of sadness because he knew he would never step onto this football field in a Cobras uniform ever again. So he sang with gusto, pride, and great joy. He was elated by their crushing victory over Durham, and he was excited for what the future held.

He fought back the tears. His heart was stuck in his throat. He treasured that field, the fans, and the football program. He was a born and raised Carolinian so wearing a Cobras uniform was the realization of a childhood dream and it was now over. And even though new dreams were waiting for him after graduation, he couldn't help but celebrate the fact that his four years as a Cobra had been filled with more memorable moments than he could have ever imagined. He was thrilled with the victory. He was excited for his future to get started. He was sad to see this chapter of his life end. Standing on the field, singing with the Chapel Hill faithful was bittersweet.

The last few words of the song left his lips and the crowd erupted in a raucous cheer. Veeder ran to the wall and climbed into the stands to celebrate the victory with the people who had always been there to support the team. This was their victory as much as it was his and he decided to share the celebration with them. The Cobra fans and students were elated Veeder had climbed over the wall. They hugged him. They congratulated him and Veeder partied with them.

Veeder signed hats that were handed to him and he took victory pictures with the fans still in the stands. Some of the other players joined him. They too climbed over the wall and embraced the Cobra faithful. The revelry in the stands went on for almost half an hour before coaches and security started to break up the crowd. Veeder didn't want the moment to end, but with coaches and team officials yelling at all of the players to get into the locker room, he and the rest of the players made their way back to the field. He disappeared up the tunnel with a boisterous chant of "Veeder!" echoing throughout the stadium.

Inside the locker room, the celebration continued as players, coaches, the athletic director, and University officials learned that only one other undefeated team remained. It was now official, the National Championship game was a forgone conclusion. And as it turned out, it was. The Chapel Hill University football team would be representing their school against Boulder Mountain Tech.

CHAPTER 24

‑‑⊙‑‑

The celebrations started as soon as Chapel Hill University had earned a spot to play in the national championship. The campus was electrified, and the celebrations extended downtown where the joyous occasion had taken over Chapel Hill.

After a celebratory dinner with his family, Veeder and Anna attended multiple parties with the other players. Anna hated these parties but had come to understand that this was part of the culture of the football team. It was a rite of passage to celebrate with the fans.

They were attending their fifth house party when Anna started feeling frustrated. She watched Veeder drink beer, hobnob with star-struck co-eds, sign autographs, and tell tall tales of his greatest exploits. He posed for a litany of photographs. She thought the pomp and circumstance of winning a football game, the celebrity status afforded the players, and the craving for attention her boyfriend had for the praise showered upon him was comical. But the fawning over football players and celebrities of all stripes was nothing new. America had created a culture of celebrity worship. She just never thought she would be thrust into the middle of it the way she had been this year as Veeder broke records and carried his team to the national championship.

Loud music assaulted her the moment she entered the house. Walking around, Anna saw people at the party abusing alcohol and other substances. She witnessed people lose control of their inhibitions and engage in activities they would regret in the morning. It bothered her. She wanted to leave but at the same time, she wanted to be supportive of Veeder.

Praying for her fellow students, Anna felt a twinge in her heart. It was time to leave. The still voice she couldn't hear over the music pounding at her eardrums had found another way to communicate and Anna had received the message.

Grabbing Veeder's arm and pulling him out onto the back porch, Anna asked, "Can we go home?"

"What's up?" Veeder stared into her eyes. "Are you okay?"

"I'm fine." Anna shrugged. "I just want to go."

Veeder chuckled. "Aren't you having fun?"

"Veeder!" A student yelled, walking across the porch. "Awesome Game! Go Cobras!"

"Dude!" Veeder raised his fist in the air. "Go Cobras!"

"Can I get your autograph?" Stumbling across the porch, the fan handed Veeder a pen and piece of paper.

"Sure," Veeder responded, taking the pen and paper. "What's your name?"

"Steve."

Veeder wrote out the autograph and handed it to him. "Here you go, Steve."

"Good Luck in the National Championship." High fiving Veeder, Steve jumped up.

"Thanks." Veeder patted Steve on the shoulder while he stumbled away.

"No." Anna pointed at Steve. "I don't like being surrounded by drunk people."

"He's having fun, he's blowing off some steam."

"But I'm not." Anna crossed her arms and let out an exasperated sigh. "This isn't my scene, Veeder."

"Anna…"

"Look, this is your moment, you should enjoy it."

"This is our moment." Veeder wrapped Anna in his arms and kissed her forehead.

"No, Veeder, it's not."

"I want to celebrate this with you."

Anna melted into his chest. "I don't want to spoil this evening."

"You're not."

"I am."

"Stay a little longer and then we can go."

"You should stay and celebrate." Anna pulled away from him and crossed her arms. "Your teammates want you here, and the fans love you. You should enjoy this moment. You've earned it. I'm just tired."

"So we'll go."

"That's not what I want. You deserve to celebrate."

"The only person I ever want to celebrate with is you."

"Really?" Anna was skeptical, staring into his eyes. She knew how much he loved the victory celebrations.

"How about we go back to your apartment and watch a movie?" Veeder took her hand, pulling her into a hug.

"A movie sounds great right about now." Anna melted into him. "Thank you for understanding. I'm sorry."

"There is nothing to be sorry about. This is the fifth party. It's getting late."

"It is." Anna sighed.

"You can even pick the movie from your collection."

"Any movie?"

Veeder cringed. "Yes."

"Even a rom-com?" Anna spied him out of the corner of her eye to see his reaction.

Veeder shuddered and squeaked out a very elongated, "Yes."

"I love you."

"We can cuddle up on the couch, watch the movie, and relax."

"That sounds really nice. I love this idea."

Swaying in the moonlight on the porch, Veeder kissed Anna's forehead. "And maybe a little later we could, you know."

"We could what?" Anna asked, pulling back from his embrace and staring at him.

Veeder raised his shoulders and eyebrows. "You know?"

"No, Veeder, I don't." Anna was getting angry at what she thought he was proposing. "Enlighten me, Veeder. What could we do?"

Veeder beat around the bush some more. "It's a special night."

"What does that mean?"

Veeder was on the defensive. "I'm just saying it's a special night."

"Say it, Veeder!" Anna was tired of playing games. "What do you want? Just say it."

Veeder lowered his voice. "I thought, maybe, we could make love."

"What? No!" Anna exclaimed in anger, pulling away from him and throwing up her arms in disgust. "No, Veeder! That's not even an option! What are you thinking?"

"What's wrong, Anna?" Veeder asked, looking around to make sure no one was watching.

"You know what's wrong!" Anna held her hands up in front of him. "We've had this conversation many times. You know how I feel. Why did you have to go there?"

"Anna, we've been together forever. We're getting married one day. What is the big deal?"

"After all these years, you still don't get it. You don't get me!" Anna started walking away. "Way to ruin the evening, Veeder!"

Veeder grabbed her arm. "Anna, wait."

"No, Veeder." Pulling her arm from his grasp and holding her hands up in a stop motion. "Let go of me. I just can't right now."

"Can we talk about this?"

"No!" Anna backed off, throwing her arms up in frustration. "Have a good night, Veeder."

"Anna!"

"You stay here and party with your friends. Have a few more beers while you're at it!"

"Anna, wait!" Veeder followed her across the porch.

"No!" Anna stopped, turned, and pointed at him. "I'm tired of having this conversation."

"Anna, you're overreacting."

"No, Veeder. I am not. And you, of all people, should know that."

"Veeder come check out this beer pong game," one of the linemen said, running onto the porch to find his captain.

"Yeah, Veeder, you should watch the beer pong game with your buddies," Anna exclaimed, turning and walking away. "I'm out of here!"

"Anna, wait!"

"Sorry, dude," the lineman said, watching Anna disappear into the house.

Veeder rushed after her but a group of students looking for autographs and selfies surrounded him and impeded his progress. He fought his way through the crowd and out onto the street, but Anna was gone. He knew she would be on her way back to her apartment, so he turned and raced up the street.

Veeder turned the corner and saw Anna walking up the street. "Anna! Wait!"

"Go away, Veeder!" Anna yelled, wiping tears out of her eyes, and picking up her pace.

"Anna," Veeder said, catching up to her, "wait! Can't we talk about this?"

"There's nothing to talk about, I just need to be alone."

Talking wasn't going to solve Anna's dilemma. Anna was saving herself for marriage. Veeder knew this. To her, this was a betrayal of her trust. This was going to be another speed bump in their relationship.

"Anna, I'm sorry. I was insensitive," Veeder said, trying to open up a line of communication.

Anna stopped, turned, and pointed at him. "No. You weren't insensitive. You were rude."

Veeder took her hand in his, but she pulled it away and stared at him. "I don't know what I was thinking. Between the national championship, the Heisman, the draft, and you walking down the aisle one day as my bride, I got carried away."

"You made a fool of me, Veeder." Tears rolling down her cheeks. "You know how I feel about sex, and you just disrespect my moral beliefs because you won a football game."

"I know, Anna." Veeder took her hands in his again. "I was wrong. I'm sorry."

"That isn't enough this time, Veeder," Anna said, pulling her hands away and turning from him. She started walking away. "I just need time to think. Go back to your party."

Veeder followed her. "I'm not letting you walk home alone this late at night."

Anna didn't answer him. She was irritated. They walked to her apartment building in silence. Both hurting, they didn't want to say something they would regret. When they reached her apartment building, Anna turned and looked at him. "I'm home. Now, go back to your party, Veeder."

"Can't we talk about this?"

"It's been a long night. I don't want to talk." Her eyes bored into his in anger. "I just need some sleep. I'll call you in the morning."

"Are we good?"

"No. We're not… but we will be." Anna said, tilting her head and half-smiling at him. "You made a suggestion. It's not like you tried to force yourself upon me."

"I'm sorry." Veeder leaned in to kiss her.

Anna turned her face, and he kissed her cheek. "Good night, Veeder."

Veeder watched her run up the front steps of her apartment building and disappear behind the front door. "Good night, Anna."

CHAPTER 25

—◦◦◉◦—

Mary Katherine loved it when Veeder joined her on the children's ward. It warmed her heart to watch him share his love of life, his infectious laughter, and his stories of football with the kids. It meant so much to the kids to feel some semblance of normalcy and to know someone cared about them. She watched their illnesses fade into the background for a few hours while Veeder spent time with every one of the kids in the room.

Veeder was a big kid at heart. Mary Katherine knew that better than anyone and she also knew when he got around kids, he loved to make them smile. He spent the whole morning playing games, reading books, and he even got involved in a spirited game of Pretty, Pretty Princess. He laughed, played, told stories, took pictures, and signed memorabilia. He had a great morning making the lives of these children, who all had life-threatening diagnoses just a little better, even if it was only for a few hours.

Veeder joined in with the kids when they booed the nurses because they told him he needed to wrap up for the day. He stayed to take pictures and he hugged each child before they headed off to their treatment. It broke his heart to see so many kids suffering. He wished he could have done more to help all of them.

"I have no idea how you do this every day, MK," Veeder said, walking down the hall.

"It's what I was called by God to do."

"Tough calling."

"The good book tells us to carry the burdens of others to fulfill the law of Christ."

"I don't know if I could complete that mission."

"We all carry others burdens in different ways. God gave you a different path."

189

"You're a scientist, MK. I don't understand all of this God-talk from you."

"I'm a follower of Christ first and foremost, Veeder. Being a scientist doesn't cancel out that fact."

"But don't they tell you in science…"

"Ah, zip it!" Mary Katherine interrupted, connecting her forefinger and thumb as she pulled her hand across her lips. "I'm not having this debate with you."

"I just don't understand how you rectify the inconsistencies."

"Look, Veeder," Mary Katherine said with kindness. "I wish you believed. I pray one day you will, but you will never convince me not to believe, so don't try."

"I still don't understand how you do this, MK."

"As I said, it's my calling."

"Doesn't all the sickness depress you?"

"I look for the good in all of it."

"What good do you see in all of this madness?"

"You." Mary Katherine beamed with pride, smiling at her brother.

"Me?" Veeder looked at her sideways. "I didn't do anything."

"What you did in that room is the best medicine. Having someone love on you and laughing with you, you gave them so much just by caring."

"All I did was play with them."

"You gave them hope. And hope is more precious than any medicine we can give them. They don't get a lot of hope here. What you did in there will make the weeks ahead bearable just because you showed them someone cared."

"Oh." Veeder was dumbstruck, shaking his head while rubbing his chin. "I still don't see how you are able to come back and face this every day."

"Christ reached out to the sick, the downtrodden, the broken, and the dying. Is it sad to see them ill? Yes. But when you look past the illness, and you see the love and the light in the eyes of each patient, my God, it changes your life."

"I've always said you were pretty special."

"So are you."

"No, MK. I'm just your run-of-the-mill football player."

"We'll see about that." Mary Katherine stopped in front of a door, grabbed Veeder by the hand, and looked him in the eye. "I need you to do me one more favor before you go."

"What's up?" Veeder sized up Mary Katherine's demeanor.

Mary Katherine pointed at the door. "Behind this door is your biggest fan. He knows every statistic. He can talk about every game you have played in and he does it all from memory."

"Why didn't he come down and hang out with us this morning?"

"He couldn't."

"Why not?"

"Hold on a second." Mary Katherine stepped into the room while Veeder waited in the hallway. He was perplexed by her odd behavior.

A few moments later, Mary Katherine came back into the hallway. She was followed by a man whose face brightened up. "Veeder McLean? What are you doing here?"

"This is my brother, Mr. Perkins."

"Tom, please. Call me Tom." He reached out his hand and Veeder shook it.

"It's nice to meet you, Tom." Veeder was still confused.

"My brother was visiting with the children in the recreation room, Mr. Perkins, and I asked him to stop by today because David couldn't join us."

"Why couldn't he join us?" Veeder asked.

"He's not doing so well. He was getting another round of chemo today." Mr. Perkin's shoulders slunk.

"Chemo?"

"He has stage IV cancer, Veeder." Mr. Perkins started rubbing his hands together and fidgeting.

"Forgive me for not knowing my medical terminology. Is that bad?" Veeder looked at Mary Katherine for clarification.

"He's dying," Mr. Perkins uttered. Veeder's heart broke upon hearing the diagnosis. "The doctors give him another six months to live."

"How can that be?" Veeder was dumbfounded, trying to rectify the information in his mind. "Isn't he just a kid?"

"Sometimes, God allows some of us to come home sooner than we would like," Mary Katherine responded, putting her hand on Veeder's arm.

"How can little kids suffer like this? It's not right, MK. It's not fair for any of these kids."

"I know, Veeder," Mary Katherine replied. "We can debate that another day but right now, I really need you to do me this favor. I need you to go into this room and give him thirty minutes of your time."

"Do you think it will do any good?"

"It would be the greatest thing that ever happened!" Mr. Perkins interjected.

"He's your biggest fan," Mary Katherine added. "You will be giving him the greatest memory of his life and a momentary escape from reality."

"I don't know how, I'm just a football player."

"And he's a kid who never got to play football. He has spent most of his life in a hospital bed hoping and praying for the day he could go outside and play any game." Mary Katherine gave Veeder the look that told him she was not going to back down.

"You said his name is David?"

"Yes," Mr. Perkins answered.

Veeder took a deep breath, walked past Mary Katherine, opened the door, and went into the room. He walked towards the bed, the monitors and IV bags catching him off guard. Veeder fought back the sadness and with every ounce of exuberance he could muster, blurted out, "David, how are you doing today?"

Mary Katherine slipped into the room behind Veeder and leaned against the wall. Upon seeing Veeder, David's face lit up in pure joy. "Veeder McLean, is it really you?"

"David, a friend of mine told me you were my biggest fan."

"I am!"

"So I told her we needed to do something about that."

"Veeder McLean is in my room!" David did a little boogie shake with his arms. "I have died and gone to heaven!"

Mr. Perkins walked across the room and stood next to his wife. "This is my wife, Ellie."

"Veeder McLean, Dad!" David yelled out again. "Veeder McLean is in my room!"

"I know, son."

"Can you believe Veeder McLean is here in my room?" David squealed, his smile growing across his face, lighting up the room.

"Nice to meet you, Mrs. Perkins." Veeder shook her hand.

"David is your biggest fan," Mrs. Perkins reported.

"I've heard that once or twice before. David, is this true?"

"Is it true?" David laughed, pinching himself to make sure he wasn't dreaming. "I have seen every game you have ever played. You. Are. Awesome!"

"You look like you could be a pretty awesome Cobra yourself, David."

"I would love to play for the Cobras, but I'm not good enough."

"I don't believe you. I could see you streaking down the sidelines, catching my passes, and running into the end zone."

"That. Would. Be. Amazing!"

"Let's try it!" Veeder picked up a NERF football that was sitting on a shelf.

"Really?" David sat up in his bed.

"Veeder!" Mary Katherine stepped forward.

"Relax, MK," Veeder said, turning and putting his hand up to stop her. "David, your parents better get their cameras out."

Veeder threw a pass across the room and David caught it. David celebrated by performing a sitting touchdown dance in his bed and Veeder danced with him. For the next twenty minutes, Veeder threw touchdown passes to David. They refined their touchdown dance and perfected an end zone handshake.

When David got tired and needed to lie back in his bed to rest, Veeder sat on the edge of his bed, held his hand, and talked football. David developed a game plan for the national championship game against Boulder Mountain Tech, and he told Veeder how their defense would try to disguise their blitzes.

Veeder was impressed at how knowledgeable David was about football. He swapped stories with David, signed memorabilia, and just laughed with him. David had the strongest spirit and greatest attitude he had ever seen.

Veeder looked at the clock and realized he had to get going. He was late for practice. He took a few more pictures with the family. Then he sat down to talk with David a little bit more before leaving. As the two were talking, he turned and stared at Mary Katherine. "MK, do you think we could bust David out of here for a day?"

"Veeder, don't." Mary Katherine shook her head.

"Mom, could we? Could we please?" David started pleading.

"I don't know, David," Mrs. Perkins replied, confused.

"He's pretty sick, Mr. McLean," Mr. Perkins added.

"I fully understand that, Mr. Perkins," Veeder said, staring at Mary Katherine in a way that bored into her heart, "but if what you told me in the hallway is true, then I don't want this to be the greatest day of David's life when we can spend more time together outside of the hospital."

"What are you suggesting?" Mrs. Perkins asked.

Veeder turned and faced Mrs. Perkins. "If David's doctors would let him come spend an afternoon with us, I would like to invite him for a tour of the stadium. He could meet the whole team and watch practice while we get ready for the national championship."

"Can I, mom? Can I? Can I?" David pleaded.

"We have to ask the doctors, David," Veeder replied. "It's up to them."

"Don't make promises you can't keep, Veeder," MK said, stepping closer to the bed.

"I'm not, MK. If you can convince the doctors to let David come to practice, he is more than welcome as my guest."

"I don't know if the doctors will allow that," Mrs. Perkins interjected.

"If anyone can convince the doctors, MK can."

"I told you he was awesome, Mom!"

"And you, young man," Veeder said, turning back toward the bed. "You need to do what the doctors say, and you need to listen to your parents. Whatever they say goes, understand?"

"Yes, sir."

"Good," Veeder said before he posed for few more pictures. He hugged David and his parents.

Mary Katherine was beaming with pride when they left David's room. "You made that little boy so happy, Veeder, thank you. But you shouldn't have talked about practice in front of him."

"Why not?" Veeder stared at her with a furrowed brow. "I gave him hope."

"False hope."

"I don't believe that."

"The doctors will never allow it."

"I don't see why they wouldn't."

"Because he's sick, Veeder."

"He's not sick, MK. He's dying."

"You're right, Veeder, he is!"

"So if he's dying, is one afternoon outside the hospital going to cost him his life?"

"No."

"Then why would they be opposed?"

"Because they don't think like you do. They think they can cure him until the moment it is physically impossible to do so."

"If you were his doctor, would you let him come to practice?"

"If I was his doctor?" Mary Katherine paused for a moment. Then she let down her guard. "Yes. I would."

"But?"

"But I'm not his doctor and I don't know if his doctor will allow it."

"Make it happen, MK," Veeder pleaded. "You saw his face; it would make whatever remaining time he has amazing."

"And if I can't?"

"I believe in you."

"I'll do my best," Mary Katherine said, resigning herself to the fact that Veeder was not going to relent in his request.

"That all I ask." Veeder hugged Mary Katherine and kissed her on the cheek. "I'm late for practice."

As Veeder left the hospital, the realization started sinking in, he was a role model. He still believed the true heroes were doctors, soldiers, and first responders, but to a kid who was fighting a death sentence, someone who shows up, spends time with them, and shares their love with them was a hero too.

CHAPTER 26

—⟨⊙⟩—

Veeder met his parents and grandparents at Raleigh-Durham International Airport. They were flying to New York City for the 1999 Heisman Trophy Award banquet. He was glad to be heading north, it would give him a couple of days off to rest before having to return to practice. It had been a long season and fatigue was setting into his body.

New York City was the perfect distraction for Veeder. He had asked Anna and Pastor Kelly to make the trip with him, but her family declined. Veeder felt it was a question of finances, so he didn't push too hard when they turned him down. The Kelly's refusal allowed Veeder to offer the invitation to his four biggest fans.

His parents and grandparents were excited to make the trip back to New York City to celebrate Veeder's success. They had joined him each of the previous seasons when he had been nominated. He lost both times but Veeder felt like he was a sure-fire candidate this time. He was confident he would win.

Veeder loved New York City. He loved spending time with his family, and they made sure to see all of the sites. They spent time in Greenwich Village, Central Park, and Times Square. They grabbed a Circle Line Cruise around Manhattan and at his grandfather's request, they met up with some of the extended family members his great-grandfather left behind when he moved to North Carolina.

Veeder was anonymous in New York City. He liked that. A few people recognized him and asked for an autograph, which made his parents and grandparents proud of how much he had accomplished. For most of the weekend, though, Veeder was able to travel around the city with very little fanfare. He wondered how it would change after the NFL draft. He wondered if he would have the same freedom when a team drafted him and made him the face of their franchise.

The Heisman Trophy banquet bored Veeder but as usual, Jill and Colleen loved every minute of it. They loved getting dressed up and spending a formal evening with James, Paul, and Veeder. They loved the attention Veeder garnered throughout the dinner, but they were more impressed with the impeccable young man he had become. He had grown up in college and had learned how to treat the press with respect since the fiasco as a freshman.

Veeder was out of his element during these types of events because he wasn't good at hobnobbing with the bigwigs. But as Veeder sat in the hall with the other finalists, he believed fate might be on his side. *Third time's the charm* he thought to himself. He felt like things were lining up for him. The Cobras had an undefeated season, they had won their conference, they were nationally ranked, and were about to play for the national championship. He was going to win the Heisman.

Butterflies fluttered in his stomach. The nervous anticipation made it hard to eat anything. Jill, noticing her son was jittery, put her arm through his to help calm his nerves. Veeder was impatient for the announcement of the winner, but he remained calm and collected on the outside. He knew there were television cameras focused on all of the finalists. He didn't want to give the media any more awkward moments they could use against him.

The moderator came to the podium, made some speech that went in one of Veeder's ears and out the other. When the moment to present the Heisman Trophy came, Veeder got excited as they opened the envelope. "The winner of the 1999 Heisman Trophy is Ron Dayne from the University of Oregon."

Veeder stood and applauded the announcement while his heart sunk into the pit of his stomach. The voters in the media had done it to him again. They nominated him three years in a row, made him a finalist three years in a row, and then in an auditorium full of people with television cameras aimed at him, he lost for the third time. Veeder smiled and applauded the accomplishments of the young man who had earned the award because he refused to let the press see him buckle under their scrutiny.

The flight back to North Carolina was a long, soul-searching one for Veeder. He questioned everything he had accomplished. Jill and Colleen sat next to him and tried to reassure him this was nothing to worry about, it was a popularity contest. But Veeder wasn't listening. He appreciated their love and support, but it didn't change the fact he had lost for a third straight year.

Veeder tried to think of what he would say to the rest of his family, his teammates, his friends, and his fans. But there was nothing to say. He was honored to be a member of the Chapel Hill University Cobras. He valued his experience over the last four years. He was looking forward, not backward. It was time to finish the job and win the national championship.

Veeder smiled when the plane landed in North Carolina. He had a great weekend with his parents and grandparents, and he was happy to be done with the political stuff. *Suck it up, buttercup. Get back to work is* what JJ would have told him, and it was what he planned on doing when he got back to Chapel Hill. His team had a championship to win and that was all that mattered. It's all that ever mattered. He didn't need individual awards; he was in it for the championship trophy.

CHAPTER 27

Veeder packed up his truck. Coach Mercer had given the team the weekend off, so he decided to drive Anna home for Christmas break. He was looking forward to a free weekend to relax after another long week of practice. He just wanted to enjoy spending time with his family and Anna.

Veeder picked up Anna in front of her apartment and drove her home. She was done with finals and wouldn't be coming back to campus after the weekend. He had to head back to school for another week of practice before getting a few days off for Christmas. They both had family obligations over the weekend, but they agreed to spend Saturday night together. Nothing fancy. Just a quiet evening out. Just the two of them.

Veeder pulled up in front of her house. "What time do you want me to pick you up tomorrow?"

"My parents have some things planned for the afternoon."

"My parents have most of the day planned as well."

"Six o'clock sound good?"

"I'll be here."

"Love you." Anna leaned over and kissed him.

"Love you, too," Veeder said, while Anna grabbed her knapsack and jumped out of the truck. "See you tomorrow."

Anna closed the door and went inside the house. As Veeder was pulling away from the curb, Pastor Kelly came out and waved to him from the front porch. He waved back and drove home.

Early Saturday morning, Veeder and his dad went out to cut down a Christmas tree. It took a while to find the perfect tree but when they found it on the far side of the farm, he cut it down, dragged it to the truck, and drove back to the house. By the time they pulled into the driveway, Jill had breakfast on the table. Mary Katherine had come home earlier in the week.

Liam, Colin, and Michael were all arriving at the house with their significant others.

Veeder and Paul hopped out of the truck just as James and Colleen pulled into the driveway. Once inside, the family enjoyed a big breakfast while Jill cranked up the Christmas music on the radio. Sean was unable to get a pass from the Army, but they celebrated him nonetheless, spending the morning laughing, singing, and decorating the house.

It took forever for Paul to get the tree into the stand, but once it was securely up, the entire family pulled out their favorite ornaments from the boxes Jill had brought down from the attic and decorated it. The tree wasn't finished until the final ornament was hung by Paul and Jill. It was an ornament Liz had given to them after JJ died. It was a picture of JJ and Liz that had been taken somewhere in Africa. The family hung it every year and toasted JJ's memory before they all sat around staring at the tree and sharing memories of their greatest Christmases.

In the afternoon, Mary Katherine and Veeder joined Colleen and Jill on an excursion to the Southern Supreme Fruitcake store in Bear Creek. Jill and Colleen bought a bunch of freshly made fruit cakes to share with family and friends. It was a holiday tradition they started after the store opened about a decade earlier. They sampled the chocolates, buying a lot more chocolate than they sampled.

Veeder picked up Anna at six o'clock and they drove into town to have dinner at Lizzie's. It wasn't fancy, but it was their place. It was where he had taken her for a chocolate sundae when they first met and it had been the place where they had spent most of their time together over the years.

They had a nice quiet dinner, and they shared another chocolate sundae. They talked about everything under the sun. College was ending and their lives were about to begin. They wondered what the future might hold for them, but they never got too far ahead of themselves. They always believed in taking life one day at a time.

After dinner, they jumped into Veeder's truck and drove to the farm. Veeder parked in the middle of one of the fields underneath the cool December sky like they had done so many times before. Veeder grabbed the blankets and the bean bag chairs out of the back seat and put them in the truck bed. Then he helped Anna climb into the truck bed. They sat back, cuddling up under the blankets, staring up at millions of stars illuminating the sky.

"It's such a beautiful night," Anna said, resting her head on Veeder's chest. "So quiet. So peaceful."

"I have a surprise for you."

"What?"

"We went out to Southern Supreme Fruitcake today."

"Shut up!" Anna sat up, pushing his shoulder and staring at him. "Please tell me that you're not joking."

"I'm not."

"Toffee?"

"Bear Creek Toffee!" Veeder pulled out a couple of pieces he had wrapped in wax paper and gave her one.

"So good." Anna took a bite, savoring every bit of the chocolate.

"I love you." Veeder kissed Anna.

"I love you, too." Anna cuddled against him. "I am so glad we came out here tonight."

"Me too."

"I love how peaceful it is just to lie here with you under God's beautiful sky."

Veeder nodded in agreement. They laid there for the longest time, staring up at the sky, and holding each other close. It felt like old times when things were easy. College had pulled them in different directions. Between their courses, the football team, and Veeder's celebrity status, it was hard to find times where they could relax and enjoy each other's company.

Anna talked about the nursing program and graduation. She couldn't wait to get out into the world, start her life, and help people. She loved everything about nursing, and even though she knew her father had spent every dime he had saved on her education, she was sure God had provided so she could go out into the world and make a difference serving Him.

Veeder listened to Anna talk about the future. He loved listening to her. He dreamed about the day when he would be playing for an NFL team and Anna would work at the hospital in the city where they settled down. It looked like their plan was going to happen, and he was happy, happier than he had ever been. He looked forward to it.

The wind blew across the field and with each billowing blast of cold air that crossed over the truck, the two of them snuggled closer together. Anna shivered. Veeder pulled her closer to him, tightening his embrace. Anna looked up into his eyes, and Veeder melted in her gaze. He leaned in and kissed her.

Lost in the multitude of kisses they shared, his heart and nerves colliding in a moment of tenderness and love, Veeder did something he had thought about many times but out of respect for Anna and her beliefs, had never acted upon. He reached down, tugged at Anna's shirt, and tried to run his hand up underneath her clothing.

"Stop!" Anna yelled, grabbing his wrist, and pulling his hand out from underneath her shirt.

"What?"

"What are you doing?" Anna pulled away from him and stared at him in disbelief. "How could you?

"I love you, Anna."

"I love you too, Veeder, but that's not going to happen."

"Why not? It's a beautiful night under the stars…"

"No!" Anna was angry because they had just had this conversation. "I'm saving myself for marriage."

"As I have been, but you're the person I am going to marry."

"Doesn't matter, Veeder, we're not married!"

"But you are the person I am going to marry."

"We're not married!"

"But you know we're going to get married, Anna. Why do we need to wait?"

"Because I don't know if I am going to marry you, Veeder!" Anna blurted out.

"What are you talking about?" Veeder stared at her, shocked.

"I don't know if we are going to get married, Veeder. I once did…"

"Anna?" Veeder interrupted.

Anna looked at him with tears in her eyes. "I love you, Veeder. I do, but nothing is changing. I can't keep having these arguments. It's draining."

"You knew I didn't believe in God when we started dating."

"And I do."

"I don't see the problem."

"I love God and you don't." Anna was deflated. She shook her head back and forth and she let out a deep sigh. "That's the problem. That has always been the problem."

"We have always been able to work through it."

"I don't know if I can anymore."

"Where is this coming from all of a sudden, Anna?"

"It's not that sudden, Veeder." Tears crept down her cheeks. "You keep doing more things that I don't agree with."

"We don't have to agree on everything."

"Your behavior doesn't line up with what I believe, and the more you act like this, I feel further and further away from you."

"Anna, we can work it out."

Anna looked at him with sad eyes. "It's getting harder to bridge the gap, Veeder."

"So I made a mistake tonight," Veeder apologized. "I'm sorry."

"It's not just tonight."

"Why didn't you say anything?"

"I did say something." Anna threw up her arms, frustrated. "You just haven't listened."

"When?"

"The partying, the swearing, the off-color jokes, the putting people down."

"I'm just blowing off steam." Veeder was defensive. "It's done in good fun."

"But it's not what I believe. It's not how I treat people. I don't like it, and I've told you that many times."

"It's just locker room talk, Anna. It doesn't mean anything."

"It means something to me. It's not something I want to be around." She looked at him, her eyes filled with tears, her heart breaking.

"So I'll stop."

"And then you pull this stunt tonight, Veeder," Anna said with a hint of shame in her voice. "You know how I feel about sex."

"I made a mistake, Anna. I'm sorry."

"Me too," Anna said, standing up and hopping out of the truck bed. "Please take me home."

It was the quietest ride they had ever shared. Neither one wanted to cry in front of the other, but both of their hearts were breaking. Their lives were changing; they were being torn apart. They loved each other, but they believed in different things. For Anna, at least, she wondered if loving someone could ever be enough to overcome those differences.

Veeder pulled up in front of Anna's house. She turned and looked at him, tears rolling down her cheeks. "I'm sorry, Veeder. I love you. I do. I just need some time right now."

"How much time?" He whispered, almost not wanting to hear the answer.

"I don't know."

"So where do we go from here?"

"I don't know that either." She touched his hand and stared at her feet. "I always believed you and I would be together for the rest of our lives. Pray for us."

"I'll try," Veeder said, knowing he never would.

"That's a start."

"Is it enough?"

"It might be. It just might be." Anna leaned over and hugged Veeder. "Goodbye."

Veeder wanted to turn and pour out his heart to Anna. He wanted to convince her to give him a second chance, but he didn't. He fought with himself to remain strong, to remain silent because it was over. His heart told him not to let Anna go without a fight, but it was too late. As he turned to fight for their love, he heard the truck door slam shut. He watched in silence as she ran into her house. Tears formed in his eyes and his heart broke inside his chest. "I love you, Anna,"

Veeder put the truck in gear and drove away.

CHAPTER 28

—⸻⊙⸻

Veeder woke up on Sunday and went to church with his family. He didn't believe in God, but he always honored their request to attend services. He decided to sit with his grandmother instead of with Anna. Colleen was glad to see him and happy things were going well with the football team. She told him she had bought their plane tickets to New Orleans and would be there in person to root for him.

The service began and Veeder looked around to see where Anna was sitting. She wasn't there. He had never known Anna to miss services unless she was sick, and he was worried. *Maybe something happened to her* he thought but he brushed away those thoughts. After services, the family congregated in the reception hall before going home to prepare for dinner at James and Colleen's house.

Veeder told his parents he had things to get done before the start of the week so he wouldn't be able to join them for Sunday dinner. Instead, he had a cup of coffee on the porch with his mother. They talked about the team and school. He avoided any conversation about Anna. He didn't know what to say and he wasn't ready to talk about it yet. When the conversation started to lag, he decided to pack up the truck and head back to his apartment.

Veeder was throwing a couple of bags of clean clothes into the truck when Mary Katherine came bounding down the front steps and walked across the front yard towards him, "Where are you going?"

"Heading back to campus."

"You're not staying for Sunday dinner?"

"Got things to do."

"I was hoping to save dad a trip and catch a ride with you."

"I thought you were done with finals."

"I am."

"Then why are you heading back to school?"

"My internship at the hospital."

"You packed?"

"Not yet."

"You better hurry up and grab your stuff. I'm leaving soon."

"Why the rush?"

"Look, MK," Veeder slammed the back door shut. "I have things to do back on campus."

"Can't it wait?"

"I'll give you thirty minutes. After that, you have to bum a ride with dad."

"I'll get my stuff." Mary Katherine stared at him before going back into the house to grab her stuff. Something was up. It wasn't a twin thing; she and Veeder didn't have that connection. It was a sister feeling. She and Veeder were best friends, and she could tell when something was bothering him.

Mary Katherine packed up her stuff. Veeder helped carry the bags to the truck and load them into the backseat. Once packed, Mary Katherine and Veeder walked back to the front porch to say goodbye to their parents.

"Are you sure you can't stay for Sunday dinner?" Jill was hoping they would reconsider.

"Can't, Mom. Got things to do."

"He's my ride." Mary Katherine shrugged her shoulders.

"Your grandmother and grandfather will be sorry they missed you," Paul added.

"I saw grandma and grandpa at church today," Veeder shot back.

"I know," Jill said, "but they love seeing you every chance they get."

"I'll see them this weekend," Mary Katherine responded.

"Where was Anna this morning?" Jill asked. "I must have missed her."

"I don't know," Veeder bristled. "She was tired from finals. I think she slept in."

"That's not like her," Jill said. "Maybe we'll see her next weekend."

"Maybe," Veeder responded.

Mary Katherine raised her eyebrows at his vague responses. Now she knew something was wrong. Veeder and Anna knew everything about each other. He would have known if she slept in. In fact, she found it strange he hadn't gone looking for Anna after services, just to make sure she was all right. For the moment, though, she decided to play dumb. She wasn't letting on that she sensed anything was wrong. She wanted to see if Veeder would talk about it on the drive back to campus.

Veeder and Mary Katherine hugged their parents, climbed into the truck, and drove down the driveway. Mary Katherine changed the radio station every five to ten seconds because she knew it would drive Veeder crazy, but it didn't faze him. He wasn't paying attention. He was deep in thought.

"I spoke to Coach Mercer on Friday."

"You did?" Veeder asked, raising an eyebrow. He was suspicious. "Why?"

"It took me longer than I thought, but the doctors agreed to let David come to practice."

"Great." Veeder just stared straight ahead.

"He's coming Tuesday."

"Uh-huh."

"Aren't you excited?"

"I am."

"You don't seem like it."

"I'm sorry, MK. I'm just preoccupied with the game plan for the national championship."

"You sure?" Mary Katherine was concerned. This whole idea was Veeder's. She was hoping for more enthusiasm about the visit.

"Yes. I'm excited to see him. We'll have an awesome day planned."

"Okay." They drove for a few more minutes in silence. "I was thinking of calling Anna and having her come up to take some pictures."

"No!" Veeder snapped. "Don't call her."

"Why not?" Mary Katherine was taken aback by Veeder's reaction. She had touched a chord, but she was not prepared for such a strong reply. "She loves this stuff."

"Because I said so." Veeder barked.

"Veeder, she loves when you do things like this for kids."

"MK, please don't." He was terse and Mary Katherine was concerned.

"What gives, Veeder?"

"Nothing."

"You've been snippy and pensive all morning."

"I told you." Veeder's tone of voice was solemn. "I am preoccupied with football."

"No, Veeder, you're not. This is different." Mary Katherine said, staring at him. "Something's up."

"Fine." Veeder rubbed his hand over his forehead, down the side of his face, and over his chin. "I might as well tell you."

"Tell me what?"

"You and Anna are friends. You're going to find out anyway." Veeder paused for a moment and took a deep breath. "It's probably best if you hear it from me."

"Find out what, Veeder? Spill it!"

"Anna and I broke up."

"What?" Mary Katherine was shocked. Her mouth agape from the news.

"She needs space." Veeder's heart pounded against his chest.

"Did she break up with you? Or did she say she needed space?"

"Is there a difference?"

"No." Mary Kathrine conceded. "There probably isn't."

"Is what it is."

"I'm so sorry, Veeder," Mary Katherine said with sympathy.

"Nothing to be sorry about, MK. You didn't do anything."

"I love you, little brother. I don't want to see you hurting."

"I'm fine." Veeder stared straight ahead at the road. It was a lie and Mary Katherine knew it. She sat there in shock, just staring at him when she noticed a solitary tear roll down his cheek and fall off his chin onto his lap. It killed her that he was in so much pain. But she didn't say anything. There was nothing to say.

She knew Veeder needed to process things. He needed time to sort it out in his head. Life to him was like reading a defense. Until he figured out the challenges in front of him and figured how to defeat them, he wasn't talking. She knew he would come and find her when he was ready to talk. Until then, she just needed to be his friend and support him.

They drove for a while in silence. It was awkward but Mary Katherine understood his state of mind and why he wanted to avoid Sunday dinner. After a while, they started to talk about David's visit to the team facilities. The doctors agreed to let him go only if a doctor went. Everyone had to agree to end the visit when David got tired.

Veeder was nodding along with Mary Katherine while she explained the ground rules, but he knew he would break every one of those rules if David was safe, smiling, and happy. He was glad to have something positive to keep him busy. It was a great distraction as he tried to figure out what went wrong with his relationship.

The rest of the ride was silent. Mary Katherine continued to fumble with the radio dial to see if she could coax Veeder out of his thoughts. She even sang along with the songs he hated just to irritate him. She tried to get him to laugh, but he never budged. He just stared ahead, watching the road. Lost in thought.

Veeder pulled into a parking spot in front of Mary Katherine's apartment building. Before she could jump out of the truck and grab her things, he turned and said, "Thank you, MK."

"For what?"

"For not pushing."

"It's not my place. I know how hard this must be. I'm just gonna follow your lead."

"I know this is hard for you, too."

Mary Katherine put her hand on his shoulder. "You're my baby brother. I hate seeing you in pain."

"But you also love Anna."

"I do, but…"

"No but's," Veeder interrupted. "You guys are best friends; that shouldn't change."

"It might a little." Mary Katherine paused, choking back her tears. "She broke your heart."

"No, MK, she didn't." Veeder paused and collected his thoughts. "It's my fault. I messed up. I broke her heart."

"It takes two to tango." MK hugged Veeder.

"Not this time. This was all my fault."

"You can play the martyr if you want, but you guys have always had it difficult. She believes in God and you don't. That's a tough one to overcome."

"It's more than that."

"But at the end of the day, that was a big part of it. Wasn't it?"

"Yes."

"It was always going to come to the forefront and rear its ugly head at some point. You thought you two would overcome it and she thought she would change you."

"That isn't what happened. I made a mistake."

"It doesn't matter what happened. The mistake was just a symptom. It all stems from the fact that she believes and you don't. It was always the underlying problem."

"So what do I do?"

"I don't know." Mary Katherine shook her head. She was perplexed. "That's a tough one. I wish I had some advice, but I don't."

"Promise me this won't change your relationship with her." Veeder stared at her with conviction. "That would kill me."

"I'll try, but I can't promise anything."

"You have to."

"I can't." Mary Katherine brushed her hair from her eyes. "You will always come first."

"Thanks."

"You want to come up to my apartment and talk for a little bit?" Mary Katherine asked, opening the door.

"No way!" Veeder put his hands up in defiance.

"I don't want you to be alone with your thoughts."

"I'd prefer my thoughts to your friends across the hall. They're always there." Veeder shivered at the thought of them hanging out in Mary Katherine's apartment. "They scare me."

"Look at the big, tough football player," Mary Katherine teased. "Afraid of a bunch of woo girls who happen to be madly in love with you."

"Shut up, MK," Veeder laughed.

"Jerk!"

"Moron!"

"Jock!"

"Nerd!"

"Momma's boy!"

"Love you, MK!"

"I love you too." Mary Katherine hugged Veeder. "Call me if you need anything."

"Thanks, MK. I will." Mary Katherine jumped out of the truck, grabbed her stuff, and walked into her apartment building. Once she was inside, he pulled away and drove across campus to his apartment.

CHAPTER 29

Veeder was happy to get back to work. It had been a rough couple of days. Football kept his mind off life. The stress of preparing for the national championship game and the breakup with Anna caused a rash to break out on his legs.

He got into the training facility early in the morning and went straight to the film room. The next few hours were spent deciphering, breaking down, and looking for weaknesses in the Boulder Mountain Tech defense. The longer he watched, little nuances in their defensive scheme became apparent. He found small gaps in their game plan he could exploit.

In the weight room, he lifted weights before doing some cardio. He wanted to be at peak performance for the game. The last five months of the season had taken a toll on his body. The aches and pains could be felt everywhere but he pressed on, pushing his body to the limit before returning to the film room during lunch. The afternoon was filled with position meetings and team practice. The coaches ended the day with a team meeting to go over the changes in the game plan for the national championship.

Exhausted, Veeder arrived back at his apartment after nine o'clock with a sandwich and an iced tea. He ate dinner with the television on before falling asleep on the couch. He woke up in the middle of the night, turned off the television, and dragged himself off to bed where he slept like a baby until the alarm went off at five o'clock in the morning.

Veeder climbed out of bed, hopped in the shower, and noticed the rash on his legs had now spread across his stomach. He felt like he was coming down with something and hoped it wouldn't hinder preparation for the big game.

He dried off, got dressed, ate a quick breakfast, and raced out the door. He had an extra skip in his step. David was coming to practice. The team had a special day planned.

David arrived at War Memorial Stadium in a hospital van at eleven o'clock. When the van stopped, Mary Katherine, Mr. and Mrs. Perkins, and one of David's doctors jumped out to greet Veeder. Mary Katherine and the Perkins all hugged him. They stood at the curb waiting for David to get out of the van. The doctor walked to the back of the van, opened the doors, and removed a wheelchair. After closing the doors, he pushed the chair towards the open passenger door of the van.

"What is that for?" Veeder asked.

"It's for David." The doctor responded, staring at Veeder.

"Why?"

"To help him conserve his energy."

"No way." Veeder was defiant, stepping up to the open door of the van. "David, do you need that contraption?"

"Veeder," Mary Katherine said with her *cut-it-out* voice.

"I. Hate. It." David clenched his fists in frustration.

"I thought you did." Veeder leaned into the van and picked David up.

"Mr. McLean, I insist," the doctor said.

"If David needs to hitch a ride." Veeder placed David upon his shoulders and started walking towards the stadium. "He can hitch a ride with me."

"Yeah!" David yelled, pumping his fist in the air.

"Mr. McLean, I insist," the doctor reiterated.

"You ride in the chair if it's so important to you." Veeder walked away, carrying David down the walkway to the front door of the facilities. Mary Katherine, the Perkins', and the doctor followed.

Veeder headed straight to the weight room, introducing David to a bunch of the players on the team. The players doted on David. Mary Katherine faded into the background. She loved that Veeder had disregarded the doctor and was giving David a perfect day. She had burned a lot of favors to get the hospital to agree to this field trip, so she knew she was going to hear about it when she went back to work.

A smile crossed David's face. His parents snapped pictures, eyes full of tears. They were overjoyed at the way the team rallied around David, treating him like a celebrity. They could never thank the players for their kindness.

Veeder scooped David up and carried him to the coach's offices, who allowed him to peruse the playlist and pick one play they would run during the national championship. The coaches had a great conversation with their young visitor and before David left, Coach Mercer handed him a letter. It was a scholarship offer to play football for the Chapel Hill University Cobras when he graduated high school. David was ecstatic and committed to the team.

After taking David's family to lunch, Veeder took David to the locker room. The Cobra players gave him a standing ovation. Every player met with him, signed hats, gloves, and took pictures. Tour complete, the family stood in front of a locker next to Veeder's with the words "David Parker" written above it. Inside the locker was a brand-new Cobras jersey with his name and favorite number on it.

David did his best to do a happy dance when Veeder told him to get dressed for practice. He looked at Veeder in disbelief and then with the help of Chapel Hill's star quarterback, David put on the uniform and walked down the tunnel towards the field. The cheerleading squad lined the path out onto the field and chanted David's name as he ran past them with Veeder at his side.

For the next half hour, the offense lined up on the five-yard line and ran plays that were designed to get David into the end zone. Mary Katherine, the Parkers, and even the doctor laughed and cried while they watched David playing football with the Cobras. The cheerleaders lined the field and rooted for him. Every time David scored a touchdown, Veeder and the rest of the players did the touchdown dance they had perfected back in his hospital room.

The coaches blew the whistle. A photographer came onto the field and took a team photo with David in the middle of the front row. Then David and his family took a seat on the sideline to watch the Cobras prepare for Boulder Mountain Tech. When practice ended, Veeder walked to the sidelines and hoisted a tired David onto his shoulders. The Perkins enjoyed seeing their son away from the hospital, being a kid again, even if it was for one day.

Veeder carried David back to the van. As he walked, a part of him was sad he hadn't allowed Mary Katherine to call Anna. He wished he could have shared this with her, but he wanted to respect her wishes. If she needed space, he wanted her to have all of the space she needed to sort everything out. They would just have to share this with her one day.

Veeder's teammates grabbed all of David's gifts and carried them out to the van. Veeder gave David a big hug as they stood outside the van. "I am glad you made it to practice today, buddy. We'll miss you out here tomorrow."

"Best. Day. Ever!" David responded, fatigue setting into his body.

"Mine too," Veeder agreed.

"I know you're going to beat Boulder Mountain Tech."

"With you on our team, how could we lose?"

"Thank you, Veeder."

"No, David." A tear formed in Veeder's eye. "Thank you. I have learned so much from you."

"You have?"

"I have." Veeder wiped the tear away.

"Cool." David smiled.

"I can't wait to bring the championship trophy with me when I visit you next."

"Really?"

"You're a Cobra, aren't you?"

"Yes," David responded, smiling again.

"Then the trophy is as much yours as it is any of ours."

"Thanks, Veeder."

"Get some sleep, buddy."

"I will."

"I'll see you soon."

"Bye." Veeder gave David another hug and helped him back inside the van. He turned around and before he could say anything, Mrs. Perkins wrapped him up in her arms, tears falling down her face.

"Thank you, Veeder. You made his day so special. We'll never forget this."

"I didn't do anything, Mrs. Perkins."

"You made my son happy. You made me happy just watching him. Your mama raised you right. God bless you."

"God bless you too," Veeder responded, not knowing what to say. He turned to shake hands with Mr. Perkins who also hugged him.

"Thank you, Veeder. I will never forget what you did for my boy."

"You're welcome, Mr. Perkins."

"This is the greatest gift anyone could have given our family. Thank you."

Veeder spoke with the Perkins family for a few minutes before they climbed into the van with David. Mary Katherine gave Veeder a kiddie punch in his side. "You did good, Veeder. Thank you for doing this."

"I agree." The doctor said, holding out his hand. "It was a great day. Even if you did break every rule we had."

"Sorry, Doc," Veeder responded, shaking his hand.

"Don't be. Laughter and love are the best medicine. You just gave that boy a huge dose of both."

"Thanks, Doc."

"I'm going to go back to the hospital with the family." Mary Katherine hugged Veeder. "I'll call you later."

"Okay, MK." Veeder watched Mary Katherine and the doctor hop into the van. He stood by the curb and waved until it disappeared out of sight. Then he walked back into the locker room so he could take a shower.

Veeder sat at his locker in the near-empty room, took off his jersey, and stared at his body. The rash of small purple dots had spread across his chest and onto his arms. He was wondering when the rash would go away.

Dwight Birkenstock, another one of the players, said from across the locker room, "That looks like measles."

"Don't be ridiculous, Dwight. It's just a rash."

"I'm not kidding, Veeder," Dwight reiterated. "That looks like measles."

"And how did I catch measles?"

"I don't know."

"I had all my shots as a kid and I got all of my booster shots before I came to college."

"I'm not saying it is measles, Veeder. I'm saying it looks like measles. If I were you, I'd get that rash checked out."

"It's just a rash man, don't be ridiculous," Veeder said, trying to downplay the situation.

"If you say so." Dwight crossed the locker room and gave Veeder a fist bump. "See you tomorrow."

"Good night, Dwight." Veeder sat on the bench staring at the rash.

CHAPTER 30

There was a forceful, incessant banging on Mary Katherine's apartment door.

"I'm coming," Mary Katherine screamed. Jolted out of a blissful sleep, she stumbled down the hallway. She was angry when she opened the door, the chain still bolted in place. "Gee Whiz chill out! What do you want?"

"I need to talk to you," Veeder said, leaning on the door frame.

"Veeder?" Mary Katherine shut the door, unlatched the chain, and opened the door. "What are you doing here?"

"Can I come in?" He was agitated which concerned Mary Katherine.

"What are you doing here at this hour? And why are you banging on my door?"

"Sorry, MK, but I really needed to see you. Can I please come in for a minute?"

"Sure." Mary Katherine stepped aside. Veeder walked into her apartment and sat on the couch. Mary Katherine sat next to him. "What's up?"

"I need you to check something out for me." Mary Katherine noticed his nervousness had turned into a state of fear which bothered her because he was fearless. It had to be something serious.

"What is it?"

Veeder rolled up his sleeve. "I developed a rash."

Mary Katherine pulled his arm close, inspected the rash from a bunch of different angles, and made some inquisitive noises. "When did this start?"

"Sunday night."

"You've been walking around like this for two days?"

"It was only on my legs on Sunday night."

"So, it's been spreading?" Mary Katherine questioned, inspecting his arm again. "Is it all over your body?"

"Not yet."

"How much has it spread?"

"A lot."

"We need to get you to a hospital, Veeder."

"No, MK!" Veeder panicked. He couldn't let this get out. "No hospitals!"

"Veeder, you've been around your teammates." Mary Katherine's face turned white. "Oh, my goodness!"

"What?"

"You were holding David. He could be infected." Mary Katherine shook her head. "This is not good. We need to get you to the hospital right now."

"No hospitals, MK, I have to prepare for the game."

"We have to find out what this rash is so we can treat it."

"After the national championship."

"If it's something contagious, you might not have a team."

"No doctors, MK!" Veeder shouted. "I'm already freaked out over this."

"I know you are but ignoring this isn't going to help you get better. And it's definitely not going to help your teammates or David!"

"What if they don't let me play?" Veeder started fidgeting. "I can't miss this game."

"And how is that fair to David? He's fighting cancer. You may have given him something that could complicate his health!"

"Oh." Veeder looked down in shame. "I didn't think about it that way."

"Or it could be something benign." Mary Katherine said, putting a reassuring hand on his shoulder. "It could be something simple they can give you a prescription for."

"I can't risk it."

"That's ridiculous. Why not?"

"I've worked too hard. We've come this far. We are so close, MK. I can't do anything to jeopardize the season."

"You're being selfish!" Mary Katherine groaned in frustration. "Think about something other than football. Think about the other people this might affect, Veeder. You have to go to the doctor for them."

"Is it measles?"

"What?" Mary Katherine was dumbfounded. "Where did that come from?"

"Dwight says it's measles."

"Dwight's an idiot."

"Yeah, he is." Veeder laughed. "He always has been."

"This could be something serious, Veeder. You have to get this looked at."

"Not now, MK," Veeder pleaded, mumbling. "I promise. Two weeks. The game is in two weeks. January 5th. I'll go on January 5th. Promise."

"You're not being fair."

"None of this is fair, MK. I have worked my whole life for this opportunity."

"What if…" MK said, stopping midsentence.

"What?"

"I have a friend who might be able to help." Mary Katherine half-smiled, she was nervous. This was her Hail Mary. "Would you go with me if it was done on the QT?"

"I don't know."

"Veeder, I'm worried about you."

"Why, MK?" Veeder asked, looking at her to see if she had something to hide. "Do you know what it is?"

"It could be one of a thousand things. It's not something I can diagnose by looking at it," Mary Katherine said with compassion. "We would have to run some tests to know for sure."

"This is getting out of hand, MK. Maybe I should just go home and we can forget I was ever here tonight."

"Do you trust me, Veeder?"

"I trust you." Veeder stared at Mary Katherine. He saw the concern on her face. He hated seeing her worrying about him. "Do you trust them?"

"I do." Mary Katherine was resolute in her conviction. "Best case scenario; you need an antibiotic and this rash is gone by Sunday."

"Worst case scenario?"

"We're not going to think about that. We're going to stay positive."

"What should I do, MK?" Veeder asked, more scared than conflicted.

"I can't tell you what to do," Mary Katherine said, trying to reassure him. "But if it were me, I would want to know what the rash is so I could get it taken care of."

"You would?"

"I would."

"And if it's really bad news?"

"We'll cross that bridge if we get there. I won't let you go through any of this alone."

"Thank you." Veeder took a deep breath and let it out. "I trust you, MK. If you trust this doctor, I trust them too."

"Let me make a phone call. Sit tight." Mary Katherine got off the couch and went back to her bedroom.

Veeder paced the room. He was scared. He wanted to be optimistic, but karma was fickle. It would be just his luck to come all this way, to work as hard as he had, and be unable to get the Cobras across the finish line. And just as fast as he let fear attack him, he dismissed all of the negative thoughts. Mary Katherine was right. He just needed an antibiotic. He would heal over Christmas and be back on the field by Monday.

Mary Katherine came back into the room, spoke to Veeder about the game plan, grabbed her things, and walked with Veeder to his truck. Mary Katherine drove them to the hospital. The short drive seemed like an eternity to Veeder as butterflies started filling his stomach.

They walked into the emergency room, slipped behind the receptionist's desk, traversed a catacomb of mini offices, and exam rooms. Mary Katherine met her friend in a small office. Veeder waited in the hall while she talked to the doctor about everything that had happened. After a few minutes, Mary Katherine opened the door. "Come in, Veeder."

Veeder walked into the room. "Veeder, I'm Dr. Rick Stevenson. I'm a big fan."

"Thanks, Doc." They shook hands.

"Mary Katherine told me about your rash."

"We need to keep this hush hush, Doc."

"We will."

"Thanks."

"But first we need to get you treated. I am going to run some tests."

"Tests?"

"Yes. I need to draw some blood."

"I hate needles, Doc."

"It'll be all right, Veeder." Mary Katherine placed her hand on his back.

"No, MK, it's not." Veeder was even more nervous. "How many needles?"

"One," Rick said. "Only one."

"You promise?"

"I promise. Once the needle is in, we can take as much blood as we need."

"Okay, Doc, let's do this."

"Let me get the nurse. Have a seat." Dr. Stevenson ducked out of the room.

Veeder took a seat against the wall. Mary Katherine sat next to him and held his hand to reassure him. "We're going to get through this, Veeder."

"You really think it's nothing, MK?"

"I don't know what it is but I'm praying for the best result," Mary Katherine replied with a shaky, unconvinced voice.

She wasn't sure what was going on with Veeder, but she knew it wasn't something that could be cured with an antibiotic. She didn't dare tell him though. He never would have come. He would have continued to play and risked everyone's health in order to win the national championship. Doing her best to hide her nervousness, Mary Katherine closed her eyes and prayed while holding his hand.

Fifteen minutes later, a nurse drew Veeder's blood. He closed his eyes. She missed his vein on the first attempt, pulled out the needle, and tried again. The nurse found a vein on the second attempt and filled up three vials of blood.

"See. That wasn't so bad," Mary Katherine joked.

The silence in the room was deafening. Waiting for the results of Veeder's blood test was excruciating. They could hear every tick of the clock that hung on the wall. It felt like an eternity. Minutes turned into an hour. Veeder fell asleep on Mary Katherine's shoulder.

Dr. Stevenson shook Mary Katherine. As her eyelids fluttered, she looked up at the clock. They had been waiting for more than two hours. Dr. Stevenson had his finger over his lips and gestured for her to follow him into the hallway.

Mary Katherine slipped out of her chair and followed Dr. Stevenson into the hallway. "What took so long, Rick?"

"I work in the ER, MK. It's been a crazy night. Things do get busy down here."

"I'm sorry." Backing up against the wall, she braced herself. "It isn't good, is it?"

"How did you know?" Dr. Stevenson asked, raising an eyebrow.

"I've known since he showed up at my door."

"Well." Dr. Stevenson ran his hands through his hair and took a deep breath. "You're right. It doesn't look good."

"What is it?"

Dr. Stevenson handed the results to Mary Katherine. "Take a look for yourself."

Mary Katherine thumbed through the test results. She stopped, staring for a long time at one page. "Is this right, Rick?"

"Yes," Dr. Stevenson was somber. "Veeder's platelet count is fatally low."

"Eight? How?" Mary Katherine was in shock, continuing to read through the report.

"I'm not exactly sure. It could be any number of things."

"What do you think it is?"

"ITP."

"ITP?" Mary Katherine paused and thought for a moment. "That would…"

"End his season?" Rick interrupted, nodding his head in the affirmative. "Yes."

"This is not happening." Mary Katherine covered her mouth, fought back the tears, and looked at Dr. Stevenson. "Please tell me this isn't happening. What do I do?"

"I made an appointment with a hematologist for the morning."

"He'll never go see a specialist, Rick. He's stubborn."

"He has to, MK. This is life-threatening."

"I know it is, but all he's worried about is the national championship."

"Your brother never should have been playing."

"You tell him that," Mary Katherine responded, staring at the test results. "He has worked his whole life for this moment."

"If this is ITP, MK, the smallest injury on the field could have devastating effects and you know that."

"What do I tell him, Rick?"

"The truth!" Dr. Stevenson was taken aback at her reluctance. "He has to know."

"Sure Rick, I'll just tell him," Mary Katherine said in an exaggerated manner, "Sorry, Veeder, I tricked you into coming to the hospital. And oh, by the way, you might have a disease that might end your football career."

"You could wait until the next hit costs him a limb or his life!" Dr. Stevenson shot back. "I'm sure your family will appreciate your hesitancy then!"

"That's not fair, Rick!"

"I'm sorry, MK," Dr. Stevenson said with compassion. "I didn't mean that."

"Yes, you did." Mary Katherine fell back against the wall, rolled her eyes, and let out a big sigh. "And I deserved it."

"He has an appointment in the morning." Dr. Stevenson touched her arm. "Get him there."

"With whom?"

"A friend." Dr. Stevenson handed her a sheet of paper. "She's a hematologist. One of the best."

"Did you explain the situation?"

"I explained the situation. She's seeing him on the QT."

Looking at the page, Mary Katherine shook her head back and forth. "He won't go."

"If he doesn't, you'll have to decide if keeping his secret is worth risking his life."

"Thanks for sugar coating it."

"I want you to realize the gravity of his condition."

"I get it, Rick," Mary Katherine shot back in anger. "I study medicine, but that doesn't make this any easier."

"I'm a doctor, MK. I have to honor his confidentiality. I'll just sign him out A.M.A."

Mary Katherine shook her head and rubbed her forehead with her fingers as the gravity of the situation sunk in. "But I'm his sister and not bound by confidentiality."

"You're not in a great position, MK. I don't envy you."

"He'll make the appointment, Rick." Mary Katherine let out a big sigh and ran her hands through her hair. "I'll make sure he is there in the morning."

CHAPTER 31

Veeder sat on the examination table, lost in his thoughts, while Mary Katherine sat in a chair against the wall. They said very little to each other after she told him about his platelet count and what it meant regarding his life. She told him that ITP was a new discovery but that doctors were working hard to understand the disease.

Veeder appreciated her knowledge of the disease but he rebuffed the information. He was angry at first, but as time passed, he didn't believe any of this was possible. He refused to believe the test results were accurate. He believed it was a false result and the blood draw they had just taken would prove he was fine.

He refused to believe this nightmare could be his new reality because it would mean the end to his dream of playing in the National Football League. He had worked hard to prepare his mind and body for the rigors of playing football. But as he sat on the examination table, staring at the medical posters covering the walls, he saw the dream of playing in the NFL slipping through his fingers.

Time crept as they waited for the doctor. Veeder's anxiety magnified. Mary Katherine tried telling a couple of jokes to lighten the mood, but Veeder never smiled. He wished Anna was with him. Her strength and patient resolve calmed him in difficult times. She was the rock in his life who had always helped him pick up the pieces when everything fell apart.

The door opened. Dr. Abbott came into the room, walked over to Veeder, and held out her hand. "Good Morning, Mr. McLean. I'm Dr. Abbott."

"Please call me, Veeder." He shook her hand and tried his best to size up the five-foot-seven doctor who had her hair pulled back into a ponytail. "This is my sister, MK."

"Mary Katherine," she said, standing up to shake Dr. Abbott's hand. "Thank you for seeing us on short notice."

"I'm sorry it took so long." Dr. Abbott pulled a stool over to the examination table.

"No worries, Doc," Veeder said.

"I was up early this morning thinking about your case and as I was thinking…"

"That he had gotten a false result on the blood tests last night?" Veeder interrupted.

"The thought crossed my mind," Dr. Abbott responded, giving Veeder a frustrated stare for interrupting. "But as I was going over your case, it didn't add up."

"That is what I told MK."

"So we just ran the test again and after looking at your results this morning…"

"Either it was a false test last night?" Veeder interrupted. "Or it's fallen further today?"

"You're not a patient person, are you, Veeder?" Dr. Abbott was agitated.

"No, Doc, I'm not."

"But he's trying hard to work on that." Mary Katherine said, shooting Veeder an icy glare.

"Right, well, keep working on that," Dr. Abbott said, opening the file she was holding.

"We will," Mary Katherine responded, trying to cut through the tension in the room.

"As I was saying. I went through the results and the notes Dr. Stevenson faxed to me and Veeder, I am sorry. It is pretty clear. You have idiopathic thrombocytopenic purpura."

"That's ITP, isn't it?"

"Yes." Dr. Abbott looked up from her notes. "You have ITP."

"My results?" Veeder's demeanor deflated.

"They went down. You're at four."

"So where do we go from here, Dr. Abbott?" Mary Katherine interjected, moving closer to Veeder, and holding his hand for support.

"First of all, Veeder, do you understand what ITP is?"

"MK tried to explain it to me last night. I understand the basics."

"ITP is a disorder that affects your platelets." Dr. Abbott said, doing her best to simplify the information. "Basically, your body's immune system thinks your platelets are a virus. In a nutshell, your body is attacking itself.

"A normal person has between one hundred fifty thousand and four hundred fifty thousand platelets per microliter. You currently have four thousand. Or as we commonly say, your platelet count is four."

"Why do you do that?"

"We drop the thousand."

"So any number you say, I should multiply it by a thousand?"

"Yes."

"And four is bad?"

"It is very bad," Dr. Abbott said, staring at him with a concerned look. "Platelets are vitally important."

"And the risks when my platelet count is this low?"

"At your current level, you risk internal bleeding and you risk having a cut that won't stop bleeding because there aren't enough platelets to form a clot."

"Why do I have the rash then?"

"The rash on your body is called petechiae. Those round dots indicate that you are bleeding internally. If you ever see those again, you need to get medical treatment immediately."

"That doesn't sound good."

"The good news is that ITP is treatable."

"How long will it take, Doc? I have the biggest football game of my life in two weeks," Veeder said, hope welling up inside of him.

"I said 'treatable', Veeder." Dr. Abbott paused and collected her thoughts. "There is no cure for ITP. It is a chronic condition you will have for the rest of your life. You will have periods of remission, but ITP isn't something we can cure in a couple of days."

"But I have the national championship in two weeks."

"You won't be playing in that game," Dr. Abbott said, ignoring her bedside manner as she delivered the news. "Depending on your response to treatment, you most likely will never play football again."

"That's ridiculous, Doc," Veeder chuckled, dismissing her claims altogether. "I have worked my whole life to get to this point. I find it hard to believe my career is over because of a few platelets."

"You don't get it, Veeder," Dr. Abbott barked, frustration getting the best of her. "You're platelets are fatally low. You could lose a leg or an arm if you take the wrong hit. And if I'm being honest, you could die if you took a horrific hit. Is a football game worth your life?"

Silence gripped the room. Dr. Abbott fought back the anger from welling up inside of her. Mary Katherine was silent. She had no words. Her brother had crossed a line in his arrogance. She wanted to give Dr. Abbott a high-five for dropping a dose of reality in his lap. At the same time, though, she also felt sad for Veeder. Everything he had worked for his entire life had just been taken away from him.

"So what do we do now, Dr. Abbott?" Mary Katherine asked, breaking the awkward silence resonating throughout the room.

"I should admit your brother and keep him under my care until his platelet count improves."

"I can't be admitted, Doc.," Veeder said. "Isn't there anything else we can do?"

"I said I should admit you, but I am not," Dr. Abbott said with compassion. "I promised Dr. Stevenson we would handle this quietly."

"What's next, Dr. Abbott?" Mary Katherine asked.

"I ordered a platelet transfusion which your brother will get in our infusion lab today. A nurse will be in shortly to get you ready for the procedure."

"What do I do after the transfusion?" Veeder asked, deflated.

"I am prescribing Decadron. It's a high dose of steroids. You will take it for the next five days." Dr. Abbott paused. "Do nothing for the next five days. Just take your meds, sit, and relax."

"You want me to sit and do nothing?"

"Yes."

"Why?"

"Because you're going to come back here next Monday morning and if the steroids work, we should see your numbers go up."

"And if they don't go up?"

"We'll cross that bridge when we get to it."

"Thank you, Dr. Abbott, we'll be here next Monday morning," Mary Katherine interjected before Veeder could say something insensitive.

"Look, Veeder." Dr. Abbott said, looking at him with compassion. "I understand your situation. I do. It sucks."

"It is what it is," Veeder said, trying to downplay the news.

"Be that as it may." Dr. Abbott smiled. "Let's see if we can't get your platelet count stabilized."

"And if we do?" Veeder asked.

"Then we can talk about what your options are concerning football," Dr. Abbott said, letting down her guard. "Don't give up hope. If you respond well to treatment, the path could be much brighter than it currently appears."

"Thanks, Doc.," Veeder said.

"The nurse will be here shortly." Dr. Abbott stood and left the room.

The nurse came into the examination room and escorted Veeder to the infusion lab while Mary Katherine went to get coffee. The nurse had Veeder sit in a chair, closed the privacy curtain, and took his vitals. She put an IV in his arm and gave him a dose of Benadryl. When the platelets arrived, the infusion began.

Veeder sat in the infusion lab, lost in thought. Still, in a state of denial, he couldn't believe this was how his football career would end. His own body, of all things, would end up being the thing that derailed all of his dreams. He saw the irony in the situation but didn't want to acknowledge or accept it. Not yet anyway. He would rebound and be ready to go in a week.

When the infusion was complete, Mary Katherine helped Veeder walk to his truck. While Mary Katherine drove, Veeder started to complain of being ice cold. His teeth chattered and he complained he was freezing, inside his body. He pulled his arms close, trying to warm himself. Mary Katherine turned up the heat in the truck, but it didn't help. Veeder's body was reacting to the infusion and Mary Katherine could do nothing but watch him suffer.

Mary Katherine knew it was important to start the medication as soon as possible. She was frustrated the nurses hadn't given Veeder a dose at the hospital. She pulled into the pharmacy, ran in to get the medications, came back to the truck with a bottle of water, and made Veeder take the first dose. Then she drove back to his apartment.

Mary Katherine helped Veeder into his apartment. He sat down on the couch and she covered him with blankets before going into the kitchen to make soup. She gave him the soup and he was grateful. He felt a little better, but he was still cold.

She decided to stay overnight to monitor Veeder's reaction to the infusion. She wanted to be there if he needed anything. She wanted to call their mother, grandmother, Anna—someone, anyone who could bring Veeder comfort during this uncertain time but didn't. It was not her place to share the news. It was not her decision to tell anyone. She had promised to respect Veeder's privacy.

She wasn't sure Veeder had accepted the reality of what was happening to him, so she knew he wasn't ready to share the news with anyone yet. He needed time to grieve. He needed time to accept. Until he was ready, she had to be willing to remain silent.

Veeder sat on the couch, bundled up under the blankets, flipping through the channels on the television until he found an old football movie. Mary Katherine grabbed a bag of potato chips and sat down on the couch to watch the movie. As they came to the end of "Brian's Song," a movie about a Wake Forest Football player who was diagnosed with terminal cancer after becoming a professional football player, she realized tears were rolling down his face.

"Am I going to die, MK?" Veeder was scared, contemplating his own mortality.

"Veeder, no." Tears formed in Mary Katherine's eyes. Her heart broke. She held his hand. "You're going to live a long life, baby brother."

"But the doctor said it was possible."

"You were frustrating her."

"I do that a lot, don't I?"

"Yes, you do," Mary Katherine said, laughing through her tears. "It's part of your charm."

"It's what I did to Anna, didn't I?"

"No, Veeder," Mary Katherine said with compassion. "You and Anna have your own demons to work through."

"She left though."

"She still loves you."

"Thanks, MK, but I think she's going to move on without me."

"Call her."

"Not now." Veeder looked at Mary Katherine, tears in his eyes. "Not because of this. ITP can't be the reason."

"You don't have to tell her about the ITP."

"Then there's no reason to call. She needs her space."

"Tell her you love her, Veeder. Fight for her."

"I do love her."

"So call her." Mary Katherine said, taking a deep breath, tears streaming down her cheeks. "That's all she wants to hear."

Veeder wiped away Mary Katherine's tears. "If I die, MK…"

"No, Veeder." Mary Katherine interrupted, pulling her brother into a tight embrace, and resting her chin on his head. "You're not going to die. I won't let you."

"If I die, MK," Veeder continued, "will you make sure Anna knows I never stopped loving her?"

"You're not going to die, Veeder."

"But if I do, promise me you'll tell her," Veeder said through his tears. "Liz knew JJ loved her and it gave her closure. I don't want Anna to ever wonder, I want her to know."

"I promise, Veeder." Mary Katherine sobbed. "I promise."

"Thank you."

"But you're going to live a long life. You'll see. I promise."

"I hope so." Veeder felt a peaceful calm wash over him. He rested in Mary Katherine's arms. "Thank you, MK. I love you."

"I love you, too, baby brother." Mary Katherine kissed the top of his head. After a while, Veeder fell asleep. Mary Katherine eased her brother onto the couch, covered him with blankets, walked back to his bedroom, knelt on the floor, and prayed. "Please, Lord, don't let my baby brother die."

She prayed for another fifteen minutes. Tears rolled down her cheeks. When she finished, she climbed up onto the bed and cried herself to sleep.

CHAPTER 32

Veeder was the first one to arrive at Dr. Abbott's office. He checked in, had his blood drawn, and sat in a secluded room waiting for the results. The steroids had rejuvenated his energy level, and he was positive the results would show his platelet count was back to normal.

He sat in the waiting room perusing magazines. Boredom replaced enthusiasm, so he pulled his baseball cap down over his forehead, leaned back in the chair, rested against the wall, and closed his eyes.

Christmas had come and gone like it always had at the McLean homestead. Jill bought too many gifts and treated everyone like they were a child again. The family spent Christmas morning at church celebrating the birth of Jesus and later in the day, the family gathered at James and Colleen's house for dinner.

Over the weekend, Liam proposed to his girlfriend. Colin and Michael both announced that their wives were expecting. With so much good news, Veeder was able to blend into the background. His grandmother made a big deal about the national championship, but for the most part, the weekend was spent celebrating engagements and baby announcements.

Veeder saw Anna at church and talked to her for a few minutes. She was in a hurry to get home. He missed her and wanted to apologize, to take her for a cup of coffee so they could talk but he didn't want to push. It had been a couple of weeks, and if she still needed space, he didn't want to seem overbearing.

"Mr. McLean," nurse Tabitha said, sitting in the chair next to him.

"I'm sorry." Veeder opened his eyes, sitting up. "I was just resting my eyes."

"No worries, we have your test results."

"I'm feeling great." Veeder smiled. "I'm betting they went up."

"I wish that was the case," nurse Tabitha said, shaking her head. "The doctor wanted me to get you ready for another infusion."

"My numbers didn't go up?" Veeder was stunned by the news. He regretted not having Mary Katherine with him to process the information. She would know the right medical questions to ask.

"I'm sorry. They didn't."

"Not even a little?"

"No."

"Stayed the same?" Veeder started to panic. Mary Katherine told him about the function of platelets. So the news that his count had not gone up was disheartening.

"Your count is at three."

"Three?" Veeder was perplexed, shaking his head back and forth. "How can that be?"

"It happens."

"But I feel like I could run a marathon right now."

"That's the steroids giving you an energy boost."

"But it didn't do anything for my platelet count?"

"I'm sorry." Nurse Tabitha shook her head. "They didn't."

"What do we do now?" Veeder was defeated. He was positive he was on the road to recovery. This was not the news he expected.

"I spoke to Dr. Mecklenburg and he has decided…"

"Dr. Mecklenburg?" Veeder interrupted. "Wait a minute. Where's Dr. Abbott?"

"Dr. Abbott is not in today but her partner, Dr. Mecklenburg consulted with her when your test results came back."

"Dr. Abbott promised she would keep my medical condition under wraps. It's the only reason I agreed to see her."

"Well, Dr. Mecklenburg isn't going to tell anyone. He is bound by the same rules of confidentiality that Dr. Abbott has to follow."

"I knew I shouldn't have listened to MK," Veeder mumbled. "I should have waited."

"As I was saying, Dr. Abbott and Dr. Mecklenburg decided to start you on IVIg."

"IVIg?"

"Intravenous immunoglobulin. It is an intravenous medication that is used to increase a patient's platelet count."

"Intravenous?" Veeder was nervous. "Does that mean more needles?"

"Yes. I'm afraid so. It's an infusion."

"When do they want me to get this?"

"Today. Now. As soon as possible."

"And it will help?"

"It's the next course of treatment for ITP patients."

"Fine." Veeder agreed without anyone to consult. "Let's get this done."

Nurse Tabitha disappeared from the waiting room to take care of the arrangements. Veeder sat, getting angrier by the minute. He didn't know who he was mad at. He was just angry, and the more irritated he became, the more his paranoia about the news of his diagnosis becoming public was getting the best of him.

Nurse Tabitha returned to the waiting room and led Veeder to the infusion lab. It was an open room with twenty bays surrounding a nurse's station. He asked if there was a private room. When informed there was not, he raced into a corner seat, hat pulled low across his forehead. He pulled the separating sheet between the bays closed and tried to hide.

It was still early. There was only one other person in the lab, but when he found out he would be receiving his infusion over the next six hours, he grew more agitated. There would be more people throughout the day and his request for anonymity was becoming less of a reality.

Nurse Tabitha checked his vitals and prepared him for the infusion. It took a couple of attempts to find a vein. Veeder feared needles and every time they missed a vein, his anxiety rose with his frustration. He felt relieved when the IV was finally running; he just had to bide his time incognito until he could slip out of the hospital.

The day dragged. Veeder read magazines, listened to a television that was blaring, but he refused to open the curtain. He dozed off in the middle of the day and was awakened by an older doctor shaking his shoulders. Veeder opened his eyes and the gentleman smiled. "Sorry to wake you, Mr. McLean, I'm Dr. Mecklenburg."

"Veeder, please." He rubbed his eyes and sat up.

"Veeder it is," Dr. Mecklenburg said, shaking Veeder's hand. "The nurses said you had some questions."

"I do, Doc." Veeder paused. "I don't understand how my platelet count is at three. I took the meds all weekend like clockwork. Can you explain that to me?"

"Not everything we try is going to work. We start with the least invasive medical procedure, and we step up the treatment if it doesn't work."

"But I don't get it. I feel like a million dollars. I could run a marathon. How is it possible my numbers went down?"

"That was the steroids, Veeder."

"So the steroids did nothing?"

"They gave you a lot of energy, but they didn't help your platelet count."

"Is that a bad thing?"

"Are you asking me or Dr. Abbott?"

"Is there a difference of opinion?" Veeder asked, raising his eyebrows, concerned.

"In the treatment plan for you? Yes."

"What does that mean?" Veeder asked.

"Dr. Abbott and I do not agree on your treatment plan, but you're her patient. Not mine."

Veeder stared at Dr. Mecklenburg, trying to size him up. "Uh, do you care to elaborate, Doc?"

"That's a discussion for you and Dr. Abbott."

"No, it's not." Veeder grimaced and glared at Dr. Mecklenburg. "I want to know your opinion."

"Are you sure?"

"Yes."

"Well, I've been doing this a long time, Veeder. There are some cases where the only treatment plan is to remove your spleen."

"Woah, wait a minute." Held up his hands. "Remove my spleen?"

"Yes."

"Why would you remove my spleen? We haven't even discussed anything drastic yet."

"Dr. Abbott is committed to trying every possible method available before surgery."

Veeder shook his head in agreement. "I don't see any problems with that!"

"Most patients don't."

"But you do?"

"In your case, I don't see how the treatment plan is going to help you."

"Why not, Doc? What am I missing?"

"You had no response to the steroids. I think we are biding time until you have surgery."

"Because I had no response to the steroids, you want to take my spleen?"

"If these minor treatments were going to work, we would have seen a small bump with the steroids." Dr. Mecklenburg rubbed his hands together. "It wasn't a small dose she prescribed, Veeder. She gave your system a pretty good shot of medication."

"That doesn't make any sense."

"And as I said, you are not my patient. Dr. Abbott wants to exhaust all other measures before opting for surgery."

"So do I, Doc! I agree with her."

"So here we are." Dr. Mecklenburg said, looking at the IVIg bottle running into Veeder's arm. "This is the next step in the treatment plan."

Veeder was quiet, yet overwhelmed, trying to size up Dr. Mecklenburg. He didn't know what to think, but he didn't want surgery.

"Do you have any other questions for me?" Dr. Mecklenburg asked.

"No," Veeder said, dejected.

"Have a good afternoon, Veeder."

"Oh yeah, I'm having a blast, Doc," Veeder said, pointing at the infusion line running into his vein.

"I will be around all day if you need me." Dr. Mecklenburg got up, closed the privacy curtain, and walked away.

The rest of the day was uneventful. Nurse Tabitha came in to change Veeder's IVIg bottle when it ran dry. Other than that, he was alone, trying to envision every option and path for his life. He wasn't a quitter. He didn't believe in absolutes. He believed if you worked hard enough, anything was possible. He had proved it many times and planned on proving it again.

When the final bottle of IVIg ran dry, the nurse stepped through the curtain, took his vitals, and removed the needle from his arm. "Dr. Abbott wants to see you back here tomorrow."

"Why?"

"She wants to check your numbers."

"And if they're still down?"

"You'll be prepped for another infusion."

"So I have to get another infusion if this one doesn't take?"

"It is a process, Mr. McLean."

"Sounds like it." Veeder was frustrated. He had received a big dose of reality and he didn't like it.

"There's no rhyme or reason to it. Some people respond quickly. Others don't. We'll find out tomorrow morning."

"Thank you." Veeder gathered his things and pulled the baseball cap down over this forehead. "Is there a back way out of this place?"

"What?" Nurse Tabitha asked, confused by the request. "Why?"

"The waiting room must be full, and I am trying to keep a low profile."

"From whom?"

"You. Don't. Know?" Veeder asked, realizing his nurse had no clue who he was.

"Know what?"

"That's good," Veeder said, smiling. "I'd like to keep it that way."

"I'm confused."

"Let's just say I need to keep a low profile. Dr. Abbott knows all about it. Is there a less public way out of here?"

"Sit tight. I need to have a conversation with Dr. Abbott." Nurse Tabitha said, leaving the bay and pulling the privacy curtain closed. Veeder sat down and waited.

She came back a while later with a packet of papers and handed them to Veeder. "Here."

"What are these?"

"Your discharge papers."

"My discharge papers?"

"They contain all of the information from today, your appointment for tomorrow, and your official check out from the lab. Dr. Abbott said if you have any questions about the packet, she will go over them with you tomorrow."

Veeder looked through the packet. "Now what?"

"You go home."

"How?"

"The employee entrance."

"Is it private?"

"Not necessarily but it's less crowded than the waiting room."

"That works." Veeder picked up his belongings. "Let's go."

Nurse Tabitha opened the curtain, looked around the lab, and motioned for Veeder to follow. He kept his eyes low and his hat pulled down over his forehead, following the nurse out of the infusion lab. They walked down a couple of empty hallways before slipping into a stairwell. When they reached the bottom of the stairwell, she stopped.

"What's wrong?" Veeder asked, wondering why they had stopped.

"Nothing. Stay here. I'm going to check out the employee lounge."

"Why?"

"Because we have to pass through the lounge to get outside."

"Got it." Veeder stayed in the stairwell while nurse Tabitha slipped through the door and disappeared. Every second seemed like an eternity. He heard a couple of doctors talking as they walked down the stairs. He pressed his back against the wall and hid his face behind the magazine he was holding but the doctors left the stairwell a flight above him.

"Come on," nurse Tabitha said, opening the door and just about giving him a heart attack.

"Don't do that to me." Veeder caught his breath, holding onto his chest.

"Sorry." Nurse Tabitha stepped into the hallway and Veeder followed her. They slipped into the employee's lounge. There were a couple of nurses sitting on the couches watching television. One of the male nurses saw them enter the room.

"Tabitha, how was your weekend?"

"Can't talk right now." She crossed the lounge with Veeder following close behind. "Be back in a minute."

"Wait," the male nurse said, excited. "Is that Veeder McLean with you?"

"No, John. Just a friend," she responded, continuing across the lounge. She had no idea who her patient was, but her friend did. It was the exact situation they were trying to avoid.

"It is." John jumped up and started after them. "That's Veeder McLean."

Nurse Tabitha raced down the hall, opened the door, and Veeder passed.

"Thank you, Tabitha," Veeder said, racing out the door.

"You're welcome." Tabitha closed the door, stopping John before he could chase Veeder into the parking lot. Veeder was in the clear. He made his way to his truck, climbed in, and let out a long sigh of relief.

CHAPTER 33

It was a beautiful night. Anna sat on her front porch, wrapped in a blanket, swaying on the swing, and staring up at the stars. Her life had changed so much over the past couple of weeks. She was learning so much about herself. Her heart ached at Christmas when she saw Veeder. It took every ounce of willpower to avoid throwing her arms around him. Part of her wanted to ask if they could start over again, but she was the one who said she needed space. *Could he ever forgive her for that?*

Anna was conflicted. She needed time to think and to sort out her feelings. She had to figure out what her future looked like. With graduation looming, she had to figure out if her future involved Veeder. That was a tough question. She had been with him since eighth grade. She was happy to have a few more weeks to relax before her final semester of school but wasn't any closer to knowing what she wanted out of life.

She loved God. God came first. She believed that to have a successful relationship, her husband was going to have to respect her faith. He would have to love and worship Jesus.

"Penny for your thoughts?" Pastor Kelly asked, standing by the porch swing holding two mugs.

"Hey, Dad." Anna smiled.

"I made you a cup of hot chocolate." Pastor Kelly said, handing Anna one of the mugs.

"Thank you." Anna blew on the hot liquid and took a sip. "That hits the spot."

"I thought it might."

"How do you always know what I need?"

"I've been making you hot chocolate since you were a little girl. It's your comfort drink when something is bothering you."

"Thanks, Dad. I love you."

"Mind if I sit?"

"Please." Anna moved over so her father could sit on the porch swing.

"So how are you holding up?"

"I'm fine."

"Are you really?" Pastor Kelly raised his eyebrows and gave her a sideways glance.

"I just have a lot on my mind."

"I don't mean to pry, but your mother and I are worried about you."

"There's nothing to worry about."

"If you say so, but you sure do spend a lot of time by yourself these days." Pastor Kelly had a twinge of sadness in his voice. "You know you can talk to me about anything."

"I know. I just have to figure some things out."

"About Veeder?"

"No, Dad." Anna paused and stared into the night. "About me. About life."

"Well, when you figure it all out, please let me know. I'm forty-eight and still haven't figured life out yet." Pastor Kelly laughed.

"That's not what I mean." Anna playfully pushed her father's shoulder.

"I know." Pastor Kelly chuckled, putting an arm around Anna's shoulders.

"I'm trying to figure out what I want to do in life, who I want to spend my life with, and what my priorities are."

"Wow." Pastor Kelly raised an eyebrow. "That's a lot to ponder."

"You're telling me."

"So what have you figured out so far?"

"Not much." Anna put her head on her father's shoulder.

"Welcome to the club."

"I thought I had it all figured out." Anna smiled, describing her vision. "Veeder and I would get married. He'd play professional football and I would work in a local hospital. We'd have a bunch of kids and we'd grow old together. Happy and in love."

"That's a pretty good dream, Anna."

"Not anymore."

"So what changed?"

"Me, Dad. I changed." Anna took a sip of her hot chocolate and stared out into the night.

"Was it his lack of faith?"

"I used to think I could live with Veeder's atheism, but I don't think I can. How do people love someone who doesn't love God?"

"A lot of people do it."

"How do I, Dad?"

"That's a tough question. I wish I had a simple answer for you, but I don't."

"That doesn't help."

"Life is hard, Anna. Relationships are harder."

"You're telling me."

"Do you know one of the most difficult passages in the Bible that young married couples have a hard time with before and after marriage?"

"I can think of a bunch. You mean there is just one?"

"Ephesians five verses twenty-one to twenty-five. Where Paul talks about submission."

"Well." Anna chuckled, rolling her eyes. "If you think about it, it sounds like a good deal for the guys."

"Is it, though?"

"It's the reason people get angry about the passage."

"You're right about that, Anna. Because they only focus on the part where Paul talks about women submitting to their husbands."

"Isn't that the point Paul is trying to make?"

"Actually, if you look at the whole passage, no. He's not."

"He's not?"

"Paul's words take on a much more loving image than we assume because the passage is about mutual submission in the loving grace of the Father."

"How so?"

"Christ gave himself to Father God in full submission and in full reverence. He did the will of the Father as He carried out His miracles. He shared His love, kindness, and compassion with the world. The passage is an illustration of what working together in perfect unity and relationship looks like. How in the confines of marriage, we can strive to live by the example Christ set forth for us."

"That still sounds like a great deal for the husband."

"That's how most women feel about it, but they miss the most important part of the text."

"Which is?"

"Men have to mutually submit. He must put his wife first much like Christ loved the church, his bride."

"I don't follow."

"Christ came to share His abundant love with the church. He washed the feet of the church, He healed the sick and those with diseases, He poured his heart out for the church, His bride, with all of His heart, and when the time came, He died for the church.

"You see, Anna, the passage isn't about dominance or control. It is about honoring one another with all your heart, mind, and soul. It is about being gentle, humble, and kind. It is about always putting the needs of the other person first and caring for the other person with your life.

"We are supposed to give ourselves to our spouse because it is the example Christ set for us. He paved the way. We just need to follow His lead and follow Him. And if we do, He will show us the way to walk in our lives. He will fill our lives and our hearts with what we truly need." Pastor Kelly pulled Anna into him and hugged her.

"How does that help Veeder and me, Dad?"

"Maybe if you just love Veeder with gentleness, humbleness, and kindness, God will fill his heart with what he truly needs, with what you keep praying for."

"And if I do and Veeder never comes to God, then what?"

"I don't know, sweetheart. That's a tough question." Pastor Kelly kissed the top of her head. "I guess you pray and ask God for His guidance."

"That sounds like a big gamble on my part."

"That's why they call it faith."

"That's a giant leap of faith, Dad, and I don't know if I am ready to make that leap."

"What does your heart tell you?"

"I believe I am supposed to marry him but if he doesn't love God, how could we ever have a successful marriage?"

"If you choose that path, Anna, I won't tell you it will be easy. Because it won't."

"Thanks, Dad. That doesn't help at all."

"But you would do the same thing if you married Veeder as you would if you married a believer. You submit yourself to your husband as to Christ. You share the life of Christ, the love of Christ, and the grace of Christ with your husband. Then you pray and let God work miracles in your marriage."

"Why is this so hard?" Anna asked with a deep sigh. "I thought life got easier when you got older."

Pastor Kelly laughed at the insinuation that life was supposed to get easier when people got older. "If I had a dollar every time someone said that to me, I'd be a millionaire."

"I'm serious, Dad."

"Anna, this is just the beginning of your life. You haven't even scratched the surface of hard yet."

"Great, Dad, that makes me excited about the future." Anna chuckled.

"You should be. It will be an amazing future."

"I don't know about amazing, but it sure is getting tougher."

"And when it gets tough, I will always be here for you." Pastor Kelly kissed the top of her head and gave her another hug. "You never have to go through anything alone. I will always be here for you."

"Thanks, Dad." Anna returned the hug and rested her head on Pastor Kelly's shoulder. The two sat on the porch admiring the stars illuminating the night sky, reminding them of the greatness of God's wonder and majesty.

CHAPTER 34

⟶⟿

Nurse Tabitha met Veeder in the parking lot and ushered him into the building through the employee entrance. She had done some research on who he was and helping him keep his anonymity was a gift she could provide. She checked him into the hematology lab from the secluded waiting area, took him to get his blood drawn, and walked with him to an exam room without running into any people. The routine seemed choreographed. Even though it wasn't, Veeder appreciated the effort she was taking on his behalf.

Veeder was reading when Dr. Abbott walked in and closed the door. "Good morning, Veeder."

"Good Morning, Doc." He put down the magazine. "Where were you yesterday?"

"I'm not in this office every day. Dr. Mecklenburg consulted with me about your results."

"I thought you understood that I was trying to be inconspicuous."

"Yes. I understand your need to hide your diagnosis from everybody. I, on the other hand, am more concerned about your health." Dr. Abbott was irritated by his attitude.

"But a public transfusion room, Doc? Really?"

"Sorry, Veeder. Nothing I can do about that."

"There aren't any private rooms I could have used?"

"They are for patients who need them. You don't need that level of care."

"I am trying to stay out of the limelight here." Veeder was angrier than he was before. "I don't need my fans or my team knowing anything about this!"

"I don't care about your popularity," Dr. Abbott shot back. "I care about your health. Whether everyone knows about your diagnosis or not is of no concern to me. You getting healthy; that's my priority."

"You need to care about my wishes!"

"Frankly, Veeder, I don't have time for your attitude. If you want someone who will work her butt off to provide you top-notch care, then stay. I promise I will provide world-class medical treatment. If you don't want quality care, there's the door," Dr. Abbott said, pointing at the door. "You are free to find someone more concerned about your celebrity status than your health, but quite frankly, that isn't me! Are we clear on that?"

"Yes," Veeder mumbled, stunned by Dr. Abbott's response.

"Are we clear?" Dr. Abbott demanded.

"Yes, Doc."

"Good!" Dr. Abbott paused and took a deep breath. "Now do you want the good news?"

"There's good news?"

"Some." Dr. Abbott smiled.

"How good?"

"Your count is at seventy-seven this morning."

"That's good, right?" Veeder tried to temper his excitement.

"It's better." Dr. Abbott was more reserved than Veeder had hoped. "It's a good start, but it's still not one hundred fifty."

"But it's not fatal."

"No. It is not fatally low."

"So what do we do now, Doc?"

"Nothing."

"Nothing?" Veeder was flummoxed. "I don't understand. You said my numbers were better. Don't we have to do something to make them better?"

"Not today. Now we wait and see if the IVIg will help your body self-correct."

"I'm not following you, Doc."

"Come back here in two days and we'll test your numbers again."

"We have to do this again?"

"We'll be seeing a lot of each other in the months ahead. We need to make sure your numbers keep going up."

"And if they go up, can I rejoin my football team?"

"Veeder, I am going to be honest."

"That's never a good thing, Doc."

"My recommendation is for you to stop playing football." Dr. Abbott was sympathetic. She understood what her advice meant for Veeder's life. "The risk of playing football is too great. You could lose a limb or much worse, your life."

A wave of sadness washed over him. "Doc, football is who I am. I don't know what else to do with my life."

"It might be time you start thinking about what life looks like without football because the time might have come."

"You mean, I'm done. There is no way I could ever play again?"

"I didn't say that." Dr. Abbott collected her thoughts. "It wouldn't be impossible but without full remission and a lot of medical intervention, I don't see how you could safely play. Or how a team would take on that kind of liability."

"What would I do?" Veeder was stunned.

"You could coach." Dr. Abbott tried to help Veeder see a world beyond football. "You could be a commentator on NSBEN. I'm sure there are many ways you can be part of the game."

Veeder and Dr. Abbott spent a long time talking about what ITP would mean in his life. She showed compassion while answering his questions and gave him a pep talk to help him see there was a whole world for him to conquer. When they were done talking, Nurse Tabitha helped Veeder escape the hospital through the employee entrance. She made sure his anonymity remained intact and that he got to his car without being recognized.

Once he was outside, Veeder walked to his truck, jumped in, and started it up. He looked at his reflection in the mirror and thought about the conversation he had just had with Dr. Abbott. He appreciated her concerns and her insights. He also heard her say he was better. He smiled. "She doesn't know what she's talking about. I'm fine!"

Veeder drove straight to War Memorial Stadium where he spent the next couple of days studying film, lifting weights, and practicing with the team. It had been his goal to win the national championship, and he wasn't going to let the opportunity slip through his fingers. Dedicated, he worked harder than he had ever worked in the past, leading by example. He was the first one into the facility in the morning and the last to leave at the end of the day. His teammates and coaches rallied around his enthusiasm and dedication. They were focused. They were ready.

After practice on Thursday night, Veeder picked up dinner and drove to his apartment. He walked through his front door, threw his keys on the table, and hit the play button on his answering machine, before sitting down to eat.

"Good Morning, Mr. McLean. This is nurse Tabitha. You missed your appointment this morning. Dr. Abbott would like to see you before the holiday weekend. She has scheduled you for labs tomorrow morning so we can get you into the infusion lab if we need to. Please call us back to confirm."

BEEP

"Veeder," Mary Katherine said. "Where are you? Dr. Abbott's office called me. She said you didn't show up for your appointment this morning. Where are you?"

Veeder forgot he had listed Mary Katherine as his emergency contact and gave the doctor permission to share all medical information with her. Dr. Abbott's office must have called her when he didn't show up for his appointment. *Oh well*, he thought to himself, shrugged his shoulders, and kept eating.

BEEP

"Veeder! Jack Johnson from NSBEN. I have a couple of questions I want to ask you. Call me back."

Veeder raised his eyebrows. *Why would Jack Johnson be calling?* He couldn't think Veeder would give him a ridiculous quote that Boulder Mountain Tech would use as motivation in the national championship.

BEEP

"Veeder, it's Mom, the farm is being overrun with reporters. Your father is chasing them off. Can you call me please?"

Veeder's heart fell into the pit of his stomach when he heard his mother's voice. He hated lying to his family. But he couldn't tell them about his diagnosis, they would never understand his decision to play. They would make him quit. *Guilt be damned!* This was the pinnacle of his career. He had a right to be selfish.

BEEP

"Veeder, it's Dr. Abbott, I don't usually make house calls but this is important. It is critical I see you tomorrow morning. Please call my office to confirm."

BEEP

"Veeder." His heart stopped, recognizing the angelic voice. "It's Anna. I was hoping we could talk. I know you're busy with practice, I don't know, maybe I just needed to hear your voice. When you get back home, call me. We need to talk. Good Luck on Tuesday. Bye."

Veeder wanted to call Anna back, but he couldn't. He needed to remain focused on the national championship. He couldn't be distracted and Anna, as much as he loved her, was a distraction. If she called to break it off, he'd be devastated. If she wanted to get back together, he'd be elated. Either way, it would take his focus off of football and for the next five days, he had to be fixated on the big game. He had to be. Anna was going to have to wait.

The messages kept coming, Mary Katherine, the doctor's office, his parents, and reporters. For twenty minutes, Veeder sat and ate, unfazed. He blocked the ITP out of his mind. His numbers were good on Tuesday morning and that was good enough for him. He felt guilty about dodging their phone calls, but the next few days were all about the national championship. His doctor and the ITP could wait. He would call them back on the 5th.

Veeder took all he could bear, he ripped the answering machine out of the wall. He didn't want to be bothered anymore. He had to stay focused, and these calls were just another distraction.

Veeder was tired. He got up from the table, threw away his garbage, and went to bed.

CHAPTER 35

I t was pitch black outside when Veeder walked to the front door of War Memorial Stadium. He slipped inside and made his way to the weight room. He put a compact disc in the sound system, turned up the volume, and started working out. Veeder was running on the treadmill a little before seven when one of the assistant coaches walked up to him. "Coach wants to see you in his office."

"Now?" Veeder continued to run.

"Right now."

"Why?"

"Don't know." He shrugged his shoulders. "He just sent me to find you."

"Can it wait?"

"No."

"I have three more miles to run."

"Coach said now!"

"Fine." Veeder shut down the treadmill, grabbed his towel, left the weight room, walked to Coach Mercer's office, and knocked on the door.

"Come in," Coach Mercer yelled from inside the office.

"You wanted to see me, Coach?" Veeder noticed that the offensive coordinator, Dillon Bentley, and the quarterback coach, Marcus Alderman, were sitting around the desk with stern looks on their faces.

"Sit down, Veeder," Coach Mercer said. Veeder sat down in the empty chair. "What time did you get to the facility today?"

"Four forty-five." Veeder looked around at his coaches.

"Was it a media madhouse out there when you came in this morning?"

"No, sir. The place was deserted."

"Have you looked outside at all?"

"No, sir. Why would I?"

"Because it's a media frenzy."

"We're playing in the national championship, Coach. Isn't that to be expected?"

"I have never seen it like this for a national championship game. Have you ever seen it like this Dillon?"

"No, Coach, I haven't," Coach Bentley replied, glaring at Veeder.

"You, Marcus?"

"Nope," Coach Alderman replied.

"It's crazy, Veeder."

"Media hype, Coach," Veeder said. "They're just doing their jobs."

"Except for the fact that I am perplexed by the questions they keep asking me."

"What are they asking you about, Coach?" Veeder's nerves welled up inside his stomach.

"Do you have something you want to tell me, Veeder?" Coach Mercer's tone was accusatory. He leaned forward, placing his arms on the desk.

"No, Coach. Just preparing for the game."

"What time is it, Marcus?"

"Six fifty-nine," Coach Alderman replied.

"Maybe this will help jog your memory, Veeder." Coach Mercer picked up a remote control and turned on the television. It was tuned to NSBEN and at the top of the hour, the NSBEN Sports News theme played on the screen. When the opening credits finished, the cameras zoomed in on the anchor sitting at the desk.

"Good morning, sports fans. Kenny Berman with you this morning and we start the day with breaking news out of Chapel Hill University where we'll go live to Jack Johnson who is reporting from War Memorial Stadium. Jack…"

"Thanks, Kenny." The image on the screen switched to Jack Johnson standing in front of the stadium holding notes in his hands. "The news out of Chapel Hill is quiet at the moment, but rumors are circulating that Cobras star quarterback, Veeder McLean, has spent the better part of the week at CHU Medical Center for an undisclosed reason. A few patients claimed to have seen McLean in the infusion labs receiving some sort of treatment. The medical personnel at the hospital have refused to comment.

"We tried to reach out to Veeder McLean for comment yesterday, but he did not return any of our calls. With the national championship just a few days away, this can't be good news for fans, players, and University officials because their star quarterback may be facing a medical situation that might disqualify him from the game."

"What is Coach Mercer saying about the health of their star quarterback?" Kenny Berman asked, a split-screen between the studio and Chapel Hill popping up on the TV.

"We have been unable to reach Coach Mercer for comment. We tried reaching out to the administration at the University, but they referred us to the Athletic Director who was unaware of any medical issues involving Veeder McLean. He referred all questions to his head coach," Jack Johnson replied.

"It sounds like this story may shake things up in Chapel Hill on Tuesday night," Kenny Berman added.

"It's still early, Kenny. This story came to my attention yesterday and the team has been short on answers. We hope to have more on this story later in the day."

"Thanks, Jack," Kenny Berman said, the camera focused on him in the studio. "That was Jack Johnson reporting live from Chapel Hill University where it looks like the Y2K bug is about to bring down its first system of the New Year."

Coach Mercer turned off the television. All eyes bored into Veeder's skull. Veeder was stunned. He was still staring at the blank screen while his heart pounded against his chest cavity. His entire world came crumbling down and he had no idea what to say.

"So, Veeder." Coach Mercer's voice was slow and methodical. "Do you have anything you would like to share with me?"

Looking dejected, Veeder took a deep breath and looked into Coach Mercer's eyes. "I don't suppose we can all forget we saw the report?"

"Damn it, Veeder!" Coach Bentley slammed his hand down on the desk. "You have been playing fast and loose with your cavalier attitude since day one! Grow up, son! This is serious!"

"Dillon, please." Coach Mercer put his hand up to stop his assistant coach's outburst.

"Come on, Ray, this is ridiculous!"

"Dillon, please!" Coach Mercer barked. "Let him speak."

Veeder rubbed his hands across his face and through his hair while his coaches argued. There was no way they were going to let this go. There was no way he could avoid the truth about his health and now that Jack Johnson could smell blood in the water, he knew he was about to get attacked by the media.

"Veeder." Coach Mercer exercised a calm resolve. "I can't help you unless you tell me what is going on."

Veeder sat back in his chair, choked down anger and fear, took a deep breath, and leaned forward. "Yes, Coach, it's true. I spent a couple of days before and after Christmas at the Medical Center."

"You didn't have the flu?"

"No, sir." Veeder hung his head and stared at the floor.

"He's a liar, Ray!" Coach Bentley yelled. "Kick him off the team!"

"That's enough, Dillon," Coach Mercer said. "You and Marcus need to leave."

"Why?" Dillon threw up his arms in frustration. "What did we do, Ray?"

"I've had enough of your outbursts. It's not helping the situation."

"He lied to us, Ray!" Coach Bentley yelled, pointing at Veeder. "Don't you get that?"

"What I know is that if you don't leave right now, I might be down a quarterback next Tuesday, but I will definitely be down a coach!" Coach Mercer stood up and pointed to the door. "Now get out!"

Coach Bentley glared at Coach Mercer, but he knew better than to challenge him. He stood up, knocking his chair into the desk before storming out of the office with Coach Alderman following close behind.

"Sorry, Coach."

"For Coach Bentley?" Coach Mercer laughed before sitting down. "Don't be."

"It's my fault."

"Bentley's always been a hothead. If it wasn't for me putting up with his antics, he'd be coaching some pee wee team back in Texas because no one else can stand him." Coach Mercer leaned forward in his chair, placing his arms on his desk. "Now what's going on with you?"

"I have a condition called ITP."

"What's that?"

"It's a platelet disorder. It messes up my ability to stop bleeding."

"That sounds serious. Do your parents know?"

"Not yet." Veeder was gripped with guilt and shame.

"Son, you have to tell your parents. They love you and will support you through this."

"I will. I am supposed to meet with my doctor. I will call them after I meet with her."

"It may be too late. They may already know."

"I know." Veeder shook his head back and forth.

"Why did you lie to me, Veeder?" Coach Mercer asked. "Why didn't you just tell me the truth when you found out about your condition?"

"Because I knew you wouldn't let me play on Tuesday night."

"What makes you think that?"

"Because my doctor doesn't want me to play."

"I need to speak with him."

"Her," Veeder said, correcting his coach.

"Fine." Coach Mercer paused. "I need to speak with her."

Veeder and Coach Mercer talked about the situation. Veeder agreed to let Coach Mercer talk to Dr. Abbott. After she had some harsh words for him, she agreed to speak to Coach Mercer. Veeder, as they had agreed, stepped into the hallway while they both spoke.

He paced the hallway with guilt, shame, worry, and fear pulsing through his veins. He hated waiting. He hated not knowing. Sitting outside Coach Mercer's office felt like an eternity. All he had worked for his entire life, everything he had accomplished, and how much this team had fought all season came down to this one phone call. He was six or seven feet away, separated by a door, and a vivid imagination.

Coach Bentley and Coach Alderman came back down the hall and disappeared into Coach Mercer's office. Veeder knew the phone call with Dr. Abbott had ended but had no idea what had been decided. He sat down in a chair, lowered his eyes to the floor, placed his elbows on his knees, folded his fingers together in front of him, and continued to wait. Twenty-five minutes passed before Coach Bentley and Coach Alderman stepped back into the hallway.

"You can go in now," Coach Bentley said before he continued down the hall.

Staring at the floor, Veeder took a couple of deep breaths. He was frozen with panic. The time he was waiting for was here and as much as he wanted this whole morning to end, he didn't like the uncertainty of the situation. Taking one more deep breath, he slapped his palms against his knees, stood up, and walked into Coach Mercer's office.

Coach Mercer said solemnly, "Have a seat, son."

"That doesn't sound good."

"Have you ever known me to beat around the bush, Veeder?"

"Never."

"So I am not going to start now." Coach Mercer paused. "It's not good."

"Coach, I am fine. I can play." Veeder pleaded but Coach Mercer held up his hand.

"Your doctor doesn't seem to think that's the case."

"We'll find another doctor."

"No, Veeder, we won't. Dr. Abbott is the only doctor I will consult in this matter."

"Coach, there are other doctors who will clear me," Veeder appealed. "You know that."

"Veeder." Coach Mercer choked back his emotions. He knew there was any number of unscrupulous doctors who would clear Veeder to play, but Coach Mercer wouldn't allow it. This condition was serious and he refused to put his star quarterback's life in danger. "You and I have not always seen eye to eye, but you are one heck of a competitor…"

"Coach," Veeder interrupted. "Please don't do this."

"You are a warrior, son. I don't think there is anything you can't do on a football field and there isn't anyone who can stop you. It's ironic that your body is the only thing that can."

"Coach." Veeder fought back the tears. "Please. You have to let me play. Football is my life."

"And that's the very reason I can't let you play. You could die on that field."

"I'm willing to accept that risk."

"I'm not." Coach Mercer shook his head and collected his thoughts. "I couldn't live with myself if anything happened to you."

"Coach, the National Championship…"

"Is just a game," Coach Mercer interrupted.

"No, Coach. It's my life."

"It's just a game, Veeder. It's just a game," Coach said with reverence. "I don't know if you will ever play again but you have so much to live for, I can't let you throw your life away for a game."

"It's my decision, Coach."

"No, Veeder, that's where you're wrong. It's my decision."

"I'll sign a waiver." Veeder lowered his forehead into his hands. "You name it, Coach, I'll sign it."

"I can't do that."

"That's not fair."

"This is the hardest decision I have ever made in my career. You are the toughest player I have had the honor to coach, and if I allowed you to step on that field, it would be for purely selfish reasons. I know you would sacrifice yourself for this team, for the University, for me. But I can't do that, Veeder. I love you too much as a person and as a friend to put you in that position. So as much as it hurts me to say this, you are medically ineligible to play in the national championship. I'm shutting down your season. The only battle you should be fighting is the one raging inside your body."

"Is that your final decision?" Veeder stared at Coach Mercer. "Is there anything I can say to make you change your mind?"

"That is my final decision, Veeder. I'm sorry."

Veeder fought back the tears. Coach Mercer's decision ripped at his heart. Knowing there was nothing he could say to change his coach's mind, he stood up and held out his hand. "Thank you for the honor of being a Cobra, Coach. I'm sorry this had to happen."

Coach Mercer stood up, pulled Veeder into his arms, and hugged him, "Not as much as I am. God bless you, son. I will be praying for you."

"Does the NFL know?"

"No one knows, but I do have to make a statement about my decision to the media later."

"I understand."

"If I were you, I would be far away from this place when the media finds out."

"I will be, Coach." Veeder turned to leave. Reaching for the doorknob, he stopped and stared at the floor. "What do I do now, Coach?"

"That's between you and God, son. Go see your doctor. She has more answers than I do. And then talk to your family. You owe that to them."

"Thank you, Coach."

"Good luck, Veeder, and please check in with your parents. They deserved to have heard this news from you, not that weasel Jack Johnson."

Veeder left Coach Mercer's office. He slipped into the locker room and grabbed his gear while the rest of the team was in meetings. Taking one long, last look around the locker room, he fought back tears. The memories of his time as a Cobra flooded back to him. He took a deep breath before sneaking out of the building through one of the back exits.

CHAPTER 36

—◦—◦⊙⟩

Veeder was back in the infusion lab within the hour. His platelet count had fallen to nineteen. Dr. Abbott was disappointed to hear he had been practicing with the team. She thought they had had a good conversation earlier in the week. She had covered the reasons why playing football would be detrimental to his health. Nurse Tabitha was sticking him with the needle when Mary Katherine, Jill, and Colleen walked into the lab and sat next to him. Veeder's heart sank. It was too late to tell them himself. They had heard the news.

After the customary round of half hugs on the side without the needle sticking into his arm and after Veeder had introduced his family members to Nurse Tabitha, the real pain began.

Jill questioned him first. "How could you have done this, Veeder?"

"Mom, it's nothing. It's being blown out of proportion."

"That's not what Mary Katherine explained to us." Veeder shot Mary Katherine a look.

"Do you know how worried we have been? You could have killed yourself out there."

"I was never in any danger, Grandma."

"Your father is in the waiting room and he is furious," Jill said.

"So is your grandfather!" Colleen added.

"It's not a big deal."

As their voices raised, Nurse Tabitha reminded the group they would be removed if they became unruly. Veeder nodded a silent word of thanks before she closed the privacy curtain.

"Not a big deal?" Jill whispered in a high-pitched voice.

"No, it's not."

"Of all the juvenile, imbecilic stunts, Veeder. Why would you do this to yourself?"

263

"I didn't do this to myself, Mom. It happened to me. I can't control my platelets."

"Why would you keep this from us?"

"I was trying to win the national championship." There was no reason to make excuses for his behavior. What was done was done.

"For a football game?" Jill yelled.

"Ladies, please quiet down," Nurse Tabitha said, walking over from the nurse's desk. "We have other patients. I am not going to ask you again."

"Sorry," Jill said.

"Very sorry, my apologies," Colleen added.

"For a football game?" Jill whisper yelled.

"It's the national championship."

"I don't care if it's the Super Bowl," Jill shot back. "I thought I raised you better."

"Mom. Grandma. Stop. I am fine. Help me out here, MK."

"Oh no." Mary Katherine held up her hands in defiance. "I tried to help you out, but after the news broke this morning, they needed to know the truth. Why didn't you call me back?"

"Et tu, MK?"

"You knew you weren't supposed to be on the field, Veeder," Mary Katherine whispered.

"My numbers went up."

"They bumped up, but look where we are! It looks like they dropped again."

"I didn't know."

"If you made your appointment yesterday, you would have known." Mary Katherine crossed her arms and sat back in her chair.

"I thought I could handle it."

"How did that work out for you?" Colleen asked.

"I made a mess out of everything."

"We've told you since you were little that your family will always have your back. You should have told us," Collen said.

"I'm sorry." Veeder was tethered to the IV bottle. There was no escaping them and their vitriol, so he chose the act of contrition to appease their anger. "I made a mistake."

For the next hour, Jill, Colleen, and Mary Katherine made Veeder's life miserable. When they left the infusion lab to go find coffee, James and Paul bombarded him with their questions. But as the day progressed, their anger turned to worry as the gravity of the situation dawned on the family. Then the tears started to fall. Even James and Paul found themselves choked up once their initial anger had subsided. They all doted on Veeder and tried to reassure him that everything would be okay.

Six hours felt like an eternity. When it was over, Nurse Tabitha took his vitals and released him from the needle trapping him in his chair. Veeder left the hospital and drove to his apartment. He was hoping to rest after a difficult day, but his family members followed him.

When he was back inside his apartment, he turned on the television and changed the channel to NSBEN. When the news broke that Coach Mercer would be making an announcement to the press, Veeder sat down and turned up the volume.

Coach Mercer walked into the press room, adjusted the microphone, and waited for the members of the media to quiet down. "I have a short statement to make and afterward, I won't be taking any questions."

The press groaned but quieted down to listen as Coach Mercer continued, "For four years, I have been blessed with a quarterback who, in my opinion, is one of the best players ever to grace a college football field. His work ethic, tenacity, determination, and drive fueled this team. We have been a nationally ranked team during his tenure and we have had one of the greatest winning percentages in school history. During his tenure as our quarterback, we have seen him break almost every passing record. Records that will probably never be broken.

"Veeder McLean has been a warrior, a true competitor, and the heart and soul of this team. His leadership is the reason that Chapel Hill University will play for the National Championship against Boulder Mountain Tech on Tuesday night. Unfortunately, Veeder will not be making the trip to New Orleans. He has some personal family obligations that have taken precedence over the game of football." Murmurs among the media members echoed throughout the room. Then the questions started, but Coach Mercer just held up his hands to quiet the room.

"And before you all rush to judgment," Coach Mercer continued, "please remember that football is just a game. Life happens and there is nothing you or I can do to change that reality. I pray for Veeder. I pray for his family. The hearts, minds, prayers, the love of this football team, and the entire Cobras community are with him." Coach Mercer turned away from the microphone for a moment, fighting back the tears.

"I respectfully ask everyone to give Veeder and his family privacy as they address the challenges that lie ahead… God bless you, Veeder. God bless your family. My prayers are with you. Thank you for everything you have done for our team and everything you have meant to our community. Thank you." Coach Mercer turned, left the podium, and went back inside the stadium while questions bombarded the empty podium.

With tears rolling down his face, Veeder turned off the television and stared at the empty screen.

Colleen took Veeder's hand. "Be strong now."

As the words left Colleen's mouth, a flashback of Jill's dream flooded her heart. She broke down, sobbing uncontrollably. It took thirty minutes before the flow of tears ebbed. When they did, she recalled the dream she had when Veeder was an infant in the NICU.

"God saved you, Veeder," Jill said through her tears. "He knew I couldn't watch you die on the field on Tuesday night. This news story is a blessing in disguise. Thank you, Lord."

"Mom." Veeder patted her back while she hugged him. "This is nothing more than a few nosy people trying to get their fifteen minutes of fame."

"This is God at work." The rest of the family agreed with Jill. Outnumbered, Veeder thought it best to leave it alone.

They ordered Chinese food for dinner, talking for a little bit before Veeder hinted for them to go home. It was New Year's Eve, and he wanted them off the road before all of the drunk people started driving.

"Why don't I stay and keep you company?" Mary Katherine asked.

"I appreciate that, MK. I do. But it's been a long day. I want to turn on a crappy movie and fall asleep."

"Are you sure?"

"I'm positive," Veeder smirked. "This millennium is ending on a crappy note, and I need to be rested for what lies ahead."

"You know this isn't really the millennium?" Jill asked.

"I know, Mom, but the rest of the world is acting like it is. Why shouldn't I?"

"True." Jill hugged Veeder and kissed him. "Call me tomorrow."

"I will, Mom."

"I am glad you are okay, son." Paul hugged Veeder. "I am proud of you. We'll get through this together. I love you."

"Love you too, Dad."

Paul took Jill by the hand, left the apartment, and headed down to the parking lot.

"Here, take this." James slipped a hundred dollars into Veeder's hand. "I won't hear anything more about it."

"Thanks, Grandpa." Veeder hugged James.

"Behave yourself and get some rest." Colleen gave Veeder a hug and kiss. "This isn't the end of the world."

"Maybe not tomorrow or next week, Grandma, but today it feels like the end of the world. The end of a dream at least."

"You'll land on your feet. You always do." Colleen gave Veeder another kiss and left with James.

"You sure you don't want me to hang out tonight?"

"No New Year's date for you either, MK?"

"We could stay up, pop popcorn, and watch bad movies."

"Thanks, MK, but I am tired." Veeder hugged her. "Besides someone has to get the old folks home safely."

"True." Mary Katherine laughed. "Very true."

"Love you, MK."

"Love you too, baby brother."

Veeder closed the door, walked over to the window, and watched them all get into Paul's truck. He waved to them as they drove away. Once they were out of sight, Veeder walked over to the couch. Instead of picking up the remote, though, Veeder picked up the cordless receiver and dialed a number. On the third ring, he heard a voice on the other end of the line, "Hello?"

"Pastor Kelly?"

"Yes. Who is this?"

"Veeder McLean, sir. Is Anna home?"

"I'm sorry, Veeder, you just missed her. She had New Year's plans with some friends."

"Oh." Veeder's heart sank into the pit of his stomach. "Thank you, sir."

"Sorry about the team."

"What?" Veeder asked, caught off guard by Pastor Kelly's sentiment.

"I'm sorry about the game. Anything I can do to help?"

"They're making it sound worse than it really is."

"I'm sure they are, Veeder," Pastor Kelly said reassuringly. "Are you okay?"

"I'm fine, Pastor Kelly, thank you for asking."

"I'll be praying for you."

"Thank you."

"I'll let Anna know you called."

"Thank you. Good night, Pastor Kelly."

"Happy New Year, Veeder."

Dejected, Veeder clicked off and threw the phone across the room as he mumbled to himself, "Yeah, right. Happy New Year to me!"

CHAPTER 37

—◦◦◦—

Veeder needed a vacation. He needed to get away from the world and focus on his new reality. He needed some time to understand how life had changed and would continue to change. The future didn't look as it clear as it once had. He needed to come to terms with everything that was staring him in the face.

Michael, Colin, and Liam had visited on New Year's Day to cheer him up. During the visit, they all decided a sibling road trip was in order. Veeder jumped at the idea of a road trip to his grandparent's cabin. No wives, no fiancés, no significant others, just the brothers and Mary Katherine. It would give Veeder time away to think about, accept, and focus on the future. A future that involved defeating ITP and if at all possible, reviving his football career.

His grandparents were thrilled about the idea and gave the boys permission to use their cabin. Jill and Paul were against the idea. Veeder's ITP worried them. Jill began to have dreams about Veeder getting hurt on the football field and selfishly, she wanted to keep him close to home so she could protect him.

Regardless of their parent's reservations, the brothers continued to pack for the trip. Veeder wanted Mary Katherine to go with them. She was his best friend, and he wanted to spend time with her. Graduation was on the horizon and their lives would change. They would take different paths in life and Veeder knew he would miss seeing his sister almost every day.

It took him a while but Veeder convinced Mary Katherine to join them. Her decision to go made Paul and Jill feel better. It gave them some comfort amid their fears. They knew Mary Katherine would watch after Veeder and keep him safe. And with that, it was decided. All of the siblings would head out to the family cabin for a week.

Veeder was at the hematology lab as soon as it opened on Monday. They drew his blood and when all of the tests had been completed, his platelet count registered at eight-seven. It wasn't enough to clear him to play football, but it was enough to clear him for a few days of vacation. He promised to take it slow and to be careful. Dr. Abbott warned Veeder not to do anything stupid, which made him laugh. The last thing he needed was a crazy adventure.

The drive out to the cabin was amazing. It had been a long time since they all had been together. They laughed, teased each other, told jokes, reminisced about stories from their childhood, and made fun of their parents. They even shed a few tears as they reminisced about JJ. And they laughed hysterically at the latest of Sean's wild adventures in the Army.

Veeder spent a lot of time staring out the window, watching the world pass by. He hoped this would be the first of many road trips they took together. It healed his heart to have this time with his brothers and Mary Katherine.

Veeder was excited about the trip to the mountains. The cabin was in a remote area. There was no television. No telephone. The nearest telephone was at a convenience store twenty-five minutes away. It was the perfect place to get lost and he was in the mood to get away so he could heal his body, his heart, and his broken spirit.

Colin pulled into the parking lot of the General Store. It would be the last chance for them to grab any last-minute supplies before heading along the back roads to the cabin. They all jumped out of Colin's Range Rover and stretched their legs. They didn't stay long, though, because they were losing daylight. Even though they had taken the four-wheel-drive vehicle, they wanted to be off the dirt roads before it got dark.

Having arrived at the cabin thirty minutes later, the sun was hanging low over the western horizon. They made haste grabbing their bags and taking them into the cabin. After settling in, they barbecued steaks on the grill, sat on the back porch, and laughed through dinner.

After Colin, Michael, and Liam turned in for the night, Mary Katherine found Veeder sitting on the back porch staring out at the stars that illuminated the majesty of the mountains. He was wrapped up under a blanket, keeping warm against the encroaching cold. She sat down next to him. "What are you thinking about?"

Veeder smiled. "Just taking in the view."

"It's amazing." Mary Katherine covered herself with some of the blanket and gazed up at the evening stars. "God's tapestry painted across the sky for us to admire."

"That's one way of looking at it."

"It's how I see it."

"I forgot how much I love being here, MK."

"Me too."

"It's been years since we came up here with grandpa. We used to hike the mountain for hours when we were kids."

"Remember the trip when grandma got a nasty case of poison oak." Mary Katherine laughed.

"I forgot about that." Veeder laughed along with her. "And she blamed grandpa for deliberately not telling her she was sitting in it when she fell."

"And what made it funny is that grandpa was fishing when she tripped. He wasn't even around, and she blamed him anyway."

"I forgot that!" Veeder laughed even harder. "What did she trip on?"

"Your football."

Veeder stopped laughing and stared at Mary Katherine. "Really?"

"Really!"

"That's hysterical!" They both doubled over in laughter.

They told stories for the next few hours. It was the perfect remedy for what ailed Veeder. It was also the break Mary Katherine needed to take a breath and regroup. Her course of study and the medical center took up all of her time and as much as she loved it, she needed respite. They both did and for a few hours, the world faded away as they sat under the stars on the porch of the old cabin.

"We've had some good times up here," Mary Katherine reminisced.

"We have." Veeder stared out into the night.

"We need to come up here more often after we graduate."

"I agree."

"Good." Mary Katherine smiled. "We'll make it an annual trip."

"I'm in."

"Then it's settled."

"You think the brothers will join us?"

"We said it was settled. They have to. They have no choice."

"Good call."

Veeder and Mary Katherine sat silent for a few minutes, enjoying the peaceful surroundings. Veeder broke the silence. "I'm going to hike up to the waterfall tomorrow morning, MK."

"That's a pretty far hike. When are you going?"

"Dawn."

"If I'm not up, wake me."

"Why?"

"I want to go with you."

"I was thinking of heading up there by myself. I just wanted you to know so you didn't worry about me."

"Not going to happen."

"I need some time to think, MK, and it's the perfect place to do it."

"Didn't you hear my conversation with the clerk at the general store?"

"No. What did he say?"

"He said the river is running high and fast with all the rain they've had. They've had a lot of flash flooding all over the region."

"How fast can the river run? It's barely high enough for a kayak or a raft on a leisurely summer day. The best you can do is tube down the river and even that's a stretch."

"He said the river is running two to three feet higher than it ever has."

"Not a chance."

"Apparently, the banks are eroding."

"That's nonsense, MK."

"He was surprised the thrill-seekers haven't come up here to run the rapids."

"Rapids." Veeder laughed. "Come on, MK! You know as well as I do there are no rapids anywhere on the river, especially below the waterfall."

"I'm telling you what the clerk said back at the general store."

"He was pulling your leg. He probably thought you were cute and was hitting on you."

"I don't know, Veeder, he seemed pretty sincere. He told me to be careful out by the river."

"I guess we'll have to check it out for ourselves."

"And by 'we'll,' does that mean I can go with you?"

"Were you going to let me hike out there by myself if I said no?"

"Not a chance." Mary Katherine smiled, sitting back in her chair, and staring out at the mountain. "I just wanted you to think it was your idea to ask me to join you."

CHAPTER 38

It was still dark outside when Veeder woke up. He dressed in silence, went to the kitchen, and brewed a strong pot of coffee. He had learned a few things about Mary Katherine over the years and one of them was she wasn't to be bothered until she had a strong cup of coffee. When the coffee was ready, he took her a cup.

Mary Katherine was slow to wake up but beyond grateful for the coffee. She sat in bed and savored the first sip. She stared off into the darkness of the room as the aroma of coffee wafted around her head. Veeder left her to wake up, went into the kitchen, put a few items in his backpack, poured himself a cup of coffee, and went outside to sit on the front porch.

Veeder stared out over the mountain watching the sunrise. He thought about life and how it had changed over the past few weeks; about the football team and all they had accomplished. He thought about school, graduation, his diagnosis, and about Anna.

He missed Anna. He wasn't at his apartment over the weekend, so he didn't know if she had called him back. He hoped she had but didn't want to find out before heading to the cabin. He needed this week to be about finding meaning in his life. He couldn't bear the thought of finding out she hadn't called or had just to tell him she had moved on with her life.

The morning was peaceful, and a calm resolve settled into his heart. He knew his team would play for the national championship that night and was at peace with the fact they would do it without him. The stress he had felt over the national championship was gone. The inner demons compelling him to work harder and to win at all costs were gone. It was a new day and whatever life had to throw at him, he would overcome those obstacles.

He felt happy for the first time in months. Maybe it was the fresh, clean mountain air. Maybe it was the time spent sitting on the back porch staring up at the stars while realizing how quiet, how vast, and how infinite the world is. Or how much of it he had missed in his quest to be the best football player on the planet.

"Thank you for the coffee." Mary Katherine stepped out onto the porch and sat on the steps next to Veeder. "That was a godsend. How did you know I was going to need it this morning?"

"I've picked up a few tricks over the years."

"You mean, you've paid attention to someone other than yourself?" Mary Katherine joked.

"To some people, maybe, but not many."

"Face it, Veeder, you're a big softie at heart." Mary Katherine hugged him.

"Please don't tell anyone."

"I won't, but I think they already know."

"You ready to go, MK?" Veeder stood and pulled his backpack over his shoulders.

"Should we wake up the others?"

"Let them sleep."

"They might want to join us."

"I didn't even want you to come with me, remember?"

"True." Mary Katherine stared back at the cabin door. "But won't they be upset when they wake up and we're gone?"

"They'll be glad we didn't wake them."

"I guess." Mary Katherine grabbed her backpack. "Ready when you are."

"Let's go."

They walked down the front steps and headed off on their trek. The waterfall was a good four and a half miles away. Rain had fallen in the middle of the night and added more water to an already saturated terrain, slowing their pace.

They walked for a while in silence, taking in the sights, sounds, and scenery. Going deep into the woods, they started ruminating about their childhood and the many trips they had taken to the cabin, joking about previous adventures, and about some of their wild escapades since going off to college.

Veeder teased Mary Katherine about being still being single when she stunned him and confessed to dating Dr. Rick Stevenson. Rick had graduated from University of Durham Medical School and was a first-year resident at the hospital. Veeder was shocked he hadn't seen the signs when he met Rick, admitting to being pre-occupied at the time. She told Veeder they had just started dating. It was the reason she hadn't said anything to any of the family. Plus, she wanted Veeder to be the first to know.

She told Veeder that Rick wasn't a big fan of the Cobras, but he liked him. Veeder told Mary Katherine that that was going to change, reminding her all of the brothers were going to have to take Rick out to dinner, just to let him know he better not break her heart. Mary Katherine objected to the ritual her brothers had about meeting her boyfriends but knew it was unavoidable. It was going to happen whether she tried to stop it or not.

Veeder was happy for Mary Katherine. He loved watching her eyes light up as she talked about Rick. She went on about how nice it was to find a guy who understood her passion for medicine, but what made her happiest is that Rick believed in God. He loved God and was someone she could share her faith with, which was a hard quality to find in her circles. Most of the guys she had dated didn't believe or put science above their faith. But Rick believed God was the creator of the earth, the epicenter of their lives, and it was God who gave them the skills they had to help people and to minister to the world through medicine.

Veeder rolled his eyes while Mary Katherine talked about God, but he knew he would never debate God with her. She wouldn't hesitate to put him in his place. So he bit his tongue and listened, noticing a joy he had never seen before. He loved seeing her happy. She deserved it.

It took them almost two hours to walk to the waterfall. Traversing the trail of the riverbed, they could hear the rushing water of the river. They stopped to marvel at the furious rush of water below them.

"Do you see that?" Veeder pointed down the embankment.

"I told you! The clerk at the general store said the river was higher than usual."

"Yeah! But that's crazy high."

"They've had a lot of rain up here."

"Yeah, MK, I get that. But the river is at least three feet above normal."

"And I'm sure last night's storm made it worse."

"If this is what the river is like, I can only imagine what the waterfall looks like." Veeder and Mary Katherine continued up the trail. It took them another fifteen minutes to reach the waterfall and it was amazing. They couldn't believe the powerful flow of water gushing over the side of the cliff and into the river below.

"This is crazy." Veeder pulled out his camera and started taking pictures.

"It's beautiful."

"Powerful, MK." Veeder pointed at the river. "Look at how forceful the current is."

Veeder and Mary Katherine took some time to walk around the waterfall. He was taking pictures while they talked about how much rain must have fallen over the past few weeks. It was beautiful but also a stark reminder of the power of nature.

They sat on an old tree stump and ate the food Veeder had packed. Afterward, they spent time exploring the area around the waterfall. Veeder took more pictures while Mary Katherine spent time taking in the scenery and the awesome wonder of God's creation. It was miraculous. God never stopped amazing Mary Katherine and she said a prayer of gratitude for the majesty of His creation.

"We should head back to the cabin," Mary Katherine said after a while.

"Just a few more minutes, MK."

"The others must be up and wondering where we went."

"I can guarantee you they are not wondering where we are." Veeder teased.

"How do you know? They could be worried about us right now."

Doug Veeder

"I highly doubt that." Veeder laughed. "I bet they are glad we are out of their hair."

"Come on, Veeder," Mary Katherine implored. "This is supposed to be a sibling's weekend. I want to go back to the cabin."

"That's fine, MK. We'll go back in a minute." Veeder walked past Mary Katherine with his camera in hand. "I want to get some pictures just below the waterfall."

"Where?"

"On the riverbank."

"Be careful, Veeder," Mary Katherine cautioned.

Veeder worked his way through the brush and the trees to get a better picture of the waterfall.

"I'm a finely tuned athlete. I'll be fine." Veeder moved closer to the top of the sloping riverbank. He lowered himself to one knee and inched closer while looking through his camera for the perfect picture. Once he had the perfect shot of the waterfall in focus, he snapped a couple of pictures and lowered the camera. "Got it!"

"Great, let's go!"

"Alright, MK, let's go back." Veeder lowered the camera and stood up. As he did, the saturated soil of the embankment collapsed under the weight of his body. Veeder slid down the bank, screaming, "Help!"

The landslide took away a couple of feet of the hillside, causing Veeder to fall down the embankment in a rush of mud that pulled him into the raging river. He slammed into the water and felt something pop in his leg as he was thrown against the rocks. Caught squarely in its clutches, the current of raging water propelled him downstream.

"Veeder!" Mary Katherine screamed. She ran to the embankment, getting as close as she could, and held onto a tree a few feet from the edge where Veeder had just been standing. She stood there helpless, watching Veeder being dragged downstream.

Mary Katherine raced through the woods to see if she could find a place where she might be able to drag Veeder out of the river, but it was no use. The rapids were too fast, and the riverbank was too soft. It was unsafe. She had to get help so she took off on a dead sprint towards the cabin.

Veeder had spent enough time with his grandfather on their outdoor adventures and knew if he ever found himself in a raging river, he was to lay on his back with his feet facing downstream. He was unable to swim to the embankment because the current was too strong and the pain radiating from his left leg reminded him, he didn't have the strength to fight against the rapids.

He didn't know how long he had been in the frigid waters or how far downstream he had traveled. He was at the mercy of the river, being tossed and thrown around like a rag doll, fighting against the raging rapids with every muscle of his body to keep his head above water.

He felt the first forceful impact of colliding with a rock, letting out a painful, blood-curdling scream. The impact forced his body sideways in the water. He was helpless, being tossed further down the river. His ribs slammed into another large boulder, knocking the wind out of him. He was gasping for air as his body was being tossed around in a rocky rapid and the best he could do was to fight to keep his feet heading downstream first.

He bounced off a few more boulders before the current whipped him around and slammed the side of his head against a rock, ripping open a gash above his right eye. Blood gushing from his forehead, weak, woozy, and washed downriver, he could feel his ability to fight slip away. He went limp. His mind started to drift. He was tired. He wanted to sleep. Eyelids heavy, sleep had begun to creep in when he felt his body get yanked from behind...

Mary Katherine covered the four and a half miles to the cabin in forty minutes. In a sheer panic, she raced into the cabin.

Colin raced off in the Range Rover to get help while Michael and Colin went back out to the river with Mary Katherine.

Five hours later, the yard around the cabin was overrun with volunteer search teams, members of the local police, the fire department, and medical personnel. They had set up a command center and were doing their best to coordinate efforts to cover the mountainous terrain as methodically and safely as possible. The Captain was approached by a member of his team. They stepped away from the command center, had an animated conversation, and then they returned with a change of plans.

"Okay, pull all of the teams back to base," he said, running his hand through his hair. He walked over to the front porch of the cabin where Mary Katherine was sitting. "Ma'am."

"Do you have any news yet, Captain?" Mary Katherine asked.

"We don't." The captain put his foot on the second step and rested his elbow on his knee. "Unfortunately, ma'am, we have to pull our search teams back to base."

"You can't do that!" Mary Katherine was animated. "My brother is still out there!"

"I understand that ma'am, but the weather is about to get really bad. We are getting reports of another strong thunderstorm raging through the area within the next hour."

"But my brother is still out there!"

"And we'll find him. Just not tonight. It's not safe."

"So you're going to quit? You're just going to leave him out there all alone!"

"There's no visibility, ma'am." The captain was calm and resolute. "The terrain around the river was unsafe before we arrived. The rain in the forecast is going to make the situation worse. I can't risk anyone's life until after the storm passes and the sun comes up."

"So you're going to let him die?"

"I understand ..."

"No! You don't!" Mary Katherine interrupted, tears streaming down her face. "If that was your brother out there, would you quit? Would you?"

"I'm sorry, ma'am." The captain turned and walked back to the command center.

"You can't quit, you can't quit!" Mary Katherine yelled after him. The captain didn't turn back. Jill, Paul, James, and Colleen came running up the driveway. Mary Katherine raced towards them. "They're quitting, Mom! They're quitting!"

"I know, MK" Jill wrapped her arms around Mary Katherine. "They told us when we arrived. The weather isn't good. They have to protect their team."

"But Veeder is still out there!" Mary Katherine cried, holding tight to her mother. Paul, James, and Colleen wrapped their arms around the two of them.

"We need to be strong." Jill wrestled with her emotions. "Veeder's tough. God is with him. He will protect him."

CHAPTER 39

The fire crackled. Each pop of wood that split under the heat of the flames sent ripples of pain through Veeder's forehead. The fierce, icy wind whipped against Veeder's face, stirring him from sleep. He rolled over, pulling into the warmth of the dry blanket wrapped around him.

"Take it easy," a strange voice said. Someone bent down next to him and placed a hand against his back, helping Veeder rollover. "You took some pretty bad hits in the river rapids."

Thunder clapped. The sky lit up. Lightning splintered the darkness. Veeder flinched at the booming sound of thunder, then struggled into a position against the rock behind him. He put his hands in front of his face because the light of the fire hurt his eyes. He had a hard time focusing. His head pounded like a sledgehammer against a metal spike being driven into the ground. He winced in pain, trying to find a comfortable position to sit.

"Easy now." The stranger tried to comfort Veeder. "Don't rush anything."

"Where am I?" Veeder moaned, trying to shake off the cobwebs. The pain in his lower left leg intensifying. It felt like a vice grip had been placed on his knee and was being tightened. He could hear the rain falling and feel the chilling wind whip across his face. He flinched every time the thunder clapped against the sky.

"We're in the forest." The stranger had a calm reassurance about him.

"How did I get here?"

"I pulled you out of the river rapids. I saw you hit your head on one of the rocks and I knew I had to do something before you drowned."

"That explains my throbbing headache." Veeder chuckled, but the laughter made his head, ribs, and leg hurt even more.

"Your head is going to hurt for a while. You probably have a concussion."

"I'm glad you were there to help. Thank you." Veeder's eyes fluttered. Everything looked fuzzy. He kept blinking to help his vision adjust to the light of the fire.

"Do you want something to eat?" The stranger moved and sat on a stone next to the fire pit. "I made some stew. I can toast some bread."

"Water. Please?" Veeder strained to speak. "Can I please have some water?"

"Yes." The stranger pulled a large canteen out of his bag, poured some water into a small metal cup, and handed it to Veeder who gulped it down too fast.

"Thank you." Veeder held out the cup. "Do you mind if I have a little more please?"

"You can have as much as you want." The stranger poured another cup of water.

Veeder drank the water, his eyes adjusting to his surroundings. They were sheltered underneath an overhang in the rock formation, protected against the storm. That still didn't stop him from flinching every time thunder cracked or a blast of lightning cut across the sky.

The wind still whipped through their makeshift campsite. He pulled the blanket against his body. He hadn't dried off from falling into the water, and each blast of wind ran through his body like little daggers of icicles.

He could feel the heat from the fire on his face. He was grateful for the warmth it provided. His new companion had a fair amount of wood stacked next to the fire pit. He didn't know if it was enough to get through the night but it looked like it would last for a while.

He studied the man and felt an instant sense of safety. There was a gentleness and kindness in His face. He couldn't put his finger on it, but the man seemed familiar to him. It was as if he knew Him even though he knew he had never met Him before.

"Thank you." Veeder handed the cup back to the stranger.

"Would you like some more?"

"I'm good." Veeder tried to stand up and grimaced in pain.

"You should relax." The stranger put up His hands to stop Veeder.

"I want to sit by the fire and warm up." Veeder tried to stand up again.

"Let me help you." The stranger helped Veeder to his feet. Standing, Veeder leaned against the man. He looked down, noticing the primitive splint stabilizing his leg.

"I made that for you. Your leg is pretty banged up."

"I felt something crack when I fell down the embankment."

"You're going to need a doctor when we get out of here, but the splint should keep it stable for now."

"Thank you." Veeder limped to the fire with the aid of the stranger and sat on a rock next to the fire pit.

"I made a crutch for you."

"Why?"

"So, we can hike out of here when the storm lets up." The stranger grabbed the blanket and handed it to Veeder, who wrapped it around himself.

"Thank you." Veeder felt his stomach growl. "Do you mind if I have some stew?"

"I made it for you. I was just waiting for you to wake up." The stranger scooped some stew out of the pot, put the food into a small metal bowl, and handed it to Veeder.

Veeder took his time eating. Both men sat quiet. He tried to think back over the day when a sudden sense of panic washed over him like a tidal wave. "Was there a woman in the river?"

"I didn't see a woman in the river."

"My sister was with me. I need to know she didn't fall in the river."

"She wasn't in the river. I am sure she is safe."

"How do you know?" Veeder yelled, trying to stand up. A stabbing pain shot up his injured leg and forced him back down. "We need to find my sister!"

"We're not looking for anyone in this storm."

"We have to. She could be hurt."

"She wasn't in the river." The stranger was resolute and firm. "I promise you."

"She could have fallen in after me." Tears trickled down his cheek. "I would never forgive myself if anything happened to her."

"Nothing happened to Mary Katherine, Veeder," the stranger said as a matter-of-fact. "She made it safely back to the cabin. She was unable to get to you, so she went to get help."

Veeder's eyes flew wide open. He stared, bewildered, at the stranger. He tried to figure out how the stranger knew their names. He stared down the man, sitting relaxed in front of him. *How did he know Mary Katherine made it back to the cabin safely?*

He became worried, staring across the fire pit at the man. He inhaled a long, slow, deep breath. "How do you know my name?"

"I have always known you. Why wouldn't I know your name?"

"I've never met you." Veeder was nervous. *Who was this man? Was He a crazy fan? A stalker?*

Fear gripped his heart. There was nothing he could do. His leg was injured, and the storm was too strong. He was at the mercy of his captor. He had to stay vigilant and protect himself until he could escape and find help.

"That's partially true but knowing someone and meeting them are not mutually exclusive."

"I don't know you." Veeder was frustrated as he surveyed the campsite.

"You're right about that, Veeder. You have never taken the time to meet me but I have always been here for you."

"You're starting to freak me out. How do you know me or my sister?" Veeder panicked. The urge to fight and run was raging. As his nerves overcame him, his legs started to bounce, and the pain from his injury rippled throughout his body.

"I have always known you. And as for your sister, Mary Katherine, I know her well. She is very special to me."

"Who are you?" Veeder yelled.

"I am who I have always been and who I will always be."

"And who is that?"

"My name is Jesus, Veeder." The stranger smiled.

"No," Veeder gasped, staring at the man in disbelief. The stranger sat in tranquility, smiling back at him. "You can't be."

"Why not?" The stranger was perplexed. Peace and kindness emanated from his face.

"Because Jesus doesn't just appear to people out of the blue like this." Veeder tried to air a sense of superiority while wondering what was happening to him. *Was he dying? Was he dead?* The questions raged in his mind. His heart broke. He never got to say goodbye to his family, to Anna.

"For a person who once told his Pastor I don't exist." The stranger recalled without passion, prejudice, or condemnation. "You seem to know a lot about what I am and am not supposed to do."

"How do you know what I said?" A tear trickled down his cheek. The realization that he was dead or dying started to sink into his heart. He had so much to say to his family and friends. He had so much to apologize for and he wished he had one more moment with all of them to tell them how much he loved them.

The stranger saw the tears on Veeder's cheek. "Do not fear, Veeder. Give it a minute. Let this sink in. It is a lot to believe. It will take a moment. You've been through a lot today."

Veeder stared at the stranger, sitting patient without a care in the world while thunder and lightning crashed around them. He was scared. There had to be some rational explanation for what was happening. He didn't know what to believe. *Could it be? Could he really be Jesus? Has my life been a lie?*

Thunder crashed and lightning hit a nearby tree, causing it to explode into a bunch of pieces. Veeder jumped and almost fell off the rock. His leg spun and jammed into the fire pit. He cried guttural, neanderthal grunts as the excruciating pain radiated throughout his body.

"Be still!" The stranger said, turning and speaking with authority into the darkness.

The storm stopped. It was as though someone had reached up and turned the spigot off. The clouds passed and the moon lit up the woods while Veeder stared in disbelief at what he had just witnessed.

The stranger stood up and took a few steps toward Veeder who recoiled, pushing his hands out in front of him to stop the man from coming too close. Panic overtook him when the stranger reached out, touched his hands, and the pain emanating from his knee just stopped.

Veeder couldn't fathom what he was witnessing. The stranger returned to His seat by the fire and positioned Himself on the rock again. Veeder stared into the stranger's welcoming face. "Why me?"

"Why not you?"

"I am not worthy." Condemnation and shame welled up inside Veeder, visions of his life played in the background.

"Everyone is worthy." The stranger smiled, the light in His eyes warming Veeder's heart.

"But why?" Veeder pleaded. There had to be a reason He would save the wretched soul of a man who had professed his unbelief at every twist and turn. Spurning loved ones who tried to share the gospel with him, especially Anna.

"You were in trouble. I helped you."

"It doesn't make sense." Veeder was lost in a moral battle of what he believed and what sat in front of him. *Truth? What is truth? How do I know any of this happening right now is true?* Veeder thought to himself while staring at the kindness pouring out of the stranger. "Why would you? I've never believed in you, why would you come to me?"

"Because I made a promise."

"To whom?" Veeder shrugged his shoulders. "I never asked you to promise me anything?"

"Your grandmother has always believed in me." The stranger's face brightened as He spoke of Colleen. "She has always been faithful, and she has always loved you."

"She is the best." Veeder smiled. "But what does she have to do with any of this?"

287

"She is amazing," the stranger agreed. "She made me promise her when we were all sitting around a picnic table not to let you 'leave this earth without seeing me face-to-face.' I am here to fulfill the promise and to reveal myself to you."

"I was seven when she said that to me." Veeder was caught up in a moment of disbelief, recalling the day he patronized his grandmother for believing in something he didn't.

This wasn't happening. There was no way the stranger sitting across the fire could know so much about Veeder's life. It was impossible. *I'm in a coma, I'm dreaming.*

"She wasn't speaking to you, Veeder," the stranger corrected. "She was speaking to me."

"You were there?" Veeder was confused. "How?"

"My spirit, the Holy Spirit, is always with you." The stranger's eyes were filled with love and compassion. "But yes, I was sitting next to you."

"How is this possible?"

"Faith."

"I've never had a lot of faith."

"True."

"But you never loved me either!" Veeder became indignant, proud, and defiant. If this truly was the Son of God sitting with him, he had a few things to get off his chest.

Veeder's arrogance and anger did not faze the stranger. His kind face radiated joy and peace. "That's where you are wrong, Veeder. I have always loved you and have only wanted the best for you."

"Even though I never believed in you?" Veeder cackled, becoming more undignified.

"Yes, even though you don't believe in me." The stranger shared a tender smiled, tilted his head, and nodded in understanding. "There are a lot of people in the world who don't believe in me, and I still love them."

"That doesn't make any sense." Veeder was incredulous. His heart hardening, he was digging his heels into his unbelief.

"I have always wanted you to believe in me. I have always wanted you to love me as much as I love you. But regardless of how you feel, I have always loved you. I always will."

"Why would you love someone who doesn't love you back?"

"Love is always a choice." The stranger winked, a twinkle in His eyes. "I choose to love you."

"You choose to love me?" Veeder chuckled, shaking his head in arrogance. "I have done nothing deserving of your love, and I don't know if I ever will."

"That is your choice, Veeder." The stranger was kind, compassionate, and smiling. "I love everyone in this world, including you. I gave up my life for you. I paid the price of your sin so you could have the love of God, my Father, and the blessing of eternal life. If I was willing to go to the cross and die so your life could be redeemed, if I loved you that much before you were born, why wouldn't I love you and pursue a relationship with you every day of your life?"

"Because I'm not worth it!" Veeder's adamant indignation grew in its intensity. If he was so worth it, he thought, then why wasn't he playing football? Why didn't Anna love him? Why wasn't he healthy?

Veeder was angry. So much had been stolen from his life and the only person he could blame for all of it was sitting across the fire pit, trying to convince him he was loved. He started to shake in anger as he tried to rationalize what was happening.

"You are to me. You are my creation. I love you and will pursue you all the days of your life." The stranger paused, looking at Veeder with love and kindness. "The real question you have to ask yourself is, am I worth it?"

"I'm still in the water." Veeder rubbed his eyes and started mumbling to himself. His core values were being challenged. He didn't know what to believe and his mind had to rectify what was happening to him. "This isn't happening. I am still in the river. Hypothermia must be setting in. I must be drowning. This must be my final moments…"

"You are very much alive," the stranger interrupted with a calm resolve.

"I can't be!" Veeder shouted.

"Why not?" The stranger was relaxed. "Because it is easier to believe you're dying than facing the reality that I actually exist?"

"Yes!" Veeder screamed in anger. "It is!"

The stranger smiled compassionately. "Why can't you accept that I love you? That I have always loved you? That all I want is to have a relationship with you and share the love of my father with you?"

"Because you're not real!" Veeder's arms flailed, his face contorted, eyes piercing the night, seething with anger.

"You keep saying that Veeder, and yet I am sitting right in front of you," the stranger said with patience. "Flesh and blood. The same today as I was yesterday, as I have always been, and always will be."

"This can't be happening." Veeder pinched his arms and slapped his face, trying to wake up from the dream. "This is not real!"

"I am very real." The stranger pulled up His sleeves and started to warm His hands over the fire. Veeder saw the holes on His hands from the nails that were driven through them when they hung Him on the cross. "I love you, Veeder. You are one of my lost sheep. I have left the flock to come find you."

"But I am not lost." Veeder professed in arrogance.

"You're not?" The stranger raised his eyebrows. "Are you sure about that?"

"Things aren't perfect." Veeder fumbled for excuses. His values were being challenged. Sitting across the fire from the stranger, he didn't know what to believe and he didn't like it. He had always been in control of everything in his life. He was scared. He was losing control. "I have to sort some things out, especially now that it looks like football won't be in my future."

"I can help you with your future. We can figure out your life together."

Veeder stopped and stared at the stranger. He was perplexed. The kindness and compassion of the stranger softened his heart. "Why would you do that?"

"Because I love you, Veeder." The stranger sat back on the rock and placed his hands on his knees. "How long will it take for you to realize that? I want you to have a life more abundant than you can ever fathom. All you have to do is accept my gift of grace."

"A life abundant? Huh? That's funny." Veeder's ire raged again inside his heart. Everything he had ever wanted had been taken from him. "I think you failed in that department."

"You mistake free will for God's will," the stranger said. "The deception of sin is that people always think what they want is always what is best for them."

"My whole life was before me!" Veeder yelled.

"Your whole life is still before you," the stranger responded.

Veeder was getting angrier. "I was supposed to play in the NFL. I was supposed to be one of the greatest quarterbacks to ever play the game."

"Was that God's will for your life?" The stranger was calm in face of the contempt Veeder held for Him.

"It was my destiny! I was supposed to have fame and fortune!"

"And in gaining the whole world, you would lose your life," the stranger added.

"God took that from me!"

"Or maybe He saved you from yourself." The stranger's words were kind and compassionate yet directed. "Did you ever think of that? What if you had died on the field on your way to fame and fortune?"

"It would have been better than where I am right now?" Veeder crossed his arms, a scowl on his face.

"Do you really believe that, Veeder?"

"Yes! I do!"

"And what about your family? What about your friends who love you? What about Anna? They have all prayed for you. They have all loved you and still do."

"They have nothing to do with this." Veeder knew he was in uncharted territory. They had everything to do with his life. He loved them. He wanted to make them all proud. He lived for them. His words were vapid, but he refused to let the stranger cut through the pain and anger.

"They have everything to do with all of this."

"No, they don't." Tears trickling down Veeder's cheek. He could feel his heart softening. He tried to fight it, but his family and Anna meant everything to him.

"Your family has been praying for you ever since you were born. I was there in the incubator with you while they prayed and asked me to help you. I was there every day when they asked for you to be redeemed."

"They were foolish to ask for your help." Veeder tried to wipe away the tears but more flowed from his eyes. The questions flooded his brain. *Why am I so emotional? Why is my heart hurting? Why do I feel so ashamed?*

"And what about Anna, Veeder?" the stranger asked. "Does she mean nothing?"

"You have no right to bring her up!" His anger gave way to trembling fear. Why was the stranger probing his heart, his existence, and his core beliefs? He wanted it to stop.

"Why not?"

"You are the reason we broke up!" Even as the words left his mouth, he knew he was lying. Veeder had no one to blame but himself for the problems in his relationship with Anna, and his heart betrayed him. Shame ripped through his heart as he stared at the stranger.

The stranger smiled and let Veeder's accusations fall on deaf ears. "Anna has prayed for your heart to be opened since the day she met you. She loves you more than you will ever know, and her heart breaks every day."

"You took her from me." Veeder tried to stop the tears but they fell harder. His heart, mind, and soul betrayed him, condemning him for the lies spewing forth from his lips.

"I didn't take her from you," the stranger stated as a matter of fact. "You didn't believe. You couldn't accept the relationship

Anna and I have. A relationship we have desperately tried to invite you into, but you fought against it. You were the one who pushed her away."

"Please stop," Veeder whispered. Concession setting in. The stranger was right about everything. He had made the choices that brought him to this moment in his life. As the bravado and lies were stripped away, the truth scared him. The façade of his life shattered, he didn't want to face the truth anymore. It hurt too much.

"Your parents, your grandparents, JJ, Mary Katherine, and Anna have all prayed for you and loved you! They have all asked for me to find you…"

"Please stop!" Veeder yelled. His head fell into his hands, crying. "Please stop. I can't take anymore."

"Do you really believe they have nothing to do with your life?"

"They do. I am so sorry. They all do." Veeder confessed. Emotional and broken, he wept.

"Would they think it would be better if you died? Are they better off by you leaving them suffering in pain and heartache?"

"No, they're not, I'm sorry." Veeder was engulfed in shame. "I wasn't thinking about them, I was only thinking about myself."

"The problem with the lies and deception of free will is that people put themselves first," the stranger was filled with compassion for Veeder's catharsis. Love poured out of His heart. "They are selfish, unloving, and self-centered."

"That was never my intention."

"It's never anybody's intention, but it's what happens. Greed, selfishness, hate, deceit, and lies fill our hearts, stealing our joy. It clouds your judgment and the love of God. My everlasting love is hidden behind those clouds just waiting for you to accept me."

"I don't know what to do." Veeder stared into the eyes of the stranger with an overwhelming sense of sadness. "Help me."

"Start by opening your heart. See the world as it truly is. See me for the first time."

"I am." Veeder's heart flooded with love. "I see you, Lord."

"Accept that I love you, Veeder. Love me with all your heart, mind, and soul."

"I will."

"Follow me."

"How?"

"Read my word. Pray. Let the Holy Spirit come into your heart and lead you."

"How will I know it is your spirit?"

"It will take some time to hear my voice at first but as you grow in your faith, well, let's just say my sheep always hear my voice calling in the wilderness. If you accept my gift of grace, you will know my voice." The stranger was tender, kind, and compassionate.

"How could you ever love me?" Veeder couldn't understand how he could be loved after everything that had happened and after all the pain he had caused in his life. He was trying hard to rectify this in his heart as the truth of his life created doubts.

"I have always loved you, Veeder," the stranger said. "That has never changed. It never will. The question is, will you love me? Will you trust me? Will you follow me?"

"I want to, Lord, I do. Please help me."

"All you have to do is believe in me. Believe in my love and give your life to me." The stranger stood up, walked around the fire, knelt in front of Veeder, placed his hand on Veeder's shoulder, and looked into his eyes. "I am offering you a new life. A new path. A life of hope. A life abundantly full of love. Do you want that life?"

"I do." Veeder found hope in the words and the love of the stranger. He was filled with an overwhelming sense of joy and peace.

"I love you, son." The stranger hugged Veeder.

"But how could you forgive me for everything I have ever done in my life?"

The stranger leaned back, smiling with a twinkle in his eye. "All you have to do is ask."

"Please forgive me, Lord Jesus?" Veeder embraced the stranger and wept on his shoulder. "Please forgive me?"

"You are forgiven." The stranger held Veeder, comforting him. "You are forgiven."

CHAPTER 40

—◦◦◦◦—

Mary Katherine woke to a flurry of activity in the yard. For a moment, she was still stuck in the vivid imagery of her dreams. Then reality brought along a wave of fear. Veeder was out there. Cold and alone.

Still dressed in the clothes she had been wearing the night before, Mary Katherine jumped out of bed and ran to the front porch. Jill and Colleen were sitting on the steps drinking coffee, waiting for any news about Veeder.

"Is there any word yet, Mom?" Mary Katherine asked.

"Nothing yet." Jill stood, pulling Mary Katherine into a hug.

"Have faith," Colleen added, joining the hug. "We're going to find him."

"Where are the guys?"

"They split up and joined different search teams so they could help look for your brother." Jill poured Mary Katherine a cup of coffee from their thermos and handed it to her.

"Dad and Grandpa?"

"They know these mountains better than anyone," Colleen said. "They headed out with another search group about an hour ago."

"And Sean called in a favor with the commanding officer at the local base and got them to dispatch two helicopters this morning."

"That's good news." Mary Katherine sipped her coffee.

"We'll find him, MK." Jill exuded confidence.

"I'm sorry for all of this, Mom. It's all my fault."

"Don't be ridiculous." Jill gave Mary Katherine another hug. "You're tired."

"I should have stopped him from going to the waterfall. I should have known better."

"When have you ever known anyone to stop Veeder from doing something after he sets his mind to it?" Colleen asked, stroking Mary Katherine's hair. "He's just lucky you were with him."

"I think we can all thank God for that," Jill added, staring out at the command center.

They knew the search would be long and arduous but the fear of the unknown still ate away at them. Mary Katherine wanted to be out searching, but the family decided it would be best for her to stay behind to assist in case of a medical emergency.

They prayed together as they talked. They prayed for Veeder to be found alive. They prayed Veeder wasn't harmed by the cold weather and the electrical storms that had crossed the mountain the night before. They were worried because the storm was more powerful than anyone had thought it would be. The thunder and lightning was fast and furious. It pounded the entire region with a torrential downpour. Then, without any rational explanation, it stopped. It was bizarre as if someone had just turned off a water faucet.

As each hour passed, fear flooded their hearts. They fought off the emotional roller coaster with stories of the ridiculous stunts Veeder had pulled throughout his life. Mary Katherine talked about how crazy and outright ridiculous her childhood had been growing up with him. Being his twin sister wasn't easy, but through all of the ups and downs, the two of them had grown as thick as thieves. They were best friends, and she didn't want that to end. She loved her brother. Her heart filled with guilt and tears escaped from her eyes.

"It's my fault, Mom, I am so sorry."

"Mary Katherine, you can't blame yourself." Jill put an arm around her.

"Every time I close my eyes, I see the look on his face when the hill collapsed into the river."

"It was an accident, Mary Katherine." Colleen tried to comfort her. "The ground gave way because of all the rain."

"But I should have known it would. I warned him about all of the rain."

"You had no way of knowing…"

"I should have helped him, Mom." Mary Katherine interrupted Jill.

"How? What could you have done?"

"I should have tried to do something!"

"You said he was being swept down the river."

"I should have gone in after him. I should have tried to save him."

"And if you had, we'd be looking for both of you right now."

"I should have, Mom. I should have tried." Mary Katherine insisted through her tears.

Jill wrapped her daughter up in a tight embrace, praying for her son, and at the same time, thanking God for stopping Mary Katherine from going after him.

Hours passed and the search crews hadn't found anything. Michael was moving west of the river with his search team. There was twenty-five feet between each of the volunteers as they combed the woods in a line that stretched for six hundred feet from the river's edge. Their movements were slow and methodical as they searched for any sign of life.

"Tim," the captain said. His voice crackling over the walkie-talkie.

"Go ahead, Captain," Tim responded into his radio.

"How far are you from Houghton's Ridge?"

"I'm about a mile away, Captain." Tim stopped walking and looked around to gauge his surroundings. "Why? What's up?"

"The military chopper spotted two people on the other side of the ridge," the captain radioed.

"Do you think it might be them?"

"I don't know. The pilot said it looked like one of the hikers was hurt."

"You think it's just a couple of hikers who got lost?"

"Doesn't matter," the Captain radioed back. "If we have hurt people on the other side of the ridge, we have to help them out."

"I'll check it out. Over and out."

"You're abandoning my brother?" Michael asked as Tim put the walkie-talkie away.

"I'm going to provide assistance to someone who may need it," Tim said before he whistled to get the team's attention.

"We're not going!" Michael was angry.

"You can stay here and look on your own, but we're going to see what is on the other side of the ridge." Tim stared down Michael while the searchers surrounded their team leader.

"You can't do this, Tim." Michael's frustration caught up with him. "We've only got a few hours of daylight left."

"If we double-time it over the ridge," Tim tried to reassure Michael, "we'll be back here in no time."

"It'll take away valuable time."

"It's a mile. We can cover that in ten minutes."

"What's going on, Tim?" one of the volunteers asked.

"The command center said the helicopters spotted a couple of hikers on the other side of Houghton's Ridge. They look like they might need our help. We're going to double-time it over the ridge, lend assistance, and if need be, split the group in half. Then we'll come right back here to continue the search."

The group debated the new directive with Tim for a few minutes but decided to head over the ridge to assist the hikers. Even Michael agreed it was the right thing to do. He could feel God pulling on his heart. He knew he would want the searchers to help someone in his family if the situation was reversed.

The group ran towards Houghton's Ridge, covering the distance as fast as the waterlogged terrain would allow. The run wasn't easy. The ground was saturated from all of the rain that pummeled the region. A number of the volunteers slipped and fell in the mud, but they were not deterred.

It took the team closer to fifteen minutes to make it over the ridge. They were scouring the area for the hikers but were unable to find them. Tim radioed back to the command center and asked the helicopters to make another pass over the ridge.

After the flyover, they were directed to head northwest of their location. The volunteers took off and ran at a brisk pace. Within minutes, they located the hikers. Tim could see one of them was using a crutch and doing his best to hobble through the wooded region. He yelled to them as he ran, "Do you need help?"

"Yes, we need help," the first man said, turning around. The second person fell to the ground, tired from the hike and unable to go any further. "I found this guy in the river yesterday..."

"You what?" Michael yelled, sprinting ahead of the group.

"I found this man in the river yesterday," the man repeated. "He was badly hurt, so we found a place to build a fire to avoid the storms."

Michael reached the person who had collapsed and rolled the injured hiker over. "It's my brother!"

"Command Center," Tim yelled into the radio. "We found him!"

Michael hovered over his brother with uncontrollable tears falling atop Veeder. "Come on, buddy, stay with me. We're going to get you out of here and get you some help."

"Michael." Veeder's voice weak. "He saved my life."

"Come again, Tim?" The radio crackled.

The rest of the team surrounded Veeder, with trained officers providing first aid. Tim yelled triumphantly, "We found Veeder McLean! Repeat. We found Veeder McLean! It doesn't look like he is doing well, though, we're going to need a chopper for a medevac!"

"Where are you, Tim?" the captain radioed back.

"About half a click northwest of Houghton's Ridge."

There was a long pause before the captain radioed back. "There is a dirt road about half a mile to your west. Can you get him there? We can meet you there with a Jeep."

"You bet your bottom dollar on it! We'll get him there, Captain" Tim radioed. The officers started to assemble a makeshift stretcher so they wouldn't damage Veeder's leg while they carried him out of the woods.

"Thank you, Mister?" Michael stood and held his hand out to the stranger. "I didn't catch your name."

"Jesus Espiritu Santo," The stranger said, shaking Michael's hand.

"Thank you, Mr. Santo, for helping my brother," Michael said, watching the team prepare Veeder for transit.

"Veeder will be fine," the stranger said. "He's got a long road ahead, but he'll be fine."

"Thank you." Michael felt a calm sense of reassurance wash over his body. The stranger bent down and placed His hand on Veeder's chest.

"Your leg is hurt badly, very badly," the stranger whispered to Veeder. "You have a long road in front of you. You need to be strong, but you are going to be just fine."

"Thank you for saving me." Veeder turned and stared into the stranger's eyes.

"You're welcome. Peace be with you, Veeder."

Veeder put his arms around the stranger's neck and pulled him into an embrace. "Thank you, Lord. Thank you. I believe. I believe."

"Only because you have seen me. Go share the blessings with those who haven't."

"We've got to move," one of the volunteers said to the stranger, bracing the stretcher for transport.

"Go in peace," the stranger said.

"Are you ready, Veeder?" the volunteer asked. Veeder gave them a thumbs up and nodded. The officers lifted the stretcher and ran at a quick pace across the muddy terrain. Veeder gasped in pain as his body bounced with every move.

It took the officers a good thirty minutes to reach the Jeep Cherokee. They laid Veeder in the back, then hustled out of the way. Michael turned to thank the man who had helped Veeder, but He was nowhere to be found. So, he jumped in back next to Veeder, closed the door, and they sped off.

They drove to the cabin. When they arrived, the Jeep came to a screeching halt. Mary Katherine, Colleen, and Jill were waiting with tears in their eyes along with the Captain and several volunteers. The medical personnel took Veeder out of the vehicle and performed as much first aid as they could.

They transferred Veeder to a new stretcher and strapped him down, then carried him to the waiting helicopter. Jill and Mary Katherine buckled themselves into the chopper. Once everyone was secured, they took off and raced through the skies toward the hospital.

CHAPTER 41

—❧—

Veeder was in surgery for hours. The entire family had descended upon the CHU Medical Center. They were crowded into the waiting room, praying, and drawing strength from each other. The doctor came out to speak with Jill and Paul. They stepped off to the side while the family waited on pins and needles, hoping for good news.

"Mr. and Mrs. McLean, I have some good news and some bad news." The doctor was stoic. He removed his surgical hat and held it in his hand.

"Is Veeder okay?" Jill asked, gripping Paul's hand. Tears formed again in her eyes.

"Your son is strong," the doctor continued. "We were worried about his platelet count, but it was above fifty, so we were able to perform the surgery. And just in time too. I believe Veeder will recover from this surgery as well as can be expected."

"What does that mean, Doctor?" Paul asked.

"Veeder broke a couple of bones in the lower part of his left leg." The doctor fidgeted with his hat.

"Broken bones heal," Jill said.

"They do but Veeder also seriously dislocated his knee. He severed a few arteries and cut off circulation to his lower leg."

"What are you trying to say, Doctor?" Fear engulfed Jill's heart.

"The damage to his leg was extensive. We did everything we could do to repair it but in the end, we were left with no other choice. We had to amputate his left leg just above the knee. I'm sorry."

"No!" Jill buried her face into Paul's shoulder and cried.

"Is he going to be okay, Doctor?" Paul held back his tears.

"I believe, all things considered, he will make a full recovery."

"Thank you, Doctor." Paul choked back his emotions.

"To be honest with you," the doctor continued. "I am surprised this wasn't more life-threatening considering the injury he sustained and the time it took to get him here. It's almost like God himself put his hand on your son's leg and held it together until we could operate. It's nothing short of a miracle."

The doctor spoke with Paul for a few more minutes and then disappeared back into the surgical area. Paul and Jill just stood there in tears, surrounded by family. They shared the news. Everyone was stunned.

Jill and Mary Katherine sat with Veeder while he slept. The nurses had informed them he had woken up after the anesthesia had worn off, but he fell back to sleep. They felt it was due to the surgery and the fatigue from fighting through everything he had to endure.

The long day had taken its toll on the family. Paul decided to head back to the farm with Liam, Michael, and Colin. James and Colleen decided to wait in the cafeteria until Veeder was up and receiving visitors, but Mary Katherine refused to leave Veeder's side. She still felt responsible for what had happened. Sitting next to him, staring at the missing part of his left leg, those feelings of guilt grew stronger.

Jill was not leaving Veeder's side either. As she had done twenty-one years earlier, she was going to sit by his bedside and do everything in her power to get her son strong again. She was worried. Veeder didn't believe. She had ignored it for most of his life, but she couldn't ignore it any longer. His lack of faith was going to make his recovery harder.

Jill feared his anger would consume him. She was worried his competitive spirit would do one of two things. Either he would shrink into a severe depression or he would push to prove everyone wrong and hurt himself even more than he already had. As she contemplated the paths that laid ahead for Veeder, she prayed for wisdom. She prayed for patience, but most of all, she prayed for strength. For both of them.

Jill also wanted to be close to Mary Katherine. She knew her daughter blamed herself for everything that had happened. The whole family tried to convince her there was nothing she could have done to change the situation. Veeder was headstrong. He was stubborn. He lived life by his own rules, but Mary Katherine refused to accept their explanations. She was haunted by the images of watching her brother disappear into the rapids when the riverbank collapsed, and she punished herself for not doing more to protect him. To save him.

No. Jill wasn't going anywhere. Her twins were going to need her more than they had ever needed her before, and she was going to be there for them. She was going to help them get through this and make sure they came out of this ordeal as stronger people.

Veeder stirred a few times but he didn't wake up. His heart, mind, and body were worn out. Anyone with a regular platelet count would have had a tough time with an amputation surgery but, adding in the complication of a diminished platelet count, this surgery took a toll on doctors and patient alike.

Veeder woke up around three in the morning. Jill was snoring in a chair at the end of the bed. Mary Katherine was half asleep in the chair next to his bed. Groggy, Veeder reached over and shook her arm. "MK, MK, make it stop. Please. Can you make mom stop snoring?"

Mary Katherine's head bobbed down towards her lap before she jerked it up and looked around the darkened room. She felt Veeder shaking her arm. "MK, please make mom stop snoring."

"Veeder," Mary Katherine said, excited. She jumped up, flipped on the light causing Veeder to hide his eyes with his hands, and hugged him. "Thank God you're awake."

"I love you too, MK." Veeder's eyes adjusted to the light. "Why did you turn on the lights?"

"She is happy to see you awake," Jill said, moving to the other side of the bed and taking one of his hands in hers. "We all are."

"That's one way to get mom to stop snoring," Veeder joked, trying to chuckle and ended up coughing because his throat was dry.

"I'm sorry, Veeder." Mary Katherine sat on the bed and looked at him with tears in her eyes. "I should have done more to pull you out of the river."

"Here drink this." Jill handed Veeder a water bottle she had opened.

"There's nothing you could have done, MK." Veeder pulled himself up in the bed and took a sip of water. "Ow. That hurt my left ankle. Is it broken?"

Jill and Mary Katherine stared at one another, stunned. The doctor said Veeder might have phantom pain where his leg used to be but at this moment, they didn't know what to say. He had only been awake for a few minutes. They didn't want to crush his spirits with the news yet.

He caught the awkward glance between them. Then Veeder slowly looked at both of them, perplexed. "What's wrong?"

"Veeder." Jill sat down on the side of the bed, still holding his hand.

"That's not good," Veeder said, nerves welling up while staring at his mother and sister. Overcome with guilt, Mary Katherine turned away to hide her tears "What's up, Mom? What's going on?"

"Your ankle's not broken," Jill continued, gathering up all of the courage she could muster. She reached out to stroke the side of his face. "Your left leg was badly damaged in the river..."

"And?" Veeder asked, concerned.

"The doctors did everything they could, sweetheart," Jill continued. She took a deep breath, cocked her head, bit her quivering lip, and looked at him. "They couldn't save the lower part of your leg, Veeder. They had to take it."

"No they didn't." Veeder flipped back the sheets of his bed. "I can feel it. It's right ..."

Veeder stopped talking when his eyes gazed upon the bandage wrapped around the end of his leg. He froze. He could hear his breathing inside his head but nothing else. He couldn't hear Jill and Mary Katherine trying to console him. He was paralyzed. He stared at his leg. His breathing and his heartbeat grew louder inside his head.

Jill and Mary Katherine were worried when Veeder sat frozen, staring at his leg. He was catatonic. His breathing was reserved and he was emotionless. He just gazed at his leg, stuck in time, motionless. They sat, frozen with fear and sadness, watching Veeder process the amputation. Finally, he spoke to himself. "You did tell me it was bad. You did. I just wish you had told me how bad it was. I wish you had prepared me a little more. A head's up would have been nice…"

"Who told you it was bad?" Jill interrupted, confused by his rambling.

Veeder ignored her question and continued mumbling, "It's okay. It really is. If this is your plan for me, then this is your plan for me. It is what it is. You said it wouldn't be easy but I'll be okay. I can do this."

"Whose plan, Veeder?" Mary Katherine questioned her brother's mental state of mind.

"You work in mysterious ways, and if this is one of those times, then this is one of those times," Veeder kept mumbling. Jill and Mary Katherine tried to understand what he was saying. "I didn't honor you before, but this isn't going to change what we went through. I will honor you with this. I'll make this work. I'll make this work for your …"

"Snap out of it!" Jill shook Veeder's shoulders, cutting him off midsentence as Mary Katherine stared at the scene playing out in front of her.

"Mom! Stop!" Mary Katherine yelled, grabbing Jill's hands. "Stop it!"

Jill stopped shaking Veeder's shoulders. Mary Katherine stared at her in horror. Veeder just looked at her with a patient smile. Jill wrapped her arms around him, tears flowing down her cheeks. "I'm sorry, Veeder."

"Are you okay, Mom?" Veeder asked. She was all but choking him.

"I'm sorry." Jill sat back and looked at her son, hands on his shoulders. "I got worried when you started mumbling."

"We both did," Mary Katherine added, still a little freaked out by everything she had just witnessed.

"I thought you had gone off the deep end," Jill blurted out.

"That's funny." Veeder chuckled. "Who knows? You're right. Maybe a week ago I would have, but not today. I was just talking with Him and sorting things out."

"With whom?" Mary Katherine asked.

Veeder pointed toward the sky. "God."

"What?" Jill and Mary Katherine gasped in utter shock.

"I was talking with Jesus. He told me the other night that my leg was hurt badly. I just wish He had told me how bad it was." Veeder looked up at the ceiling and said towards heaven. "A head's up about my situation would have been nice, that's all I'm saying."

"Wait a minute." Jill was confused. "When did you start talking to Jesus?"

"When He pulled me out of the river?"

"Jesus didn't pull you out of the river," Jill said. "Michael said a Spanish guy named, Jesus Espiritu Santos, saved you."

Veeder laughed at Jill's admission.

Mary Katherine's eyes flew wide open, staring at Jill. "What. Did. You. Just. Say?"

Jill was confused. "What? Michael said a man named Jesus Espiritu Santos pulled him from the river."

"Mom," Mary Katherine swallowed hard and took a deep breath. "In Spanish, Jesus Espiritu Santos roughly translates to Jesus, Holy Spirit or the Spirit of Jesus."

"What?" Jill's eyes grew wide, goosebumps jumping up all over her body. "Wait a minute? No. Wait. Veeder, who were you talking to?"

"I was talking to Jesus. I was telling Him that if this is the plan He has for me, then I accept it. He will use this for His glory. Whatever He has planned for me, I am willing to fulfill it as long as the glory falls on Him."

"What happened to you out there?" Jill asked.

Veeder told Jill and Mary Katherine the whole story of how Jesus had saved him from the river and about the debate they had in the middle of the storm. Veeder ended up telling the story a few times over the next few days as the family members had many questions for him. Colleen was happy to hear Jesus had honored the promise. She knew He would but was glad He had remembered because she had forgotten all about it.

The doctors also made Veeder tell the story to a couple of psychiatrists. They came up with a medical rationale for what had happened. Something about trauma interfering with his mind which created a false narrative helping Veeder cope with the realization that he had been through a horrific event.

Veeder and the family disregarded the doctor's explanation. They knew that God lives with us at all times and will show himself in a myriad of ways. Veeder knew better. He had met the man in person and nothing could ever change the truth: Jesus is real!

CHAPTER 42

Two days after Veeder's surgery, the entire Chapel Hill University football team descended upon the hospital to spend time with him. They had lost the national championship but had made a game out of it. The play David called went for a touchdown. After they scored, the team told the press about the young man who had called the play. The announcers made a big deal about it on television, even announcing David during the broadcast as the architect of the play. Veeder hoped David and his family had watched the game and heard their names during the broadcast.

Veeder told Coach Mercer he was petitioning the league for one game of eligibility the next time the Cobras were in the national championship because he was coming back to lead the team to victory. The team showered Veeder and his family with love and support. They pledged to be there for him while he recovered from his injuries.

A week later, Mary Katherine pushed Veeder in his wheelchair down to the cafeteria so he could look out the windows and hang out in a different environment. Veeder spent a lot of time in the cafeteria because he hated being in his room alone. It felt confining to him, like a prison cell. He liked being out so he could meet people in the hospital and pray with them. Veeder spent a lot of time in the hospital visiting other people and praying for them.

He spent time in the cafeteria reading his Bible and playing games with his family members. He had many questions for his grandmother about the Bible and the meanings of the various passages he was studying. She had done such a good job teaching him all about football, he thought, who better to teach him about God?

But like all situations, people went back to their normal lives. So, Veeder relished the idea of getting some time alone to start thinking about what his future held. Mary Katherine had some duties to attend to in the hospital, so she said she would have a cup of coffee with him before starting her shift.

Mary Katherine pushed him over to a table next to a window looking out over Chapel Hill. "Is this table good, Veeder?"

"This is fine."

"Large French Vanilla with milk and sugar?"

"That would be great." Veeder stared out the window. "Thank you, MK."

Mary Katherine went to get the coffee. Veeder opened his Bible and started to read. He was lost in his thoughts, processing the words on the page when a cup of coffee was held out in front of him and a familiar angelic voice asked, "Do you mind if I join you?"

Veeder looked up and smiled. His heart skipped a beat. "Anna."

"Hi, Veeder."

"Hi."

"How are you doing?" With a hint of sadness in her eyes, Veeder took the coffee from her.

"Sit, please sit." Veeder looked back across the cafeteria and saw Mary Katherine smiling at them. She lifted her coffee cup and dipped her head before leaving the cafeteria. "I'm doing okay, Anna. Better than I thought I would be. How are you?"

"I've been missing you."

"I have missed you too."

"Read any good books lately?" Anna sat next to him, staring at the book in his hand.

"As a matter of fact, I have." Veeder smiled, holding up his Bible. He paused. "I meant to call you, Anna…"

"It's okay." Anna interrupted.

"No, it's not." A sheepish smile crossed Veeder's face. "My heart has been breaking ever since Christmas. I wanted to say hello at church, but I was afraid to. I was going to call but I didn't want this incident to be the reason…"

"Stop." Anna held up her hand. "Your injury has nothing to do with my reaching out to you. I called before New Year's because I missed you."

"I am so sorry for everything, Anna. Can you ever forgive me?"

"I already have. What is done is done. I am focused on the future. Now, what can I help you with?" Anna winked at him and smiled. "I'm pretty good at helping people out with this stuff, well, you know, since my dad's on the payroll and all."

Veeder chuckled. "He told you about that?"

"Yeah, he told me about that," Anna responded, laughing along with him.

Veeder smiled, wrung his hands together in his lap, looked at his feet, and sighed. "Anna, you didn't sign up for this."

"Sign up for what?"

"I have a long road of recovery in front of me. You have your whole life in front of you. I wouldn't hold it against you if you walked away right now and never turned back. You don't have to do this, you know."

Anna moved closer to him, put her hands on the collar of his shirt, and looked directly into his eyes, "You let me worry about me. I know what I can and can't handle. I chose to be here today, and I'm not going anywhere."

Anna paused and then she planted a slow kiss on Veeder's lips. As they pulled apart, Veeder let out a sigh of relief and love. "Does that mean you will still marry me one day?"

"Now you're getting ahead of yourself." Anna winked with a flirtatious smile. "Let's get through the book of Matthew first and we'll see where that takes us."

"Would you mind if we prayed together?"

"Mind?" Anna half-laughed, caught off guard by the question. "Veeder, I have waited my entire life to hear you say those words."

"I bet you have." Veeder chuckled, held Anna's hands, bowed his head, and closed his eyes. "This has been one of the greatest days of my life, Lord Jesus. Thank you for bringing Anna here today. Amen."

Anna beamed with pride as she mouthed the final word of praise with him. "Now, what can I help you with?"

"You have already done more than you will ever know. Thank you, Anna." A solitary tear rolled down his cheek. "I could never live with myself if you couldn't forgive me."

"Water under the bridge."

"I am sorry you have to see me like this," Veeder said, biting his lip and lowering his head.

"Like what?"

"Weak." Veeder was soft-spoken. "Broken."

"You were always weak and broken, Veeder," Anna responded, picking up his Bible and smiling at him. "But with this book in your hand, it's probably the strongest I have ever seen you."

Veeder looked up at her and smiled, his heart beating against his chest. "Amen."

Thank you for reading *Intercepted.* I am honored and humbled. If you enjoyed reading this book, please leave a review at Amazon.com and/or Goodreads.com so other people can experience this novel as well.

Thank you!

ACKNOWLEDGMENTS

There are so many people I need to thank for their help in putting this book together. There were many eyes and hearts encouraging and inspiring me to get this story from my head to my computer and finally, to the bookstore.

Thank you, Nicole Hampton, for your invaluable guidance and insights into this novel. You were truly sent from God when I needed it most. Your thoughtful ideas and suggestions helped me to make critical decisions about the story. It was amazing to work with someone who knew what I was trying to do and what I wanted to accomplish. Thank you, Nicole, for always challenging me to take this book to a higher level. You will always be more than a mentor and a friend; you have become family and my life is more blessed because He sent you in my direction when I needed it most. Thank you.

Thank you, Allison Houck, for doing a final read through of Intercepted. Your comments and suggestions made the writing so much stronger, and as much as I fight with my commas, you reminded me of the importance of the Oxford Comma.

I owe a huge thank you to Tom Derosier for the artwork for the cover. I never made it easy for you. The only direction I gave you when we initially sat down at Starbuck's is "I'll know it when I see it." After talking with my daughter, Chloe, you utilized your artistic genius and did what you do best, and I cannot thank you enough. You also gave my family a new inside joke which has been oh so much fun!

Thank you, Jessica Tilles, for taking me under your wing when it came time to format and put the finishing touches on the cover of the book. Your kindness in our original communications spoke volumes to your character and professionalism. Thank you for all of your help in turning my manuscript into a book. Your attention to detail and the small touches that you accentuate throughout the book make a world of difference. Thank you.

Thank you, Chloe, for all the ways you have helped shape this story. I still remember those car rides to and from school when I shared a sketch of the story, and you came up with the title of the book. You saw the multiple layers of the meaning of the word and how it is so apropos when applied to this story. Thank you also for the vision you had at the dinner table after Tom sent over the first set of designs for the cover. He may not have incorporated every aspect of what you depicted in your conversation with him, but your creative ability to visualize when I can't (yes, the inside joke) made a world of difference in the development of the cover design. Thank you.

Thank you to my son, Josh, who has been helping me visualize the font size and colors on the cover of the book. I also appreciate all of your insights into a digital and social media marketing plan so we can reach as many readers as possible. Your understanding of social media mixed with the business classes you have taken in college have helped me learn new tricks of the trade. Thank you.

Thank you, Mark, Sue, Aunt Renate, Uncle David, Josh, and Stephanie, for your initial read through of the book so many years ago. Your honest insights, opinions, and engagement with the characters in this tale helped me to hone the direction of the story and fix what you, the readers, saw in this story as I wrote the next iterations of the book. Thank you for your help and your time.

I will never be able to properly thank my beautiful wife, Stephanie. Between teaching, coaching football, helping in the community, and raising our two awesome kids, you have been my biggest fan as this book took on life. You have been my rock, supported me through the long days and nights of writing and editing, and then writing and editing some more, and in the frustrating times when I was overcome with writer's block. You kept reminding me that all good things will happen in His time and that made all the difference. You were the answer to my prayers so many years ago, and you continue to be the answer to my prayers every day. Thank you for your patience as Intercepted slowly came to fruition. I hope it was worth the wait and most of all, that you love it.

And finally, thank you God for bringing all of these people into my life and for being a part of this project. You knew I would need them to complete this project. Thank you for your vision, your love, and your grace. Amen.

ODDS AND ENDS

—⌒◎⌒—

As I was writing the book, many of the test readers asked about the locations in the story. "Are they real or a figment of my imagination?" Please let me shed some light on some of the questions I was asked as many places are real but were used fictitiously in the story.

Goldston, North Carolina is a real place. Some of the descriptions of Goldston used in the book are accurate as of the writing of the story. As we all know, with progress comes change, so those descriptions may become obsolete.

Goldston Old Fashioned Days is a real event that takes place every year in October. The event, to my recollection, started in the mid-1980s (1987, I think). This event holds a special memory for our family. When we flew here to investigate our new home state, this was the first event we attended. We have been back many times over the years.

Lizzie's Diner is a fictitious place based on a real place in Goldston; Lizzie's Grill-N-Chill. As far as I can ascertain Lizzie's Grill-N-Chill was not in existence in the time frame of this book. My daughter, Chloe, and I visit often. We love their chicken salad and homemade chips.

Southern Supreme Fruitcake & More is a real place in Bear Creek, NC. This establishment, to my recollection, started in the 1980s and was in existence during the time frame of this story. If you couldn't tell by Anna's reaction in the book, I am a big fan of the Bear Creek Toffee.

Now known as The Shiny Diner, Gypsy's Shiny Diner started in 1997 and was open for service on July 4, 1998, when Veeder and Anna stopped in for a romantic evening. My wife is a big fan of 50s Diners. This was a special treat in our new home state. And whenever I go, I make sure to save room for pie.

Ron Dayne was the 1999 Heisman Award Winner.

Jimmy Buffet actually played a concert at Carter-Finley Stadium on July 4, 1998. In a stroke of absolute luck and a little bit of investigation, an old WRAL article online revealed that there were strong thunderstorms all night that canceled many of the fireworks shows. From what I have been able to find in my research, the concert went on as planned.

ABOUT THE AUTHOR

Born in New York City, Doug grew up in Connecticut while still exploring the city he called home. He spent a lot of his youth exploring his imagination. He dabbled in plays, screen plays, poetry, lyricism, essays, writing stories, and singing in various bands.

After graduating from Roger Williams College, Doug went on to work for educational non-profits and school systems. He never lost his enthusiasm for writing, creating, and performing, though. Over the years, Doug has been a writer, an actor, a lead singer, a comedian, a DJ, a fantasy football commissioner, a poet, a lyricist, and a really bad guitarist. He finally honed all of those skills so he could teach middle school students and bring education to life for the next generation.

Doug lives in North Carolina. He is a middle school teacher, a football coach, a loving husband, and a proud father who spends his free time creating stories like Intercepted, his debut novel. His goal is to bring characters you love to life and to share their stories as they relate to the world around us all.